TALES OF THE
SHADOWMEN

Volume 9: La Vie en Noir

TALES OF THE SHADOWMEN

Volume 9: La Vie en Noir

edited by
Jean-Marc & Randy Lofficier

stories by
**Matthew Baugh, Nicholas Boving, Robert Darvel,
Matthew Dennion, Win Scott Eckert, Martin Gately,
Travis Hiltz, Paul Hugli, Rick Lai, Jean-Marc Lofficier,
Nigel Malcolm, DavidMcDonald, Christofer Nigro,
John Peel, Neil Penswick, Pete Rawlik,
Josh Reynolds, Frank Schildiner, Bradley H. Sinor**
and **Michel Stéphan**

translations by
Matthew Baugh and **Michael Shreve**

cover by
Nathalie Lial

A Black Coat Press Book

ISBN 978-1-61227-145-3. First Printing. December 2012. Published by Black Coat Press, an imprint of Hollywood Comics.com, LLC, P.O. Box 17270, Encino, CA 91416. All rights reserved. Except for review purposes, no part of this book may be reproduced or transmitted in any form or by any means, electronic or mechanical, including photocopying, recording or by any information storage and retrieval system, without permission in writing from the publisher. The stories and characters depicted in this anthology are entirely fictional. Printed in the United States of America.

Table of Contents

THE BLACKCOATS

Paul Féval

adapted by Brian Stableford

Ill. J.-M. Ponzio

Introduction
The Treasure of the Black Coats

Edith Piaf liked to sing about *la vie en rose*, "life in pink," in other words, life seen through rose-tinted glasses. This volume of *Tales of the Shadowmen* is another kind of song altogether, one dedicated to *la vie en noir*, the darker side of life. And what could be darker than the Black Coats, that sinister brotherhood of criminals created by the visionary Paul Féval in 1863?

Unusually for *Tales of the Shadowmen*, you will find that several stories in this volume are orchestrated around a central theme: that of the legendary Treasure of the Black Coats.

For those wishing to read these stories in their internal chronological order, they are:

1808-10: Rick Lai: *Gods of the Underworld*
1873: Matthew Dennion: *The Treasure of Everlasting Life*
1911: Pete Rawlik: *Professor Peaslee Plays Paris*
1930: Matthew Baugh: *The Tournament of the Treasure*
1930: John Peel: *The Benevolent Burglar*
1931: Christofer Nigo: *Death of a Dream*
1952: Frank Schildiner: *The True Cost of Doing Business*

The treasure of the Black Coats is first mentioned in Paul Féval's *The Parisian Jungle* (ISBN 978-1-934543-03-0). It is, in fact, the most important loose end left hanging at the end of the book. Its secret was supposedly contained in the "scapular" worn around the neck of the supreme master of the Black Coats, Colonel Bozzo-Corona, an exceedingly old man who was once the famous bandit Fra Diavolo.

The Invisible Weapon (ISBN 978-1-932983-80-7) later hinted that the treasure might be an illusory prize maintained by the Colonel in order to keep his unruly subordinates in order, but that, in fact, the organization's running costs might have dispersed their profits more rapidly than its hopeful heirs suspected. On the other hand, another passage suggests that it was buried in the vicinity of Sartène, in Corsica, probably in the ruins of the Convent of La Merci, which had once been the base of Fra Diavolo's bandits.

The Companions of the Treasure (ISBN 978-1-934543-26-9) was the novel in which Féval bit the bullet and set out to explain what really happened to the treasure. In it is a scene where the ever-devious Colonel shows it to Vincent Carpentier, after bragging of having spent a whole night in the Vatican plundering the Roman Catholic Church's riches. This scene takes place in a secret room located under the Colonel's Parisian lair, on the Rue Thérèse. There, Vincent sees gold bars, jewels, chalices, columns made of gold coins, paper money, investments, loans, etc...

The Treasure is the Colonel's ultimate source of power. As he puts it: "I am Gold. I am Wealth. I am Power. You must not compare me to Kings or Emperors or anyone who lives upon the Earth. I have only two rivals: one in Heaven and the other in Hell. For only God, if God exists, and Satan, if Satan exists, can say like I do: Everything in the world is mine, for I own it *all*!"

As with so many of Féval's novels, *The Companions of the Treasure* left some dangling ends, and many more questions unanswered. The most fascinating one revolves around the nature of the Treasure itself, which prompted translator Brian Stableford to write an elaborate afterword to the novel, in which he put forward a bold theory, a lengthy excerpt of which we reproduce below:

"As with all mysteries, the central question of *The Companions of the Treasure* comes down to a matter of *whodunnit?* In its immediate predecessors within the series—in terms of the order in which the books were written—the answer to that question was Colonel Bozzo-Corona, but that answer was complicated in both '*Salem Street* and *The Invisible Weapon* by deliberately-planted doubts as to who or what the Colonel really is. The suggestion was explicitly made in both those volumes that he is, in some sense, the Devil, or at least the Devil's earthly agent. He is, metaphorically if not literally, evil personified—or, more accurately, a particular species of evil personified. It is possible that when he began to write *The Companions of the Treasure*, Féval did not mean to kill the Colonel so abruptly and unceremoniously, and it is arguable that it might have been a more interesting novel had he not done so. Had he left a slim possibility open that the Colonel was still alive, the scene in the graveyard might have been much more challenging and Julian's anxieties much more understandable. That is, however, a minor point; the true import of the plot of *The Companions of the Treasure* is that it finally reveals exactly who and what the Colonel had always been.

"On several occasions, Féval takes the trouble to observe and remind us that there are three persons, individuals or characters in the Brigand's painting: the father, the son and the treasure. The first time he does so, he actually uses the words *personnes* rather than *personnages*. The natural inclination of a 19th century reader—even one who recognized the obvious parallel with the Holy Trinity—would be to construe *personnes* and *personnages* metaphorically, but the novel's plot makes much more sense, and can only make sense, if it is construed literally. The same is true of the many references to the gold that depict it as a demon.

"The treasure of the Black Coats really is a person, individual or character, and its particular character is that of an unholy spirit, which is an essential component of a trinity of three persons in one. As in the two novels preceding *The Companions of the Treasure* in the Black Coats sequence, the superficial answer to *whodunnit?* in this novel— as the fatal words inscribed on the rear wall of the safe make clear, despite the fact that the Colonel is dead and buried—is Colonel Bozzo-Corona. The real answer, however— which takes aboard the question of who and what the Colonel really is—is that the demonic treasure did it, and that the Colonel and Julian are merely different aspects of the same adversarial individual.

"The feeble human being that is the trinity's most evident manifestation did not transport the treasure to Paris from Sartène; it came of its own accord, by its own means—and the manifestation that it paraded in front of Vincent's eyes was, in effect, a bombastic illusion, which required no fencing in order to transform itself yet again for the benefit of other eyes on other occasions. It did not kill Vincent because it had possessed him, and had work for him to do (as it keeps insisting by way of Vincent's speech); nor did its component parts succeed in killing their counterparts, when they were led to try by the hatred innate in their natures, unless and until the unfolding drama required them to succeed. The demonic treasure produced the Brigard's painting itself, by its own mysterious means, and played out the charade in the cemetery in exactly the same spirit that it maneuvered Julian around its game-board and wrote its mocking message on the rear wall of the safe. There are, in fact, no outrageous coincidences in the novel's plot, but only— as the narrative voiced and the characters continually assert—the workings of an implacable and ironic Fate. It is all a black comedy, played out partly for amusement and partly for the purposes of instruction.

"Why did the gold-demon do all these things? It did them, firstly and most importantly, because that is what unholy spirits do; their entire *raison d'être* is to tempt, to cheat and to punish. They are, in essence, agents of moral fabulation—or, more pedantically, agents of apologue. Secondly, however, it did it simply because it could. It is a character in a story, and characters in stories are exactly what their authors say they are, and can do exactly what their authors say they can do, requiring no other authority than the words on the page. Such agents of moral fabulation are, perhaps, slightly redundant in a place like Paris, which—as Féval scrupulously points out— has evidence of the destructive power of avarice perennially at hand, even when it has not just suffered awful humiliation at the hands of the Prussians and the Commune; on the other hand, though, where on Earth can they find better opportunities?"

So, is Brian Stableford right? Is the mysterious Treasure more than simply a pile of gold and jewels, but a malignant self-aware entity that is the embodiment of greed and avarice—and the seemingly eternal Colonel merely its pawn, its agent on Earth, whose purpose is to drag and crush unworthy mortals in its clutches of wealth?

In this volume of *Tales of the Shadowmen*, we put the question to our team of talented writers, and several of them decided to tackle the theme and provide their own answers.

But the Treasure of the Black Coats is not the only dark facet of life covered in this volume. You will also find stories about the evil Fantômas and the mysterious Yellow Shadow, the crafty Doctor Cornelius and the megalomaniacal Sun Koh, the ruthless Irma Vep and the frightful Bride of Frankenstein; in these pages, you will read tales of vampires, creatures and zombies, and things from otherworldly realms, and likely gasp at the most monstrous couple of parents ever imagined—how is that for the dark side of Life?

Jean-Marc Lofficier

The alphabet favors Matthew Baugh who almost always opens each new volume of Tales of the Shadowmen. *Matthew had long wanted to write a tale featuring Robert E. Howard's Steve Costigan, and the theme of the battle for the Black Coats' ever elusive treasure presented him with such an opportunity. Travel with him to the South Pacific to attend...*

Matthew Baugh: *The Tournament of the Treasure*

French Polynesia, January 14, 1930

The *Sea Girl* had docked in Papeete after a long haul from Tampico by way of Magallanes. I hadn't been to French Polynesia in a long spell, so I decided to take some shore leave. Before I headed out to see the sights, which is to say the bars, I went to the local athletic club.

"Steve Costigan!" a familiar voice bawled as I put my hand on the door. I turned to see the ugly mug of Ned Dargan creased in a grin. He ambled over and we punched each other's shoulders in greeting. The last time I'd seen Ned was the day after I'd kayoed him in the ninth round of a bout in San Francisco, but he weren't one to hold no grudges.

"What are you doing in Tahiti?" I asked.

"A couple of gents hired me in Frisco," Ned said. "They paid me five hunert smackers and flew me out on a chartered plane for some big fight."

I blew out a soft whistle at that. "They must think you're somethin' special. Who do they got you fighting?"

"I dunno."

"What?" I said. "I ain't never heard of no fight where you don't know your opponent."

Ned hitched up his shoulders. "It's some kinda tournament. I seen a couple of other heavyweights in town; Slug O'Leary and Mullargan."

"What?" I repeated. O'Leary's was as tough as they come and had once fought my brother Mike to a twelve round draw. Mullargan was an up and comer what everyone said would be a contender soon.

"So, who hired you?" I asked.

"Big, fat guy called Gutman and a little prissy guy named Cairo."

"You think they could use another fighter?"

Ned grinned. "Can't hurt to ask. They're at the American Bar; I'll take you to 'em."

That suited me, especially as I was headed there anyway to meet my shipmates Bill O'Brian and Sven Larson. It was early morning and there was lots of natives and a few seamen on the streets. We had gone about three blocks, which was most of the way to the hotel, when I noticed a woman who didn't fit in. She was a real dish, American by the look of her, slim and blonde, and dressed real classy.

"Excuse me," she said glancing back and forth between us. "You're Americans, aren't you?"

"Yes, ma'am," I said.

"Do you know where I can find a sailor named Ned Dargan?"

"That's me," Ned replied.

"My name is Virginia Harper and I need your help. The people who have hired you... they've taken my husband."

Ned and I exchanged a bewildered glance.

"They kidnapped him?" Ned asked.

"No." She wrinkled her brow, like she was struggling to find the best words. "I can't prove that they're holding him against his will, but they are. That woman has some sort of unnatural hold on him and she's forcing him to fight in a tournament."

"What woman?" Ned said. "I only met Mr. Gutman and Mr. Cairo."

"She's called Madame Ingomar. She appeared several weeks ago and had some sort of influence over our Chinese cook, Sing Lee. The two of them have done something to Townsend. He's not himself any longer and doesn't even seem to recognize me. I questioned Sing Lee and was able to learn that Madame Ingomar wanted Townsend for a fighting tournament."

"Your husband's a prize-fighter?" I asked, surprised that such a classy dame would be with a common pug.

"My husband is Townsend Harper of the New York Harpers," she said.

"Ma'am," Ned said. "If he's in the tournament and he ain't no boxer, he'll get murdered."

"No, Townsend is very strong. I'm afraid that he might kill someone if he fights." Tears welled up in her big blue eyes. "Oh, there must be some way to keep this from happening!"

I figgered it was just the case of a woman getting the jitters about her fella getting into the ring, but I could see Ned starting to melt. Unlike me, he is a sucker for a pretty face.

"Leave it to me, Ma'am," I said. "I'll set him straight."

"Hey!" Dargan protested. "The lady asked *me* to help."

"It don't make no sense for her to rely on a stumble bum like you when I'm around," I said.

"Oh, yeah?"

He balled up his big hands and stepped toward me.

"Oh, no!" Mrs. Harper said, turning a bit pale. "You mustn't fight!"

"Don't worry, Ma'am," I said, polite-like. "This'll just take a minute."

"Less than that," Ned said, just as gallant.

We squared off but before either of us could throw a punch, the doors of the American Bar burst open and an AB seaman come flying out to land in the gutter.

"Bill O'Brian!" I said, startled.

A second later the doors sprung open again, this time allowing a huge squarehead Swede to fly through.

"Sven Larson!" I cried.

"Friends of yours?" Ned asked.

"Those is my shipmates," I said. "You wait here whilst I check on them. I'll be back to batter you senseless in a minute."

"If you break off now, I count it as a forfeit," he replied. "That means I gets to help the lady."

I didn't like that much, but didn't see much choice. A man's duty to his pals has got to come ahead of opportunity. I hurried up the street to where Bill and Sven lay in the dirt. Bill was clutching at his side and Sven was out cold with a notable dent in his skull.

"Bill," I cried, moving to his side. "What happened? You look like the two of you was worked over with a crowbar."

"Naw," Bill said, betwixt his gasps of pain. "The guy that did this laid us out with his bare hands."

"One man?" I said. The thought astonished me because my shipmates was two of the toughest salts I had ever sailed with.

"Yeah," he gasped. "He's in the American Bar. But don't go after him, Steve. Ain't nothin' human can hit like that guy."

That got my temper up. Human or not, there ain't no man I'd shy away from fighting. The very thought of it made me see red.

"You get yourself and Sven patched up," I said. "I'll see you back on board."

I slammed open the swinging doors and looked around for whoever had beat up my friends. There was a mix of sailors in the room, but none of them looked particularly fierce. None that is, except for a retired Limey fighter named "Seaman" Pallant who I spied at a corner table with a strange little assembly.

There was two women sitting there, a blonde and a Eurasian gal. Each about as nice-looking as you could ask for, dressed to the nines and smoking cigarettes in long holders. With them was a middle-aged man what must have weighed in at more than three hundred pounds, none of it muscle, and a little guy in a prim suit with his hair slicked back. I figgered they was the two guys that had hired Ned Dargan. The last man was past thirty and about six feet tall with an athletic cut to his jib. He was dressed like a laborer but didn't look like one. He didn't look like no fighter neither, as his mug didn't show any of the signs of abuse one picks up in the ring. He was a dubious looking character, even bigger than Sven Larsen, who is 6'4" and fights at 245 lbs. I reckoned he must be the culprit.

"Hey, you!" I shouted as I strode across the room toward him. "I don't care much for the way you handled my shipmates!"

The big man stood and looked me over kind of superior-like, which raised my temperature even higher, then he said something to the woman in French. That settled me on my course right there. I don't dislike Frenchies in particular, but speaking a foreign language in a place called the American Bar is just bad manners. I strode to him and stared up at his ugly mug.

The big Frenchie shoved me back and took a big overhanded swing. It was a powerful punch but didn't have no skill. I had no trouble ducking under it and sinking my right hand wrist-deep into his midsection.

The big man grunted and backed up a step, which gave me the chance to land a one-two combination that rocked his head from side to side. He shrugged the punches off and lunged at me with arms outstretched. I slowed him with a straight left that mashed his nose into a bloody mess but he fought through the pain and wrapped his massive arms around me and lifted me up.

There ain't no real boxing defense against that kind of move. Fortunate for me, I have learned a lot of things in my life that the Marquis of Queensbury would not have approved of. I pummeled the sides of the big man's head as he crushed the air from my lungs but, as my feet were dangling off the ground, I couldn't get no power in my punches. I changed tactics, grabbing hold of his ears and pulling his head back. Once his face was exposed, I leaned forward and clamped my teeth on the ruin of his nose.

The huge man screamed and let loose, dropping me to the floor. As I struggled to get my breath back, he grabbed a table, which the patrons had already evacuated, and raised it over his head. He brought it down on my back as I started to rise. The force shattered the table and drove me to my knees, which irritated me no end. Whilst the big man was looking around for something else to hit me with I rose up and landed a right cross under his heart. He staggered back and cast about for a weapon but I moved in, peppering his face with a series of lefts and rights.

He grabbed at me in desperation and managed to catch hold of my belt. Using the grip, he hoisted me over his head and threw me across the bar, shattering the big mirror that hung over it. I rose and vaulted the bar. The big man had picked up a whiskey bottle and now broke it against a wall and threatened me with the jagged end. This angered me further as I have always contended that bringing weapons into a fist fight is a low and cowardly act. I caught his wrist with my left hand and drove my best right cross into his shoulder. He barked out a cry of pain and dropped the bottle from numbed fingers.

I swung my right hand in a backhanded blow that snapped his head to the side, then I moved in close and worked his body with a series of left and right hooks. He retaliated with clubbing blows to my shoulders and back but his punches were getting weaker and I mostly ignored them. I finished with an uppercut that started so low my knuckles nearly brushed the ground. It landed on the point of his jaw with all the force of my legs and torso behind it. The big man took two steps backward, then tipped over, like a cut tree.

I glanced around at the seamen, who had started picking up the tables and chairs. The little group had taken advantage of the fracas to slip away, all but the blonde woman. She sat at her table watching me with a look in her dark eyes that made me feel like a rat does when the ship's cat spots him.

"*Mon Dieu*," she said. "I would not have imagined that anyone could defeat Bebert like that."

"Aw, he weren't very tough," I said modestly as she reached out to feel the muscles of my arm. "I can't figger how he could have worked over my two friends like that."

"Your friends?" the lady gave a titter of laughter. I can't say why, but the sound of it prickled the flesh all down my spine. "It wasn't Bebert who fought them, it was Madame Ingomar's companion, Bulan."

"That Eurasian woman was Madame Ingomar? Then that man must be Townsend Harper?"

"I believe that is his name," she said taking a long drag on her cigarette. She let the smoke blow out into my face before she spoke again. "She prefers to call him 'Bulan.' He's fighting in a little tournament we're putting on at midnight. Since you disposed of Bebert so effectively, I would like you to be my champion."

"Thanks, Ma'am, but I ain't no champ yet. Not unless you count being the champeen of the toughest windjammer on the Seven Seas."

"I am called Fatala, and I will pay you a thousand American dollars." She ran a hand across my chest and smiled. "There will be... other compensations."

The way she said it made my toes curl up. "That's mighty big stakes," I said.

She smiled again. It was a hungry sort of smile and this time the curling feeling went all the way up to my belly.

"The Colonel's treasure is the greatest prize imaginable."

"So it's some army guy putting on this fight?"

"No," she said. "Colonel Bozzo-Corona is no longer in possession of his fortune. I'm part of a small consortium which has chosen to relieve him of it.'

"I don't foller."

She disengaged my hands and moved away a few feet to place a new cigarette in her holder. Then looked up at me from under her eyelashes.

"Can I trust you?" she asked.

"Miss, I'm as honest as a parson."

"Very well," she said. "The Colonel is the head of one of the oldest and most powerful criminal organizations in the world. He has many resources that have helped him to remain in power, but the foremost is his fortune which outstrips the treasuries of most nations."

15

I gave a soft whistle. If she was playing me straight, this was the biggest windfall of my life.

"So, how'd you get this treasure?"

"The details are unimportant. Suffice to say, my associates and I took it from him while he was on an ocean liner. He won't even know it's missing until he reaches Australia. In the meanwhile, we discovered none of us wants to split the fortune. That's why we came up with the idea of the contest. Whoever has the strongest champion takes it all."

I gave some thought to the morality of the whole thing. On the one hand, I don't take to stealing. On the other hand, if this Colonel was the rat she said he was, it was doing the world a service. Besides, this was a chance to square things with the slob who'd beat my shipmates down.

"I'm yer man," I said.

Fatala's yacht carried her and me and the unconscious Bebert to a little place called Opunohu Bay which was about 20 miles from town. It was a long, narrow inlet with a big rocky bluff on one side. There was three other yachts and a tramp steamer sitting at anchor.

Fatala led me to shore, where the moon had risen, making the beach sand as white as bone and the lush foliage as black as night shadows. There was a number of men that I took to be her partners and their fighters. Fatala gestured to a crude boxing ring made from tall bamboo torches driven into the sand and strung together with rope.

"The fights begin in three hours," she said. "Do whatever you need to prepare yourself."

"I'll need some togs to change into," I said.

"I have arranged for that. I have also arranged for something that will give you an extra edge."

She slipped a little glass bottle filled with some kinda red liquid into my hand.

"If you find your strength flagging, drink this," Fatala said. "It will restore your vitality, increase your strength, and make you immune to pain."

"Some kinda drug?"

She smiled. "Something rare, and powerful enough to guarantee your victory. Do not use it until you have to."

"Lady, I ain't never doped for a fight."

"You should think about that very carefully," Fatala replied.

I ain't scared of much but there was something in her voice that sent a chill through me. Then she smiled again and kissed me on the cheek.

"*Bonne chance, mon brave.*"

When she had left I looked around at the others on the beach, which was as unlikely looking a crew as you can imagine. As I stood there a blocky form came from the shadows behind me. I spun and nearly laid him out before I recognized Ned Dargan.

"Steve, what are you doin' here?" he asked.

"I'm in the tournament," I said.

"I'm fighting for Mrs. Harper," he replied. "If she wins, we're gonna swap the treasure for her husband."

"How come they're letting her have a fighter at all? I thought this thing was just for members of the gang."

"It's Mrs. Harper's husband," Dargan said. "Madame Ingomar told her goons to get rid of us when we showed up, but he wouldn't allow it. He lit into them like nothin' I've ever seen. That woman's got him messed up where he don't remember his own wife, but he still ain't gonna let no harm come to her. The gang agreed to let her participate to keep him happy."

I glanced over to where Harper, or Bulan, or whatever, was stretching out his muscles. He looked fit enough, but hardly no match for a fighting man like me, or even Ned. The Eurasian woman watched him from a throne-looking chair set up on the sidelines. She was attended by a number of Orientals of a sort I didn't recognize. They was short and so broad-shouldered as to resemble apes.

I glanced at the next group and saw Mullargan shadow boxing whilst a handsome little fella, no more than three feet tall and wearing an expensive suit looked on. He was surrounded by half a dozen men, all at least six feet tall and well muscled, as anyone could see, them being shirtless.

"The little guy is named Oden," Ned whispered. "He gives me the creeps."

I spotted Gutman and Cairo next and recognized the huge man who would be fighting for them.

"That's Butch O'Leary, ain't it?"

"Yeah," Ned said. "They're calling him 'Slug' these days. The fat man and Cairo found him in port after I quit their outfit. He ain't a bad guy, he just don't know what kind of crowd he's fallen in with."

"Anyone else?"

He nodded. "There's Jack Holligan, fighting for some European guy named Marius and some tough-looking ship's captain named Dawson fightin' for himself. It'll be a three round tournament with opponents drawn at random."

"Hey," I said, noticing a woman a little ways away having a heated discussion. "Ain't that Mrs. Harper arguin' with that heathen Chinee?"

"Yeah," Ned said. "We'd better make sure she's okay."

The little man got a worried look as he saw us approaching. He didn't look like the rest of Madame Ingomar's crowd. He was taller and slimmer for one thing, and his face didn't have the same kind of killer-look. In fact, he was a pleasant looking chap, for a Chinaman.

"I am sorry, Missy," he was saying as we walked up.

"You should be, Sing Lee," she said. "My father trusted you, my husband trusted you, and I thought of you like one of the family. I can't understand why you've betrayed us like this."

Me and Ned took up positions behind the slender woman as if we was sentries. The Chinaman glanced at us, alert but I didn't see no fear in his eyes.

"I think of you as my family also," he said, "but I have other loyalties. I am a member of a very old and powerful society. When the Si Fan called on me, I could not refuse."

"Such a strong loyalty that you've stolen my husband from me," she said.

"I would give him back to you if I could, Missy, but it is beyond my power."

That was all too mysterious for me and before I had a chance to think about it I heard a blast on a conch shell. Everyone moved back to the makeshift ring. Some of the various flunkies brought out more of them throne-chairs for Fatala, little Mr. Oden, Gutman, and Mrs. Harper. Cairo seemed kinda put out that she got a seat and he didn't but he subsided at a word from the fat man and stood in the background, pouting.

A huge man, probably seven feet tall, with a neat little beard and moustache of the sort Frenchies and Krauts and other foreigners sometimes wear stepped into the ring. I reckoned he must be the Marius character Ned had spoke of.

"My distinguished partners... Mrs. Harper," he said. "There is no need to reiterate what we are doing here. The rules are simple: opponents will be selected by lot and the winners will proceed to the next round. There are no fouls or forbidden techniques and there is no quarter given. The men shall fight until only one can stand, at which point I will proclaim him the winner. At the end of three rounds, the surviving champion shall claim the Colonel's treasure." At this, he gestured to a small table with a teakwood box inlaid with gold. One of Madame Ingomar's ape-like Chinamen and one of Oden's shirtless musclemen stood guard over it.

A pretty Tahitian girl stepped up to Marius carrying a top hat so little that I imagined musta been Oden's. He reached in and pulled out two slips of paper.

"The first contest is between Ned Dargan and Captain Dawson," he announced. "Gentlemen, take your corners."

Ned, who had changed into his fightin' togs, stepped past me to his corner. He was 6'1" and 209 lbs. which put him about the same height as Dawson and maybe 30 pounds lighter. I ran my gaze over the big man who had stripped off his shirt but was otherwise still in his seaman's get-up. There weren't much trace of softness in his bulk. He looked as strong as his name and meaner than a rattler with hydrophobia.

"Watch out for this swab," I whispered to Ned. "He looks like more of a brawler than a boxer."

"I ain't worried," Ned said and held out a pair of regulation boxing gloves. "Here, be a pal and lace these up, willya?"

"You're wearing gloves in a fight like this?"

"I don't wanna break my hands punching that mug in the head, do I?" he asked with a grin.

I helped him on with the gloves and finished as the girl with Marius blew the conch. The two men advanced on each other. Dawson opened with a looping left which Ned slipped easily. He responded with a pair of neat left hooks which caught Dawson in the ribs and made him stagger. That was the way it went for the first few minutes, with Dawson making a bunch of clumsy attacks and Ned keeping his distance and landing clean shot after shot.

That musta' made Ned confident 'cause he decided to land a kayo. It was a mistake, for Dawson rushed him and the two went into a clench. He slammed his forehead into Ned's face, then swung a rabbit punch to the back of his head. Whilst Ned was stunned, Dawson looped an arm around his neck and drove blow after punishing blow into his face.

"Hey!" O'Leary cried. "That's a foul!"

"There are no fouls," Marius replied, as calm as could be.

With a great heave, Ned broke loose and drove Dawson back with a flurry of rights and lefts. He rang Dawson's bell with a one-two combination to the kisser and the big man went to his knees. That's when Ned's natural sportsmanship tripped him up. He backed away, as if to let Bull take the count, only there wasn't no referee. Dawson came to his feet with a handful of beach sand that he flung in Ned's face. Whilst Ned was struggling to get his vision back, Dawson landed a vicious uppercut and he went down. Dawson's crew whooped and cheered and there was some murmuring from the rest of the crowd. The big sailor pounced on Ned then, kneeling astride his chest and raining down a series of punches on his head.

Ned tried to throw Dawson off, but the boxing gloves kept him from getting any kind of grip. He covered his head as best he could but Dawson kept dropping bombs, even when it was clear Ned couldn't defend himself no more. That made me see red; I sprung into the ring and hauled Dawson off of Ned, who had stopped struggling.

"Shove off!" Dawson snarled and took a swing at me. I blocked it and gave him a two-handed push that dumped him on his rear. He rose to his feet staring bloody murder at me and I hunched into my fighting stance.

"Enough!" Marius cried. "The fight is over. Captain Dawson is the winner."

"Your time's comin', bilge rat," Dawson said to me with a nasty grin.

"It'll be a pleasure to rearrange your ugly face," I retorted.

He went back to his crew with his arms lifted over his head in victory and a smile on his ugly kisser whilst I helped Ned to his feet and guided him to sit under some palm trees. Mrs. Harper moved to meet us.

"I'm sorry Ma'am," Ned said through mangled lips. "I let you down."

"Hush," she replied. "There's nothing to be done for it."

She tended to his wounds as I turned my attention back to the ring. Marius had just announced the next match between Seaman Pallant and Jack Holligan. I was surprised to see Pallant fighting; he'd retired a few years back and, whilst he was still a tough enough mug, he wasn't in trim to face a younger man in the ring. Holligan, on the other hand, was a young colored fighter who people was already comparing to the likes of Jack Johnson and Ace Jessel. He was 6'2" and 210 lbs to Pallant's 5'10" and 195 and a good 15 years younger. His smiling features was a real contrast to Pallant's mashed nose and cauliflowered right ear.

As I predicted, the limey never had a chance. He made a game show of it, but Holligan easily danced away from his attacks and pasted him at will with his left jab. That went on for a bit with Holligan taunting Pallant before he finally moved in. when he did, he snapped the limey's head back with a hard straight left, then struck him a thunderous right cross to the jaw. The punch practically took Pallant out of his shoes. He hit the sand and stayed there till a couple of Madame Ingomar's thugs carried him off.

Marius called my name next, along with Mullargen's, which suited me fine. He was a sandy-haired guy with the smug look of someone what's never been beat. He was tall, 6'2" to my 6'0" and we both weighed 195 lbs. I'd heard he had a reputation for being able to put his opponents away with one punch.

I noticed that he'd dressed the same as me, in fighting trunks. We'd both ignored the gloves and just taped his hands up real good.

As we squared off I could see he had some real pretty ring skills. I tried for a hook to the body but he danced away and stung me with a couple of straight lefts. That irritated me and I swung a left hook, which he ducked and caught me in the short ribs with a left of his own that made me grunt.

The next few minutes was infuriatin' for me. I kept trying to close with him whilst he used his longer reach and speed to stay outta range and kept stinging me with blows to the body and head. He was good enough to slip past my defenses three times out of four and, brother, could he hit. Inside of five minutes he had my nose gushing blood and one eye swole nearly shut.

That's when I figgered I'd best change tactics. I gave up all thought of defense and just focused on driving in close to him. He hit me with a snappy combination that bounced my head like a rubber ball but I persisted and got inside his range. Once I was in close, I began throwing short hooks to his body. He gasped as I sunk my right fist deep into his midsection. I followed that with a right and felt his ribs bend under it. Mullargan scrambled back to escape but he lost his footing on the loose sand and fell.

"Don't let him up!" Fatala screamed. "Finish him now."

"Come on Sailor," Dawson's taunting voice added. "This ain't no Marquis of Queensbury fight."

I disregarded them and backed off so's Mullargen could get on his feet. He gave me a little nod and we moved in on each other again. This time he didn't waste no time dancing around but came in with a flurry of punches that dazed me but didn't do no real damage. They wasn't meant to, though, they was to put me off balance for his one-punch finisher; a right uppercut that packed all the power of his body behind it.

The punch caught me flush on the chin and lifted me off of my feet. I blacked out for a minute and was only snapped out of it when my shoulders landed on the sand. I opened my eyes and Mullargen was standing over me but it seemed like there was a red fog betwixt us. He stared at me in shock as I clumb to my feet--probly because nobody had ever gotten up from one of his special punches before. To my surprise, he stood back and let me stand.

I gave him a little nod and we started again. This time he went back to his first strategy of stinging me and dancing away. Something had changed though; I could see it in his eyes. He'd hit me with everything he had and I was still coming. It had rattled him and his punches didn't have as much in 'em. It was like he was spending most of his effort staying out of my reach.

That gave me the chance I needed. I crowded him close to the ropes and, and when he didn't have no space to run I laid into him with left and right hooks to the head. He covered up with his arms but that left his kidneys and short ribs open and I commenced to beat on them. He started coming out of his crouch and I caught him with a right hook that crossed his eyes then drilled him with an overhand left that put him down for the count.

Two of the big, shirtless sailors helped him out of the ring whilst I clambered out to where Fatala was waiting.

"Fool!" she snarled. "What were you thinking, letting him get back up?"

"What's the problem," I asked. "I won, didn't I?"

"If I lose this tournament because you choose to be merciful... they will never find your body."

Before I could recover from surprise, she stormed back to her throne-chair and started puffing away on a cigarette. I ambled over to Ned Dargan who was looking better and sitting on a log next to Mrs. Harper.

"Say, that was pretty classy of you, Steve," he said.

"I just ain't one to hit a guy when he's down," I replied with a shrug.

"That eye looks pretty bad," he said, unfolding a clasp knife with shaky hands. "It oughter be lanced."

"Belay that!" I said. "You're still loopy from that beating you took and liable to jab me in the brain-pan.

"I'll do it," Mrs. Harper said.

She took the knife and, under Ned's direction, made a cut to the swollen area under my eye. She turned a little pale when the blood spurted out but didn't otherwise show no sign of distress.

"Thanks, Ma'am," I said. "I can see again."

"Good," she replied.

She was gonna say more but suddenly went rigid. Following her gaze I saw her husband stepping into the ring across from Slug O'Leary. He was about six feet tall and probably weighed 190 lbs, which made him look like a pigmy next to O'Leary who is 6'3" and 240 lbs. of muscle. Tournament or no, I decided I was gonna step in if it looked like he was getting hurt bad. I liked Mrs. Harper and didn't want to see her more upset than she was already.

I shouldn't'a worried. O'Leary stepped forward and took a swing but Bulan--as he had been interduced--side-stepped it and landed a punch on the bigger man's face. It weren't a blow with any real science behind it, but it took the big man off his feet. Blood was trickling from O'Leary's nose and mouth as he rose and he spat out a tooth. He tried another punch but Bulan caught his wrist. He grabbed O'Leary's belt with the other hand, lifted him like he was a child, and flung him clean out of the ring.

Slug landed hard and it took him a couple of seconds to rise. In the meantime, Bulan just stood there in the center of the ring. Slug climbed back over the ropes but it weren't two seconds before Bulan had smashed him down again. This time he didn't get up.

I couldn't believe what I'd seen but I didn't have no time to think about it. Marius stepped out again.

"Round two," he announced. "Dawson and Costigan, take your places."

I locked eyes with Dawson and he gave me a smirk. I realized that I want to bash in his ugly mug about as bad as I'd ever wanted to hit anyone. We came straight at each other and stood there, toe-to-toe, trading punches with neither of us making no attempt at defense. I had to give it to him, Dawson was as tough as they came and his punches was like getting kicked by a mule.

He must not have liked the results he was getting, 'cause he pushed into a clench. While we was struggling for position, he drove his left knee up between my legs. I felt a burst of intense pain that radiated out through my limbs. Before I could shake it off, Dawson tripped me and started kicking me with his over-sized feet. I knew that he only weighed about 235 or 240, but them stomps felt like he was as heavy as an elephant.

Fortunately, I've had a well rounded education, meaning that I knows a thing or two about rasslin' as well as boxing. I caught Dawson's foot with both hands and give it a powerful twist which dumped him to the ground. He scooped up a handful of sand as he rose but I'd seen that trick when he'd used it on Ned, and charged him, driving my head into his massive gut before he could fling the sand.

Dawson went down with me on top of him. He pasted me one across the mouth but, lyin' on his back as he was, couldn't get no weight behind it. I leaned in and slammed my fist into his forehead. It hurt like blazes but it hurt him even worse. I repeated the blow and felt something inside my hand give. Despite that, I drew back for one more smash, but it wasn't needed. Dawson was out cold.

Fatala was all smiles when she met me at the ropes.

"That was most impressive," she purred. "I'm pleased that you can be ruthless."

"Yeah," I said. She was a pretty enough dame, but her own ruthless streak was causing me to go sour on her.

"Let me give you a reward," she said, draping her arms around my neck and drawing me in to a lingering kiss. Whilst I wasn't feeling none too friendly towards her, I figgered it was best to be polite like and kiss her back.

"I saw that your arm was hurt," she whispered as she brushed her lips across my stubbly cheek. "Take the drug I gave you earlier; it will help."

"No disrespect, miss," I replied, but I told you: I don't dope for a fight."

"The rules of the prize ring have no place here," she whispered, drawing back a little.

I shook my head. "I ain't a cheat."

"Very well," she said. "Don't take the drug if you're certain you can win without it. If you fail me, though, you will regret it."

I stared into her eyes for a minute and got that chill again. I can't say why, but I got the feeling that she would happily kill me if she decided it was a good idea. There was more cold-blooded murder in those eyes than in Dawson and his whole crew of cutthroats.

I ambled down the beach a bit as Marius called the names of the next fighters: Bulan and Holloway. I opened my hand and frowned at the little glass bottle, then tossed it into the bay.

"You spurn Madame Fatala's gift?"

I turned to see the little Chinaman, Sing Lee, who had come up on me real quiet.

"What about it?"

"Most men would have accepted."

"I ain't never doped for a fight and I won't never."

"Most admirable," Sing Lee said, "but most dangerous. She is one of the deadliest criminals in Europe. Some say that she is Fantômas himself, come back in female form. Perhaps you should have accepted."

I snorted, derisive like.

We both glanced over to the ring where Holloway was dancing around Bulan. He was playing it cautious, having seen what happened to O'Leary.

"Lissen, pal," I said. "That Bulan character ain't no ordinary fighter, is he?"

"He is not. Bulan is not a human being. He was created in a laboratory by Missy Virginia's father, Professor Maxon."

"Huh?"

"The Professor had a dozen successes, but they were all deformed monstrosities," Sing Lee continued. "He was missing the key element, the tissues of a human being. Finally, opportunity presented itself. A young American named

Townsend Harper drowned off the island where we were living and his body washed ashore. I took samples from his body and added it to experiment 13. Bulan is the result of that experiment."

"Huh?"

"You must be wondering how I, a humble cook, could help guide this experiment without the Professor's knowledge. I am actually a scientist of some small skill. I was sent to monitor his experiments by Madame Ingomar's father, who has long desired the secret of creating a homunculus for himself."

"Huh?"

"The homunculus is an artificial man," Sing Lee said. "You see…"

He continued on but I sorta tuned him out. He weren't makin' no sense and I wanted to see the fight. Holligan had been doing okay against Bulan but the smaller man had finally managed to corner him and was raining blow after crushing blow on his defenses. Holligan clenched with him but Bulan just locked him up in a bear hug. Holligan struggled fiercely but it weren't no good. In just a few minutes Bulan tossed him to the ground where he feebly crawled away.

"That brings us to the final match," Marius shouted, stepping into the ring. "Bulan, representing Madame Ingomar versus 'Sailor' Steve Costigan, representing Fatala."

I strode to the ring and ducked through the ropes and, before the conch sounded, marched up to Bulan.

"Mister," I said, "I don't know why you're doing what you're doing but I think you're a dirty bilge-rat."

He glared at me but didn't say anything.

"You got a nice wife—a real classy lady who's all tore up over the way you're acting. After the grief you've given her, roughing you up is gonna be a pleasure."

"What are you talking about?" The look on his face was such genuine puzzlement that it irritated me.

"Are you saying you don't remember her?" I demanded, jabbing my finger in the direction of Mrs. Harper. She stood when he turned to face her and looked all hopeful but her face fell when he turned back to me.

"I don't know that woman."

"Costigan!" Marius cried. "Back to your position or you forfeit the fight."

I did what he asked, but when I turned back I saw Bulan looking at Mrs. Harper with a troubled expression. Then the conch shell blew.

I launched into Bulan, who still seemed kinda distracted. That worked out for me because I got in a good left to the head before he thought to defend himself. I followed up with my right but my hand exploded with pain when the punch landed. Bulan, in the meantime, shrugged off the blows and swung a looping overhanded punch at me. It shoulda been easy to duck, but it came so fast that I couldn't. I barely got my good arm up in time to block it. It hit so hard that I was numbed to the elbow.

He followed with a punch to the gut that felt like it pressed my belly button up against my spine. Compared to that punch, the best shots of Dawson and Mullargan and all the heavyweights I ever faced was nothing but puny slaps. I don't think Dempsey hisself could have come close to a blow like that.

I leaned into him, trying to keep on my feet, but he wasn't havin' none of that. He gave me a shove that tossed me a dozen feet to land in a heap. He got distracted again, looking off at Mrs. Harper, which gave me the chance to rise and head toward him. I gave a fierce roar as a swung at him, but he just slapped my hand away and gave me a punch that knocked loose one of my right molars. That wouldn't have been so bad but the tooth got lodged in my windpipe and started choking me.

Bulan was real obliging though. He gave me a left to the belly that popped that tooth out neat as you like. Course, it also messed up my breathing, but you got to take such favors as you get 'em.

He dropped me again with a right to the head. The sand felt real comfortable, and a swab with even a lick of sense would have stayed down for the count. I ain't got that much, I guess, and I sure ain't got no quit. I used my good arm to push myself up then rose to my feet and attacked once again.

Bulan got a puzzled look on his face at my determination, but that didn't stop him from smashing me down. I rose again and he struck me down again. We repeated that three more times.

"Why don't you stay down?" he said as I rose a fourth time.

I couldn't muster the breath to speak so I answered him with a left to the jaw. That really irritated him and he grabbed me in the same bear hug he'd used on Halloran. The hold pinned my arm against my body but missed my injured right somehow. It was agonizing but I forced my hand up until I could fishhook my thumb into the corner of his mouth. It must have hurt him, but I couldn't tell by the way his grip continued to tighten. I felt my ribs bend to the breaking point.

"Townsend!" I heard Mrs. Harper's voice cry out. "Please, stop! You're going to kill him."

I don't know if that got through to him but his grip slackened just a bit. I poured all my strength into my throbbing right arm and forced his head back. When I had enough distance, I slammed my forehead into his face. His grip came loose and I hammered at him with a left, which surprised me by connecting. I followed that with a backhand blow with the same hand and, when that worked, I began working my left arm like a piston, raining blow after blow on Bulan, who didn't seem to be making no effort at defense. I didn't stop to think about that. My whole world had narrowed down to the rise of my fist and the jarring impact each time it came down. I wasn't aware of nothing else until I threw a punch that didn't meet no resistance.

I staggered back a step and became aware of Bulan stretched out on the sand at my feet. Someone moved up beside me and I almost punched him before I recognized Marius.

"The winner!" he cried and raised my right hand in victory.

That caused me no end of pain so I jerked it away from him and glared at the members of the gang in their throne-chairs. Mrs. Harper clambered through the ropes and knelt by her husband, cradling his head in her lap.

"My champion has won!" Fatala said, rising to her feet. "The treasure is mine."

"Nuts to you, lady," I replied and saw her expression change from triumph to shock. "I know I come here as your champion, but I didn't fight that last match for you. That was for Mrs. Harper."

The lady looked up at me with a tear-streaked face and a stunned expression but it was Madame Ingomar who spoke.

"Virginia Harper and I have an agreement," she said. "She can have her husband back in exchange for the treasure."

"No!" Fatala shrieked. "This is not to be allowed. He entered this contest as my champion, the victory is *mine*!" She took a step toward the darker woman but a pair of the ape-like Chinamen stepped in between them, hands on the hilts of their big daggers.

"Ladies, please..." Marius said.

Before he could get any more out, there was a burst of gunfire. Bebert had stepped out of the jungle with a Tommy-gun in his hands and fired another burst over the heads of the assembly.

Fatala let out a crazy laugh. "I anticipated some sort of treachery, so I chose to be prepared."

It seemed to me like she was taking a long chance. All of them big-time crooks and every one of their deformed Chinamen and bare-chested sailors and pirates and various thugs and villains was eying her and Bebert. It was just a matter of time before someone went for a pistol or flung a blade and the standoff turned into mayhem.

I thought there would be a problem as Fatala approached the little teak box but the guards stepped away. She opened it with a triumphant flourish, then her face changed.

First, it went blank with shock, then turned to fury, then she started laughing, a horrible, ghoulish cackling that I knew I was gonna be hearing in my dreams for a long time. Finally she stopped and took a little piece of paper from the box.

"It's from the Colonel," she said. "He knew all along."

"What of the treasure?" little Mr. Oden asked.

"Gone. He has reclaimed it already. But he says he has left us with a gift."

"What gift?" Gutman asked.

As if in reply, there was a hollow sounding *whoomp* as Dawson's steamer erupted into a column of flame that lit up the bay. Sailors and various mugs ducked for cover as pieces of flaming wood and metal began to rain down. A second later one of the yachts blew to smithereens and I decided that bitin' the dirt was a good idea. There was another explosion as a second yacht went up, then another, then another.

When I looked up there wasn't anything left of them boats. The others began to clamber to their feet with no sign of resumin' hostilities. Even Bebert let his gun hang at his side.

I didn't stick around to see what the gang did. Me and Ned took Mrs. Harper and her husband, who was already coming around, and found a footpath heading to Papeete. O'Leary and Sing Lee had tagged along as well. I didn't know if the gang was gonna take the same path out, though I suspected they wouldn't while Bulan was with us.

"I don't get it," I said. "I couldn't'a beat you if you'd kept fightin'. Why'd you just stand there and take it?"

"I don't know," he replied. "My memory was gone, but there was still something about Virginia's face. I couldn't fight when she told me not to."

"Well, if you decide to go professional, you could get any title you like," I said.

He shook his head sadly. "No, friend. Championships are for real men. You heard what Sing Lee had to say; I'm just a soulless monster."

"That is not what Sing Lee said," the Chinaman interjected.

"No," Mrs. Harper chimed in. "Could a man without a soul have thrown off that woman's control like you did?"

"I don't know…" Bulan said.

"Well I do," I said. "I ain't no expert on souls, but nobody can fight like you without heart, and that's as good as a soul any day."

"Perhaps so," Bulan said, looking all thoughtful.

"All right," I said. "Now, let's pick up the pace. I gotta catch my ship before she sails. This has been fun and all, but it ain't goin' in the record books and I got a fight in Brisbane to get ready for."

There is a gap in Harry Dickson's career, about which we know very little: it takes place between Harry's service in World War I—presumably as a spy of some kind—and the opening of his consulting detective agency in Baker Street in or about 1929. Nicholas Boving has chosen to present us with an untold tale of Dickson's pre-Holmesian career, teaming up the American Sherlock Holmes with the indomitable Bulldog Drummond against the works of a mad scientist whose story is torn from the pages of Maurice Renard's sf classic Doctor Lerne...

Nicholas Boving: *Wings of Fear*

England, 1923

The iron bound door slammed behind him with a bang of awful finality. Hugh Drummond shrugged. If there was a way in, there was a way out. It was an immutable law. The trick was to find it.

A voice came out of the darkness.

"Drummond? Hugh Drummond?"

Drummond froze and slowly turned.

"Who wants to know?" he asked.

A tall, rangy man came out of the shadow.

"Harry Dickson."

Drummond smiled; an expression that totally transformed what was generally considered an ugly face into a thing approaching, if not handsome, at least acceptable.

"Good God! What the Devil are you doing here?"

Dickson frowned.

"Three damned great thugs dressed as gamekeepers jammed shotguns in my back. It seemed prudent to obey them. What about you?"

Drummond shrugged.

"I'm staying at a pub a couple of miles from here, just doing a spot of shooting and fishing, and generally getting the stink of London out of my system. I was taking the landlord's dogs out for a bit of a post-prandial run when I saw this place sitting on the end of the causeway, just asking to be poked into. And, like you, I got rounded up by what was probably the same bunch of so-called gamekeepers. The dogs had the sense to bolt for home." He smiled a bit sheepishly. "Serves me right for being so nosy. But more to the point, why are you here, and how long have you inhabited this ritzy place? This isn't exactly the old metropolis of London."

"About twenty-four hours." Dickson gestured with his chin. "It's a long story, so pull up a rock."

When Dickson had finished his explanation there was what is sometimes called a thundering silence, for he had just told a story that, on the face of it, would have got him laughed out of every decent club in London. Not that Dickson, unlike Drummond, belonged to any decent clubs.

"You mean, this thing is genuine, not some stitched-together hoax?" asked Drummond.

"According to the Natural History Museum's curator of dinosaurs, or whatever you call him, it's a living, breathing, flying worst nightmare from Hell."

"Sounds like my aunt Matilda. So it's real?"

"Absolutely" said Dickson, nodding. "Imagine a cross between a pterodactyl with a ten foot wingspan, a crocodile's head and claws like a monstrous eagle, and you'll get some idea."

"You paint a pretty picture of something that ought to be extinct. Where did it come from?"

"A farmer caught it snapping up one of his sheep. Gave it both barrels of his twelve bore. He said it came out of the setting sun like one of those fighter planes."

"And he didn't try to sell it to the local press?"

"Never got the chance." Dickson shook his head. "Seems some swell called Hannay was staying with a pal in the area."

"Not Major-General Sir Richard Hannay?"

"That's the one. Anyway, don't interrupt. This Hannay spirited the thing away and sent it post haste to the Natural History Museum." He cocked an eye at Drummond. "You know Hannay?"

Drummond nodded.

"Same club, dear boy. But go on, go on."

"Well, it seems a couple of days later, Sir Walter Bullivant, you know, the..."

Drummond nodded. "I know who he is."

"Anyway, he got a hand-delivered note with a photo and descriptions, and a demand for ten million pounds, or the writer was going to let loose dozens of the damned things all over England."

"How did you get involved?" asked Drummond. "Oh, of course, you were some sort of spook during the war."

"Bullivant wanted it kept quiet: a secret investigation. He remembered me and roped me in."

"Why not the police?" inquired Drummond.

"Bullivant said he didn't want a bunch of coppers tramping across the West of Scotland asking questions and scaring the locals."

"The farmer?"

"Given untold gold and threatened within an inch of his life."

Drummond's next question was deceptively quiet:

"Found out anything yet?"

Dickson wasn't deceived. He knew his man of old. The slightly loony front hid a startling capacity for getting at the truth, and then dealing with the problem effectively. There was a twinkle in his eye.

"I left the best bit for last. The letter was signed."

The silence was palpable.

"Does the name 'Peterson' mean anything to you?"

The palpable silence deepened. Drummond's face got uglier and granitic. Slowly he stood up, went to the door, then turned.

"I suppose you know you've got my full attention."

"Rather thought I would," said Dickson, smiling.

Drummond looked upwards. "Then this is..."

"The lion's den, yes."

"How the Devil did you find it? I mean, dear old Carl is a wily bird. He doesn't usually exactly advertize his presence."

"How are the mighty fallen." Dickson looked self-satisfied. "The trouble with this kind of place is, they aren't quite ten a penny; at least, not livable castles sufficiently far from nosy neighbors. And you can't exactly go around knocking on doors asking if they're for rent, or do they have nice dungeons and assorted barns. I mean, you might raise one or two eyebrows."

"With you so far old bean," nodded Drummond.

"Discrete inquiries with local bobbies, the aforementioned farmer, and one or two chaps who specialize in arranging rents and sales and so on, and I managed to zero in on this place. Added to which, I narrowed it down when I mention a fellow accompanied by a stunningly beautiful woman. You'd be amazed at how many chaps remembered dear Irma."

"No wonder Bullivant roped you in."

"Elementary, my dear chap. Any detective could have done it."

Drummond digested the information.

"One wonders how dear Carl has managed the impossible this time. I mean, for God's sake, dinosaurs are extinct and you can't just whistle up something like that."

Dickson's face had also lost its humor.

"You can if you have a tame mad vivisectionist called Doctor Lerne who's been known to carry out successful organ transplants, both between men and animals. It seems this Lerne was a student of Moreau, or something like that..."

"Sorry old bean, you've lost me," said Drummond, puzzled.

"Moreau."

"More of who?"

"Doctor Moreau," sighed Dickson. "Name means anything?"

Drummond's brow furrowed, then enlightenment dawned.

"Good God! The fellow who had that dreadful island? But that was years ago."

"That's the man."

"The how the deuce does he fit in?"

Harry shook his head. "He doesn't. But Lerne is ten times more capable than Moreau ever was."

"And you know this how?"

"Peterson came and gave me an orientation lecture just after I was nabbed."

Drummond's slightly oafish exterior slipped away like a snake's skin. Dickson wondered why he bothered with it, but realized it was actually a very good disguise.

"And old Carl vouchsafed this unto you?"

"Word for word."

"So this really is a stitched together monstrosity after all, a one-off that got shot," said Drummond, his expression lightening.

His optimism was lowered several rungs by Dickson's answer:

"Unfortunately no. The thing is literally a biological creation. God knows how Lerne did it, and the Natural History Museum is utterly mystified. There was a report of a bunch of dinosaurs discovered in a valley in the Auvergne near Gambertin… Perhaps that was the source of Lerne's samples? Who knows? But there it is. And according to the brains, if he's done one he can do as many as he likes." He managed a smile. "It seems Peterson has a bit of a sense of humor because he's called it *Diablosaurus Petersonii.*"

"And you say he signed the letter as well?" asked Drummond, frowning. "That was stupid: Carl must be slipping. Anyway, he has no sense of humor: more a god complex." He turned and stared through the bars. "The problem is, how the Devil do we get out of here and put a spoke in his wheel?"

"Well, unless he intends to starve us to death, at some time someone's going to come along with our dinner. All we have to do is…"

"Biff them over the head, do a bit of wrecking, collar Carl, and put the rest in the hands of the police. Problem solved. Can't think why I didn't think of it '

"If you're going to be negative and put it that way," said Dickson, looking slightly put out.

Drummond smiled cheerfully. The thought of action always brightened his outlook on life.

"Not at all, dear boy. Your scheme is perfectly sound. The only fly in the ointment might be that they'll come in gaggles and have guns, and we've got our hands firmly tied behind our backs."

Irma Peterson fitted a cigarette into her long holder and lit it. She blew a plume of smoke and looked across the room to where Carl Peterson stood silhouetted at a tall window.

"So our nemesis is finally behind bars. I wonder how he found us.

"His usual inane luck," replied Peterson, shrugging.

"The other will tell him if it's a coincidence, of course."

"I do not believe in coincidences."

"What do you intend this time?"

Peterson continued his study of a pair of hunting falcons.

"A final solution naturally. I cannot risk his meddling."

Irma seemed amused.

"He does have a way of spoiling things, does he not?"

Peterson turned to face her.

"There are more than twenty diablosaurs in the barn already. They are no doubt hungry. Even Drummond cannot escape such creatures."

Irma raised one perfect eyebrow. It seemed that even she found such an end disquieting for a man she reluctantly admired. Without comment, she picked up a magazine and absently flicked through the glossy pages.

Peterson strolled slowly to an escritoire, chose a cigar from a humidor and lit it with evident satisfaction.

"I shall be with Lerne," he said. A mantelpiece clock chimed for attention He glanced at it. "We dine at eight. After that I shall see to Drummond and the other interfering fool."

Major-General Sir Richard Hannay looked across the large desk at Sir Walter Bullivant. The great man seemed worried.

"No word from Harry Dickson?" Hannay inquired.

Bullivant toyed with a pencil then threw it down in a gesture of frustration.

"Nothing. He's missed his schedule. It's been twenty-four hours. I tell you, Hannay, I'm worried."

"There may be any number of reasons. He may be close to his man and not able to risk giving himself away."

Bullivant's expression didn't change.

"Perhaps. But his mandate at first was to observe and report back. Dash it all, I'd send in the army if I thought it would do any good. The deuce of it is that it's on a spit, accessible only by a causeway and cut off by high tide, and he has a steam yacht. The moment our man smelled a rat, he'd be gone and in international waters. We'd be back where we started with this horror still looming."

"You're convinced he's genuine?" said Hannay.

"Horribly." Bullivant waved a dismissive hand. "The money is nothing. But once he's got it, what's to stop him unleashing the things anyway. God knows he hates us enough."

Hannay crossed one tweed covered leg over the other. His tone was casual.

"I don't suppose it would help if I went up and took a look?"

Sir Walter jumped at the offer.

"Would you? I mean, could you? What about your wife?"

"Mary's at Cannes with Janet Roylance, and Peter John's at school. So, you see, I'm my own man at the moment, just roughing it at my club. I'd welcome a bit of action."

"I'd be damned glad if you would," said Bullivant.

Hannay got up.

"As old Peter Pienaar would have said, we shall make a plan."

Five minutes later Major-General Sir Richard Hannay left the august portals of the Home Office and was striding across St. James's Park towards his club. There was a twinkle in his eye and a spring in his step. He would take the night train to Glasgow.

Carl Peterson entered the laboratory in the ancient Castle Dubh. He stood in the doorway watching the genius of his newest confederate, Doctor Lerne. His thoughts on the subject of the good doctor were not pleasant, and he wondered what the man would have said if he knew what would occur once his usefulness was at an end. He also thought the castle's name was appropriate, for it was black indeed.

"Good evening Doctor," he said. "I trust that all goes according to plan.'

It was not a question, but the doctor was oblivious to the veiled threat. He unbent his back from peering into a microscope and pushed his small round spectacles to the top of his thinning forehead.

"You trust correctly. What may I do for you Mr. Peterson?"

"Exactly what you are doing Doctor, but perhaps at a slightly accelerated pace."

Doctor Lerne turned back to his study of the microscope slide.

"These matters cannot be hurried."

His tone was a touch acerbic. Peterson answering smile was thin and lacked any degree of warmth.

"I have obtained two test subjects for you," he said.

Lerne jerked up.

"Who? Where?"

There was a quiver in his voice and stare in his eyes that betrayed a mind on the verge of madness or in the grip of drugs. Peterson ignored the question.

"How many diablosaurs have we now?"

"I have decided to call them *kraks*."

Peterson raised an angry eyebrow. "What they are called is for me to..." He stopped. Best to let it ride. He needed the doctor for the time being and, as Shakespeare had written, what's in a name. Lerne might call the creatures kraks, but the world would know them as *Diablosaurus Petersonii*, and tremble.

"How many, doctor?"

"Twenty three. More are... hatching as we speak." He advanced a couple of steps. "Well, what of these... subjects?"

Lerne's enthusiasm for the demonstration was replaced by his even keener enthusiasm for his creations. He beckoned eagerly.

"Come Mr. Peterson, come. Let me show you."

Peterson smiled inwardly. The man was undoubtedly mad, but also undoubtedly a genius. How else could one possibly describe someone who had achieved the impossible and literally created life? He allowed himself to be led into the huge stone barn attached to the castle by a newly constructed passageway.

The passage opened up into a closed off section constructed of steel bars. Beyond the bars was the barn, and in it were arranged in serried rows, a series of strong steel mesh cages.

In themselves, the cages were no different than those used to transport dangerous animals to and from a zoo. But in those cages there strode and hopped on huge raptor's talons, hissing like leaky steam valves, and clacking horrendous beaks as they flapped leather wings in attempts to escape their confinement, the fearsome creatures Peterson had named Diablosaurs.

Carl Peterson was a man whose emotions were as cold as ice water, but even he was glad of the strong bars protecting himself and the doctor. Genius indeed the doctor might be, but it had been his genius to realize the potential the creatures offered. Money indeed, and more than he could use in a lifetime, but, overall, had been the prospect of revenge over the country he had come to hate. An unpleasant smile lurked at the corners of his thin lips. Also revenge against his nemesis, that bungling oaf Bulldog Drummond.

He gave a low growl of anger as a thought crept unbidden into his mind. How had the fool found him? Irma had suggested coincidence: it was a possibility, even though he had no time for coincidences. How else could Drummond have...? He whirled about and returned along the passage to the laboratory. There he stopped while Lerne caught up.

Peterson drew on his cigar and examined the half inch of ash.

"I think we shall have a demonstration this evening after dinner"

He turned to go. Lerne called out, his voice agitated:

"I insist, Peterson. I must know who these... subjects are."

Peterson looked at him coldly.

"It is of no concern to you, doctor." He drew on his cigar and sauntered out of the laboratory. He called over his shoulder. "One hundred, doctor. I require one hundred. It is in our... agreement, remember?"

Not more than an hour after Drummond had been so unceremoniously shoved into the cellar; Major-General Sir Richard Hannay leaned back against the dry stone wall and steadied the telescope in the vee of his walking stick. The range was a little over a half mile. Castle Dubh stood out against the sea silvered by the morning sun. He did not find the sight particularly inspiring.

"The only chance is to go in after dark," he said to the man lounging at his side.

Archie Roylance was equally unimpressed.

"Never did much like night raids. I like to see my enemy."

Hannay lowered the telescope.

"That's because you were up at a couple of thousand feet. Down on the ground, darkness is your friend."

"Does the general have a plan?" Archie's tone was a touch sarcastic.

"A pincer movement should do it."

"There'll be guards roaming or I'm the Queen of Hearts."

"We need to cross the causeway," said Hannay, nodding. "What time is low water?"

"Round about ten, I think."

"And the moon?"

"First quarter and it rises at midnight."

Hannay raised his telescope and peered again at the castle. He snapped the scope shut.

"I think I'll send a telegram to Glasgow. There are a few lads from my old regiment who'd probably welcome a bit of sport."

"And the plan?" Archie insisted.

"We take as much explosives as can fit in a decent-sized push cart, and blow the place up. A ton should do the trick."

Archie Roylance had his own plan.

"Why not just whistle up a gunboat and blow the place to smithereens?"

Hannay rounded on him fiercely.

"Absolutely not. My God! Think of the outrage and questions in the House. The press would have a heyday and heads would probably roll. An explosion can be put down as a mystery, or an anarchist outrage. Bullivant could manage that, but not one of His Majesty's ships shelling private property."

Archie retreated, slightly abashed.

"I suppose you have a source for the explosives?" he asked.

Hannay shrugged as if such a thing was an everyday requisite.

"A lorry can deliver them within two hours of my call."

Archie Roylance reached out and took the telescope. He examined the castle.

"I wish I had that kind of pull," he brightened. "We'll need guns: rifles and whatnot."

"Rifles are a no go with these things," Hannay said. "They're like damned great eagles: vicious and fast Archie, you're in charge of shotguns, more if possible. Get a dozen. Beg, buy, borrow or steal. And cartridges: lots of cartridges. Bird shot won't do unless it's turkey."

"The farmer got one."

"He was lucky. See if you can get #2 shot, but #4 will do."

Archie Roylance unhitched himself from his seat on the wall. "And he did his master's bidding. I'll be back by dinner time at the latest."

Bulldog Drummond had about him the air of a disgruntled bear. He gave a massive sigh. "Right about now, I could do with half a dozen eggs, a pound of bacon, and at least three pints of good ale."

"I was thinking along the lines of a steak and kidney pie," said Harry Dickson. "What time d'you reckon it is?"

"Getting rather late for dinner," Drummond growled.

"My thoughts exactly. I fancy we're on short commons tonight."

Drummond grunted. There was about him the air of a man concentrating to the full and exerting huge strength. Dickson looked at him.

"You all right, old man?"

Drummond gave one last grunt of effort and suddenly his hands were free. He winced as he massaged life back into numbed extremities.

"Persistence; that's what does it Harry. Never give up."

"Why didn't you tell me?"

Drummond stood up.

"Didn't want to get your hopes up." He dragged Dickson to his feet and untied his hands. He grinned wickedly. "We now have two aces up our sleeves. Sooner or later someone will remember us, at which time we shall catch them with their pants down and make our escape. However," he cautioned. "When they come, we must be models of meekness and self-pity, our hands safely behind our backs."

"You don't do meekness and self-pity."

Drummond scratched his chin. "I'm not much of an actor, but the poor light should cover that defect. In the meantime, let sleep re-knit the raveled sleeve of care or whatever."

And, suiting the actions to the words, Hugh Drummond lay down and within a couple of minutes his snores reverberated through their cell like an express train in a tunnel.

With a last snore like a warthog emerging from a wallow, Drummond woke. For a moment, he lay still, absorbing information about his surroundings. Then he remembered and sat up.

"What time is it?" he asked.

Harry Dickson had been awake for some time. He was standing by the door with an ear to the thick paneling.

"You've been snoring like a pig for eight hours, probably more. How do you do it?"

"Easy," Drummond said. "I just close my eyes and *voilà*."

"Ass. I mean sleep at a time like this."

"Old soldier's habit, Harry. Sleep when you can. No sign of life I suppose. No succor, no beer, no bacon and eggs?"

"No sign of anything. And the time is nearly ten."

Drummond stretched and got up.

"So no dinner then. Probably do you good anyway; you're fat and pasty from city living."

Dickson was about to answer defensively when there was a bang on the door.

A voice called out: "Step away from the door. If you do not, you will be shot."

Drummond raised an eyebrow.

"Now that doesn't sound like any waiter I know."

As they moved back against the wall Drummond said *sotto voce*: "Remember we're tied up. Keep your hands behind your back."

The door opened to reveal three large men dressed in rough tweeds, one carrying a shotgun and the others with Luger automatics.

"What ho chaps," Drummond said breezily. Then, he frowned. "But what's the meaning of all this? My friend and I, just a couple of innocent hikers and you..."

One of the Lugers flicked at him warningly. The owner growled:

"Shut up."

Two of the men entered the cellar, taking up positions along the walls. One remained outside. Drummond considered having a go at them, but realized the impossibility of such a venture.

"What now?"

The Luger jerked towards the door.

"Go that way. Follow that man. Try nothing stupid and you may live a short while more."

"Why do they always say things like that: so melodramatic," Harry Dickson sighed.

"Comes with using guns instead of brains," Drummond replied as he sauntered towards the door. He nodded at the man at the entrance:

"Lead on, lead on."

Drummond strode into the room behind the gunman, and stopped. His face broke into a wide smile.

"Hello Irma my sweet; how perfectly ghastly to see you. I hear Carl's dreamed up some real-life harpies. It must be so comforting to know you have sisters after all." He glanced at Peterson. "Not so invincible anyway; the one that got away responded rather adversely to a farmer's shotgun."

"It did not escape," said Peterson, smiling. "It was sent as a gypsy's warning. To show that what I threaten is real."

"You took a chance, letting it go like that. Might have gone anywhere."

"It was hungry. The nearest food was on the mainland: I made sure of that."

"Speaking of hungry," Drummond said. "Doesn't the Geneva Convention have something to say about treatment of prisoners? Harry and I have been locked up for ages, and not so much as a sandwich."

Irma Peterson drew on her cigarette holder and blew a thin stream of smoke. She looked at Drummond appraisingly.

"You never learn, do you, my ugly one?"

Drummond turned to Dickson, then back to Irma.

"Now that's not very polite. Harry is considered quite handsome in some less discerning circles."

Carl Peterson unhitched himself from his stance at the fireplace.

"You're a meddling fool Drummond," he said.

"It's what I do best."

"Well, this will be the last time."

"My dear old Carl; you've said that before, and yet, here I am."

"This time, it is different. This is my last hurrah, my grand exit from the stage of, shall I say, unorthodox enterprises. I am untouchable. Your government knows it and will comply with my demands without let or hindrance. After which I shall...disappear."

Drummond took a couple of steps into the room. All banter had been wiped from his tone.

"My government will do nothing of the sort." He shrugged. "Besides, you'll be dead, so the matter is irrelevant."

Peterson was unmoved.

"Rather the reverse is true. It is you who will be dead, while I will be on the high seas on international waters." He waved a hand at the tall windows. "Moored just out there is a steam yacht."

Drummond glanced at Irma.

"I'd watch out for that personal pronoun, if I were you. Sounds as if your usefulness might be waning."

Irma shook her head and smiled.

"Nice try, my Hugh."

Drummond's mouth turned down.

"Not going to work, eh?"

Carl Peterson interrupted: "As a point of interest, just how did you find me?"

"I didn't. Harry did. You see, he's clever while I just sort of blundered in, in my usual way."

Peterson went to the escritoire, took a cigar and lit it. He glanced at Dickson.

"Just how did you find me?" he asked.

Drummond laughed.

"Dear old Carl, did you seriously imagine we wouldn't find you?"

Peterson ignored him, concentrating on Harry. Harry shrugged.

"A nice warehouse in London or Manchester would have done the trick, but no, you had to go all medieval, buy this pile, do a heap of renovations and stick out like sore thumbs. Country folk are notoriously nosy. And I thought you were supposed to be clever, a master criminal. I'm disappointed."

"It's old age," Drummond said. "Grey matter getting soggy. Sad really."

Peterson strolled casually to Drummond, looked at him as one might an interesting specimen, and slapped him hard across the face.

It was mistake.

He should have known better.

Drummond hit him, once, very hard, and it suddenly became apparent to one and all that neither of the securely bound men was secure after all.

Since arriving at the castle, since waiting in the cell, and since entering the room, Drummond had had one on his mind: mayhem. One of them, at least, had to escape. As he prattled, he had been eyeing everything that might conceivably be used as a weapon. He had settled on a set of very useful-looking set of brass tools in a rack by the fireplace. The heavy poker and a pair of tongs looked particularly serviceable.

Carl Peterson reeled backwards, tripped over a rug and landed heavily on his back, his nose bleeding profusely.

Dickson applied his elbow hard into the solar plexus of the guard behind him, who was stupidly standing too close. He ducked as the second guard charged. The man went over his shoulder as Dickson applied a Jujitsu move, landing heavily and hitting his head against a table leg, where, for several long seconds he ceased to be sure of his surroundings.

The third guard started to bring up his Luger, but it all seemed to happen in slow motion as Drummond sidestepped, strode to the fireplace, grabbed the brass poker and it the man across the shins. He dropped with a shout of agony and Drummond scooped up the Luger.

Irma screamed. Not with fear or hysterics, but with rage. She went at Drummond like a wild cat, hammering at him until Dickson dragged her off.

An oil lamp, which Drummond had noticed and which had, up to that point had leant a certain warm ambiance to the room, was swept up in one flowing movement and thrown. It shattered against the tall window frame and exploded. Within seconds the curtains were ablaze, and the fire had caught the spilled trail and was racing across the wooden floor.

And that would have brought matters to a successful conclusion, had not four large, hobnail-booted and tweed-clad men, aroused by the noise, appeared through an adjoining door. They were armed with shotguns, and no one in their right mind argues with a shotgun at close range.

But Drummond was not entirely in his right mind. Without a second thought, he charged them, roaring to Dickson to get out. Dickson hesitated for a split second, then realizing the logic, sprinted for a side window, dodging and feinting around the upright and fallen like a rugby fly half, and threw himself through the window, taking frame and all in his dash for freedom.

Drummond fought like a madman, but even his great strength was no match for four hefty men pinning him down. In the end, he surrendered rather than be battered to death and have no hope.

Peterson staggered to his feet, hand to his nose. His eyes blazed his fury. He pointed one quivering hand at the door to the cellar.

"Take him," he hissed through clenched teeth. "Take him to the barn and throw him in with the diablosaurs."

"No weapon, Carl?"

"I'm afraid you won't find a sword sticking out of a rock," Peterson snarled.

"So I won't get to rule Britannia and call myself Arthur? I'm disappointed, Carl."

"I think you will find little to laugh about when confronted by the kraks."

He whirled to face the fire. The smoke and crackling flames that had taken hold of the dry wood of the ancient building told him better than words that his dream was coming unstuck in a big way. A portion of the ceiling plaster collapsed as he snarled his rage. Irma, ashen faced, staggered towards him.

"What about Doctor Lerne, Carl?

Carl Peterson shrugged. "Indeed. What about him?" He wiped blood from his nose, crossed to the escritoire and rescued the humidor of cigars. "Time for us to make for the lifeboats, my dear." He paused to select a cigar and light it. "Perhaps some of the...kraks...will survive."

The gamekeeper thugs shoved him hard and Drummond staggered into the caged area. The steel barred gate clanged behind him and he heard the bolts shot home with an unmistakable finality.

A gravelly coarse voice with a foreign accent called out:

"The cages are opened by chains pulling on the locks." There were a couple of humorless laughs from the others. "I'm going to start opening them."

Drummond watched with a cold chill as slim chains tightened and the cage doors started opening.

"So long Drummond. Say your prayers. It's been a pleasure."

For a moment, Drummond stood like a statue, absorbing information: surroundings, deployment of the cages, exits—one, weapons—none, number of kraks—too many, outlook—very sticky and dark, chances of getting out—slim. Then one of the kraks either spotted him or smelled fresh meat because it swung its terrible head and the large, beady eyes seemed to flame with blood lust. It took a couple of lumbering steps towards him, and rustled its leathery wings.

The hairs on Drummond's neck stirred. He knew he was in for the fight of his life, worse and bloodier than any he had taken part in before: worse than the trenches where a man's life was measured in days, or even hours.

His eyes darted to the shadowed corners of the barn. Somewhere, there had to be something. A grim smile flitted across his face as he saw it, a small stack of reinforcing steel, the leavings from the construction of the fencing that kept the kraks imprisoned.

It was a race. Drummond took a dozen giant strides. The krak hopped, awkward, land bound. In the air, it would be master of its element, but not on the ground. Still, it was quick, horribly so, and the fearsome beak opened with a harsh hiss of anger, to reveal double rows of teeth that would with ease tear the hide from an elephant.

Drummond snatched two six foot lengths of one inch round steel bar and whirled, the bars spun in his hands like Indian clubs.

The krak hesitated momentarily, its primitive brain trying to process this new information. But it had no more experience than a new born child, nothing but raw instinct that drove it to kill and eat. It charged.

Drummond might have managed the kraks one at a time, for with one rod he caught the first one a crashing blow across its snapping beak, and the second rod smashed onto the bony, featherless skull. A gout of sticky blood splashed onto him and his lips curled in disgust. But there were already others let loose, and like all such nightmares the smell of blood drew them irresistibly.

For a few ghastly seconds, Drummond watched as they ripped the dying creature apart and ate its still-quivering body parts. He knew that he was witnessing not only life and death in the long-ago age of dinosaurs, but also what might become the present if they escaped the barn. The image conjured was too terrible to contemplate.

Vaguely his mind registered the smell of smoke. He had a flash vision of the curtains blazing. But nothing could take his mind off the appalling sight of the two kraks devouring the third. He had seen many horrors during his time as a soldier, but nothing had ever prepared him for that.

Sir Arthur Bullivant put the phone down and noticed with detached interest that his hands were shaking slightly. Other than calling out the army he'd done what he could. Harry Dickson had his orders: meet with Hannay and put him in the picture. But what of Hugh Drummond? The man had got out of some deuced tight places, but it seemed his chances in this one were dashed slim. Peterson's fiendish game might have been scotched, but those damned horrors were still alive and could break loose. God knows, Peterson might let them go anyway as an act of revenge.

He ran a hand across his eyes. He was tired. He sighed, reached for a cigar and lit it. His hand had steadied. The small flame burned true. He thought that after this matter was safely resolved he would retire. He had served his country as well as a man might, and lost his only son it its service. Surely that was enough. In the meantime there was work to do.

There were about a dozen rough-looking men in work clothes, cloth caps on their heads and scarves knotted about their necks. They looked at and listened attentively as Hannay spoke, the man whom they revered and had fought with in the war to end all wars. They would do as he ordered without question. Hannay pointed to a canvas covered lorry.

"There's a ton of dynamite in there, with detonators and fuses; and in Sir Archibald's car you'll find shotguns and cartridges. The plan is quite simple. This is raid with the object to destroy that building and everything in it. And I can tell you, the things Mr. Dickson called diablosaurs are creatures from Hell. They must be destroyed; not one left alive. Are you with me?"

There was a chorus of deep rough voices, and their meaning was without doubt. They'd follow the Major-General through Hell if asked. He held up the orders Dickson had been given by telegram from Sir Walter Bullivant.

"This job's about the most important you'll ever do. Listen to this." He read the text aloud: "You have full Governmental authority in this matter. The Prime Minister concurs. You must. Repeat. Must eliminate creatures at all cost." There was no room for misinterpretation.

Hannay took out his watch. "In half an hour the causeway will be uncovered, we'll drive the lorry as far as possible and then I'm afraid it's a load apiece. After that half of you go ahead to take care of any so-called gamekeepers—and I don't much how rough you get." He smiled . "Remember, guards at night are jumpy. But you chaps know what to do."

A man who seemed to be the agreed leader chuckled grimly. "You leave it to us, General."

Archie Roylance started handing out shotguns and cartridges and a khaki clad soldier started the lorry. And that was as far as they got.

Archie suddenly Roylance pointed urgently and shouted. "Look. The dashed place is on fire. Oh, well done, .Hugh!"

Dickson paused in the act of taking a shotgun.

"We've got to get him out of there."

"What price those bally explosives now Dick?" Archie grinned.

But Hannay was already among his men, issuing new orders.

"Too late for the dynamite. Someone's beaten us to the post. The job now is to get rid of those creatures. We must take the barn at all cost. You all have shotguns." He swung around to Dickson: "How many of the damned things are there?"

"Peterson said something about twenty or so," replied Harry, shaking his head."I should think probably more."

Hannay turned back to the men.

"You heard Mr. Dickson. You know what to do."

Almost before he had finished the men were heading for the castle at the double. He faced Archie and Dickson.

Archie watched them disappear into the darkness.

"Good Lord. I don't know if they'll scare anyone at the castle, but they most certainly scare me."

Hannay gave a wry smile.

"They're the salt of the Earth Archie. They come from a rough world, one that the likes of us do not understand. But by God they know how to fight."

Dickson broke in: "What the Devil are we standing here for?"

"The man's right." Hannay grabbed a shotgun from the car. We'll take the castle. Peterson and Irma may still be there."

Dickson followed suit, racing after him. Archie panted as he limped along in the rear.

"Would you be? The man has a steam yacht."

As they approached the castle, they heard a fusillade of shots like a pheasant shoot at some great estate. The shotguns were blazing. Dickson stopped, scanning the smoke filled darkness. He touched Hannay's arm.

"What about Drummond?"

Hannay's face was emotionless. Dickson saw by his expression that he was not going to weaken.

"Those damnable things come first, Dickson. Hugh Drummond can look after himself."

"What if he's injured? What if those things have got him?"

Hannay broke the shotgun, slipped in a pair of cartridges and snapped it shut. "Then, we're already too late."

Hugh Drummond had fought for his life many times. But never had he faced such overwhelming odds as when the rest of Peterson's diablosaurs began to drop from the cages and advance with dreadful purpose; hissing and shaking their leathery wings. Inconsequentially, he wondered what Phyllis was doing right then: probably just getting home from having dinner with one of her friends.

The two closest lifted their evil heads from the remains of their gruesome feast. It didn't take a genius to figure out what second course they had in mind. Drummond backed towards a corner: it was the only way. He had to have his back against something or they'd overwhelm him in seconds. He was brought up short as he felt the cold steel of the grill, and hefted the weight of the rods. What price a rifle? God knows, he might get a couple, and then what? What he needed was a machine gun. He needed firepower, not a couple of clubs.

And what could he do to stop creatures like that, things with brains so primitive they knew no fear, only the instinct to kill and feed?

And then, the one to his right took the initiative, or maybe it ran out of patience, or its blood lust was a shade stronger: for it charged, head low and neck outstretched like an attacking goose. Drummond's reaction was measured, leavened with instinct. With split second timing and a force that would have decapitated an ox, he swung the steel rod and caught the diablosaur across the neck. The creature's neck snapped like a rotten branch, but its momentum kept it moving and its nervous system didn't know it was dead until it crashed into Drummond, sending him staggering. He slammed against the grill, banging his head hard. He reeled and dropped to one knee as his brain tried to clear the concussion.

His confusion lasted no more than a few seconds, but by the time he had shaken his head clear and looked up, the nearest diablosaur was making its charge. Drummond eyes focused, he saw the horror, tried desperately to get to his feet, knowing it was already too late.

And then the creatures head disintegrated in a mess of blood and bone, and he heard the two flat bangs of gunshots: a left and right. He whirled in disbelief, to see half a dozen men with shotguns sticking through the bars. A moment later he felt as if he was back on the front as a continuous barrage of shotgun blasts filled the barn with mind numbing noise and choking smoke from black powder.

Drummond had no choice but to cling to his corner, just staying out of the way. He peered through the smoke and saw the creatures being blown to shreds, one after the other. Their screams of rage came clear over the gun blasts as they flung themselves towards him, minds still centered on their prey. But they also turned on each other, for meat to them was just that, and the scent of blood maddened them.

But slowly the noise of the shotguns eased until there was just the occasional bang as one of the shooters took care of a diablosaur still showing signs of life.

Drummond got to his feet, slowly and a little shakily. A voice with a strong Glasgow accent shouted something. He didn't understand at first, but it shouted again.

"Get oot the wa, Sir, I'm gin te blow the lock."

Drummond's brain cleared. He waved a hand and flattened himself against the wall. There was a bang, some fierce oaths, and the cage door slammed open. A couple of men in rough clothes, carrying shotguns, hurried in. One of them, a big raw boned hulk of a man, grabbed Drummond's arm.

"Are ye alright, Sir? Ye look a gae bluidy mess."

Drummond managed a smile.

"You should see the other fellow," he said.

There was a dull crash that shook the barn. For a moment Drummond didn't understand, and then a small flicker of flame at the corner of the barn roof told him the main castle was falling in.

"Best get out of here," he said. "This place is going to be an inferno shortly."

The big man nodded. "Best place for the damned things is Hell."

Drummond slapped him on the shoulder.

"I owe you fellows. My life wasn't worth a button till you showed up. Damned good shooting. Now get out."

And before the man could answer or stop him Drummond had made a dash for the door connecting to the main house.

The big Glaswegian skidded to a stop in front of Hannay, and made a smart salute. The war might be a memory, but once a soldier, always a soldier, and he revered the Major-General.

"I couldna stop him, Sir. Just uppit and ran straight inta the hoos."

"Not your fault, Sergeant."

The sergeant saluted again. "There's none o' they devil creatures alive, Sir. I'm thinkin' we got the lot."

Hannay returned the salute. "You and the men did a damned fine job. Now, spread out in a cordon across the island and make sure no one escapes."

He turned as Harry Dickson touched his arm.

"Drummond's in there, Hannay." He pointed to the castle which was burning beyond any hope of stopping. And even as he spoke a part of the roof collapsed, sending a huge column of sparks spiraling into the night sky.

Hannay's face was grim. "I know Harry."

"We've got to try. Let me take a couple of the men. Damn it all, he's in there. We can't just do nothing."

"Hugh Drummond is a friend of mine too, Harry. He should have come out with the lads. He's big enough, and God knows he's ugly enough to look after himself."

"You know he's gone after Peterson."

Hannay nodded. "I know. But Hugh's made his choice. We can only pray for the right outcome. I won't send another man to his death."

As he spoke another section of the roof caved in. Dickson knew the Major-General had made some hard choices during the war and sent men to their deaths, many of them, and in his heart he knew the man was right.

"And Peterson?"

"His damnable scheme has failed, thanks to you." Hannay said. "I shall speak to Bullivant of course."

"Damn Bullivant."

"Dick's right, you know." Harry saw Archie Roylance at his elbow. "But old Hugh's been in some dashed tight spots before. Besides, he hasn't had breakfast yet."

As he fought his way up the long flight of stone stairs and along the corridor that led to the castle hall, part of Drummond's brain acknowledged the stupidity and probable futility of his actions. A man with the brain of a flea would have got out of the place as fast as a running stag, but Drummond was not always known for the logic of his actions. It was the other part of his brain that drove him; the part that said he wanted above all else to see Carl Peterson's corpse on its funeral pyre, to know that the master criminal was finally dead, in his coffin and the lid nailed down. And also, a tiny corner of the same brain held the faint hope that perhaps the lovely Irma had managed to slip away.

He got to the end of the corridor, choking and gasping as the dense smoke caught his lungs. It was beyond time to get out. *For God's sake, get out!* Logic was screaming at him to do the sane thing. And then his outstretched hands felt the wood of the door, already hot to the touch. He cried out as the brass handle burned his fingers, but he turned it, ramming his shoulder against the door and bursting it open.

The room was a hell of smoke and fire, swirling, roaring, wood crackling and timbers falling. He peered through the inferno, eyes watering. Another chunk of ceiling fell, spewing flame and sparks at him. He was forced to acknowledge that nothing could have survived. Carl Peterson was assuredly dead, and the Devil had claimed his own.

Drummond covered his face with his jacket lapel, made a dash for the same window from which Harry Dickson had so unceremoniously exited, and leaped through it. He landed heavily, rolled, and was up on his feet in a second. He took a half-dozen steps away from danger, and then Hugh Drummond passed out.

It seemed that hours passed, a lifetime perhaps as images swirled in his mind: unsettling images of foul things. Irma Peterson's head merged with one of the creatures from hell, flying at him with mouth wide and incisors elongated into vampire fangs, to explode in a burst of red mist. And Carl Peterson, his arms around Phyllis, a knife at her throat, laughed, taunting, until they too faded into nothing but vague forms shrouded in fog.

Drummond woke with a start. It was dark. Above him were the pinpoints of stars struggling against the nascent moon. He smelled smoke and sat up. Behind him, a mere few yards away, the heat of the fire reaching him even against the breeze, the remains of the Castle Dubh blazed. He stood up, head splitting and the foul taste of burning flesh in his mouth.

He turned at the sound of voices. Somewhere men shouted and lamps bobbed as the men ran. They were coming towards him. He waited, not knowing whether he would have to fight again, or flee. He managed a croaking laugh. Flee? What kind of word was that? He braced himself as a tall figure emerged from the darkness and stopped a couple of yards short.

Harry Dickson shouted, and the relief in his voice was there for all to hear:

"Good God! We thought you were dead!"

Drummond tried to laugh again, but it stuck in his throat. Relief swept through him in waves. He threw his arms wide.

"So did I; several times."

Another figure emerged, tall and soldierly. Drummond managed a smile.

"Good to see you General."

"By God, Drummond, you gave us all a bad fright."

"Not as much as I gave myself." Drummond's face hardened. "What of those damned things?"

"Dead, the lot of them. The lads got them, I hope."

The craggy form of the sergeant appeared at Hannay's shoulder.

"Like shooting fish in a barrel, Sir. And the lads are gae glad ye came out awright."

Drummond reached forward and grasped the man's hand.

"My life sergeant. I owe you and your men my life."

The craggy face split into a smile. "Just ye be sure we dinna have to claim it Sir."

Archie Roylance limped forward.

"What of Peterson?" he inquired.

Drummond shrugged.

"God knows. But no one could have survived that inferno."

"But you didn't see bodies?"

Drummond shook his head.

Roylance turned to Hannay. "It's all London to a brick he's got away. The man's as slippery has a wet eel. Is the steam yacht still there?"

Drummond seemed disinterested.

"Doesn't matter Archie. If he has there's nothing we could do anyway."

But Archie wasn't about to give up. "What about that gunboat, General? Can't you pull strings and whistle one up?"

Hannay shook his head.

"No point. By the time a boat steamed down from Scapa, or wherever the fleet's gathered, Peterson would be in international waters."

"Navigation error?" Archie said hopefully.

Hannay gave a wry smile. "He may work outside the law, but His Majesty's navy does not."

At that moment, their attention was sharply diverted by a terrified scream. They swung around as if pulled by a puppet master, to see a figure wrapped in a flapping white laboratory coat. It was Doctor Lerne.

The craggy sergeant was about to take off after him, but Hannay stopped him. "Wasted effort Sergeant."

"Good God," Archie Roylance breathed. "He might as well have a bull's eye painted on his back."

Faintly across the rough moor and heather the cry of terror was repeated: a cry for help that was not going to be answered even if it were possible, for out of the night sky came one of the diablosaurs, the things Lerne had in his hubris named kraks. It had seen the flapping white and was zeroing in on it like a dive bomber.

They watched in rigid silence as the dreadful spectacle unfolded, it seemed almost in slow motion. Lerne ran, twisting and turning, and even at that distance it was clear his face was contorted in terror. Words were not needed, for all who watched knew the man stood no atom of a chance.

Suddenly, the wings folded in the way of an eagle attacking its prey, the great talons came forward: hooked, long and sharp as a tiger's claws, and the fearsome beak opened.

The krak hit him; half lifted the struggling screaming man, then dropped him. Blood sprayed. The krak struck again, and that time its beak ripped.

The sergeant, a hard man who had seen many terrible things, made a guttural sound in his throat.

"Good Gawd Almighty," was his deliverance.

"I doubt the Almighty will want much to do with him," Roylance said.

"Justice is served," said Hannay in a voice that was devoid of pity.

Dickson's answering voice was tight and grim. "But one of the damned things got away."

"One we can cope with," Hannay said. "A hundred would have spread panic the like of which this country hasn't seen."

Carl Peterson stood on the port wing of the steam yacht's bridge: his nose had a sticking plaster across it and his eyes hidden behind dark glasses. He was not happy. At his side Irma stood, a mink coat draped across her shoulders against the night cold, and cigarette in her long holder. The wind whipped away the smoke. She took a sip from a martini glass.

"What now?" she said.

Carl Peterson gazed out to sea to where the crescent moon shone a thin path across the waters to the west.
"That way lies America," he said. "They say it is the land of opportunity." He drew on his cigar. "We shall see."

Tales of the Shadowmen *wouldn't be quite complete without a story featuring the first and foremost French superhero, Leo Saint-Clair, a.k.a. The Nyctalope. The character appears to have taken both writers and readers by a storm and, despite publishing not one but two volumes of pastiches—*The Nyctalope Steps In *and* Night of the Nyctalope*—we have received even more stories featuring this indomitable explorer. This tale, by "Robert Darvel"—the nom de plume se-lected by a well-known French expert in popular literature in homage to Gustave Le Rouge—takes place concurrently with the events described in* The Nyctalope on Mars, *when Leo is torn between going after his fiancée Xavière de Ciserat, who was taken to the Red Planet by the XV, and his explorations in Af-rica...*

Robert Darvel: *The Man With the Double Heart*

For Boutel... Lehman... Harry Morgan...
Gorlier of course... Et Joan ! Joan of Arc !...

Africa, 1910

Part One: White

While he was on his way to the Congo, Leo Saint Clair—the Nyctalope—decided out of the blue to fly over Camgueba Falls. These spectacular falls were located in the middle of Mbambala, a small country on the border of the Congo whose poor subsoil protected it from the benevolent appetites of French geolog-ical engineers.

The majestic waters of the three rivers, the Ngam in the east, the Gombbi in the west and the Blrhoum in the middle, met there. The three rivers flowed through different Loess soil and their raging torrents carried along the natural sediments, one of clay, one or marl and one of basalt. It was a sight to behold the yellow, green and red rivers gradually mingled and twisted and woven together by brute force! And to behold with what fury these three mixed but still separate rivers rushed into the void. What a cataract! What a waterfall! One thousand feet, yes: one thousand feet of a devastating, frenzied fall! Not one hundred or five hundred but one thousand feet! And then there was the multi-colored gush of water, the shimmering gush, green ocher with bright red glints, wild, foam-ing, the blending blood of the three mighty rivers of the Mbambala region! And then the single river, far off, with the same strength and fury, flooding and driv-ing on the remains of the confined lands, the conquered lands where wild goats bleated, in a bristling tangle of tree trunks that formed islets scattered by the conquering flood, sublime like the flag of a future nation...

Eager to enjoy the spectacle, Leo Saint Clair floored the horizontal impulse lever of his electric aerodyne and went flying at breakneck speed, 135 mph, in the hot sun.

It was exactly 5:35 pm when Leo Saint Clair spotted the torrent of foam rising over the treetops. What better prelude than this upright column! A pillar of foam upholding the sky! A furious, fervid creature trampling on lazy Africa and shaking its rainbow mane! The sight was so magnificent that the Nyctalope felt his heart swell with pride. Yes, pride! Because he knew that it was thanks to his eyes—the eyes of a white man watching—that it was so amazingly beautiful.

How many Camguebalese felt such excitement in their heart for such a marvel? Not a one! On the contrary, the Savages hated the fact that the falls disturbed their ancestral fishing habits! Because the Camguebalese might have had no heart or soul, but they had stomachs! Their eyes were uninterested but their gluttony infinite, whereas the white man who forged the sacred desire to rise up thanks to his belligerence, the white man who changed cunning into knowledge, awkward groping into tried and true technique, the white man who worked from sunup to sundown and from sundown to sunup to achieve the technical prowess to invent marvelous vehicles like this electric aerodyne driven by domesticated forces, yes, the white man: there was the true spectator of the wonders of Wild Africa!

Under the belly of the fantastic airship the awesome foam rolled by. Leo Saint Clair veered off to the west to satisfy his demiurge's curiosity in 360 degrees. He seized the liquid splendor and made it shimmer in the sunrays. The extraordinary aerial maelstrom calmed his beauty-craving soul.

"Oh! To conquer! To conquer the world!" he exalted.

With a wide sweep of his hand he pointed out the fantastic horizon to his copilot, a young, mute Moroccan by the name of Kephal who had been accepted, adopted, pampered and raised by Professor Clavigny de Chambrun at the end of some serious events, and whose honesty the professor had guaranteed was matched only by the ardor of his race when he presented him for the first time to Saint Clair.

"Look at the awesome foam coming from the rivers' fury! Yes, let's fly over it!"

Leo Saint Clair brought his electric aerodyne into a tight turn, wings vertical, and then worked the commands and approached the widest of the three rivers, the Ngam, red with clay from the mountains to the east of Camgueba. He maneuvered the lever trying to keep the aerodyne so close to the surface that he felt the soles of his shoes (as thick as they were) vibrate from the foam hitting the cabin underneath. Dazzled and delighted, even though struggling to hide his fear, Kephal saluted the dangerous move with his own form of body language.

"Make sure your straps are tight, Kephal!"

Under the airplane millions of gallons were falling into the void with a tremendous roar and crash. When he got to the steep edge where the crazy, turbulent mass of water was rushing into the abyss, Leo Saint Clair suddenly pushed the lever. The aerodyne tipped forward and dove, like it was being dragged down by the torrent, hauled along like a tree trunk. The vehicle flew down the fall. Pulling the lateral lever, the Nyctalope spun it so that the cockpit was next to the water. The foam was roaring 30 feet away, even less! Fifteen feet, ten feet from the cockpit, right in front of the two men. Young Kephal Clavigny de Chambrun clenched his straps but did not have the courage to watch the amazing sight. It was clear that he was suffering an attack of cowardice, undoubtedly afraid that Saint Clair would drive the machine straight into the abyss that was about to swallow them up. At the last second, the Nyctalope spun the plane a second time to bring it back into its original position and pulled the lever. The aerodyne came up at a right angle, passed through the roaring foam, sprang out of the frothy shroud and flew low over the water until it became calmer and slower. Then Saint Clair veered to skim the treetops. More agile than a great ape, the shadow of the machine hugged the relief of the heights in its lively, bouncy crawl.

"Criiiiii!" Kephal said. Poor voice of the mute. Poor cold, dry, metallic echo you might say...

Then the Nyctalope flew over the river heading back upstream. "I can't help it! The desire is too strong! Don't worry, my boy," he assured, "I'm not going to do it again."

Indeed, the aerodyne was going back to the falls, but this time at a reasonable speed and at a pretty safe altitude over the river. After giving in to the thrilling call of danger, Leo Saint Clair was now piloting his plane with moderation.

On each side of the river rolling hills of bush marched by, a mad expanse, indescribable excess, and farther away, much farther, the ocher mist of the savanna, a dusty country crossed by great herds. Saint Clair drank in the view of the infinite territory unrolling beneath his wings.

"Africa! Impressive Africa!"

But all of a sudden his joy turned into a cry of rage, a cry of fear. Had a crackling sound just passed through the cockpit? What was that?

The Nyctalope thought that maybe the foam had caused some disturbance... He looked at the control panel...

The controls were not responding! And the aerodyne was heading straight for the waterfall, the turbulent watery grave was right in front of the distraught pilot! With all the strength in his arms and all the muscles at the disposal of a soul that had more fight than anyone on earth, the pilot pulled against the lever. His whole body strained... Exhausted. It was no use, the fabulous machine answered his effort with incomprehensible apathy. The moment was dire, atrocious!

"Xaviere! Xaviere!" the desperate Nyctalope groaned, his final thoughts focused on his beloved so that his love might cross the African ether all the way to France where the daughter of Admiral de Ciserat was waiting for him.

Next to him young Kephal Clavigny de Chambrun could no longer hold back his wild spasms of despair. It was clearly beyond his psychological limits—his head fell back and he passed out. Troubled, Saint Clair watched the falls for a moment as it was about to swallow him up and then looked back at his co-pilot.

What he saw at that dramatic moment defied human logic. A wide gash cut his throat in two; his bronze skin split open… and shiny sparks, like a portable electro-mirror that the XV use, an arc, an electric arc gushed out of Kephal's throat! It was unimaginable, unthinkable!

Kephal Clavigny de Chambrun was not a flesh and blood Moroccan but a complex apparatus!

Kephal Clavigny de Chambrun was a machine!

The ethereal electric arc kept gushing out of his throat. Thanks to the supernormal keenness of his vision, the Nyctalope could see the waves of the arc that were mixing with the waves emitted by the aerodyne's commands. In a flash of pure, intuitive energy, the Nyctalope knew why it had broken down. It was bewildering! It was more than likely that Clavigny de Chambrun, fanatic and crazy, with his indescribable technological knowledge, had decided to kill anyone who had ever doubted his goals. Yes! The man was sickly jealous if not completely deranged because of the past that had accused him of fantastic things that were in perfect harmony with such sophisticated criminal activities. Abominable outrage! And to think that Saint Clair had flown over thousands of kilometers—from the Var where the retired professor lives—with this instrument of destruction at his side. From the start of the journey, the killing machine was working out its attack and in his snap decision to come and see the falls Leo Saint Clair had dug his own grave!

But, the reader will ask, who is Anselme Clavigny de Chambrun?

He is an engineer who had once worked with Camille Flammarion and his team but who had split from them, judging them unconditionally to be too tentative in their appreciation of the limits of science. Even if the scientific popularizer from Juvisy-sur-Orge had proved to be very curious about the territories beyond scientific dogma: hadn't he given a eulogy for the spiritualist Allan Kardec? Hadn't he focused his work on confirming live on Mars? All this was a façade! Or so Clavigny de Chambrun had harshly claimed. And during a meeting he had shouted it out rather passionately, denouncing the blind dogmatism fossilized under the mystical veneer of these petty scholars who keep refusing to search with true and sincere devotion beyond known lands. "Me, I assure you, I promise today to devote myself body and soul to this research that you deny and believe me, the next time I come among you it will be to gloat over your shame in the face of my discoveries!"

Then Clavigny disappeared for many years until that day last week when Saint Clair got a letter from the doctor—whom everyone had forgotten—inviting him to pay a visit to his laboratory in Roquebrune-sur-Argens where he worked completely cut off from the world.

"Monsieur Saint Clair, you have always been one of my acquaintances who remained kind toward me. Therefore, I have kept for you the fruits of my labor."

Although Saint Clair was planning to fly to the Congo, he decided to make a stopover at Clavigny's and so he sent a letter back accepting the invitation, but only for a short visit due to his obligations. On the appointed day he landed his aerodyne at the foot of the Rock de Roquebrune and climbed up to visit Clavigny on the winding path of the Basse-Rouquaire following the given directions. Clavigny welcomed him. Clavigny with a hollowed face, bright eyes, theatrical gestures, dressed in brown, a tight-fitting frock coat and a red vest. Although not overcurious Saint Clair wanted to see his workshop, but he had to remain unsatisfied when the professor said he wished to show him later.

"I just want to be sure, Monsieur Saint Clair, that your friendship to me is the same as I remember. I will call for you soon. In the meantime, I won't be so impolite as to delay your travel any longer." Then, while he was walking Saint Clair back, he added, "Oh, I understand that you were headed to the Congo. You would be doing me a great service if you were kind enough to take with you my assistant and adopted son Kephal who has to go to Katanga on some manganese business. He won't be a bother: the poor boy is mute."

Saint Clair accepted and that was how he met Kephal Clavigny de Chambrun, the young man with a pleasant bearing and fine manners, in reality an instrument of Clavigny's vengeful madness against scientists and against Saint Clair in particular!

How absurd and wicked to confirm the preeminence of a technology that is obviously superior to that being developed in France by turning it into a death machine!

No doubt overwrought by the violent acrobats, the frightful automaton just snapped. About to be exterminated, it decided to act in his final moments to neutralize the electrical waves with its own like it was ordered to do at some point during the trip.

All of a sudden... An impossible vision! A grotesque vision: the Moroccan's head came off! And there, visible like a fractured bone, was the mechanical larynx.

Saint Clair focused all his attention on the waterfall that roared a hundred feet away from the cabin. The Nyctalope was calm again. With the cause of the breakdown known, weighed and dissected, he was now able to keep a level head and gather his thoughts to deal with the situation and the final goal: survival!

He rattled the lever. In the interference it still did not respond. Destroyed along with the center receiving the propulsion force coming from the relay-transmitter from Tamanrasset in the Hoggars...

Less than 80 feet before the end... 70...

With a simple movement of his hand, a swift movement that was as precise as a machine, definitive and unhesitant, Saint Clair pushed the big red button.

The cockpit became silent.

Saint Clair had just cut off the propulsive force! The electrical radiation streaming out of the porcelain bowels of the aerodyne was reabsorbed into the air. Lacking a target, the opposing current, the parasitic current generated by the machine that had been Kephal Clavigny de Chambrun jolted. It dissipated in a final, useless crackling.

Then Saint Clair threw his fist at his copilot. The blow sent the head rolling behind the seats. Saint Clair shoved his fingers hard into the bowels of the machine, grabbed the larynx and yanked. Now, when he restarted his aerodyne, the rotten, vibratory interference would have no chance of working. But would he have time to work the controls? Would he be able to? The waterfall was only fifty feet away!

No! But the controls were free, all the controls, like those that did not need the propulsive force, like the lift levers and pivoting arms...

The Nyctalope maneuvered the two lateral levers, one pulled toward him and the other pushed away. The port flap straightened up, the starboard did the opposite. The electric aerodyne kicked to the left.

The foam was there like a burst of saliva spitting against the belly of the machine out of some giant mouth. Its prey had escaped!

After dodging the falls, the aerodyne was flying perpendicular to the river now, skimming over the rift that cut the forest in two. The Nyctalope was forced to follow it so closely that he could not pull the machine away as its momentum faded with less and less lift. So the aerodyne went down, diving into the green foliage...

It was like a tide of luxuriant limbas, blue eucalyptus and acacias attacking from the rift, ready to swallow up the tiny bird in distress.

In spite of the risk of tipping over, the Nyctalope took his right hand off the lever to press the red button. The engine hummed, started up again... But alas, at a time when every movement had to be precise, the decapitated body of the dummy Kephal toppled over in the listing cockpit as the aerodyne slowed down, not producing enough centrifugal energy to maintain its speed or position. The mechanical man's right arm flopped over and the hand hit the lever. It was really as if the dead machine was using its last kinetic kick to cast its enemy into the void. The destabilized aerodyne plunged, upside down, into the trees.

It crashed with an awful noise.

A branch ripped off the glass protection. Something hit the Nyctalope in the face, knocking him out almost instantly.

"Xaviere," he had just enough strength to say in his final breath. Then there was darkness, real darkness, the only darkness that the Nyctalope failed to penetrate: the darkness of death.

If I have given an accurate and minute description of what will turn out in the end to be but an episode, it is to better present the reader with the extraordinary qualities of Leo Saint Clair. Thus, the reader will understand that the rest of this prologue on the border of the Congo will be written quickly not for easy reading or from laziness on the part of a serial writer pressured by his editor, but rather to give a painstaking account of the uncommon and exceptional strength with which the Nyctalope overcame a destiny that would have been fatal to anyone else.

When he woke up, Leo Saint Clair, who was miraculously unharmed except for a scratch on his forehead, found himself under a roof of interwoven leaves: that of a bamboo hut. He was lying down, arms and legs spread out, wrists and ankles tied to stakes that were stuck solidly in the ocher earth. Over the next three days, which went by without him being freed, he learned that he had been found by a tribe of natives who lived in the forest. The savages were split into two camps as far as what to do with their unexpected guest. On one side were those who wanted to eat his white flesh and on the other those who thought him some kind of divinity, arguing that he had fallen from the sky. While words were flying, Leo Saint Clair was given plenty of food and drink by a devilish little Negro with an intelligent look, always the same, who accomplished his task with gracious devotion and curiosity. The Nyctalope had the feeling that this devoted little devil, applying himself with a passion and thoughtfulness that surpassed the simple duty of feeding the prisoner, must have benefited from the charitable teaching of missionaries. Leo Saint Clair quickly communicated with him and after a few words between the two, had confirmed his intuition: Odilon—that was the name given to the little savage by the missionaries—Odilon, who jabbered crude French with a Belgian accent mixed with melodious and guttural intonations, knew that it was bad to participate in the mistreatment of the white man.

"Me not able to free without them make me awk-awk!" Odilon said, rolling up his big white peepers.

"And who will kill you for such an act of mercy?"

"M'Cougné!'

"Is this M'Cougné the chief of the tribe?"

"No."

"Who is the chief?"

"Niyadi."

"Untie me and I will go to him."

"Niyadi not 'him'. Niyadi 'her'. Niyadi a woman!"

A woman! A woman at the head of the tribe! Now that really spiced things up. The Nyctalope was intrigued. Intensifying his tempered enthusiasm and eloquent authority, he found the words to convince Odilon to cut him free. In order to keep his savior safe, he promised to say that he had freed himself and to wait for nighttime to escape; thus Odilon would not get in trouble.

And that was what happened. Odilon sawed through the vine shackles with a sharp stone that he left on the beaten floor of the hut. At midnight Leo Saint Clair got up and walked out of his jail, which was not being guarded. The night was dark, very dark because the light from the last quarter moon was too weak to break through the thick foliage of the limbas. The savages were sleeping, for the most part, wherever they happened to close their eyes. A few guards were nodding off here and there. Even if, by chance, they woke up from their animal lethargy, they could not see the shadow that was walking right under their square noses. The Nyctalope moved confidently thanks to his night vision. He headed for the hut described by Odilon as being the most impressive in the village, if a word like "impressive" could be attributed to such rough and amusing constructions.

Leo Saint Clair entered the rudimentary Elysian shack and found a woman lying on a mat. She was adorable, black and naked, as naked as one could be and the most ravishing Black he had ever seen.

His senses were all topsy turvy.

Niyadi! The Venus of the limbas! The goddess of the forest! Niyadi immediately aroused Leo Saint Clair to African Love.

Wrecked, betrayed, marooned in the heart of this cannibalistic Africa, the Nyctalope was consumed only by passion. Leo Saint Clair, fallen from the sky onto the bed of this fatal beauty at the dawn of this night of carnal revelation was presented to the tribe and celebrated as the queen wished. No one counted the days that their burning passion lasted, their strange, insatiable passion! It happened outside of time, apart from days, beyond any other contingencies but that of hearts and bodies. It was the wave that drowned Man and Woman, a wave of harmonious tumult, generated by souls united in Love. A wave so strong, apt to smash so much that only the gentlest, sweetest reef could force it back...

Xaviere... Xaviere... a time hidden by a passing cloud, like a frail meadow flower, distant and beautiful Xaviere de Ciserat, whom Leo Saint Clair thought about one morning, his loyalty, his flame that was almost extinguished by the froth and foam of his frantic senses.

He had to find her again. He had to deny the black beauty. The farewell was heart-rending. Niyadi begged him. He promised her with his hands on his heart. He left in the morning after their final night together. He left with four guides who led him to the river Ngam that he just had to cross to reach the border of the Congo. Frantic, shaky, fighting against his divided soul, the Nyctalope bid farewell to the Blacks—only one of them would accompany him to civilization: the young and devoted Odilon who had become like a brother to him.

A last impulse before returning to Xaviere: he wanted to leave a souvenir for Niyadi. He searched his pockets. To Momtouanou, the most trustworthy of the three Blacks, he gave Kephal's metal larynx, which he had never dreamt of parting with. A paltry present for a queen? A relic barely good enough for a scrap merchant? No! The beloved black queen would be able to recognize her lover's precious gift.

He turned around and left. With Odilon at his side.

He was going to rejoin Xaviere.

Part Two: Black

What did he find out, much later, when he had Jolivet over to his apartment in Paris? Xaviere! Xaviere de Ciserat had been kidnapped! Jolivet left and Saint Clair would learn that the abduction was the work of Koynos at the instigation of Oxus. That Xaviere was being held by XV on Argyre Isle, on Mars! Although frantic and panic-stricken, Leo Saint Clair pulled himself together and with self-control swore that he would rescue Xaviere. He would rescue the fourteen women kidnapped along with his fiancée. He was already drawing up plans he would have to take over the radiomotor station in the Congo otherwise the waves could not carry the crystal radioplanes to the red planet. For this he would be helped by his faithful companions—Jolivet, of course, and Max, Klepton, Gaynor, Bontemps, Merlak, and Tory, Pary, O'Brien, Pacard, Tardieu, Johnson, Dirving, Dupin and Admiral de Ciserat, the father of his fiancée and her sister Yvonne. He could already see it, the aerial fleet ready for departure. He saw it shoot into the cosmos on its marvelous mission. He was eager for the coming preparations. His mind was in ferment when all of a sudden someone rang. Who was it? Odilon! Odilon the Negro! Since he had not been with the other (only Jolivet and Bastien had met him), the Black was told all about the Nyctalope's adventures. Odilon felt a touching kindness for all women who could fill up the hole left by his distant queen. And he was even more eager after seeing the pictures of the women that Saint Clair showed him during their conversation. Seeing the defeated look in his young friend's face, Saint Clair thought that in some way or another he knew something about the despicable abduction and that he came to Paris to express his sympathy. Kidnapped, Felicie and Yvonne... and Xaviere!

"Well, Odilon?"

"Niyadi!"

"Niyadi?"

"Kidnapped!"

"Her, too?"

Leo Saint Clair was dumbfounded. Odilon was the only one here to know about their relationship, brief but leaving the mark of its torrid and indestructible delights in the body and soul of the Nyctalope. No one knew about the existence of the Venus of the limbas. Kidnapped? By whom? It could not be the work of Oxus!

How did it happen? Down there, Odilon explained to Saint Clair who was still skeptical, in Mbambala, people glinting with metal appeared in the sky and took the queen away in their nets. People like a cloud of locust. With brown skin shining like copper.

This detail reminded him of Kephal Clavigny de Chambrun. And then Leo Saint Clair understood: they were doubles of the machine that had tried to destroy him! And if they had managed to find Niyadi, to ascertain the bond that united the black lover and the Nyctalope, it was undoubtedly thanks to the steel larynx unwisely kept in his pocket and then unfortunately given as a present. A locating object...

Thus Clavigny de Chambrun was still chasing Saint Clair out of his inexplicable hatred. Clavigny de Chambrun, whom the Nyctalope had tried to find again as soon as he got back from the Congo before being dragged into the maelstrom unleashed by Oxus and the XV. To no effect: when he went back to Roquebrune-sur-Argens he had found Chambrun's lair completely empty, deserted. Saint Clair had questioned the inhabitants of Muy, a nearby village from which you could see the Rock of Roquebrune, and many of them confirmed that one night soon after the Nyctalope's first visit, a huge, indescribable oval mass rose out of the Rock. This mass, this dirigible you might say, even though it was made of copper, shined like countless fires in the moonlight. Absolutely silent, it rose up and disappeared into the nocturnal heights.

Was Niyadi's kidnapping a result of Clavigny's stubborn vengeance? Clavigny who, according to witnesses, had acquired knowledge and techniques that, as he boasted at the time of Flammarion, came from sources that were not terrestrial?

How had Odilon come to know about the tragedy? The Negro pulled a letter out of his pocket and explained that it had been left at the door of his humble house in Gentilly, addressed to the attention of Leo Saint Clair. With a shaky hand the Nyctalope took it. He tore open the envelope... He read the message... His face inscrutable... Did it confirm his suspicions? He did not say a word but stared at Odilon. The young black would know no more. The tragedy dated back two weeks now and Odilon had delayed coming while he awaited confirmation from the subjects of the African queen whom he had kept in contact with from France.

Then in a devastated, jumpy voice, the Nyctalope said, "Xaviere... or Niyadi! What an awful dilemma. Both kidnapped at the same time! I can't save them both! One of them has to die for the other to live!"

In the Nyctalope's mind the countless glints from the radioplanes flickered. Their brightness, which had just now reflected the fires of glorious hope, was tarnished by a wicked veil.

If he did not save Niyadi, she would die. If he flew to her rescue, Xaviere would be the one to perish!

Xaviere or Niyadi? The White or the Black?

The Nyctalope suddenly jumped up. He had it! He went down into the big parking garage under his Parisian house and sat at the wheel of his electric automobile. Odilon was right behind him. He stood there waiting for a sign. A wave inviting him to climb in. He sat next to Saint Clair. Ignition, the fantastic automobile started up...

"Where are we going?"

"To Cruchard," Saint Clair said.

"The inventor?" Odilon had been introduced on his arrival in France.

"The inventor! Cruchard has been working on an invention and if he's perfected it, it could put an end to our dreadful dilemma!"

"What is this extraordinary invention that could have been so useful to Corneille?" Odilon asked, panting—and the reader can see the progress made by the Negro in his refined elocution and solid culture.

"A doubler!"

"A doubler?"

"A machine with the marvelous ability to make two beings out of one so that binucleated in the smallest parts of my body and soul, I'll be able to save both Xaviere and Niyadi!"

"I hope to God that Monsieur Cruchard has had the needed resources to finish his machine," is all Odilon said.

At 75 miles per hour it barely took the automobile 30 minutes to pass the gate of Asnières and reach the house of Professor Cruchard in Cormeilles-en-Paris. As soon as the vehicle stopped on the lawn, the Nyctalope jumped out and ran to the house. Two minutes after his impetuous arrival Cruchard the engineer knew about everything. He contemplated the request very intensely. Was the device working? The answer took time to come... It came... Yes! By extraordinary luck the engineer had put the finishing touches to his work the day before.

"Follow me," Cruchard said. And the three of them went down to his laboratory. Ignoring the hundreds of fabulous achievements scattered around, the inventor led them to a work of modest appearance.

"There it is," he declared.

There were two cabins, 12 feet apart, connected by a glass arch framed in brass, rising and falling in a peculiarly designed curve. At the top of this curve a crystal globe was embedded. Cruchard pulled a lever and a crackling noise could be heard. Some furious but domesticated energy lashed the crystal globe. Then the inventor whistled. A cat came and rubbed against his leg. He introduced it, "This is Jeanne d'Arc, the house pet. Beloved, pampered Jeanne, who is going to be our guinea pig to show you how harmless the machine is."

The engineer put Jeanne into the cabin on the right and closed the transparent sliding door. Then he worked various levers. The energy formed a halo around the animal, which showed absolutely no sign of being troubled by the experiment. The energy rose through the arch until the discharge was concentrated solely in the crystal sphere.

The professor opened the door and the cat snuggled into his arms. He waved his visitors over to a couch and they all sat down. Odilon looked questioningly at the Nyctalope. Nothing happened. Nothing was happening.

"We're not watching a magic show," Cruchard finally said. "Science is not instant magic." The professor looked at the grandfather clock. "We have to wait 40 minutes," he advised. "The molecular clock..."

Ah, the molecular clock...

Five minutes went by, then six... 10... 20... 30... Everyone was staring at the door of the second cabin. An endless wait. Then the electrical activity in the sphere diminished and flowed back down the arch. 35 minutes... 39... The electrical activity died.

At 40 minutes the door flew open, watched by the three pairs of eyes. It had been pushed open by a gray cat that looked exactly like Jeanne. Jeanne who was still cuddling with the professor!

All of them jumped to their feet.

"Thus," Cruchard declared, "you see the functional capacity of my invention. Monsieur Saint Clair, it is at your disposal," and he bowed.

Without further ado the Nyctalope stepped into cabin one. After a last look at Cruchard, he nodded his head proudly to give the green light. Cruchard maneuvered his commands and just like the cat the electric sparks sizzled over the man's body. Excited to soar into the future, he felt no fear. Once the replica of his molecular essence was siphoned into the arch and transmitted to the crystal, he left the cabin. He told them he intended to leave without waiting 40 minutes to get to the base in the Congo where his travel companions were about to take off for Mars.

"Odilon, you stay. I couldn't find a better guide than you." Then turning to the professor, he added, "Cruchard, ready an aircraft so that I can fly to Mbambala where my second heart is pulling me. Goodbye! And vive la France!"

The fiery man flew to the Congo, to Mars, answering Xaviere's call of distress and her 14 unfortunate companions.

But it is said that nothing ever goes as planned. All of a sudden, at 39 minutes and 40 seconds the cabin door was pushed open, twenty seconds before the expected exit of the molecular double! Odilon jumped to his feet to dash forward. The professor held him back as the door gaped open and there on the floor was… an abomination. A body that was not a body but an anarchic mass of flesh quivering with something that was not life… but the result of residual electrical energy. The experiment had inexplicably failed for the man where it had succeeded for the cat!

No, there was an explanation: you see that little rejected thing like unformed flesh. That's the heart, the Nyctalope's artificial heart that created a distortion, an electrical perturbation as a foreign body.

Odilon screamed in terror. He howled in pity. Leo Saint Clair had left, flown off to Xaviere. Niyadi could not be saved. The Negro fell into Cruchard's arms, trying to relieve his desperation through a violent burst of emotion. As the two of them were teetering on the brink of horror, an ethereal voice rang out, penetrating their senses though not reverberating off the frail skin of their auditory organs; a voice with no source… The voice of Leo Saint Clair! Which explained to them that the experiment had succeeded, but with unexpected results. At least, it had partially succeeded.

"Only my mind has been correctly duplicated," the man said with extraordinary calmness from the inexpressible depths of the ether. And then, "I will save Niyadi! I need to find a body and I will save my sweet Venus of the limbas!"

Odilon moved away from the professor, fell to his knees, put his hands together and begged, offered, "Leo, take my body! I give it to you as a gift!"

"No, not you, brave friend!"

The young Negro argued with all his mental abilities, with all the persuasive prowess learned from different teachers: what body could be better for the Nyctalope's passionate heart? Didn't Odilon come from Niyadi's tribe? Wasn't he the ideal vehicle for the mind of his queen's lover?

"But a body cannot house two minds, isn't that right professor?" Nyctalope asked and declared at the same time.

The professor agreed sadly.

"What will happen to your own mind, Odilon?"

"I will wait for your return, safe in a jar," the young man offered with unprecedented generosity. Not just his body, he was also offering up his mind.

"Not a jar," the professor interjected. He presented a cylinder equipped with straps, originally an air tank meant for breathing underwater, which they could fill up not with oxygen but with Odilon's mind. Not too bulky and shaped so as to resist enormous underwater pressure, it would be the ideal receptacle for the mind of the brave young man, who would be protected from accidents and could accompany the Nyctalope on his mission of honor and love.

So it was decided and with the help of Professor Cruchard, Odilon's mind was transferred appropriately, by the right technical means, into the steel bottle. His precious, abandoned body wobbled two or three times while it was placed in the reception cabin to receive the Nyctalope's mind. Then he strapped the spirit container onto his back and after a simple goodbye to the professor, who gave him as promised his own airship, the Nyctalope soared off, a guest in a new, young, black body in order to save his African lover.

Very soon afterwards he saw the Camgueba waterfalls, the green canopy, the rift and the village. The Nyctalope brought the silent machine to a stop on top of a majestic limba. Agilely and smoothly he climbed down, branch by branch, and was soon standing in the middle of the forest village. No one came to meet him. The reason was that the place looked totally abandoned: huts open to the wind, gaping roofs and the jungle was swiftly and stealthily gaining ground.

"No queen, no community," Leo Saint Clair understood. "The confused savages have scattered like bees."

And then he found the bodies, torn apart by predatory cats. He leaned over and examined the wounds: the wild cats had feasted on bodies that were already dead, clubbed to death—the undeniable, hateful signature of a scared, cannibalistic race. What happened? What tragedy?

All of a sudden there was a noise behind him. An exclamation. "Mbala! Mbala!"

Mbala, the native name of Odilon. Leo Saint Clair turned around. In front of him stood a subject of Queen Mbambala who looked familiar.

"Momtouanou!"

Momtouanou was one of the three guides who had led him to the shores of the Ngam, the very one whom the Nyctalope had given the larynx as a gift for Niyadi. Momtouanou ran to whom he believed was Mbala. The two black bodies hugged each other and then the Negro started babbling incomprehensibly. And yet he had to understand his speech. Precious information could be given… How, how to understand him?

Then Leo Saint Clair remembered the trances he had seen here. Those wild, frenzied gatherings where the Africans communed together, those mad rites, those intense, violent rites wherein their spirits bound together like the three rivers flowed together toward psychic fusion. He remembered the kind of mushroom that the Negros ingested to alter their consciousness… He knew where to find it… Could he thus enter into communion with Odilon, the pure mind in the steel cylinder? Could Odilon communicate mentally with the Nyctalope and become the ideal interpreter of Momtouanou?

Firmly resolved, Leo Saint Clair brought the Negro with him, without saying a word, into the forest. He kneeled down at the trunk of a limba, dug with his hands, cleared away a root and pulled off a spongy, purplish mass, yes, a kind of mushroom. Then the Negro understood. He jumped up and down, excited no doubt to be able to get in touch with the dispersed spirits of the tribe. The mushroom was cut into thin slices and crushed to extract the juice. The two men agreed to sit together in the least ruined hut so that no wild animal might attack them during their trance. The decoction was ready. Without flinching, with wild determination, Leo Saint Clair took a big gulp before handing the mortar to the Negro, who put his fat lips to the rim and guzzled it down.

Later, from the ethereal trees of the trance, Leo Saint Clair greeted Odilon's mind, with which he communicated in French, as well as Momtouanou's, who was particularly elated when he perceived the two consciences, that of Mbala that he was expecting to meet and that of the admirable white man, beloved by the queen, who had come to save her.

Leo Saint Clair urged Odilon to learn everything he could from Momtouanou's mind and tell it to him. They had to act quickly before the end of the trance. Out of the cylinder, Odilon asked questions, examined, probed... He translated everything he heard in the rough, unfathomable Mbambala dialect, which the Nyctalope unfortunately did not know: he was like a bee on the edge of a black orchid.

Finally, the trance ended, leaving the three minds wearied and stuffed and completely exhausted they fell into a delightful, refreshing sleep. Then the Nyctalope woke up. He was alone and once again had use of his own faculties; Odilon's mind had gone back into its steel tank. But Momtouanou had got too excited and could not control himself. Being alone and cut off from his tribe, forgotten by his people, he had rushed too frantically into the trance. His long, bruised body lay on the packed ground, foaming at the mouth with dry, white eyes like two pebbles... He was dead.

Here is what Leo Saint Clair knew of the situation, what the trance had told him:

Right after the extraordinary kidnapping of Niyadi, M'Cougné—the one who had wanted to eat Saint Clair during the three days of arguing—named himself chief of the tribe. Whoever contested his authority was murdered pitilessly, which the Savages know how to do. Once the opposition was wiped out, the M'Cougné clan wanted to stay in the village, but too many wild animals were prowling around, crazy from the victims' blood, so faced with this danger it was decided to go and live somewhere else. They deserted the village, leaving the carcasses to the predators. And Momtouanou? Momtouanou had escaped the massacre by digging a hole under the roots of a tree. He was hiding in it when M'Cougné and his clan went on their killing spree and he stayed there when the lions, tigers, monkeys and other scavengers came to clean the place out. He only crawled out when he saw Mbala show up.

Had Momtouanou seen Niyadi being kidnapped? No. On that day he was gathering crane's eggs off near the rocky rift. When he came back the deed had been done, the queen abducted by the metal beings. And brought where? Momtouanou did not know, could not say...

Leo Saint Clair was alone now in the deserted village in the middle of the African forest without a clue, without the slightest trace... How would he save Niyadi? How was he going to get her back? What direction was he going to turn? Where was he going to search? What was he searching for?

The copper! The imperishable metal that the Moroccan duplicates were made of! Leo Saint Clair knew how to find this copper, whether it was buried in the jungle or stationed in the sky because Cruchard's airship was equipped with a metal detector. He just had to fly over the treetops and if the abductors, the mechanical looters were there or had left a trace of their plundering, it would be child's play to find them!

On board his airship the Nyctalope started his frenzied round, skimming over the canopy and when no signal came after he had extended his search, circling over the vast forest and higher up in the warm air, he pushed the range of his detector to the maximum. Three whole days passed, entirely devoted to the tireless search. Three days in vain, with no results. Leo Saint Clair was about to give up... His mind drew up other, desperate plans, other strategies to fall back on in case of total failure of this first, risky investigation. Finally on the morning of the fourth day, while he was drifting high in the sky, the lights started blinking! The signal indicating the location of metal started vibrating! The analysis was clear: the meter showed that it had to be located in a range of two miles above the airship. Two miles... At the edge of the troposphere!

That could only mean one thing: there was an indescribable presence able to keep itself suspended in the air, that is, a clearly artificial construction. And Saint Clair thought again about the descriptions by the people in Muy, about the strange apparition in the night described as a copper dirigible.

Jubilant, Saint Clair pulled a lever and the airship rose, the nose of the fuselage pointed proudly toward the place where his black mistress was undoubtedly waiting for him. As he went higher and higher he considered the dangers he would face. He was going to have to confront a bunch of metal soldiers. Remembering the steel larynx of the artificial Kephal de Chambrun that could damage the inner workings of the navigation system, he worked out an elaborate approach that was risky, to be sure, but that had to assure his victory.

With one eye on the display, the Nyctalope soared up silently into earth's atmosphere. And suddenly behind a cumulonimbus cloud a dirigible balloon appeared. Saint Clair estimated its length to be 100 yards, which was colossal, but what was more extraordinary was the color of the airship. It looked like gold! Glistening with countless solar fires, a celestial star whose curves were controlled by science... By a non-human science! Leo Saint Clair gasped, teary-eyed. But although he was amazed and flabbergasted, he was still on his guard. There was no doubt about it: here was where Niyadi was being held. He saw a door open in the side of the ship and two shining lights came out, heading straight for him.

Aiming the lens in the fuselage that transmitted a magnified image of flying objects, he shouted, "Copper Kephals!"

The Kephals came up slowly. They did not have the Robida aerial torpedo tubes or Danrit cannons; they were just flying men, made of copper, but already from their open mouths the electric arcs were crackling, meant to paralyze the commands of the intruder. It was high time to put his four-point plan into action: evade the metal sentinels, get into the dirigible, slip on board and save his lover. Leo Saint Clair felt his heart swell (even though artificial) as an expression of his fierce desire, his fierce will to pit himself against the enemy hiding his evil designs inside this dazzling copper sun.

He worked the commands of his airship. With lightning speed the vehicle turned around and sped away from the golden dirigible as if being piloted by cowards— spineless curs overcome by fear at the sight of the extraordinary, terrifying star. He headed for the ground in a double spiral, out of control. Now that he was out of sight of the Kephals, the airship made a wide turn, rolled behind the cumulonimbus and then hidden by the cloud rose straight as an arrow up to fantastic heights. Now he was above the dirigible. He came back down, unseen, light as a butterfly, and landed deftly on the upper hull. Saint Clair took a deep breath. He opened the door and got out.

He felt like he was stepping onto a planet to be conquered, where he had to dive into the bowels to save his black lover. Far in front of him, at the end of the horizon rounded by the dihydrogen, he could see the stabilizers and rudders. Leo Saint Clair stood up straight, proud, sure-footed, solidly planted, his chest facing a calm wind.

The dirigible was a semi-rigid model with a frame containing the smaller, internal balloons and an external membrane made of copper wire fabric supported by cables. Without a shudder Leo Saint Clair started walking toward the abyss. He followed the frame along the cables. When the curve became too steep, he turned around, grabbed on and continued his descent nimbly. His Negro body was as agile as a monkey. The wind blew enough that the cylinder on his back where Odilon's mind was kept groaned as if the ethereal being was expressing his fear of heights... Or was it a fear of being diluted in the troposphere?

The Nyctalope soon reached the level where the hull was no longer housing the sustentation gas but rooms for people—because there was no gondola underneath, only mica portholes from stern to the bow, sticking out of the airship like a ventral fin.

The Nyctalope saw the dock where the two Kephals had come out of to chase him a little while ago. The ramp was raised vertically like a drawbridge in the side of the airship, but there was a foot or so of space around the edges with a flexible membrane that undoubtedly served as a buffer in case the wind blew hard. The Nyctalope moved aside the rubber and slipped in. It took some work and agility but he managed to enter the airship.

He was in.

Silently, as ghostly as a cat, he slid from shadow to shadow and crossed the empty spaces or some full of crates. He dashed down windowless passageways and others with portholes. He scurried up and down stairs, turned and veered, advanced with the instinctive movements of a hunter while his mind analyzed every detail and always, always trying to decipher some clue that might lead him to the nerve center of the flying palace. Now he was walking in a hall that was so lavish it had to lead to private quarters. Less than ten minutes later he was standing behind Clavigny de Chambrun.

The professor was alone, sitting at a desk facing a large window. He was dressed in the same brown, tight-fitting frock coat. He was staring at the clouds. Saint Clair, who had been careful to lock the door when he entered, walked up behind him. Then Clavigny turned around. His red vest lit up his face, which looked even hollower than the last time, and his eyes more feverish.

"Who are you, damned Negro?" he asked in a weary voice—the voice of a broken man, a man who had given up. "Did she bring her flunkeys, too? Who are you?"

"Leo Saint Clair."

Clavigny waved off the crazy declaration and the Nyctalope thought he heard him mumble "damned negro liars" and other such things. It would have been easy for the Nyctalope to convince him with a few words describing what a Native of Camgueba could not know about the life of a French citizen if he had never stepped foot there, but he kept quiet. Wouldn't it be easier that way to make Clavigny talk?

During the three days of his aerial search, Leo Saint Clair had gone over and over this interrogation in his mind. What was Clavigny's goal? What purpose did his insane actions serve? How far did his hatred carry his extraordinary technology? Saint Clair had decided that it was really a series of acts that had nothing to do with Oxus and the XV... The presence of the Kephals identical to his copilot linked together the phases of the criminal campaign; the continuity of attacks started from before his accident at the Cambuega Falls through the same will that was now fostering these later events. How could Clavigny de Chambrun have foreseen that I would run to Cruchard for help?

Then, with exhaustion from the endless aerial search kicking in, Saint Clair's thoughts took a strange turn. Was it Africa itself that was taking vengeance on the Nyctalope? Was it Africa, the Spirits of Africa, conjured up by the "magic" of his black lover, that were sucking up the ecstatic manifestations of his white heart? He had already abandoned his white body for a black one—was all this trouble taken just to devour his white soul?

No, no, no! Saint Clair had been thinking behind the controls of his airship. These thoughts are just the noxious emanations from my black flesh eating away at my mind...

"Why does the white man want to kill Saint Clair?" the Nyctalope asked, deciding to fool his enemy about his real identity so as to stay a step ahead in the coming confrontation.

"How do you know that?" Clavigny raised an eyebrow.

"My queen told us after Saint Clair told her."

"And what do you care about the rivalries of white men?"

"You fight like baboons against each other."

"I'm fighting against Saint Clair because that man…" Clavigny waved his hand again and sighed, "What's the use of talking about my hatred to a Black for whom a battle, as grandiose as it might be, is, in reality, nothing but a skirmish between baboons…"

Would Saint Clair know more about this? Hatred… Would hatred be like God, unfathomable, impenetrable? No…

Clavigny looked out the window. He kept silent. Saint Clair believed that he would tell him nothing more. Finally, after a long silence, the engineer spoke.

"Yes! Yes, I got in contact with extraterrestrial minds. Yes, I received their knowledge, the mastery of cosmic forces that haunt matter like so many spirits. Yes, I learned how to draw from the sources of the Universe the energies that not a single timid scientist will ever dare think to study, however thirsty for knowledge he is. O Negro, poor Negro! What would you understand if I told you of the drainage of mercurial fluid, of the Alpha condenser that gives my flying men the essence of their suspension element? Nothing. You would think nothing. In this you are just like that clique completely impervious to true knowledge, that condemns my activities as if they were crimes of the future, or vengeance against it!"

"You tried to kill Saint Clair," the Nyctalope objected.

"Not true! I wanted to give Saint Clair a demonstration of my knowledge and the fiend saw a criminal act when his acrobatics had simply disrupted my Kephal…"

The Kephals are certainly magnificent automatons but nothing more than simple airships endowed with a human face. Mercurial Force! Please… The lies of a vanquished man trying to absolve himself by denying his criminal nature, Saint Clair was convinced… Here was the madness of a man who had failed to rise above Men, who was burning with this final bitterness after the inertia that he himself had called ludicrous had reduced his inspiration and success to a trivial joke.

Saint Clair knew the sad truth after asking, "Why did you kidnap Niyadi?"

Clavigny screamed, "I didn't kidnap that crazy girl! Niyadi is here of her own free will! She's the one who contacted me and then rejected me!" And then he moaned, "Ah, you sorry, white lover, she told me… then she threatened me: Take me to Saint Clair! Take me to Saint Clair!"

Epilogue: Red

Clavigny just killed himself…

He took a gun and shot himself in the head. In front of the Nyctalope, before he could convince him of his identity. Nothing more would be revealed. Clavigny had just killed himself but right before taking his life he told the Negro standing in front of him, the Negro who had come out of nowhere to hear his last words, planted there like the primitive shadow of a chaplain, he told him to pray for his soul.

"Oh, your magic charms can be effective but at least they don't catch fire. Negro, do you know that the dihydrogen that's keeping this dirigible in the air is highly flammable? You're going to find that out, and your queen, too: I've turned on the firing system for the explosives."

And then... the powder, the brain, the awful crack of the skull...

Saint Clair was stunned. At that moment an awful explosion rang out. The dirigible rocked but did not catch fire because the rudder was the target. The apocalypse in the sky was delayed. Saint Clair ran out of Clavigny's room. Where was Niyadi? Certainly not in the hold! He approached another luxurious apartment and pushed the door open. There in the center of the huge room was a kind of four-poster bed made of gold and bamboo. Niyadi's bed. The Venus of the limbas was lying on it, lounging, almost nude. The queen looked up at the intruder. She spoke—in her dialect that the Nyctalope, unfortunately, did not understand. He begged her to speak French; she knew the little that he had taught her between their caresses.

"Oh Mbala," she said, "what are you doing here?"

"I'm not Mbala."

"Okay, your white name, then... Odilon?"

"I'm not Odilon. I'm Leo, your lover. I've come to rescue you."

Niyadi laughed. "France has mixed up the boy's mind."

"No, Niyadi, I'm Leo Saint Clair in Odilon's body!"

The woman burst out laughing. "Oh, Odilon-Mbala! The fantastic stories of the white griots, the tellers of tall tales, know how to make their listeners lose their minds better than our pour babble."

"I beg you to believe me, Niyadi! I'm going to prove to you that I'm your Leo. Listen..." And Saint Clair told her certain details of their past fondling, described their intimacy, repeated the sweet nothing born of their burning passion...

Niyadi dismissed them all, saying, "Mbala, Mbala, Leo shouldn't have told you such secrets. But he's so passionate and he has so many reasons to be so proud."

At that moment another explosion shook the dirigible, throwing Saint Clair onto Niyadi's bed. She pushed him off. "I want nothing to do with a black body—and scrawny little black at that!"

"I'm Saint Clair!"

"If you're Saint Clair in Mbala's body, where is the real Saint Clair?"

"Alas, on Mars! Listen Niyadi: your flying prison is about to go up in flames. You have to follow me."

"It's not a prison. It's my palace in the sky. I came here to wait for Saint Clair and I'm going to wait for him."

Despite the emergency, despite imminent death, Saint Clair wanted to understand. "O Queen, tell me what happened."

And the Venus of the limbas, lounging there magnificently, her throat fluttering, her throat of velvet and gold, gave in like a child. She told her story and took frivolous pleasure at seeing who she thought was Mbala listen to her while devouring her with his eyes and panting.

Here it is: after Saint Clair left, Niyadi denied all the black lovers who left her unsatisfied. She pined for her lover. One day M'Cougné, even though the strongest of her subjects, also failed and she remembered the story of Saint Clair's accident. She went to find the aerodyne. She knew of the white man's genius. When she discovered the Kephal, she dreamed of making this superb, sleeping creature her lover. Watching, examining, her mind on the threshold of science, she groped about, understood, analyzed. Her slender fingers entered the machine and guided by a strange intuition she managed to reconnect the larynx, which she had immediately known was part of the automaton—the larynx given to her by Saint Clair! The Kephal was working again. He was easily located by Clavigny who was eager to come and get him. When he arrived, Niyadi jumped out. Wrapping her charms around him like a vine around a tree, she convinced Clavigny to take her with him. The professor refused at first, protested, but finally gave in. And soon rising over the poor village in the forest Niyadi thought she had found her happiness. Then, disappointed by Clavigny (unfortunately suffering from monorchism, with only one testicle) she asked him to use all means possible to bring her true, her only lover to her—Leo Saint Clair. And thus the letter sent to Odilon.

"Which happened while the war against Oxus was raging!" Saint Clair growled.

The tyrannical mistress was impatient. Clavigny was upset that his Kephals as well as his marvelous dirigible, perfect instruments of a perfect revenge, were becoming accessories to a bedroom drama at the whim of woman. How to tell her that according to the latest news captured by radio waves Saint Clair would not be coming to join her because he was flying to Mars!

"Clavigny killed himself," Saint Clair said suddenly.

"He was just an old monkey," Niyadi said.

"He wanted to take us with him."

"If you think that the white man could enjoy destroying such beautiful things built with his own hands, go on, Mbala. This is my palace. I'm staying and waiting for Saint Clair, who will come back from Mars for me. Go!"

And Niyadi pushed Mbala away. Her eyes were red and nasty. Having seen her get angry with her subjects, Saint Clair knew that it was wise to fear her at these moments. He backed up, away from the bed, out of the room. All of a sudden there was catastrophe, a huge explosion. The dihydrogen was ablaze! The dirigible was going to crash down like a flare!

"My airship!" Saint Clair screamed.

Too late. Sitting on the dirigible, the machine had certainly been pulverized.

It was the end!

No! There was one hope: the Kephals! The flying Kephals! Saint Clair ran to where he thought he had seen the imitation Moroccans when he was searching for Niyadi. He grabbed one of them while the infrastructure of the dirigible collapsed. A gaping hole opened under his feet and Saint Clair dropped into empty space. He was riding the Kephal. Above him, the fires of hell were burning the heavens. A mighty blaze. The shock wave from the explosion hit Saint Clair. He was knocked over and then thrown off his copper mount. Alone now in the dizzying sky, falling like Icarus. He knew he was about to die.

In an admirable gesture, he put Cruchard's tank on his belly and opened it, releasing Odilon's mind into the warm air. "Goodbye," he murmured. "May you be welcome in the heart of every being that inhabits your Africa!"

As he was falling to earth, and to his end, he looked up. Above him, behind the ashes of Clavigny's fabricated sun, the Martian star was twinkling. The Nyctalope, a trivial black body, a useless black body, prepared to die without regrets: he knew that on the surface of the red planet he himself was leading a glorious battle against the evil beings who had kidnapped his fiancée Xaviere.

(translated by Michael Shreve)

Marti

Visions of the Nyctalope (A Portfolio)

Earlier this year, the French website *Comix Heroes* decided to organize a competition of young artists, the subject being the first and foremost superhero of French popular literature, the Nyctalope.

Tales of the Shadowmen has always prized the contributions made by many artists to the field of popular literature, from Gino Starace's Fantômas to Jim Bama's Doc Savage. We have, in previous volumes, published thematic portfolios by various artists, and are therefore proud to present in the following pages eight renditions of the character, as a thematic continuation of Robert Darvel's story.

Blastalx

Bruce

Alex Daft-Wolf

Eudocimus

Job

Johann

Marti

Yves Moulin

Surt

We remain in darkest Africa for our next adventure, which stars legendary hunter and explorer, just as famous as the Nyctalope, Allan Quatermain! Matthew Dennion has crafted a story, which is centered around the theme of the Treasure of the Black Coats, but which depicts the clash between two powerful, evil masterminds, who orbit around it like two malevolent moons around a planetary giant...

Matthew Dennion: *The Treasure of Everlasting Life*

Africa, 1873

The kettle hanging over the fire began to whistle, indicating it had reached the boiling point. Despite the heat of the African savanna, the Englishmen in Allan Quatermain still craved a cup of hot tea in the mid-afternoon. Quatermain gently lifted the kettle from over the fire, poured the hot water into a cup, and began mixing his tea. He walked out the door of his home to sit on his porch and enjoy the afternoon.

As he seated himself and surveyed the landscape, something out of place caught his eye. In the distance, he could see smoke which shot into the sky in a straight pillar. The hunter mused that the pillar of smoke wafted backwards as if the object it was emanating from was moving. Quatermain used his hand to shield his eyes from the sun. He could see a large object beneath the smoke pillar. Had he not know better, Quatermain would have sworn that he was witnessing a train rolling down a set of tracks. The only problem with that explanation was that the nearest set of train tracks was hundreds of kilometers away.

Whatever it was that was sending the pillar of trailing smoke into the air was heading directly for Quatermain's house. The adventurer leaned back in his chair and took another sip of his tea. With the life that he had led, few things surprised him at this point. He was well aware that whatever it was would reach his home shortly, and he would deal with the strange object when the time came as he had so many other phenomena in his life.

The object slowed down as it reached Quatermain's house. A crowd had gathered composed of the various workers employed on the homestead. The object stopped a few meters short of Quatermain's front porch. As it came to a stop, Quatermain was able to fully observe its appearance. It was clearly some manner of massive transport. The transport was nearly two stories high and composed of steel. It had wheels not unlike a train with the exception that the tracks seemed to run around the wheels themselves. This format allowed the tracks to remain in constant motion around the wheels in order to propel the machine forward. The most peculiar aspect of the machine was that it was shaped like a massive rhinoceros. It had a huge horn at the tip of its nose through which smoke and steam were expelled.

Quatermain walked down the steps to his house and stood in front of the machine. His workers remained a few steps behind him. While the natives wanted to run in terror from the horned demon, they felt that Macumazahn, The Watcher-by-Night as they referred to Quatermain, would protect them. The diminutive Hottentot Hans walked up next to Quatermain:

"I don't know, baas. I don't think I like the look of this."

Quatermain silently nodded in agreement. He took a slight step backwards as the machine made a sound like pieces of metal being scraped together. The hunter watched as the top portion of the chest section pulled loose and descended to the ground revealing a staircase leading out of the transport.

Throughout all of his adventures, Quatermain had never seen a stranger duo of men than the two he beheld at the top of the stairs leading into the machine. One man was a giant-tall and lean with massive hands. The massive being's eyes stared blankly forward as if he was looking into an abyss. In contrast to the first man, the second man was a dwarf. He carried a cane in his right hand and smiled down at Quatermain and the gathered natives with a smug look of superiority.

The giant lifted the dwarf in his long arms and descended the stairway placing the small man directly in front of Quatermain. The dwarf smiled as he spoke:

"The legendary Mr. Allan Quatermain, I presume?"

Quatermain nodded.

"I am indeed Allan Quatermain, but I am hardly legendary. Who, sir, may I ask, are you?"

The Dwarf bowed.

"Doctor Miguelito Loveless, and this is my assistant, Voltaire. We have had a long journey, Mr. Quatermain. May I trouble you for a drink and then we can discuss my reasons for seeking you out?"

Quatermain gestured for them to follow him, and the three men entered the house, with Hans following behind them.

Loveless settled into a chair as Quatermain handed him his tea.

"Thank you, Mr. Quatermain."

Quatermain took a chair opposite him.

"Doctor Loveless, I am a curious man. May I inquire as to the nature of the machine you utilized to find me?"

The dwarf smiled.

"Oh, the Rhinoceros. Quite impressive is it not? It is a steam-powered vehicle, not unlike the current locomotives which travel across the railways. The design, however, is much more complicated than a simple steam engine, though. I wish I could take credit for designing the propulsion system, but the idea itself was first used to construct a steel elephant which was used to explore India several decades ago. I simply used those designs and reimagined the transport as a rhinoceros. The machine allows us to cross vast stretches of land with relative ease and total safety. Enough of the machine though, Mr. Quatermain, I would prefer to keep the rest of its secrets to myself for the time being. Let us discuss the reason for my being here."

Loveless stood up and hobbled forward.

"I am not only the world's most advanced scientific mind, but, to speak frankly, I am also a master criminal, and a member of a criminal organization known as the Black Coats."

At the mention of the Black Coats, Quatermain slowly reached for the hunting knife he kept at his side.

Loveless laughed.

"Mr. Quatermain, there is no need for that, I assure you! I mean you no harm, nor do I desire any of your possessions. I do, however, require your assistance with a matter of the utmost importance."

Quatermain released the grip on his knife.

"How can I be of assistance to you?"

Loveless began to pace the room as he spoke:

"As a scientific genius, I am afforded a certain status within the High Council of the Black Coats—the inner circle of criminals, if you will. These are dangerous men, Mr. Quatermain, dangerous men indeed, and none is more dangerous than their leader, Colonel Bozzo-Corona. The man is both brutal and brilliant at the same time. He needs to be, in order to maintain his position of leadership. More than this, though, is required, and he has something which all other members either fear or desire. There is a legend of a treasure in the Colonel's possession—a treasure reportedly so great that simply possessing it allows one mastery over the entire organization. Members of the group have long speculated about what the treasure could be. Reports abound, from a large sum of gold to a mystical weapon. Myself, I have a different theory, Mr. Quatermain. I believe the treasure is the secret to everlasting life."

Quatermain began to respond when Loveless cut him off.

"Please, Mr. Quatermain, hear me out. The disadvantages of being a man my size are numerous, but there are several advantages. For instance, I can hide in spaces much too small for a normal man to conceal himself. Additionally, people tend not to look directly at a dwarf. Rather through disgust, or some sense of misguided social norm, people avoid staring at dwarfs. These advantages allow me to enter areas that other people would find difficult. On numerous occasions, I have entered the Colonel's private chambers. I have examined his most personal texts and records. Do you know that the Colonel has been in command of the Black Coats for nearly a century? A century! There is no way one man could live so long, let alone maintain his position of power for such a time unless, of course, that man was immortal.

"Ancient texts in his room suggested a hidden city in Africa that contains the secret to eternal life. When I found these texts, I knew I had discovered the nature of his treasure. The texts, however, gave no exact location of this city, and that is where you come into this, Mr. Quatermain. My sources indicate that you have recently discovered such a city, and encountered a woman who herself was an immortal."

Quatermain stood up

"You mean Ayesha? That crazy witch queen in Kor? She's not immortal, she just thinks that she is, and the people around her simply believe her out of superstition."

Loveless shook his head.

"I understand you helped her battle another immortal. One who shook off bullets like drops of rain and who was only stopped by a unique axe."

Quatermain was in disbelief.

"That man must have had some manner of armor on, and the only unique thing about the axe in question was the strength of the man who wielded it. Doctor Loveless, I cannot believe that you, a man of science, would believe in native myths and stories of magic!"

Loveless stopped pacing.

"There is no such thing as magic, Mr. Quatermain. What people call magic is simply science that we do not yet understand. Scientists and doctors are aware that the application of certain substances can alter the way the body functions. Alcohol can dull pain as well as cognitive processes. The consumption of particular foods can increase the potency of a man's immune system. It is far from the realm of possibility that there exists in nature a substance which strengthens our bodies' resistance to damage from time, disease, and injury. Who better than Doctor Miguelito Loveless, the world's foremost scientist, to study, harness, and master this substance?

"As regards to myths and stories, you, of all people, should know that behind all native myths, there is a hint of truth. Look at all of the supposed myths which point to a source of immortality in Africa. The woman you mentioned is only one example. What of the reported Phantom in Bangalla? The Ghost Who Walks? He has been documented to have been protecting his country for centuries. The writings of Solomon Kane describe queen Nakari, who lived for several millennia... Countless other examples exist of immortals in Africa."

Quatermain grew tired of the debate.

"This is a pointless argument, Doctor. If you have come to hire me to guide you back to Kor on a fool's errand. I have to inform you that no amount of money will convince me to return to that mad city. As such, I will bid you farewell."

Loveless gestured toward Voltaire, whose massive hand shot out and grabbed Hans by the throat. Loveless strolled to the window and pulled out what Allan thought to be some manner of blow dart gun.

"Mr. Quatermain, to clarify, I had no intention of purchasing your services for this expedition, and if you will come over to the window, I will demonstrate why you will guide me back to Kor."

The hunter watched as the dwarf opened the window and placed a small sphere in the blow dart gun. Loveless pointed to a large tree next to the house. He took a deep breath, put the blow gun to his lips, and exhaled. The tree burst into flames as a shockwave shook the entire house. Quatermain stood with his mouth agape. Loveless turned to him.

"You see, Mr. Quatermain, a single kilogram of this material is more powerful than a stick of dynamite. With offensive capabilities such as this, and the protection afforded by my rhinoceros, the queen of Kor will have no choice but to surrender her secrets or watch her kingdom be destroyed. Just as your only choice is to guide me to Kor or watch as I destroy your home and all of the people you employ."

Quatermain was shaking with anger.

"Fine, Loveless. I will lead you to that God-forsaken city, as long as you promise not to harm my people."

Loveless bowed.

"I give you my word as a gentleman. You may take as many people as you need to convey your supplies for this journey. You will lead in a wagon, and I will follow in my rhinoceros. It will be a slow process, but keeping you out of the rhinoceros will ensure my safety. Voltaire will stay here with the Hottentot. Should you attempt to abandon me and return home, know that he will kill your friend."

Quatermain did not reply; he simply began directing his staff on what supplies to prepare for the journey. Loveless smiled, for he was sure that he would find what he was looking for in Kor: the treasure of the Black Coats, the secret to the Colonel's immortality. Once he had that secret, overthrowing the Colonel would be within his power. He knew that, within a short time, he would control the most powerful criminal organization in existence for eternity.

Quatermain tossed and turned in his tent, as he attempted to sleep. The first day's travel to Kor had been a disturbing one. He reviewed the day's events in his mind. The group had set out early in the morning with Quatermain's wagon train leading the expedition, and the massive steel rhinoceros in the rear of the caravan. Around mid-day, the party had come across the Waziri tribe, a group Quatermain had heard of, but had not yet encountered. The tribesmen, however, were well aware of the legendary Macumazahn. The tribe had stood atop a hill overlooking the savanna. Hunters from the tribe were preparing to enter the grasslands below, filled with zebras, giraffes, gazelle, elephants, and buffalo.

The natives were unsure what to make of the great steel beast as it rolled past them. They feared normal rhinoceros for their power and short tempers, so the massive one that moved before them awed them. Loveless took advantage of the opportunity. Turning his machine to its full speed, he sent the monstrosity barreling into the grasslands. The animals tried to run, but they were no match for something that could move as quickly as a locomotive. The Waziri and Quatermain's people watched as giraffe and buffalo were crushed under the massive weight of the machine. The screams of the beasts were blood-curdling. Quatermain had killed many animals in his day, but the deaths were always quick, within one or two shots at most. Many of the beasts were strewn across the field with their bodies half-crushed as they writhed in agony.

Once Loveless had the natives' attention, he unleashed the explosives. Opening a porthole located in the rhinoceros' eye, the dwarf began to direct his exploding pellets at the fleeing animals. Massive explosions blazed across the plain, sending pieces of the animals scattering into the air. Dozens of beast had been needlessly slain before Loveless had ended the carnage. He then turned his monster around and stopped it before Quatermain and the gathered Waziri.

He opened the porthole and addressed the hunter:

"Quatermain! Explain to the tribe that I am a great rhinoceros god. Tell them they will do my bidding, or be slain without mercy just as I slew the animals on the field. Tell them they will accompany us on a great journey to defeat a terrible witch!"

Quatermain sighed, realizing that he was sending many of these tribesmen to their deaths. He also realized that there was a chance they would live after confronting Ayesha's forces, but there was no chance of survival against Loveless and his machine. With a heavy heart, Quatermain relayed the dwarf's message to the tribe in their native tongue. Once they agreed to Loveless's demands, the dwarf chuckled inside of his machine. He gloated to Quatermain:

"Thank you, Mr. Quatermain. While I had little doubt that my rhinoceros would be a match for the armies of Kor, having our own army will insure the outcome. Once I have become immortal and overthrown Kor, the remaining tribes will also be convinced of my godhood. They shall be added to the resources at my disposal. With an army added to my cause, the Colonel will soon grovel at my feet."

The words echoed through Quatermain's head, and the smell of burnt flesh permeated the air as he lay in his tent. He still did not believe that the dwarf would find the immortality he sought. He was convinced, however, that many people would die as a result of his quest. Whether or not Loveless overthrew this Colonel was irrelevant to the hunter. What did concern him was that, with the massive rhinoceros in his arsenal, much of Africa could easily fall under the rule of Doctor Loveless. Quatermain sat up in his tent. Sleeplessness was not unknown to the hunter; there was a reason the natives called him the Watcher by Night.

He had resigned himself to sitting in front of the campfire until dawn when, suddenly, he felt a sharp pain in his neck. He reached back to find a tiny blow dart which he pulled from his skin. He looked at it for a moment as his vision began to blur. The hunter then fell backwards unconscious.

Allan Quatermain awoke several hours later. He was surprised to find a note with a hat attached to it sitting on his chest. It only took Quatermain a second to recognize the hat as belonging to his friend, Hans. For a moment, his heart skipped a beat and he feared the worst: that Loveless's blood lust had injured Hans as further motivation to reach Kor as quickly as possible.

Quatermain composed himself and directed his attention to the letter:

Dear Mr. Quatermain,

Please allow me to introduce myself; I am Colonel Bozzo-Corona, the man whose treasure Doctor Loveless is currently trying to steal, and whose position he is scheming to usurp. To allay your current fears, please know that your friend Hans and your ranch are in my possession. Your home and employees are unharmed and will remain so if you follow my instructions. You will direct Loveless 20 kilometers north-west of your current location. You will take him into a valley surrounded by hills on all sides. Once there, you will then direct the tribesmen to follow you in attacking Doctor Loveless's machine. The natives will be fearful of attacking it, but with the great Macumazahn leading them, I am confident they will fight valiantly. Inform them that you have been assured by the gods themselves that divine assistance will be provided to support them in their attack. Once the natives begin their attack, additional forces will be provided by an associate of mine to aid you in the battle.

I will be observing the battle myself from the apex of the northernmost hill overlooking the valley. When Loveless is engaged, confer with me atop the aforementioned hill, and I will provide you with the means necessary to defeat his machine.

If you follow my instructions, and if you survive the battle, your friends and home will be returned to you unharmed and without further consequences.

Sincerely,

Colonel Bozzo-Corona

Quatermain threw the note down in contempt, and his face turned red with anger. First, Loveless held his friends hostage, and now the very man the dwarf feared had his home and friends in his possession! He shook his head, knowing that the request to challenge Loveless and his demonic machine head on was a suicide mission. The Colonel would need half the artillery of the British Army to even stand a chance against that powerful machine. Whatever additional forces he had amassed, Quatermain was sure they would not be enough to defeat the rhinoceros.

The hunter considered his situation and decided he had no other choice than to follow the Colonel's instructions. A slight change in the direction of the expedition would arouse no concern as he was the only member of the group who knew where they were going. The hunter set to sharpening his knife and cleaning his rifles. Whatever challenge lay ahead of him, he wanted to be as prepared as he could to face it.

After a day of travel, the group reached the destination the Colonel had dictated. Quatermain's heart was heavy; his people and the gathered Waziri followed him to the apex of the first hill overlooking the valley. The hunter surveyed the terrain. It was green and lush with only a few trees scattered around it. The sun shone brightly as birds flew through the air and a cool breeze gently blew through the grass. It always amazed Quatermain how artists tended to portray wars and death on a massive scale occurring with a black sky on some bleak battlefield. He had been in enough battles to know that, more often than not, nature did not change its look to fit the battlefield people dreamed up in their minds. Most of the wars Quatermain had fought in occurred on beautiful days just like this day, and on gorgeous battlefields similar to the valley before him. Quatermain looked over his shoulder and saw the steel rhinoceros begin to ascend the hill behind the gathered natives. The thought occurred to him that there were less pleasant days and places to die.

The rhinoceros slowed considerably as it attempted its ascent. The hunter thought to himself that, at least, this mysterious Colonel had chosen his battlefield wisely. Surrounding the rhinoceros with steep hills on all sides would impede its speed and maneuverability. Loveless was still, of course, hidden behind a wall of moving steel. Furthermore, for all Quatermain knew, he had the ability with those exploding pellets of his to blast his way through the walls of rock and dirt that would surround him.

Quatermain gestured for the tribesmen to follow him into the deep valley. When the caravan arrived on the valley floor, Quatermain doubled the speed of their pace and headed for the hill where the Colonel indicated he would be waiting. The sweat poured down the hunter's face as he raced to his destination. The rhinoceros had not yet begun to descend into the valley when the rest of the caravan had attained the northern hill. If at all possible, Quatermain wanted to confer with the Colonel prior to Loveless entering the valley. The sooner he could coordinate the Waziri with the Colonel's forces, the more effective their attack would be.

The hunter had spread word of the attack on the rhinoceros when they had reached the valley. The natives were concerned, but they trusted him, and their fears were further quelled when he informed them of the Colonel's promised divine intervention. He hoped that, whatever information the Colonel had on the weakness of the machine, would be useful, because, without some form strategic advantage, the upcoming battle would be a slaughter.

Quatermain led the natives up the north hill as the rhinoceros was beginning its descent. Quatermain directed his gaze to the top of the hill to see two men standing at its apex. The first was an elderly man dressed entirely in black, leaning on a cane. He had long, flowing white hair, but, despite his wizened face and bent posture, looked surprisingly charismatic. A mysterious energy radiated from his dark, scheming eyes. Quatermain assumed this imposing figure was the mysterious Colonel Bozzo-Corona. The second man was an elderly gentleman with the same look of disdain mixed with fear on his face that Quatermain possessed.

The Colonel held out his hand.

"That will be close enough for now, Mr. Quatermain."

Placing a large speaking trumpet to his lips, he addressed Doctor Loveless in the steel beast.

"Miguelito, this is Colonel Bozzo-Corona! I am aware of your schemes and have come to inform you they stop here! Mr. Quatermain, as well as the assembled natives, are now under my control, and are prepared to attack. Turn your machine around and head home. Once we have returned to the citadel, we will discuss the future applications of that magnificent machine, as well as your punishment!"

Loveless slid open the vent near the machine's eye.

"My dear Colonel, I had hoped to delay a direct confrontation with you until I had attained a longer lease on life, but I am more than willing to crush you now and succeed you as leader of the Black Coats. With my machine, defeating the natives will be as easy as a locomotive running over a group of attacking ants." The dwarf smirked. "So please allow me to extend to you the opportunity to surrender now, and lead me to Kor yourself."

The Colonel shook his head.

"Miguelito, you disappoint and underestimate me at the same time. Do you think I would consider a confrontation with your machine with only a tribe of savages and a game hunter?" The Colonel gestured to the man beside him. "You are only one of the many talented people I have uses for. Allow me to introduce Doctor Dolittle. He possess a singularly unique talent, and since I am in possession of his grandchildren, I now posses it as well. Yes, Miguelito, I too can kidnap and blackmail in order to persuade people to conform to my will."

The ground under the feet of those on the hill began to shake and a low rumbling noise could be heard in the air. The Colonel placed his hand on Dolittle's shoulder.

"The good doctor here has the ability to talk to animals," he explained.

A trumpeting sound echoed through the air as from the hills to the East and West of the valley dozens of elephants charged down into the battlefield. Dolittle had a difficult time convincing the King of the Elephants to agree to attack the machine, especially when he learned they would be battling alongside Allan Quatermain. The hunter was known to have killed many elephants in his past. But Dolittle's pleas were aided by a young bull known as Cornelius, who had witnessed the slaughter Loveless orchestrated on the plains days earlier. He had convinced the King that the steel rhinoceros was the greater threat, and that allying themselves with Quatermain against this common foe was their best course of action.

The natives stood in disbelief as elephants slammed into either side of the metal monster. The rhinoceros shook violently from side to side as the elephants repeatedly gored the machine from both flanks.

Realizing he needed to act in order to snap the natives out of their shock, Quatermain climbed to the top of the hill and fired his rifle over the natives at the machine. The Waziri screamed and charged the machine head on while the elephants continued to attack from the sides. The spears and clubs the tribesmen hurled against the rhinoceros bounced as harmlessly off it as paper would being thrown at a mountain.

Quatermain ran over to the Colonel.

"Even with the elephants impairing the machine's movement the natives won't last long against that monster. What can we do to stop Loveless? What weakness does that beast have?"

"As you can see, Mr. Quatermain, Doctor Loveless is now engaged from three sides, leaving his back vulnerable. I have obtained the designs of the machine which inspired Doctor Loveless to build his rhinoceros. If he has not deviated from the original plans, there should be a vent at the top of the machine's back. You must get behind the beast and scale it. Once you reach the top, your elephant gun should be powerful enough to blow that vent open, thus allowing you inside—and direct access to Doctor Loveless."

Quatermain leveled his rifle at the Colonel.

"If I can stop that dwarf, both you and he will leave me and my people alone. If you do not leave us in peace, be assured I will make it my business to find you."

The Colonel glared at the hunter.

"People have died for less than this threat, Mr. Quatermain. However, I am a man of my word. Should you live, you will have no further quarrels with the Black Coats."

A series of explosions ripped through the Waziri and the elephants.

"The savages and the beasts have no hope of defeating Loveless's machine. They are merely cannon fodder to draw Loveless's attention. If you desire to see any of those warriors survive, I suggest you make haste."

Quatermain cocked his elephant gun and raced down the hill toward the machine.

The battle raged on with both the Waziri and the elephants taking losses as Quatermain reached the machine. He jumped on the tracks used to propel the monster and found a few handholds along its back which he used to scale it, while explosions continued to echo through the valley.

Once he reached the top, he quickly located the vent the Colonel had mentioned. Carefully aiming his heavy rifle, the hunter blasted it open.

He dropped into the interior of the mechanized nightmare just as Loveless was turning his attention from the battle to see what happened to the vent. The two men stared at each other for a moment. They fought to maintain their balance as the fury of the elephants shook the transport violently. Loveless leaned on his cane as Quatermain drew his hunting knife and approached the madman.

With surprising speed, Loveless sprang at Quatermain, using his cane to strike him across the left knee. Quatermain winced and swung his knife at the dwarf, who jumped to the side and thrust his cane between Quatermain's legs, causing him to trip.

Quatermain's face struck the floor. He rolled over and was struck again with the cane across the face. Once more he attempted to stab the dwarf only to be struck across the wrist with the cane. The hunter lost his grip on the knife and saw it go skidding across the floor.

Loveless stood above Quatermain wielding his cane like a saber.

"As I mentioned to you previously, many people see my size as handicap. However, when one is in a close quarter battle, it helps to not only be a smaller target, but to be able to maneuver easily. Soon, I will have the Colonel as a prisoner. He can lead me to Kor thus eliminating the need for you. Goodbye, Mr. Quatermain."

As Loveless lifted his can above his head, the machine shifted under him, causing him to pitch off balance. Quatermain seized his opportunity and kicked Loveless in the stomach, sending him rolling backwards.

The hunter dashed across the floor and regained his knife. Loveless used his momentum to control his roll and stopped himself at his captain's chair. He then reached under the chair and pulled out a pistol, which he aimed at Quatermain. The hunter cursed himself for having only kept his elephant gun, giving the Waziri his other firearms in a futile attempt to better their chances in their battle with the machine.

With no cover, Quatermain froze for a moment, sensing that his life was at its end. He then noticed several of the small exploding pellets Loveless had created carefully placed on series of shelves above the captain's chair. The hunter hurled his knife at the shelves.

Loveless, seeing the weapon's trajectory, quickly rolled into the open space beneath the steel control panel. As the knife hit one of the capsules, the entire front section of the steel rhinoceros blew open.

The machine stood still in the valley, its face a smoking wreck. As the smoke spread across the valley, the cheers of the Waziri tribesmen could be heard in conjunction with the victorious trumpeting of elephants.

Loveless awoke to find himself in a bed placed inside a well-furnished room. Sitting in a chair next to his bed was the Colonel. Standing just outside the door, he could see the massive forms of both Voltaire and the Black Coats' fearsome executioner, the Marchef.

The Colonel leaned over the bed.

"Good morning Miguelito. You have made quite a mess of things lately haven't you?"

Loveless started to respond but the Colonel cut him off:

"If you value your life, you will remain silent. The only reason that you are still among the living is because I am wise enough to appreciate your aptitudes in science and mechanics. However, my wisdom does not quell my temper regarding your recent actions. First of all, let me inform you that both Mr. Quatermain and Doctor Dolittle have had their families and friends returned to them. Currently, they are both resting at their respective homes. Due to your actions, the Black Coats have now acquired two formidable adversaries in those individuals.

"Second, you sought to steal my treasure. Not only did you attempt to steal it, you even went so far as to misidentify it!" The Colonel laughed. "The legend of Kor was just a hobby of mine, not my actual treasure, you fool! I might actually have assisted you in finding that city had you asked my permission. Instead, you set off on your own, not to only locate Kor, but to use its supposed powers in an attempt to overthrow me! This action was something that I could not overlook; thus forcing my intervention and the inconveniences to Mr. Quatermain and Doctor Dolittle."

The Colonel began to pace the room.

"The question now is: what to do with you? As I said, I have allowed you to live so that your scientific skill can continue to benefit our brotherhood. Your punishment shall be as follows: you will be sent to America. Your activities will be confined to that wild area for the remainder of your life. Any attempt to operate in Europe will be met with quick repercussions. I will be kept informed of your latest inventions, and they will be at my disposal, should I require them. You will henceforth turn over fifty percent of all your gains to the Brotherhood. Your primary objective will be to gain control over the area known as California, which you claim is rightfully the property of your family."

The Colonel crossed the room and stood before the Marchef.

"Once you gain control of that land, you will learn the difference between the rewards bestowed on a loyal member of our Family, and the punishment applied to a potential usurper. Your land will become our property. My Marchef is sometimes concerned about what happens to the children of people whom he kills. He so hates to see young innocents suffer. I intend to reward his loyalty at your expense. Once you have gained control of California, you will create a sanctuary for these children, and you will personally supervise it. I dare say, the children should find a dwarf such as you an amusing caretaker."

The Colonel placed his hand on the Marchef.

"Is this an acceptable reward?" he asked.

The giant simply nodded affirmatively. The Colonel then turned back to Loveless.

"Miguelito, you understand that if you refuse these terms, your life will be ended here and now without a second thought?"

Loveless nodded as he stared down at his bed.

"Good!" said the Colonel. "Then we are in agreement. But remember, should you attempt to usurp my power, or seek my treasure again, you will wish I had killed you today."

About this story, Win Eckert writes: "Just as Philip José Farmer's Wold Newton Family tree and studies of his Wold Newton mythos are supported by explanatory essays, readers may also need assistance in navigating the interconnected branches of the various official Wold Newton Origins stories and unofficial "sideways" tales. The first story in this sequence, "Is He in Hell?" was published in Tales of the Shadowmen 6. *Thereafter, two short sideways follow-up tales, "Nadine's Invitation" and "Marguerite's Tears," which appeared respectively in* Tales of the Shadowmen 7 *and* Tales of the Shadowmen 8. *These sideways tales can be read separately from the main storyline, and conclude with this new story. Meantime, the official Wold Newton Origins storyline has carried forward with "The Wild Huntsman" in* The Worlds of Philip José Farmer 3. *Finally, without providing spoilers, those wishing to know what comes after "Violet's Lament" should seek out my story "Zorro's Rival" in* More Tales of Zorro."*

Win Scott Eckert: *Violet's Lament*

Blakeney Manor, Richmond, England, February 1815

The bells pealed two o'clock in the morning as Siger Holmes skulked into Sir Percy Blakeney's vast library—one of the finest and most complete in Europe—and closed the door gently behind him. Once again, he had a need to consult those books upon which he had relied, on so many prior visits to Blakeney Manor.

Consult them, perhaps, for the final time.

Gathering several dry and cracked leather-bound volumes, he placed the most important book, the *Ruthvenian*, on the top of the stack and settled into a comfortable chair. The fire in the grate was low—the men had concluded their *digestifs* in this very room hours ago—but he dared not stoke it, despite the chill of the season. Instead, he gathered his dressing gown about him and curled up in a comfortable chair.

The flickering candle on the table beside him cast a yellow pool of light, under which he held the book, carefully turning to the desired pages.

The *Ruthvenian* was at least one-hundred years old; it had been written by Armand Tesla, a researcher into vampiric and other occult lore. Although the tome focused on the family Ruthven, in which Tesla claimed that vampirism ran strong, and had done so for centuries, the volume also contained much valuable lore about vampires in general, and Holmes had come to view the book as a veritable vampire bible.

He wondered briefly if the present Lord Ruthven had succumbed, or would. He shook his head. He had not believed in vampires—or ghosts, or goblins, or were-creatures—until Marguerite's funeral. Her empty casket, and the falling droplets of blood as she flitted away into the night sky with her—her—he could barely bring himself to think it—her *lover*—made him believe.

The library door opened a crack and Holmes started. A shaft of light, cast from another candle, framed a figure in the doorway. The late-night visitor darted into the chamber and closed the door as quietly as he had.

"I'm sorry to startle you, Uncle."

Holmes' hawkish features softened as exhaled strongly, almost extinguishing his own candle.

"Violet, my dear, what are you doing here at this time of night?"

"Now Uncle, I could ask you the same," Violet said. Her lips turned upward slightly, but there was no humor in her smile.

Holmes was her uncle by marriage, and he and his wife, Violet—after whom the seventeen-year-old girl had been named—certainly played the roles of treasured uncle and aunt in her life. Siger and Sir Percy were as close as brothers, and their wives Alice and Violet were in fact sisters; as such the Holmeses were frequent visitors to Blakeney Manor.

At 55, Sir Percy Blakeney was getting on, although still active. Some of his many children had married or were betrothed. But not his daughter Violet. In contrast with her siblings, she had no interest in being courted, despite her great beauty, and instead insisted on daily fencing lessons from her father, and late-night scholarly and political debates with the *cognoscenti* who always seemed to be passing through the manor halls. She had a special attachment to Siger, and enjoyed the challenge posed by his great intellect. He, in return, took a special interest in the girl who seemed to bear the loss of her mother Marguerite—Sir Percy's first wife—with an outward stoicism that was belied by her regular probing questions about her mother and father's adventures together during the French Revolution.

As close as they were, however, Violet's next question astounded Holmes: "Uncle, have you finally found *her*?"

"What do you mean, my dear?"

Violet's eyes flashed, one of the few times she had ever shown anger toward him. "Don't dissemble, Uncle, it's beneath you, and you've trained me too well, not only to see, but to observe."

Holmes' smile was grim. He gestured for her to continue.

"Every time you come to visit, you make late-night visits to the library. What you may have missed is that ever since I was a little girl, I've noticed this and come into the library after you've finished."

"I'm impressed, Violet. Pray continue."

"I've made note of which books were out of place, which have been disturbed, where dust was cleaned away." Violet tossed her dark hair, a gesture in unconscious imitation of her late mother, and continued. "I've searched the books themselves and have seen the little markers you left for yourself, thinking no one else would notice or even use these books. This has something to do with mother's death. You must tell me."

Holmes' sharp features were grave as he shook his head. "Nothing good can come of this."

"I insist."

He sighed and steepled his hands and rested his chin on them. "In the time before your mother passed, she wasted away, slowly, very slowly, year after year. I blame myself for not making the connection sooner. I only put it together after she passed. I'll never forgive myself for that."

Violet took his hand in hers and silently urged him to continue.

"There was a woman, a friend of your mother's, and a frequent visitor to her from the Continent," Holmes said. "It was not until after Marguerite died that your father made an offhand comment about this woman's...*exceptional* interest in your mother. I had long suspected this woman of some treachery, or machinations, in other areas. But I didn't connect her to your mother's condition until it was too late."

Holmes filled his pipe, lit it, and took several deep puffs. He continued. "I mentally reviewed the history of your mother's illness. I realized she had taken a turn for the worse each time this woman paid a visit. The woman was pale, her skin like ice to the touch. I became conscious of the fact that with each visit, your mother's complexion had become more and more pallid, so that it was almost colorless."

"When did this begin?" Violet asked.

"I believe they first met in Bath, in 1795. Later that year, in December, your father and mother held a large gathering, at Blakeney Hall, up in Yorkshire, at which she was present."

"Yes, at Would Newton. I remember father's stories about the fiery star which fell from the sky."

"A stone, actually..." Holmes murmured. "But to continue...she came to visit your mother here, at Blakeney Manor, several times after that, until...the end."

Violet squeezed his hand, her dark eyes wet with unshed tears. Holmes met her gaze. "I was a man of logic, of science. This prevented me from discerning the truth sooner. But after your father's comment about this woman, after I began to suspect...I came here, to this library. I consulted these tomes.

"The night of your mother's funeral, I, and another, unearthed her coffin," Holmes said. "It was empty."

"*Then she's alive?*" Violet interrupted.

Holmes shook his head, his gray eyes filled with sadness. "No. Not in the way that we think of life." He opened the *Ruthvenian* to another section, and pointed to the relevant introductory passages, which she rapidly scanned.

Violet looked up at him. "And you believe this?" she challenged.

"I do. Too late, but yes, I do."

"What have you been researching this evening?"

In reply, Holmes turned the pages to a different chapter which described different types of night creatures and how to destroy them.

"Then you've found her," Violet whispered.

"Yes. My agents on the Continent have tracked her down…"

"What is her name?"

"Countess Nadine Carody," Holmes replied.

"Is my mother with her?"

"I don't know."

"And you are intent on going after this Countess?"

"I admit it."

"I'm going with you."

Holmes drew on his pipe, and sighed. "I know."

Blakeney Manor, Richmond: 28 Feb. 1815
My Dear Sir Percy,

I regret my sudden departure from Blakeney Manor, and hope you will understand when I explain that matters pertaining to the conclave you hosted at Would Newton, lo those twenty years ago, have once again, and unavoidably, drawn me to business on the Continent.

As you will recall, prior to the conclave, we suspected that Colonel Bozzo-Corona and the Countess Nadine Carody were somehow in league. As events unfolded, we were never able to confirm the nature of their relationship, although I did see the Colonel's man, Lecoq, at the Countess' Paris townhouse in the month prior to the conclave.

Although the agreements we reached with the Colonel and the Brothers of Mercy at the conclave are, at this point of course, moot in the face of Bonaparte's depredations, word comes, coincident with his escape from Elba, of the Colonel and the Countess.

I will explain fully upon my return, but I ask you not to follow me.

It is also with deep regret that I must inform you that Violet observed my preparations for departure from Blakeney Manor this morning and confronted me. In fact, she insisted upon accompanying me—"for my own protection," apparently—explaining to me, with unassailable logic, that her skill with a sword is unparalleled and any adversaries will underestimate her, thinking her a mere helpless girl. I am truly sorry, but was powerless to dissuade her; as you well know, Sir, it is impossible to refuse her once she's set her mind on a thing.

I vow to you Percy, upon my honor as your brother and as the child's godfather, that she will be protected with my very life.

Believe me, dear Sir,
Your obliged and faithful humbl. sert.,

Dr. Siger Holmes

Etsch Valley, Tyrol, Austrian Empire, April 1815

The deep forest smelled of pine and loam. Leaves hung heavy under morning dew not yet evaporated by the sun just rising over the Alps in the distance.

It was the rising sun that threw them. They hadn't expected a confrontation after daybreak.

Siger Holmes tripped over a great tree root which had burst from the ground ages ago. His companion caught his arm and he steadied himself.

The woman appeared, seemingly from nowhere—had she dropped from a tree branch high above them? Her skin was pale as fine porcelain, her hair jet black; her equally black eyes were rimmed red and seemed to burn like coal embers in the forest shade. A long monk's habit covered her from white throat to the ground.

Holmes' companion reached under a cloak, and he shot out a restraining arm.

"Wait," he whispered.

A red squirrel chittered, rebuking him for even that unobtrusive disturbance.

A dark blur leapt toward them and the woman sprang forward, intercepting it before the newcomer reached Holmes and his friend. The two forms clashed and tangled, rolling in the leaves and tearing at each other with sharp claws. They ripped at each other's pale flesh with razor teeth.

They leapt apart and landed like cats, hissing and growling. The woman had lost her cloak in the fight and now crouched low to the ground, naked, blood spurting from jagged rips on her white breast.

The other was a man, Holmes could see now. Or at least the creature had the form of a man. His hair was coal black, like the woman's, and his red eyes flamed. The tips of his ears came to tiny, but distinct, points.

The two hunkered down, ready to pounce at each other again.

The man bounded forward and flew toward the woman in an arc. Rather than responding in kind, she bent lower and faced upward as he descended upon her. As he reached her, claws extended to tear off her face, a long hardwood stake appeared in her hands. Holmes, shocked, could not tell where it had come from; it was as if she had conjured it from thin air.

She lodged the blunt end in the ground and held it fast, aiming at his approaching chest. The man landed on the sharp end and gravity and momentum did the rest, plunging the stake through his heart, chest cavity, and out its back, releasing a great crimson geyser.

The pallid woman rolled her victim over and ripped open the thing's chest. Prying apart the ribs, she dug around a bit. She found her prize and triumphantly stuffed he heart in her mouth, chewing greedily, cherry red rivulets of blood streaming from the corners of her mouth and over her naked, upturned breasts.

Finally, the woman's battle-feast concluded, she looked up and addressed Holmes and his companion, who had remained stock-still through the whole episode.

She smiled, redly. "I am Ziska."

"And are you friend, or foe, Ziska?" Holmes challenged.

"A friend, Dr. Holmes, or else you would both be dead by now, at the hands of the Giaour."

"Then we thank you," Holmes replied.

Ziska shrugged. "He was newly undead, and presented only a mild challenge." She licked her lips. "I would see you and your friend attain your goal."

"Well?"

"Those whom you seek are at the castle," Zizka replied.

"Very well…"

Ziska smiled, somewhat ghoulishly, and continued. "They are defended by several others—one less, now," she amended, gesturing to the bloody corpse, "although the one you seek believes her guardians are true to her."

"Then you seek to betray her," Holmes said.

"I have already done so, merely by speaking to you, and by my intervention here," Ziska said.

"Why?"

Ziska eyes burned more brightly. "My reasons are my own. Let me see your weapons," she commanded.

Holmes' fellow traveler stirred, and once again he held up a restraining arm. He withdrew his pistol and presented it to her.

"And the ammunition?" she asked.

He retrieved it from his overcoat pocket and held it in his hand.

Ziska eased the stake from the Giaour's chest. It made a slick, slurping noise as it slid out.

"Should you be doing that?" he inquired. "Doesn't the stake need to remain embedded?"

"I have torn out his heart and consumed it," Ziska said. "There's no coming back from that."

She touched the tip of the stake to the pistol and spherical lead balls.

Ziska turned to Holmes' companion. "The sword, please."

Violet Blakeney looked askance at Holmes and he shrugged. She drew the blade, a double-edged *spada da lato* or side-sword, from its concealing cloak and held it out to Ziska.

Ziska touched the stake tip to the metal and held it there for several seconds. Then the stake vanished from her hands as mysteriously as it had appeared, and Violet replaced sword in scabbard. Holmes was unsettled.

"The outer hatch to the castle cellars will be unlatched two days hence at sunrise. The tunnels from the cellars lead to the chapel. I must go now," Ziska said. "I will be missed."

"Thank you for your assistance," Holmes said. "Will we see you again?"

"The future is uncertain," she replied. "But, one thing *is* certain. You are being followed." She grinned devilishly and disappeared.

Holmes and Violet whirled and stood firm, facing the path they had trod mere moments ago, watching as four dark figures resolved from the mist and shadows.

The four men approached unarmed, despite Holmes' drawn firearm. Violet reached under her traveling cloak to draw her sword from its sheath, and Holmes held her back with a gesture. "Not yet," he whispered. "We may need yet rely upon the element of surprise."

The growing morning sun penetrated the thick foliage.

The four stopped ten feet away from Holmes and Violet. The youngest man smiled and touched his hat brim in a brief two-finger salute. "Hello, Doctor Holmes."

Holmes faced the other man, frowning. "Do I know you, sir? You seem familiar."

The other's grin widened. "You knew my father, Doctor Holmes. I am Lecoq."

Holmes held his pistol steady. "That's far enough, I think, M. Lecoq."

Lecoq—he looked to be barely out of his teens—stopped and held up his hands in a gesture of peaceful intent. "Come now, Doctor. We are all friends."

"We?" Holmes echoed. "Who are these with you?"

"Ah yes, may I introduce my colleagues: M. Durand, M. Thénardier, and M. Mondego," Lecoq said.

Durand, perhaps in his late thirties with hints of gray at the temples, nodded slightly. The other two were larger—probably Lecoq and Durand's bodyguards or "enforcers." They stood behind Lecoq and Durand and stared, saying nothing.

"And your companion, Doctor Holmes?" Lecoq raised his eyebrows in frank appreciation. "I am charmed, Mademoiselle. Leo Lecoq, at your service."

"My daughter, Violet," Holmes replied. "I'll thank you to redirect your gaze to mine, Sir."

Lecoq shifted his eyes as Holmes bade, but his smile didn't reach them. "As I mentioned, Holmes, we are all friends."

"That remains to be seen. Why are you following us?"

"The Colonel would like to know why you have returned to Europe," Lecoq replied.

"And is all of Continental Europe the Colonel's territory now," Holmes asked, "that all simple travelers must explain themselves to him?"

Lecoq's eyes became tiny flints. "You are no simple traveler, Holmes. Never simple. And not just a traveler. The Colonel makes it a point to stay abreast of the activities of important men. You should be flattered, Sir. He considers you one of those men. And of course you are allies."

"We were," Holmes interjected.

"You are allies," Lecoq continued, "bound by the accords reached at Would Newton."

"Any agreements and plans made at Would Newton have long since gone awry," Holmes said. "Lupin's half-brother left our control—and the Colonel's—long ago. Witness his recent escape from Elba."

"Yes, the Colonel does regret that the Little Corporal has not been more... reliable. Nonetheless, we were, and are, all still in this together."

"The time for togetherness, all for one, one for all, is long past. Even as we speak, Bonaparte has retaken Paris."

"Your point being?" Lecoq said. "You are a long way from Paris, Doctor Holmes."

Holmes changed tactics. "I would like to better understand what the Colonel knows about the whereabouts of Countess Nadine Carody," he said. "They were in league, all those years ago, were they not?"

Durand turned to Lecoq and spoke for the first time. "This is getting us nowhere."

Lecoq gestured for silence and stared at Holmes and Violet.

"Very well then," Holmes continued. "We will continue on our way to the Castle of Monteleone."

"How did you know the Colonel—?" Lecoq cut off his own question, too late.

The corner of Holmes' mouth quirked. "So the Colonel and Countess Carody are holed up there together are they? Very good, thank you for letting me know."

He stepped back, gesturing to Violet. She followed, slowly turning away but keeping the four men in sight out of the corner of her eye, and her hand under her cloak on the hilt of her sword.

"Doctor Holmes! Wait, if you please," Lecoq called.

Holmes and Violet turned once again.

"I confess. The Colonel's eyes are everywhere," Lecoq said. "He has kept up with the attendees of the so-called conclave at Would Newton."

"Confess to something I haven't already deduced."

"The Countess Carody has allied with Murat, the King of Naples."

"Napoleon's brother-in-law," Holmes said.

"Yes," Lecoq replied. "We were also on our way to Murat's castle at Monteleone."

"To report to the Colonel."

"No, Sir," Lecoq replied. "To rescue him. He is the Countess' prisoner."

Holmes and Violet made camp for the night in the strangely silent woods, in a small grove off the trail to Tcherms. They planned to decamp at three o'clock a.m. and continue along the shrouded forest trail, timing arrival at their destination, the Castle of Monteleone, after sunup.

Lecoq, Durand, Thénardier , and Mondego had insisted on accompanying them. "We are aligned in this, can't you see, Doctor Holmes?" Lecoq continued to argue as they prepared a small fire.

"And why would you say that?" Holmes inquired.

"The Countess, it must be the Countess. She is the only reason you would be here. You have no reason to seek out the Colonel."

Holmes shrugged.

"We must join forces against her!" Durand added, and now Lecoq made no effort to silence his companion.

"You, Mademoiselle Holmes," Lecoq said. "What is your interest in this? Why do you also seek the Countess? Surely your father here would agree it is too dangerous. How have you persuaded him to allow you to accompany him?"

"Well, I—"

"That will do, Violet," Holmes said.

Lecoq turned his attentions back to Holmes. "Why do you mistrust us, Sir? As I said, the Colonel deeply regrets that Lupin's half-brother escaped our influence. But our intentions and mutual interests—"

"Surely you know, young man," Holmes interrupted, "your father must have told you, that the conclave, and the resulting alliance of which you speak, was conducted under an air of deceit and murder?"

"My father died when I was young, Doctor." Lecoq's expression was unreadable.

"And the Colonel did not tell you?" Holmes inquired. "Never told you of the three murders, all unexplained? All carried out in different and horrific ways. All signaled by nine terrible tollings of an awful bell. All unsolved to this day. And in the thick of it, Colonel Bozzo-Corona, your father Lecoq, Kramm, Carody, Gerolstein. We concluded our business for the good of Europe—we thought at the time—but don't think for a moment that your Colonel and his contingent have never been suspects."

At this affront, the two hulking men leapt up and before Lecoq could call them off, Mondego grabbed Holmes' traveling cloak in a giant paw and lifted him bodily in the air. The other fist came at Holmes' jaw in a great arc while Thénardier, standing behind Mondego, egged on his friend: "Teach 'im to insult the Colonel! Give 'im 'is just desserts! Maybe after yer fists and my boots've bloodied 'im a bit 'e'll sing a different tu—"

Mondego's mammoth fist connected with Holmes' jaw, knocking him in a daze, just as Thénardier's taunts cut off. The doctor landed by the fire, still in a stupor, and yelled in terror and surprise when Thénardier's head, ripped off at the neck and geysering spirals of blood, also landed and rolled beside him.

The head's eyes blinked once and the gaping mouth, no longer connected to lungs, made small croaking noises.

Siger turned and retched into the fire, made nauseous as much by Mondego's blow as by the disembodied head's now-dead eyes staring into his.

He turned and tried to rise, failed. On hands and knees, he managed to raise his head and grasp what was transpiring.

Mondego lay on the ground in front of him; four giant, ragged claw marks across his chest burbled wet and crimson. Lecoq and Durand were up a tree, to the left of the clearing.

On the other side of the fire, Violet Blakeney faced a creature, white of flesh and red of mouth, with eyes burning in the pitch night. Her cloak was thrown off and her sword was drawn. The steel flashed in the orange firelight.

He called weakly: "Violet, no, you cannot face such a creature as this with a mere sword."

The beast—for it was a beast, despite the human appearance and dark evening clothing of an Eastern European sophisticate—agreed, grinning wetly at her. "Listen to him, little girl. Count Aubri declares it to be so. There is no resistance in you. You cannot win."

Violet paused, and lowered her sword a foot.

Count Aubri's red eyes swirled in pleasure. "That's it, girl. Succumb. You have already lost. But perhaps you may yet win; please me and my gifts might be yours."

Violet looked blankly into Aubri's damned eyes; the sword dropped even further. She licked her lips.

"Yield to me." Aubri reached out a lone talon, caressed her cheek, drawing a trickle of blood. The sword pointed at the ground. "Open you hand. Release the sword. Release the sword and join me in a dark kiss, little girl."

Violet sighed and she crumpled to her knees, the sword still dangling from her loose fingers. Aubri bent over her to take the blade from her hand.

"Violet!" Holmes yelled again. The girl blinked—and the steel flashed in a one-hundred-and-eighty degree arc, neatly removing the vampire's head from its neck, showering Violet in scarlet gore.

The head bounced and came to a halt next to Thénardier's, undead and dead eyes staring at each other.

Violet turned and ran to Holmes. "Uncle! Are you all—?"

"Violet!" Holmes yelled. "The *body*!"

She turned back to see Count Aubri's headless figure bounding on clawed hands and feet at incredible speed toward the bodiless head resting by the fire. She leapt into its path and thrust the blade through its back and out the chest on the other side. Her aim was true; his heart was pierced and he collapsed.

Violet pulled out the sword and before the creature could reanimate, flipped it over, pulled out a heavy knife and drove the tip into the chest cavity. With much effort, she sliced and cut, finally drawing out the dead heart on the tip of the blade.

She tossed it in the fire, where it flared and crackled.

Violet went to her uncle and helped him sit up, as Lecoq and Durand approached. She gave Holmes some water, and tended to his bruised jaw, while the other two busied themselves burying the bodies of Mondego, Thénardier, and Count Aubri.

Later, Holmes and Durand slept, while Violet and Lecoq kept watch. He spoke to her: "She knows we're coming."

"So?"

"Who are you, really?" Lecoq asked. "Why are you here?"

"We told you," Violet said.

"No. During the fight you called to him," Lecoq said. "You called him 'uncle.'"

She sighed. "He is my uncle; he is my father's brother-in-law, and my godfather."

"And you are, then?" Lecoq pressed.

"Violet Blakeney."

"Aha. Yes. The daughter of Sir Percy."

"One of them, at any rate," Violet said.

"And why do you seek the Countess Nadine Carody?"

"She killed my mother."

"Ah. It becomes clear," Lecoq said. "You wish revenge."

"Of course," Violet replied.

"And yet...knowing Countess Carody's...*appetites*...can you really be sure your mother is dead?"

Violet was silent. Lecoq took another approach.

"Why is your father not here? And how did you kill Count Aubri with a mere steel sword?"

"Enough questions," she said. "Your turn for some answers. If the Countess knows we are coming, is she actually holding your Colonel hostage? Perhaps your Colonel sent you and M. Durand to dissuade us from seeking him and the Countess out..."

Lecoq laughed at her. "*Mon Dieu*! How could such thoughts enter such a pretty little brain! You saw what that thing did to Mondego and Thénardier!"

Violet glared and put her hand to her blade. "I also saw what it *didn't* do to you and M. Durand."

"We hid in the trees, I confess—"

"Yes, please do confess."

"—I confess to momentary startlement as the creature attacked, but surely not to the perfidy you accuse me of."

"I confess," Violet returned, "that your flowery words mean nothing to me. I confess I believe you and M. Durand are biding your time, looking for an opening to turn the tables on us, perhaps even kill us in order to save your Colonel from the Countess."

"Violet, my dear Violet, I must protest!"

"You may address me as Mademoiselle Blakeney."

"But—but, my dear Mademoiselle," Lecoq protested, "your bloodthirstiness gets the best of you! I assure you—"

"That'll be enough, Lecoq." Holmes was awake, staring at them, his eyes hard. "It's time for Durand and me to take the watch."

He shook Durand awake, roughly, and then spoke more gently to Violet. "Go to sleep, my dear. Tomorrow will come too soon."

Castle of Monteleone, Austrian Empire

As the sun pierced the veil of night, Violet, Holmes, Lecoq, and Durand crept through the dank tunnels beneath the Castle of Monteleone.

"According to the *Ruthvenian*," Violet whispered, "we should find the Countess in her coffin."

"No, child," Holmes replied. "Nadine Carody must be of a different breed of vampire than that described by Tesla in the *Ruthvenian*. I have seen her walk in broad daylight many times, although she shaded herself from direct sunlight. Nonetheless, I hope the *Ruthvenian* will be instructional when it comes to defeating her."

They followed the twisting, turning warrens, and stole up a cramped passageway of stairs, exiting at the base of the castle's three-story, 14th century chapel.

The sanctuary was dim, the morning sun only beginning to seep in through stained glass framed by narrow arched windows.

"Welcome."

The voice, a woman's, came from nowhere and everywhere.

The four newcomers turned, faced the pulpit.

From above, floating gently down as if they were motes of dust riding invisible air currents, came three dark figures.

In the forefront was the ethereally beautiful Countess Carody. Her heart-shaped face and wide eyes, like dark whirlpools of oil, were framed by straight and lustrous chestnut hair which fell to her waist. She wore a long white gossamer gown which flowed behind her as she descended. Her breasts were small and pert.

Although he knew she was Hungarian, the Countess reminded Holmes of an exotic Spanish princess—or at least what he imagined such a creature might look like.

Behind her and to either side were Ziska and a man in a dark suit. Ziska was naked as she had been when Holmes and Violet had met her in the forest. The man, as pale as the others, had heavy dark brows, and graying black hair which crept down his forehead in a pronounced widow's peak.

The three alighted gently on the cold stone floor, Countess Carody in front and the other two at the points of a vampiric triangle.

"Doctor Holmes, it's so nice to see you again," the Countess greeted. She looked at Violet and her tongue darted out, flicking red lips. "And you've brought some friends."

Holmes withdrew a small silver cross from a chain around his neck and held it forth. "Come no closer." Behind him, Lecoq and Durand drew their knives.

The Countess smiled, almost sadly. "I am not your garden-variety night creature. In case you didn't realize…the sun is up; I and my minions are also up and about."

Lecoq said, "Where is the Colonel? Give him to us and we'll leave these other two to you."

Countess Carody shook her head. "You don't understand… All of you—not just the doctor and the lovely Violet—are mine now. And the Colonel." She gave a small wave of her hand at the wrist, and above them, in a corner of the chapel ceiling three levels up, the shadows receded like an ocean tide.

Colonel Bozzo-Corona hung from a chain which wrapped around his chest and extended up into the ceiling. Another length of chain was slung loosely around the elderly man's neck.

"M. Lecoq, M. Durand, if you interfere," the Countess said, "I will snap the chain around his chest and his neck will slip into the chain noose. He will die before any of you can reach him. Of course, you will die as well, and Count Yorga—" she gestured to the male vampire behind her "—and Ziska and I will have a fine meal."

Yorga grinned, wet fangs gleaming. "I will have this lovely creature," he said, staring at Violet. "I can hear her blood throbbing, pumping. I will have it…"

He took a step forward and Countess Carody turned, her left arm outflung, blocking him.

"Hold!" she said, facing him. "The girl is mine—"

"You always claim the best morsels," Yorga growled. "This time—"

A sharp *crack* issued and a bloom of crimson burst forth from Count Yorga's tunic. He looked down in shock—the shock of an immortal creature done to death—and collapsed.

The Countess whirled back and faced Siger Holmes' smoking pistol.

"*How?*"

"A wood-laced ball, if I'm not mistaken," Holmes replied.

"And now you must reload," the Countess said. "You won't get the chance."

She charged at Holmes and Violet flung herself in his way, drawing her sword from its scabbard.

She whipped the blade around in a frenzied blur, and the steel edge met the Countess' outstretched, taloned hand at the wrist, slicing it off neatly.

Countess Nadine Carody spun and backed off, writhing, screaming, and clutching the stump which jetted scarlet everywhere and smoked faintly as if cauterized.

"*Bitch!*" she hissed. "Get her, *now!*" she ordered Ziska.

Ziska feinted toward Violet, then spun and flew at the Countess, raking her cheek with her talons, leaving deep red grooves.

While Holmes struggled to reload his pistol, Violet held her sword at the ready, seeking an opening amidst the tumbling, clawing, slavering she-vampires, hoping to get another blow in against the Countess.

Meanwhile, Lecoq and Durand sought purchase on the rough chapel walls, hoping to climb them and free their master.

Violet and Holmes watched as Ziska and the Countess bit and slashed, the Countess' diaphanous gown shredding in the battle.

For a moment, the Countess seemed to gain the advantage, stabbing deep into Ziska's chest with her remaining clawed hand. She barely missed the heart and Ziska disappeared from the Countess's grasp, reappearing behind her. She sank her jaws into the back of the Countess's neck and ripped, exposing bloody sinew and vertebrae.

The Countess rotated, her head half-detached at the base of the neck, and once more thrust lethally sharp claws into Ziska's chest. Her aim was true this time and blood gushed from Ziska's mouth, drenching both their naked bodies in bright red gore.

Ziska's eyes rolled up in the back of her head. As she collapsed in a heap of crimson flesh, a clear shot opened and Holmes pulled his pistol's trigger. The Countess rolled to her left, dodging the shot with inhuman speed, and landed on her feet like a cat, facing Violet and her sword.

"Come here, sweet thing," the Countess said, her head still listing freakishly to one side. "Put down that sword. Come here, and taste my kiss, and we'll love eternally."

While Holmes made to reload once more, Violet swayed, disoriented by the Countess's lulling, lilting voice, and her blade lowered.

"Just like…our love…was eternal?" Ziska croaked as she bled out all over the gray stone floor.

"Don't listen to that *betrayer!*" the Countess screamed at Violet. Then, more softly: "Come to me, child, come to me."

Violet's sword arm dropped once more.

"*Violet!*" Holmes yelled. The girl started, and then turned her gaze slowly back to Countess Nadine Carody. Clearly the Countess' persuasive powers were stronger than Count Aubri's had been.

Holmes looked up at the two Frenchmen, climbing to release their leader, and saw something black flit in the gray shadows above the suspended man.

The black thing dove from the upper corner ceiling of the chapel at incredible speed and alighted in front of the dazed Violet. Whisking the blade from her daughter's hand, Marguerite Blakeney whirled and completed Ziska's work, lopping the Countess's head from her neck in an eruption of scarlet gore.

Marguerite then thrust the sword in the Countess' breast and through the heart. She went to Ziska and bent over her. "Thank you. You transformed the sword, the bullets...laced them with hardwood."

Ziska nodded, blinked, and coughed up some blood. "Yes...Nadine's little troika went on too long...adding more 'prizes' to her harem all the time...it couldn't last." Her eyes closed, perhaps for the last time.

Violet stared, coming out of her stupor. "Mother...?"

Marguerite nodded, and came over to her child. She kissed Violet's forehead, and held her for a long time. "I'm sorry, little Violet, I'm so, so sorry."

She whirled, plucked Violet's sword from the Countess' chest, and thrust the blade into her own heart. She fell to her knees, and mouthed, "I am sorry," once more.

A red teardrop trickled from the corner of her dead—truly dead—eye.

Violet wept.

"I cannot return home. I can't face father after this."

"But Violet, you are in my care," Holmes said. "I staked my life to Percy that I'd bring you home safe."

"Tell him, he taught me well and I can take care of myself. Tell him, not to worry, Uncle. Besides, Father can never know about Mother. It would kill him..."

Colonel Bozzo-Corona approached and put a hand on her shoulder. "If I may. I owe you, young lady, a debt of gratitude. I wield a great deal of power in France and Italy, a great deal, if I may say so. The Countess, allied with Murat, wished to take that power; she wished to break me."

Violet looked him in the eye and shrugged. "Go on."

"I can offer you a position in my organization," the Colonel said.

"Just one moment—" Holmes started.

"What kind of 'position?'" Violet asked. She placed her hand on her sword hilt, purposefully.

"Now, now," the Colonel replied. "Nothing of that sort, nothing of that sort at all, I assure you. Anyone would underestimate you, a mere slip of a girl who wields a blade like the best Corsican masters! That, my dove, would be an invaluable asset to me in my business dealings."

"And that's all?"

"That is all," he replied solemnly. For some time now, I have been planning an expansion of my operations into Spanish California." He paused and indicated Durand. "You shall pose as his daughter."

Lecoq spoke up, looking speculatively at Violet. "And perhaps, Colonel, I shall go as well?"

Faster than thought, Violet's sword-tip was below Lecoq's chin. She pressed gently. A small drop of blood splattered on the ground.

The Colonel smiled again. "Apparently not, my dear boy."

"Right answer, Colonel," Violet said.

"Violet, please come here," Holmes said. He had gone to sit on the dais and she came over to him.

"Violet, you cannot seriously—" Holmes said.

"I don't wish to stay in Europe, Uncle" Violet said. "I would rather go far away, far, far away, and leave all this behind."

"Running away is not the answer."

"Uncle, I don't fit in. I have no intention of being married off like the rest of my sisters. I don't know what awaits me in America, but there is no life for me here."

Holmes look down, trying to hide welling tears and failing. "What am I to tell your father?" he whispered.

Violet was also tearing up. "Father will understand. Tell him, and Alice, and everyone, that I love them. Above all, do not tell him about Mother."

Holmes nodded, forlorn. He took her hand in his, and they sat quietly together for a long while.

Then Holmes said, "I will miss you very much, my dear. I will miss our talks."

Violet wiped away salty tears. She kissed him on the cheek.

"I love you, Uncle."

Then she stood and walked away, toward her new destiny.

One of the most popular characters of Tales of the Shadowmen *is undoubtedly that mysterious traveler in space and time known as Doctor Omega, created by Arnould Galopin in 1906. This year, several writers have seized upon the eccentric Doctor and spun new yarns about him. This one, by Martin Gately, also makes use of another equally odd and enigmatic time traveler, Dr. Moses Nebogipfel, introduced by H.G. Wells in "The Chronic Argonauts" in 1888, which may well have inspired Galopin's creation...*

Martin Gately: *Wolf at the Door of Time*

Doctor Omega eased back on the temporal throttle, bringing the passage of his Space and Time ship—the *Cosmos*—to a virtual stop within the aether. The ship was momentarily buffeted by highly charged energy clouds until the Doctor delicately nudged the controls and the craft moved out of the central turbulence into the more gentle time eddies of the gravity foam boundary. Turning slowly in the foam was the object that had first caught his attention in the chronoscope: a derelict time vehicle—an eight meter cylinder of brass, crystal and ivory, beautifully constructed and only lightly covered with bosonic frost. It had not been lost in the aether for long, perhaps only a few days ship's time, a week at most. The most startling thing about the craft was the ragged hole in its fuselage as if *something* had burst out of it.

The Doctor identified a hatch at the end of the cylinder and maneuvered the *Cosmos* closer until its docking coupler was able to reach out and bring the two ships together. He then reconfigured the environmental controls of the *Cosmos* so that a breathable atmosphere was created and sustained within the derelict. The Doctor donned a fur-lined jacket—it would be cold on the other ship—and grabbed a lantern from the stores. He passed through his own airlock with ease but had to use a sonic wand to open the intransigent frosted hatch into the cylinder. The aged scientist moved carefully into the gloom of the derelict; the cone of illumination from his lantern picked out the empty pilot's chair and sweeping control console with its jewel handled levers and coral toggle switches. Then, in the corner of the chamber, he saw what must once have been a steel cage. The bars of this cage had been bent outwards as easily as if they were pipe-cleaners. The Doctor shuddered involuntarily at the thought of a creature possessed of that level of strength and ferocity and wondered if he had not best return to the *Cosmos* to collect something to use as a weapon. No, the chances were that whatever this creature was it had exited the craft via the ruptured hull some time ago; but that brought its own problems and severe concerns were already starting to coagulate in the back of his mind.

Doctor Omega swept his light over the deck in front of him. Curled up in a fetal position on the floor was a figure in a helmeted environment suit. The suit

110

seemed highly anachronistic: while the derelict itself could easily be the product of a late Victorian age genius experimenter, the almost insectoid suit looked to have been developed by an advanced civilization; at a guess the Arcadian Hegemony of late 42nd century Earth. The Doctor crouched down and put his lantern on the deck, then reached out to rouse the prone figure by shaking his shoulder. The figure stirred suddenly and then aimed at the Doctor what he immediately recognized as a *staseur* energy pistol.

"Go ahead, shoot!" instructed Doctor Omega. "I can assure you that it will have very little effect. The energy weapon suppression field of my ship also envelops yours. Perhaps you would be better served by telling me who you are and how you got into this sorry predicament, eh?"

The man raised the visor of the environment suit helmet and looked squarely at the Doctor.

"My name is Doctor Moses Nebogipfel," he stated flatly. "And all of this has happened to me because I was foolish enough to transport a mesonychid in my time machine."

"Hmm. To say foolish would be putting it rather mildly," admonished Doctor Omega. "In terms of evolutionary biology, that was rather like kicking out the bottom layer of a house of cards and expecting the structure to stay up…"

"I don't know what you mean," said Nebogipfel with a look of genuine of puzzlement.

"The mesonychid is a key ancestor for an entire branch of mammalian development. If you removed it from its proper place in space and time before it produced progeny, you will have potentially devastated the ecology of great swathes of the Earth. You understand what the mesonychid is, surely?"

"Yes, it's a colossal and vicious prehistoric wolf," answered Nebogipfel.

The Doctor rubbed his brow and shook his head. Perhaps he had been overly lucky over the years with his choice of companions—such men as Fred, Borel and Tiziraou—it meant that, very unfortunately, he had become unaccustomed to dealing with idiots.

The Doctor shone his lantern on the floor of the cage, noting the massive almost hoof-like paw prints in the compacted foul-smelling excrement. Then he ran the beam over to the gaping tear in the hull.

"The wolf was alive when it went out into the aether?" the old scientist asked.

Nebogipfel merely nodded.

"This is far more serious than I thought," exhaled Doctor Omega.

Later, while Nebogipfel supped hot cocoa from a chipped ceramic mug aboard the *Cosmos,* Doctor Omega piloted the two docked craft towards the Fresnel Tertiary Boundary—the Void equivalent of periscope depth—and deployed the chronoscope. It would allow him to observe the material universe—the 'normal' Euclidean space outside the aether.

Doctor Omega's eyes had been pressed hard against the chronoscope viewer for nearly twenty-five minutes when he gave a snort of triumph and switched on the large flat monitor screen so that Nebogipfel could also see what he had found.

"The wolf has absorbed a phenomenal amount of Feinberg energy and is being hurled forward just above the secondary gravity foam layer. You can see the arc of its path quite clearly. It is as if the beast were a rubber ball thrown very hard in a confined space; so just as the kinetic force propelling the ball would cause it to hit a surface and bounce off, so the valence of the charge will make the mesonychid materialize in space and time. To begin with the materializations will be short, but as the energy dies the beast will manifest in time for longer and longer periods until finally it will come to rest, like a crazily bouncing ball ultimately coming to a stop on a single floor tile," explained the Doctor.

"But it's only a wolf," whined Nebogipfel. "What damage can it really do? Most likely it will be shot by a hunter and that will be the end of it."

"Perhaps that will happen, but we must follow the creature through time and do what we can to mitigate its effect on the continuum. At the moment, I hesitate to use the chronoscope to look into the far future of Earth because I fear what I may see. Let us try to view the wolf's first manifestation. The first temporal arc ends in the year 1577 AD in the village of Bungay in Suffolk, England."

The screen flickered for a moment and then showed a crackly black and white image of a church with a tall, proud spire and cockerel weather vane; then moved in closer, closer until the walls of the church seemed to part to allow a view of the congregation sitting on pews in the middle of their prayers. The pictures from the chronoscope were silent, like ancient newsreel footage, and perhaps that was a blessing when, seconds later, the clergyman's mouth issued forth screams rather than benedictions and the worshippers ran in terror towards the altar away from the dreadful thing wrapped in black lightning that had appeared at the back of the church.

The wolf was as dark as jet and all of its fur was stood on end due to the tachyonic static. It was like no wolf that had walked the Earth in tens of millions of years. Its snout and jaws were impossibly elongated, like a creature from a fairy tale picture book. Its cheeks were bulbous and rounded with thick knots of muscle capable of snapping its mandibles together as powerfully as a mantrap. Its teeth were nearly three inches long and looked as if they more properly belonged in the mouth of a crocodile. The eyes blazed, and, though the scanner was only delivering a monochrome image, Doctor Omega knew deep in his soul that they were glowing red—red as hellfire. To these simple folk it must have looked like a hound straight out of Hades.

There was really nothing they could do but watch helplessly as the wolf attacked the people and tore off limbs and heads. The pews were splintered under the beast's hoof-like paws and, most dreadful of all, it grabbed a child in its mouth and shook it to pieces. The beast then pounced on a man and still had his severed leg in its maw when a swirl of inky bubbles lifted the creature away into the void and it was gone from the church as inexplicably as it had arrived.

"That was nauseating, simply horrible," cried Nebogipfel as fat tears ran down his sallow face.

"Horrible, yes—and you are responsible! Why on Earth were you transporting that creature through time? Have you absolutely no sense at all? No sense of the grave responsibility you have as a time traveler not to pollute nor divert the flow of history?"

"I'd travelled to the 42nd Century and settled there for a while; the people there urged me to bring back specimens from the far past for their zoological gardens. There are so few interesting animals left in that time period and they wanted something exciting so I…"

"…Went back to the Eocene and stunned with your *staseur* what with your limited scientific knowledge you mistook for merely some form of primitive hound-like proto-wolf?" interrupted the Doctor. "Transporting animals for profit…hardly original… I have heard of it before to a lesser extent, but nothing as monstrously foolhardy as this."

Nebogipfel looked up at the monitor as if for absolution or inspiration and instead saw that the chronoscope had tracked the end of the next temporal arc; the mesonychid was materializing again.

"It is now 1643," observed Doctor Omega. "Somewhere near the village of Grimpen on Dartmoor. Possibly the circle of Neolithic stones that you see in the background was in some way conducive to the materialization."

Nebogipfel flinched as he attempted to watch the unfolding scene as it was displayed on the screen. A huge, brutal-looking man, dressed in the rich, lace-trimmed finery of a nobleman of the period was viciously attacking a beautiful young maiden out on the bleak vastness of the moors.

The off-white monoliths gleamed dully in the moonlight like a jagged row of broken teeth as the attacker knocked the girl down then tugged and tore at her garments, before finally pulling from his belt a knife and filleting open her bodice to expose heavy, lolling breasts. The man seemed to be salivating uncontrollably as he loomed over her. She clutched at her chest, not through modesty, but from the beginnings of the pain of cardiac arrest.

The picture flickered and Doctor Omega fine-tuned the controls of the chronoscope to restore the image. When the picture came back, it was in garish hues. The girl's lips were blue from cyanosis though her face was a slate grey. The immense rangy lupine form of the mesonychid was advancing now on the nobleman: the black lightning of its previous materialization had resolved itself into a cherry red and gold halo-like glow. The beast looked at up the sky and howled before it leapt and Doctor Omega immediately regretted his fine-tuning. The chronoscope had picked up sound and the howl was the most earsplitting and unnerving thing that he had ever heard. The mesonychid plucked at the throat of the man and long scarlet threads caught between its long teeth. Three men on horseback entered the scene, momentarily blocking the view of the fallen man. One of the men shouted something that might have been "Sir Hugo!" and then they cantered away in terror. The image faded into silvery static.

"You criticize me and yet you have done nothing to save those people!" accused Nebogipfel as he undid the seals of his environment suit and started to extricate himself from it.

"What would you have me do at this stage? You understand so little that I would have to devote most of your life to teaching you the basics of temporal mechanics before we could commence to have an intelligent discussion! You know nothing of the cavitation wave effect I'll wager. You understood my analogy with the bouncing ball so I'll give you another. When I materialize the *Cosmos* in time and space, a harmless wave of energy displaces the molecules that are already there to create a cavity that the ship can occupy. It has no detrimental effect on molecules that are native to any given point in spacetime, but the creature is charged with fantastic amounts of energy from the aether. The wave would give it sufficient impetus to start another temporal arc. Like a billiard ball directly in front of the pocket—it only takes a tiny nudge of kinetic energy to send it down the hole and completely off the table."

"So we can't ever materialize in the same place as the wolf?" asked Nebogipfel.

"Every time we did, we would simply push the beast further on in time. No, we must track it until the energy has dispersed and deal with it then."

"And what of those who are slaughtered by the creature in the interim?"

"I will think on it, but I suspect that there is nothing I can do for them," said the Doctor as he lit his pipe.

Joseph Balsamo approached the hovel in the woods carefully. The stories of man-eating wolves in this locality had greatly unnerved him, but he had a duty to perform and he would not shirk it. A guttural growl from the far side of the structure made him feel as if his stomach were performing somersaults. If he encountered the Beast or one of its progeny now, how would he defend himself? He had been a fool to come here alone and unarmed. The great hound slunk around the side of the hovel and bounded towards him making him cry out with fear. Then as the dog leapt at him there came the embarrassing realization that the creature meant him no harm and was trying to lick his face.

"My dog will not hurt you, sir," said Jean Chastel as he too appeared from inside the hovel's curtained door. The huntsman shouldered his arquebus musket and gave a broad grin as his pet continued to direct its slobbering affections at the stranger.

"Come inside and have some wine, my friend. I can tie Max up outside."

A little while later, Balsamo eased himself onto the rough stool while Chastel poured wine into two old cups.

"I am a novice from the Order of St John of God and I am here on a special mission," explained Balsamo—this was actually a lie, albeit a fairly harmless one. Balsamo had been ejected from the order some time ago, but he could not shake the feeling that the strange dreams he'd had of late were connected with his time with the brotherhood.

"Yes, yes - of course, the ammunition," interjected Chastel.

"*You* know about the ammunition?" asked Balsamo surprised.

"My friend, every clergyman for miles around has travelled here to bless my bullets; either that or sent me the shot they think I should use—most of it doesn't even fit my gun. But I'm glad of the company so you are most welcome here."

"You are truly hunting the Beast alone? Aren't you afraid? They say it has killed over a hundred people…" said Balsamo with genuine admiration.

"I suppose I wouldn't be much of a wolf hunter if I was so very frightened of wolves, but yes, I am more than a little afraid, for I have seen it, more than once, and it is no ordinary wolf. And I don't just mean in size. It is as different from a forest wolf as a lion is from a cat. It does not belong here. Nevertheless, it has rutted and bred with our wolves producing many a tainted offspring. They carry the look of the thing; the length of snout, the heaviness of the paws. Some of these I have already killed. I call them the wolf-mules, for they are barren creatures and neither male nor female. I doubt if they could live a proper lifespan," explained the hunter.

"There is something I must tell you," began Balsamo. "About a month ago, I started to have odd dreams. At first, I ignored them but the man in my dreams became more and more insistent."

"Man?"

"Yes, an old man with long white hair—an untidy lock of hair at the top—wearing a long black coat such as one might wear to a funeral. He wanted me to make something for him; he said that mine was the most sensitive mind in this locality; actually, I think he said time period, and that I already knew something of alchemy and that would help," said Balsamo, once again somewhat embarrassed."

"What did this 'dream man' want you to make?"

"Well, at first, I thought it was a huge hollow cylinder made of silver and filled with cables spun from gold and platinum all inset with crystals and jewels and I asked him how I could build it when the richest man on Earth could not have afforded the riches to put inside it and he explained that the cylinder was something like a bullet and would be no more than an inch or so long. It was impossibly intricate. It nearly drove me to distraction making it because it was so difficult. In the end, he said I should give it to the huntsman Jean Chastel in the forest of Mont Mouchet and that you *must* use it to kill the Beast. He said it is the only way we can be rid of it," and with that Balsamo took the silver cylinder from his pocket and handed it to Chastel.

"It's beautiful, but it is far too large for the barrel of my arquebus," said Chastel and he held the cylinder near the muzzle in order to demonstrate.

The cylinder emitted a sound something like birdsong for a split second before it adjusted its size so that it could easily slip down the barrel.

"The work of the Devil!" exclaimed Chastel.

"I think not. It is not the Devil who wants to destroy the Beast of Gévaudan. Make sure you do use that bullet—I really need to get some proper sleep. Thank you for the wine," said Balsamo as he got up to leave.

Four days later, the mesonychid stepped out of undergrowth in front of Jean Chastel and sat down on the forest path. The creature had learned that musket fire bothered it little more than insect stings and it was totally unafraid. Chastel leveled the arquebus at it and aimed carefully. The immense thing's eyes troubled him; they were a dull dark grayish red, like dying embers. There was an incredible arrogance about the creature that said: "Do your worst!" —like a bruiser in a bar spoiling for a fight who knows that your best punch will only faze him. Chastel gently squeezed the trigger lever on the musket and a liquid silver cage seemed to form around the wolf for a heartbeat, then there was a multi-colored flash of light that somehow reminded the hunter of stained glass windows and the Beast was gone.

Having seen the miraculous bullet change shape, the huntsman was not entirely surprised at this turn of events. He owed a debt to the strange young alchemist and the white-haired man from his dreams that he would never be able to repay. Now he was left wondering how he could claim the reward on the wolf with no wolf carcass to show. His own ingenuity soon solved this. Two days later he killed a wolf-mule—the largest he had seen—few would question that this was a wolf capable of killing over one hundred men, women and children. The Beast of Gévaudan was gone—gone back to the hellfire from whence it came, for all he cared.

Doctor Omega shook Nebogipfel gently by shoulder to wake him. Nebogipfel sat up in his cot and rubbed his eyes. The Doctor offered him a steaming cup of fresh tea which he gratefully accepted.

"The situation has improved a little while you were sleeping," stated the old man.

"Hmm?" yawned the rather incompetent time traveler.

"The Beast is trapped in a bubble in the aether for the time being. Now I know you understand little of such things and we have no time for long explanations," began the Doctor as if to a cap-wearing dunce. "Essentially, I have equipment aboard the *Cosmos* that can make a precise duplicate of a short stretch of the timestream and by using the power of this craft's engines I can fold a fragment of the universe into an enclosed pocket in which it will repeat itself until it runs out of energy and the bubble collapses. The Beast's reality bubble holds about six days of history from Villers-Cotterets in rural France in the 18th century."

"But that's incredible! Then, this is no mere time machine! You can manipulate and create your own realities…Yet, how did you get the wolf into the bubble?"

"With some minor adaptations of the chronoscope, I was able to cobble together a sort of mental projector and place words, images, commands even, into the mind of a rather brilliant but amoral young man in 1767 and he built for me using his not inconsiderable skills a device that transported the wolf out of normal time using just the odd scraps he scrounged from a local jeweler and the bits and pieces he had on his own alchemy bench."

"Well, this is an enormous relief. So with the whole issue of the wolf resolved you can perhaps assist me in repairing my machine and I can return to my own time period," smiled Nebogipfel nervously.

"Not so fast!" exclaimed the old man. "I only said that the situation had improved, not that it had been sorted out once and for all. Yes, the mesonychid is trapped, but only temporarily. When the bubble breaks down the wolf will arc back into normal spacetime, but its levels of tachyonic energy will be vastly diminished. I doubt if its momentum through time will carry it much beyond the early 20th century."

"How is the wolf's energy being drawn off within the bubble? What is it being expended on?"

"A good question, Nebogipfel. He is granting wishes to another inhabitant of my little pocket universe. A rather self-pitying sabot-maker called Thibault who wants nothing more than an easy yet grandiose life. Each wish reconfigures the reality within the bubble and uses up part of the tachyon charge."

"Why would a wolf be granting wishes?" asked Nebogipfel.

"It thinks it is the Devil," answered the Doctor.

"Oh, no! That really can't be good."

"It is somewhat alarming, but quite useful for our purposes. For a wolf, the mesonychid has a gigantic brain and greater than primate intelligence; but this will not be generally known until the mid 21st century. I am using the psicnic projector to exchange thoughts between the wolf and Thibault creating a sort of artificial telepathy between them. Thibault was afraid of the wolf to begin with and asked if it was the Devil. The mesonychid can find no better explanation of its existence and is happy to accept itself as being the Devil."

"Why? Why does a prehistoric wolf have a massive brain? Modern wolves don't have a primate-like intelligence so why should it?"

"I told you it was a key ancestor. Didn't you stop to think what it might be the ancestor of? The mesonychid is the land-based ancestor of all dolphins and whales. Without the presence of this single specimen of mesonychid in the whale lineage, the biological history of the world is re-written. Entire species of whale have simply never existed. Worse still, while you slept I summoned up the courage to direct the chronoscope to the extreme far future of Earth; to a time when I know the oceans are dry and great pods of sky-whales fly above the planet consuming aerial krill—it is a time I have visited on many occasions— but no longer. The sky-whales have never existed and instead of their deity, Zoomashmarta, the remaining humans worship a titanic bloated wolf; a wolf that eats only human flesh. I saw farms dedicated to breeding humans for it to eat. It has been mutated by its long exposure to the void and grown so large that it dwarfs the sea dwelling whales that it has served to replace," explained the Doctor shuddering.

At this Nebogipfel broke down in sobs and made inarticulate howling noises which the Doctor was not sure whether to categorize as hysterical or merely histrionic.

"Console yourself! With the remedial actions I have taken we can hope that the future I saw will not come to pass. We will now play a waiting game. In a few days, the reality bubble will collapse and the hunt will be on again."

The great wolf walked into Thibault's cottage on its hind legs and dropped the bloody doe carcass onto the floor.

"You wished for meat," said the black wolf. "Well here it is. I did not even have to hunt for it in the forest, I just imagined a deer and the deer appeared in front of me. I like this new world in which I find myself, it is all so easy here."

"I'll be able to sell on this venison to the charcuterie in Laon and make enough money to buy a fine new suit of clothes...I'll be able to woo Agnelette or perhaps a woman of rather higher status. Why should I not set my sights higher now that the Devil himself is my ally?" asked Thibault.

"Why not indeed? Why do you wish for a single mate? All of the women in this realm are yours to take. When I arrive in a new world, every bitch of my kind must submit to me or die. I rip off the heads of cubs that I have not sired and drive away the adult males – that is the best way. For food, I like your species. You are slow runners and your meat is sweet," said the Wolf while Thibault's eyes widened with terror.

"You...you would not eat me?" quaked the little shoe-maker.

"No, you I have marked out as special amongst the humans. Our minds are somehow joined and I take pleasure in altering this world to please you. I like the way that your hair changes each time I grant one of your wishes."

Thibault had noticed this too. In the broken looking glass that hung on his cottage wall he inspected his scalp periodically and saw the thick blood red hairs which were sprouting from the center of his parting. To begin with he had been able to cunningly brush his hair so that the strings of scarlet could not be seen. Now it was useless and people were starting to stare or worse to ask him to account for the hairs for they suspected that he was a werewolf. The black wolf had been seen walking away from Thibault's cottage on at least a couple of occasions and the simple folk of the locality had drawn the obvious conclusion that the human occupant of the cottage and the bipedal wolf were one and the same.

"Why do you not walk on all fours like a normal forest wolf?" asked Thibault. "You are making everyone think that I change into a wolf."

"Since our minds joined, I find it easier to walk this way," explained the Devil-wolf. "For a long time, it seemed as if that great body of water—the ocean—called to me. I had urges to run and play in the sea to raise my young there and never leave the dark waters. That desire is dead in me now. I wished instead for a land of plentiful slow-moving prey who cannot defend themselves, who leave their children undefended and sleep soundly at night in weak wooden shelters that I can break down with my heavy paws. I am in that land now, and it is almost perfect; my heart is filled with bliss when I think of the impotence of the human hunters and how their metal projectiles scarcely break my skin."

And so, in the days to come, Thibault's wishes became greater and greater in number, as did the glowing cables of red erupting from his scalp. Thibault became the Lord of Vez—the most powerful nobleman of his region, the master of an impregnable castle guarded by an army of wolves. He was now a giant of a man, a prodigious warrior who exacted the most terrible revenge on those who had tortured him in punishment for his old sideline of being a successful poacher. This night, Thibault and the Devil-wolf stand atop the battlements of the castle and watch the sky together. The sky is slowly opening and beyond it can be seen a howling wild void of dust clouds and swirling star-froth. It feels like the end of the world and it is.

"If this is the final night that will ever be," began Thibault, "then bring me every woman that I have ever desired and I will make love to them all in my bedchamber right now."

"This is the end of everything," said the black wolf. "And my power is fading...go to your bed...I will do my best to bring about your wish."

Thibault went to his room and lit a lamp, then, for want of anything better to do, changed into his night attire. A few minutes later, the door swung open and the exquisite sixteen year-old Agnelette entered the room, still wearing the simple grey linen cap and country dress that she had on the last time he saw her. He went over to her and removed the little cap allowing the cascade of blond hair to fall to her shoulders. Yet, there was no recognition in her eyes. Her eyes were black and dead. She started to disrobe and her movements were like those of a wind-up automaton. Was this really Agnelette? Thibault drank in the beauty of her form as she tugged off her undergarments. The pink tipped breasts were just as he had seen them in his dreams. Finally, she was naked and something was horribly wrong. In the place where Thibault had always imagined there would be just a downy, feathery triangle of curls there was an impenetrable mass of blood red glowing hairs—each individual hair as thick as an earthworm. It was as if some vile poisonous sea anemone had taken root in the place he desired most of all.

Thibault recoiled in horror at the sight and the door opened again. Now, Madame Magloire—the bailiff's wife whom Thibault had ached with desire for a long time—came in and swiftly divested herself of her clothing. Her limbs were long and sensuous and her bosom two jutting cones of creamy flesh. It was all too much for Thibault to bear, especially when he saw that she too had the great scarlet serpentine fibers, a huge dangling mass of them hanging most of the way down her thighs.

In short order, the delightful little maid Lisette entered and made herself nude, as did her mistress, the Comtesse de Mont-Gobert; and—this last addition was the most physically beautiful of all, for her sinuous shape was truly bewitching—if only her eyes were not dead, if only her pubis was not marred by the angry-looking tendrils. Unable to help himself, he reached out to touch the Comtesse. The red hairs stung his fingers as if they were jellyfish tentacles and when he pulled his hand back it was covered in deep welts. He looked at each of the naked doll-like women in turn; each of them had the same blank face and the same red growth. This was not at all how he had imagined his last night on Earth.

"Wolf! Wolf!" cried out Thibault. "What I wished for is not happening properly. Use your magic again!"

The exhausted wolf crawled into the bed chamber and lay down on the rug.

"The magic has run out, my friend," explained the wolf. "I told you I would do my best, but this is the end of everything."

Thibault threw his arms around the wolf's neck and hugged him. Then Thibault, the castle and the French countryside melted away, and only wolf was left; tumbling and spinning in the aether.

"This calls for something stronger than tea," smiled Doctor Omega as he opened the little wooden wall cabinet and extracted several bottles of varying sizes and a couple of glasses. "I wonder if the cryogenics unit can spare us some ice for our cocktails."

"Cocktails?" queried Nebogipfel.

"Of course, I always celebrate in style," without further explanation the Doctor added *Dubonnet*, orange bitters and gin to the glasses, then some shards of ice from the cryo-overflow tube, before concluding with French Vermouth. "The reality bubble trap worked very well. Almost all the wolf's energy has been used up. After we have finished our drinks I will deploy the chronoscope for what could very well be the last time."

The two men relaxed and sipped at their delicious cocktails while looking absently out of the porthole at the milky swirls of quantum foam. Suddenly, a white streaking shape with a red and silver trail passed by so close that they could almost have reached out of the porthole and touched it.

"The mesonychid!" shouted Nebogipfel. "And it almost hit us!"

"I don't think so, but let me check that object with the chronoscope just to be sure..."

The old scientist put his eyes to the viewer and swiftly locked the sensors on the departing shape.

"It is a meteorite, an ordinary chondrite to be specific, but highly charged with ionizing radiation from the Void."

"A meteorite?" queried Nebogipfel. "But this isn't ordinary space. How could a something other than a time vehicle enter the aether?"

"It is possible in certain circumstances. There are those that I refer to as the 'discarnate entities.' A few of these, such as Zoomashmarta, have come to dwell within this wormhole. Some are worshipped as gods at different points in the timestream; the points at which their influence is strongest. But if Man knew what little power the gods did wield, he would question the purpose of prayer... These beings sometimes draw things into the void for their own mysterious purposes. To help or hinder mankind as they have judged fit. In this case, I doubt if it is a coincidence. The meteorite is exiting the void in late 1795. That is remarkably near to when the wolf has been manifesting itself in time. Hmmm. A meteorite charged with bosonic particles might cause beneficial mutations. I wonder if someone is trying to give mankind an advantage in the long-term battle against the mesonychid; perhaps even Zoomashmarta himself."

The *Cosmos*, still conjoined with Nebogipfel's ship, which he revealed to Doctor Omega he had rather unimaginatively christened *The Argo*, continued their gradual progress through the aether, questing for any sign of the termination point of the wolf's latest jaunt through time.

The Doctor allowed Nebogipfel to take a turn at the viewer having taught him how to manipulate the controls. It was over an hour later that the intense gaze of the younger man lighted on a faint energy trail that curved through the roiling foam heading out towards the year 1916. Nebogipfel alerted Doctor Omega straightaway but they were unable to lock the chronoscope onto the wolf's exact position. Their best estimate was that the creature was roving the battlefield of Mons sometime in the late summer of that year.

Captain Yeskes of the Fifth Northumberland Fusiliers awoke in the stench of the muddy charnel pit. Death was all around him. For weeks he had been losing patrols in no-man's land, patrols that had not been victim to either phosgene gas or the German shelling. Now he knew the reason why. The thing that the men had spoken about was real. He had quashed the rumors when he heard them; devised punishment details for those who had even whispered of a monstrous hound that slunk about the great shell holes and abandoned trenches. These were surely stories for children to tell, not grown men fighting for their country. Yet, he had consoled himself that some of these soldiers were little more than boys. Two men had said they had seen the beast up close. They said it was shaped like a massive wolf, almost as big as a dray horse. It had dragged injured soldiers into a gargantuan pit of liquid mud. They called the pit its larder for it was full of dying men and the split human bones that it had opened to sup on the marrow. They said that it must have a human brain because it was more cunning than any ordinary beast. They theorized that it was perhaps some new German weapon. Yeskes put them on a charge and had them flogged. Now, as he lay in the larder pit himself, he wished he'd pulled out the most detailed map he had of the blasted hinterland between the two opposing sets of trenches and got the men to estimate as precisely as they could the position of the beast's pit before directing every single allied artillery piece to fire on it.

The summer sun had hardened most of the battlefield's sucking mud, but not here in the wolf's pit. Yeskes had sunk in almost up to his thighs and he was ever so slowly continuing to sink. He reached for his holster while he still could and pulled out his service revolver. His arm was swollen and painful to move due to the bite he had sustained. The thing had also swiped a heavy paw at his head like a cat playing with a mouse and his forehead was caked with a thick crust of blood. His throat hurt abominably and he was burning up with fever. If the thing came back now it would be tempting to blaze away at it with the revolver—a couple of shots at least—before he turned the gun on himself. He had no intention of being eaten alive.

He sat and waited for the wolf creature to drop back over the rim of the muddy crater and advance on him. He had to keep awake until then. After a while, with his mind drifting back to his childhood he became aware that he was hallucinating. An old man with silvery white hair in a black frock coat was moving down the pit's slopes towards him. Not climbing down, but sort of drifting as if levitating. The old man's hair and white shirt glowed with an unearthly transfiguring light and there was a bluish electric halo about him. Well, thought the injured man, since one legend of no-man's land had proved to be true then why not another? Surely this could only be the Companion in White, the angelic, Christ-like figure who appeared to and sometimes aided dying soldiers?

The "Companion in White" spoke to one of his fellow angels who remained unseen.

"Nebogipfel, there is a man in the crater. Increase the projection energy to hard-light settings. I must help him," the strange vision intoned.

The angel seemed to gain greater substance and settled on the mud to walk about like an ordinary mortal. Captain Yeskes lifted his arms up as if in supplication and the angel reached down and pulled him clear of the quicksand-like drag of the mud with prodigious strength and therefore surprising ease. The angel tore at the rough material of the Captain's battledress jacket exposing the deep and bloody puncture wounds where his arm had been mauled by the wolf. The Companion in White then removed his frock coat and ripped at his own shirtsleeve until he had torn off sufficient material to create an improvised bandage.

"Are you real?" asked Yeskes.

"In the very strictest sense, no. I am a projection beamed to this location from beyond the aether, but that is hardly anything for you to worry about my young friend," said the angel.

"A drink of water...a cigarette?" requested Yeskes through parched lips.

"I very much regret that I can supply neither at this moment, Captain. I must get you out of this pit and back to your own lines."

And with that the angel started to lift up Yeskes. But then after a couple of steps, he set him back down on the earth very gently, then reached for Yeskes's webbing belt and removed the long-bladed bayonet. The mesonychid was padding down the slope softly, stealthily, towards them. Incredibly, it looked somewhat lean and undernourished. The conditions here on the battlefield did not suit it and it had contracted mange thereby losing much of its black fur. This contributed to giving it a canine rather than lupine look, something like a mammoth, freakish lurcher crossed with Fenris of Norse mythology. The angel reached down for his frock coat and then held it in front of him like a matador's cape while still holding the bayonet in his right hand. The wolf glowered at the men with its dull red eyes and then leapt with jaws agape. The Angel sidestepped and jabbed at the wolf's haunches with the bayonet as it flew past in a move that the great bullfighter Juan Belmonte would have envied.

The wolf's momentum carried into the very center of the mud pit and it flopped into the liquid morass. Captain Yeskes looked on expecting the beast to be sucked down into the mire and never seen again. But he had not counted on its fantastic strength, nor its innate, instinctive swimming. The thing originated from a time when no mammals swam, and yet the skill was somehow hardwired into its brain. It kept its head up and fought against the sucking power of the pit; its limbs rhythmically pounding, unseen, beneath the surface.

Doctor Omega was in a quandary now. His plan to lure the beast into an area of heavy shelling had failed and he now had a responsibility to preserve the life of the young army Captain. But if the wolf bit the time traveler's hard-light simulacrum the bio-electric feedback would short out the sensors attached to his real body aboard the *Cosmos* possibly killing him. If he reverted to a soft-light specular projection or ripped off the sensors he would no longer be able to assist Captain Yeskes. It was an impossible choice. The old man thought nothing of his own safety but if he was slain how might the mesonychid ever be stopped? He barked an order to Nebogipfel to reduce the projector levels to soft-light.

"I can't! There's something wrong with the power controls," shouted Nebogipfel, sounding terrified.

Captain Yeskes watched astonished as the angel jerked and convulsed as if experiencing severe electric shocks. The beast was now only up to its hocks in mud and was edging up towards Omega and Yeskes. Yeskes aimed his Webley revolver squarely at the wolf's head and squeezed off two shots. This weapon was far more powerful than the ancient muskets that the creature had been hunt-ed with in the 18th century, especially at this close range. The bullets pierced its armored hide and thick dark blood spread out over its fur like a wine stain on linen. Shocked and enraged though the wolf was, it neither paused nor retreated. Yeskes checked that there was a third cartridge in the cylinder and then put the barrel to his temple. He shut his eyes, attempted to pull from deep within himself the unequivocal urge to end his own life and failed. The wolf's fetid breath rolled towards him like a hot, sickly cloud. He knew his fate would be to be torn asunder and consumed. A groaning, wheezing sound filled the air. The sound was loud, alarming, slightly unearthly and mixture of a repetitive mechanical grinding fused with something like whale song.

The Captain opened his eyes and saw the wolf fading away; shoved out of the here and now molecule by molecule as the cavitation wave from the combined materialization of the *Cosmos* and the Argo struck it. The Companion in White had disappeared as well. Yeskes looked up and balanced on the edge of the crater was a long ivory colored tube with a blue capsule attached to it. The sight of the ivory tube reminded him that he still needed a cigarette. Shock, dehydration and loss of blood finally caught up with him and his head slumped onto the ground.

"Yes, we need to get the Captain to a hospital," agreed Doctor Omega. "But I have thought the better of returning him to his own lines. We'll take him to a military infirmary in England. If he makes an official report here about the mesonychid the evidence will support its existence and valuable resources will be deployed in looking for it that would be more effectively used elsewhere."

"How much further down the timestream do you think the wolf has gone? It was hardly carrying any charge at all."

"Perhaps only thirty or forty years at most," replied the Doctor. "One more thing, Nebogipfel. I always like to give praise where it is due and your quick thinking in activating the materialization circuits saved my life. The fault in the projection power controls was my responsibility. I have made far too many improvised changes to the electrical systems aboard the *Cosmos* recently."

The two men placed Yeskes onto a cot then headed back to the control room where the Doctor dematerialized the ship in order to shift its position in space.

"As I was saying, I am in your debt Nebogipfel, but your exile on Earth must continue and I must remove from you the ability to travel through time and space until you have properly learned your lesson."

"My exile must continue? What do you mean? I am not in exile?" said Nebogipfel baffled.

"Your supracranial development and ability to cobble together a time vehicle make it quite obvious to me that you and I are of the same race. At some stage, your memory has been partially erased and you have been subjected to hypnotic conditioning. That conditioning is now starting to degrade. Such punishments are commonly handed out by my people to those who meddle in time. The final proof is your name: Moses Nebogipfel. A name that is not a name."

"Quite plainly it is my name! You are going senile, Doctor."

"I think not. It is an anagram, a rather clever anagram, the solution to which almost certainly makes up the hypnotic key words to restore your memory. I must make a note of them."

Doctor Omega looked out of the porthole.

"Ah, we have arrived at the District Voluntary Aid Hospital in Torquay on the English coast. That will do quite nicely. If we bluff our way as medical men we should be able to get Captain Yeskes admitted fairly easily," smiled the Doctor, feeling rather pleased with himself.

Nurse Miller returned to the dimly lit nurses' station at the far end of the ward and sat down at the desk. She quietly rooted around looking for some scrap paper and then started making some notes. Her whispered talk earlier with Captain Yeskes had been fascinating. His recovery was coming along nicely but it was quite obvious that he could not yet differentiate between his fever dreams and the reality of the horror of the trenches. This yarn about a 'hound of death' dragging men to their doom was quite fantastic. It was all so evocative and atmospheric that she determined to use it in one of her stories one day. Yes, she was a budding amateur author but her tastes ran more to crime fiction. Nevertheless, the idea had plenty of mileage in it. She'd fit it in somehow.

"Regarding, your exile, I don't think that the 20th century or even the 19th are really very suitable. Too much technological temptation. Otherwise, I'd suggest that rather lovely Italianate village in North Wales near Penrhyndeudraeth," stated the old time traveler.

"Oh no! Not Wales, please…I was in a village there not so very long ago and it really didn't agree with me. Why can't I serve out my exile in the Arcadian Hegemony?"

"In the far future society founded by that renegade starship commander— Captain Strange? I think not since it was doubtless he who was responsible for sending you to get the mesonychid. And don't think I fell for that nonsense about putting the beast in a zoo for people to gawp at. Strange would have wanted it as a biological weapon to use in his grudge match against the Federation! He probably planned to have them cloned by the million," declared the Doctor.

"Captain Strange's wife is rather beautiful. I'm afraid I fell heavily in love with her," confessed Nebogipfel.

"Then you extracted the wolf from the Eocene to curry favor with her? You little fool! She's out of your league…she's made a career of partnering herself with some of the greatest space-heroes and villains of history. She eats men like you for breakfast," chided Omega.

The old man considered for a moment. Where might the best place be for a man who allowed lust for a gorgeous woman to lure him into breaking the laws of time? What could possibly cure him?

"I have it! You will spend the rest of your exile in a monastery that is well known to me. Randgrith Abbey near the Village of Wulnoth in the mid-11th century. You may even come to enjoy monastic life and after 10 or 15 years I will return the *Argo* to you, so make sure you stay in the vicinity. It will materialize for one day only and if you do not claim it, I shall destroy it. If I ever catch you undermining the basic structure of the timestream again…well, let's just say that will be the end of you," warned the Doctor.

The Nyctalope advanced cautiously forward into Kirov Oblast Municipal Park. This part of the city had been totally abandoned to the King Wolf and his brood. The surrounding buildings were empty and lightless. Thick drifts of snow softened the city's hard, man-made edges and the shadows were short under the high full moon. The Nyctalope had been fully briefed on the wolf plague. Never before had so many wolves massed in a single place. Never had they dared to enter and permanently dwell in a city in such large numbers. Two hundred Soviet troops had been sent in to clear the wolves from the city. Only six had returned to the perimeter headquarters. The survivors reported that these were not ordinary wolves. Odd in appearance, ferociously savage and intelligent. They were ruled by a tyrant wolf. The soldiers were strangely diffident in describing the attributes of this King Wolf. It seemed they feared they would not be believed. An officer plied one of the men with vodka until he revealed that the King Wolf was over five meters long and two meters high at the shoulder. Its feet were more like hooves than paws. It was under serious consideration by the Chiefs of Staff to use saturation bombing to destroy the wolf brood. At this point Comrade Frunzoff took personal charge of the problem. He was aware that Leo Saint-Clair—known to some as the Nyctalope because of his ability to see in pitch darkness—was currently visiting Moscow on a temporary assignment from the French Secret Service.

Saint-Clair was more than happy to assist. He had long been concerned at the growing disintegration of relations between East and West. Only a few years before we had all been allies against the Nazi threat; if we continued down this road, then the resulting stand-off had the potential to ultimately destroy the world in an atomic conflagration. Saint-Clair called for special mechanical equipment to be shipped from France to Moscow. The Nyctalope assembled the equipment himself in great secrecy and then travelled with it by road to Kirov.

The Nyctalope wore white snow camouflage ceramic armor with his customary helmet with periscope attachment. On his back was a powerful battery pack which could be linked to a either a handheld radio transmitter, as it currently was, or to the pommel of short sword which currently hung from a scabbard at his belt. This allowed it to deliver a jolt of electricity powerful enough to fell an elephant. His only other weapon was a MAS-38 sub-machine gun specially adapted to fire electrified bullets. The armored warrior flicked a switch on the radio-transmitter and the four semi-autonomous robotic drones which accompanied him moved forward in unison - these modular drones were the special equipment that had arrived from France and they were armed with high-explosive mortars and automatic shotguns; they also carried infra-red sensors that allowed them to shoot at moving targets even in darkness.

There were times when the Nyctalope regarded his ability to see in the dark as something of a curse. This was perhaps one of those occasions. In a sense, he'd rather not have seen the size of the approaching wolf pack, nor the immensity of the King Wolf. He flicked the red switch on the remote control transmitter and the automatic shot-guns in the drones commenced firing. The King Wolf seemed to hang back, using its servitors as cannon fodder. Though many of the wolves had fallen, the pack was getting too near. The Nyctalope switched two of the drones to mortar firing mode. The heavy crump of the mortars echoed around the park and the air was peppered with bloody fragments of wolf-flesh as the beasts were blasted to smithereens.

Saint-Clair switched all of the drones to mortar mode and ran forward blazing away with the MAS-38. He was almost on the King Wolf now. He stumbled over a dead wolf as he approached but carried on firing, unloading a whole clip directly into the monster's throat. The King Wolf grabbed him by the arm and bit down hard…but the ceramic armor held. The Nyctalope yanked the sword from its scabbard and plunged it into the thing's eye. He fumbled with the power lead, then after half a second discharged enough voltage into its skull to fry its brain. The creature bucked wildly and knocked the Nyctalope high into the air. The drones kept firing on the wolves; they would do so until their ammunition was exhausted.

When the Nyctalope regained his senses, the wolves were all dead and an old man in a black frock coat was bending over the body of the King Wolf, prodding it with a strange buzzing wand.

"What…what are you doing?" asked Saint-Clair.

"I need a sample of its blood, my friend. I must recreate the wolf and put it back in its proper place in time and space…it doesn't belong here," he explained. "There is a lot of human nucleic acid in its gut too. Hmm. I don't think I should get into the business of bringing back the dead—not really my province, eh?"

And with that the strange old man strode off into the snow towards an odd looking shell-shaped craft which Saint-Clair had not noticed previously.

The Nyctalope trudged wearily out of the park. By the perimeter fence a trio of figures waited for him. A young, balding man with steel- rimmed glasses in the uniform of a Russian army captain (if Saint-Clair judged his epaulette stars correctly). The young captain was just shrugging off his back the twin tanks of a flamethrower and placing them carefully onto the snow; with him was an avuncular man in a raincoat smoking a pipe and a young girl in a white fur coat who could not have been more than twelve. The blond child was armed with a scaled down version of a Degtyarov sub-machine gun and had a red star painted (hopefully rather than tattooed) on her forehead.

"Monsieur? I am Captain Gogol of Army Intelligence. May I offer you my congratulations?"

"Thank you. I take it you are fully aware of my diplomatic status and that no debriefing by Soviet Intelligence is appropriate?" questioned Saint-Clair.

"Of course, Comrade Frunzoff has kept us fully apprised," smiled Gogol.

"What exactly are you three doing here?" asked the Nyctalope. "This is no place to bring a child."

"Hardly. But then Little Oktobriana is not an ordinary child. Along with my friend Avakoum Zahov here, we three are the last line of defense for the Soviet Union. Had you failed...well, it would have been down to us to kill the King Wolf or die trying."

The Nyctalope arched an eyebrow quizzically. The man was deadly serious. And suddenly the Frenchman had the unaccountable feeling that the three of them must have triumphed countless times in similar circumstances to enable Gogol to exude such reckless confidence.

"Come, let us help you recover your equipment," said Zahov. "It will be a walk in the park, eh?"

Nebogipfel sat alone in his monastic cell at Randgrith Abbey. His scalp was still sore from the tonsure he had received and his skin itched from contact with the rough homespun fabric of his habit. Scrunched up in his hand was the page he had stolen from Doctor Omega's notebook. On this slip of paper the old man had written the three simple words he believed would be the key to opening the locks that had been placed by his people in Nebogipfel's mind.

He read them aloud: "Song. Poem. Beliefs."

Long shut synapses commenced to open.

"My God, I know who I am," he whispered.

This first installment in Travis Hiltz's new time-hopping saga, entitled "Lost in Time," features various characters looking for the mysterious Doctor Omega. Like the classic French novel which inspired it, this story harkens back to the golden age of science fiction, when anything was possible in the intermingled worlds of sf and fantasy. Now, read on as Denis Borel, the Doctor's accidental companion and narrator of the original novel, meets a mild-mannered-by-day Vicar who is anything but that at night...

Travis Hiltz: *What Lurks in Romney Marsh?*

Cornwall, 1776

Life is peculiar. One moment, you are a talented, yet underappreciated, violinist on holiday in Normandy; the next, you are invited by an eccentric scientist to travel through space and time, and before you can get used to that experience, you find yourself stranded in the marshlands of Kent, a hundred years before you were born...

Denis Borel frowned.

"A bit too flip," he muttered, tucking a pencil stub into his battered diary and putting it in a coat pocket. "Too flippant by far."

He sighed and looked across the field. The countryside was lush, rolling and green. It had a quiet beauty that could inspire painters or poets, but to Denis, sitting on a stump, it was as oppressive as the dreariest of prisons.

It had been three months since radioactive turbulence had struck Doctor Omega's space-time craft, scattered its crew and left two of them stranded in the small village near Romney Marsh.

Nearly every day since, the young violinist had returned to the place of their arrival in the increasingly desperate hope of finding some hint of rescue, escape, or the whereabouts of his other traveling companions: the diminutive Martian, Tiziraou, or Doctor Omega himself.

Denis sighed again, stood up and trudged back towards the village he had been calling home. His clothes were drab and well-worn, but appropriate to the time period: knee breeches, long coat, waistcoat and blocky black shoes with a buckle on the front. One of the few cheerful things about his exile was that Denis felt he looked quite jaunty in a tri-corner hat.

He soon left the wooded fields and came to the wide dirt road that served as the main thoroughfare for the village of Dymchurch. He strolled past cultivated fields and farmhouses and was soon on the edge of the village itself.

Under other circumstances, Denis would have described Dymchurch as rustic, and even quaint, a loose collection of homes and shops, mostly done in wood or grey stone, with the occasional whitewashed building. Denis trudged along, taking a narrow side lane that lead past a blacksmith's shop. Behind the blacksmith's were an overgrown yard and a small shack with a sagging thatch roof.

Denis pushed through the front door, hung his hat on a crude peg nailed into the wall. The hut consisted of a single room with a wobbly-looking table in the center, a couple of equally unappealing wooden chairs and a rough cot with straw for a mattress. Seated at the table was a burly man with muscular arms and an impressively thick black beard. He was in his shirtsleeves, breeches and a pair of clunky boots that seemed to be held together with twine and wishful thinking. Scattered across the table was a vast collection of odds and ends, and bits of machinery as well as unidentifiable junk that seemed to have no visible use. The bearded man was sorting through this treasure trove, picking out the odd kick-knack and seeing if it fit onto a larger, cylindrical piece of metal with a smoky glass sphere on the top.

"How was the 'great outdoors'?" he rumbled, not looking up from his intent rummaging.

"Frustratingly green and scenic, Fred," Denis muttered, sinking into the other chair and helping himself to a pewter mug on the table. He took a gulp, winced and put the mug back down. "Not a hint, or even a crumb of hope..."

"Denis," Fred grumbled, polishing a greasy bolt with an equally greasy rag, "I am trying to reconstruct a temporal codex ampliphier using the few things that came with us when we were flung across the time stream and bits of 18th century technology. That doesn't get any easier when I have to listen to you moping. I don't want to take the time away from making to work to throttle you, so I've been tactful and understanding for the last two months, but my patience is nearing an end. So either spit it out, or do something useful, like make dinner."

Denis got up and trudged over to the tiny hearth. He poked at the coals and stirred at a pot of gluey beige gruel. He gave a shudder and put a wedge of cheese and a hunk of bead on a wooden plate and then returned to the table.

"That's just the problem, I think," Denis sighed, sitting back down. "My less than successful attempts to 'do something useful.' You, at least, have the knowledge to try and cobble together some kind of signaling device, while all I can add to our rescue attempts is staring at a field, in the hopes that something happens and a certain gift when it comes to string instruments..."

"Don't sell yourself short, lad," Fred said, helping himself to the hunk of bread. He tore it in half and dunked a piece in his mug. "Your playing at the tavern and giving music lessons to the local children has kept us in pocket money. Kept from starving and gotten us a friendly in with the locals."

"Nice of you to say, but I can't help but feel that things would have gone better if Tiziraou or the Doctor were here..."

"But, they aren't," Fred interrupted, looking up and tossing his rag down on the table. "And we have no idea where or when they are or if they are still aboard the *Cosmos*, or even if they or the ship survived the turbulence. Both the Doctor and the little Martian could have been flung through history and the universe like we were, and be hoping that we will rescue them."

"I just keep hoping they will be able to trace us to the time and place we arrived, but it persists in staying just a field…"

"Well, I may have something that'll help us," Fred said, tossing an object over to the younger man.

It was the charred remnants of a paperback book. The cover was gone and only about a quarter of any given page was legible.

"What is this?" Denis said, gingerly leafing through the ragged staired pages. "It looks like an almanac…?"

"It is. I had it in my workshop, just the right size for keeping one of my workbenches from wobbling. It was one of the bits of flotsam that got flung into the time stream with us." Fred explained, reaching over and taking it back. He leafed through until he found a certain page than handed it back to Denis. "That bit."

"Shooting stars over…Romney Marsh…?" Denis read in a puzzled tone. "There was a comet sighting or meteor crash here...?"

"There will be," Fred corrected. "It won't happen for a couple days, but it may be just what we need."

"How so? What is this 'falling star'?"

"I'm not entirely sure, but while you've been watching that field, I borrowed a telescope from that fellow that runs the tavern, and used those books the vicar loaned you to do a little astronomical research. I'm having a problem finding any trace of our shooting star."

"Is that important?" Denis asked.

"It could be. If it isn't traveling through space…"

"You think the shooting star traveled though time?" Denis interrupted. "Could it be the *Cosmos*?"

"It could be," Fred shrugged. "But, at this point, I'll settle for any rescue…"

"Any rescue? You make it sound like there are a fleet of ships traveling through time out there…?"

"You can't be so naïve to think the Doctor is the only one," Fred grumbled. "You've met his friend from Oxford, as well as that madman, Rotwang. Then there is Doctor Moses Nebogipfel and that Englishman…what was his name. .? Anyway, the point is, if our visitor is coming through time, there is no guarantee it's the *Cosmos*. I'll be willing to go with anyone willing to offer us help, or at least get us somewhere with a level of science that gives us a better chance of cobbling together some way to signal the Doctor."

"I'd settle for indoor plumbing, myself," Denis muttered.

"I can't argue that," Fred chuckled. "Anyway, no idea if my guesswork is right, but, if the meteor isn't a rescue ship, we can at least use it to power my temporal codex amplifier and get a signal off."

"What if it's just a meteor?" Denis asked. "You and Doctor Omega are always telling me meteors are just pieces of stone and ice, floating through space?"

"Most of them are, but they also contain elements we can use as a power source, or even just absorb the thermal energy of it traveling through the atmosphere. The important thing is, this shooting star is our best hope in months of getting back to the *Cosmos*."

"What can I do to help?" Denis said, brightly, sitting up straighter in his rickety chair.

"We have a couple days, so I need to make sure the amplifier is going to work. We'll need maps of the area and a small boat…"

"A boat?"

"Look around you, Denis. Chances are the meteor will land in the marsh or just off the coast. To get close enough to it for our needs, we'll need a boat."

"Hmm, true," Denis nodded, sitting back and rubbing his chin thoughtfully. "The vicar loaned me those books; I wager he'd have local maps as well. He knows a great deal about what happens in this village. He'd probably know someone that could loan us a boat."

Denis stood up and began dusting himself off.

"While you work, I'll go stroll over and have a chat with Doctor Syn."

The Vicar of Dymchurch's home was plain, but comfortable, a suitable home for a scholarly bachelor. Its only bit of ostentation was the man of the cloth's impressive library. Each room seemed to contain a bookcase.

Doctor Christopher Syn was a tall man, with a high forehead, a prominent, noble nose and piercing blue-grey eyes. It all combined with his general stoic expression to give Syn an air of authority that reminded Denis of all his most respected teachers. Even at his most relaxed, there was a feeling that the good Doctor was watching you, sizing you up.

"What do I owe the honor of this visit?" Doctor Syn asked, once they were seated and he had sent his sexton to fetch them tea.

"I wanted to return your books," Denis said, retrieving them from a much-abused looking cloth satchel. "They were quite informative. I was also hoping I could impose on your generosity once more."

"I would be a poor vicar to deny the newest members of my flock," Doctor Syn replied, one corner of his mouth going up in a smile. "How can I be of assistance?"

"Well, as you know, my companion and I have accidently found ourselves settled in your fine community…"

"No word from other traveling companion?" Syn asked. "A Professor or Doctor, I believe…?"

"No, nothing yet, but we believe our best bet to be reunited is to stay in one spot, as he is most certainly searching for us. My request in fact involves learning more of our temporarily adopted home."

"I will be happy to offer what assistance I can."

"As you know, I've been enjoying hiking about the area and was wondering you had some local maps I could make use of…perhaps point out some spots of interest?"

"Maps…yes, I do believe I have some…I think in the rectory, I'll have Mipps hunt them down for you."

"If I may impose on your generosity once more, my friend Fred is looking to do some fishing and I was wondering if you knew of anyone in the village that had a small boat we could make use of?'"

"A boat?" Syn asked, with a raised eyebrow.

"Just a small rowboat," Denis said. "We aren't planning to round the Horn, merely a bit of fishing.

"I couldn't say for sure…Mister Mipps, you'd know better than I, anyone in the village with a boat that our new friends could make use of?"

The vicar's sexton was a shorter, gruff-looking man, who, despite his well-groomed clothes, still had an air of someone it was well advised to keep an eye on.

"A small boat…?" Mipps pondered, scratching his in need of a shave chin. "Peters, I believe has one. Hasn't gotten much use out of it, since he banged up his leg. He would probably let you gentlemen have it if you tossed a few coppers his way. I could have a word with him, as I have some errands to run."

"That would be most appreciated, Mister Mipps," Denis nodded, finishing off his tea and then standing up. "Thank you both. You've been a great help during this trying time."

"Think nothing of it," Doctor Syn said, standing.

He gestured for Mipps to clear the tea things, as he escorted his guest to the door.

"A word though," the Vicar said, once they had reached the foyer. "You'll want to be cautious on your fishing expedition. While I am not one to indulge in gossip, the stories concerning smuggling in this area are not all fanciful tales. The British navy, as well as the smugglers themselves, I would imagine, take a dark view on any unknown boats that drift into their reach. I would not venture far from the shore."

"Maybe it would be best if we stuck to local streams on our first outing," Denis suggested, retrieving his hat from the rack in the foyer.

"The marsh can be treacherous in its own way," Syn said. "When I find those maps for you, I can point out areas to avoid as well as those to visit."

"More smugglers, or are you speaking of the local legends?" Denis asked, with a smile.

His host smiled in reply, but Denis was disconcerted to notice it did not seem to reach his piercing eyes.

"What stories have they been regaling you with at the tavern?" he asked quietly.

"Oh, the usual sort: ghosts and night creatures. Birds that use their song to lead unwary travelers off the safe paths and there was something about a scarecrow that walks the marsh...fanciful stuff to tell around the fire."

"Hmm," Syn said and nodded, not seeming to share Denis' light-hearted opinion of the tales told about the Romney Marsh. "Well, just exercise caution in your naturalist ramblings."

Denis thanked the Vicar for his help, wished him a good day and strolled back to his ramshackle lodgings, pondering that the Reverend Doctor was a very serious-minded man and probably didn't appreciate Denis' enthusiasm for the stories.

"I suppose a ghostly scarecrow is a bit much," Denis muttered to himself as he walked. "Haunting a field I could see, but why would a scarecrow be in a marsh...?"

Two days passed and, good as his word, Mister Mipps arranged for them to rent Peters rowboat, and even brought along the promised maps. Upon the third day, as the sun was touching the horizon, Fred and Denis were putting the boat into the murky water.

Fred manned the oars, with the cylideral temporal codex amplifier on the bench next to him. Denis sat in the stern, the map laid out on his lap.

"If we follow this stream," Denis said, tracing a path on the map with his finger, "it will lead us deep into the marsh, but after that...?"

He shrugged.

"We may have to haul her over land a bit," Fred grumbled, deep in his beard.

"One thing that I don't understand," Denis said. "Getting close as we can to the place the meteor strikes, aren't we in danger of getting...well, too close? It doesn't do us much good to power up the signaling device if we are moored in the center of a dangerous bull's eye."

"It's a gamble," Fred muttered, craning his head around to scout ahead as he rowed. "Once we have a better idea what the meteor is, we should have time adjust our plan."

Not feeling terribly relieved, Denis sighed and continued to study the map. He shifted, trying to get comfortable on the rough wooden floor of the boat.

"It's a bit of a roundabout trip," he mumbled. "But, I suppose following the stream will let us avoid crossing paths with that navy frigate."

"Yes," Fred nodded, absently. "All we have to worry about is smugglers, quicksand and your ghostly scarecrow."

'Yes," Denis agreed glumly. "And all for the lucky chance of being pulverized by a hunk of stone from outer space. 'Tis a fulfilling and stimulating life, traveling with Doctor Omega."

"It could be worse," Fred suggested. "It could be raining."

The pair meandered their way through the marsh. There were spots where the trees and tall grass crowded up close against the sides of the rowboat. Places where the stream would stretch out, wide and shallow and force the two to get out and carry the boat across the spongy damp ground.

After two hours, they pulled the boat aground on a hummock of land and Denis dug several sandwiches, wrapped in paper, out of his coat pockets. They ate, rested and studied the map.

"It's going to be full dark soon," Fred said, between chews. "Good clear night though. We don't want to use the lantern any more than we have to."

"You really think there are smugglers?" Denis asked. "It's hard to believe, in such a small, quaint village."

Fred shook his head at his companion's naiveté, brushed crumbs out of his beard and got to his feet. They were soon on their way, paddling through the marsh, under a cloudless black sky.

Denis, even during his turn at the oars, couldn't stop from tipping his head back and taking in the vast tapestry of stars overhead. This lead to him losing his hat several times and having to pause to fish it out of the water.

The stream eventually merged with the marsh itself and the going got trickier. The muddy water shifted from mere inches to waist-deep with little warning and tree roots protruded from the ground, lurking within the water, ready to catch an oar.

"We're getting close," Fred said, peering at the map and then adjusting several controls on the temporal amplifier.

"It's hard to believe it's going to happen," Denis added. "It's so quiet out here...so peaceful..."

"Almost too quiet," Fred muttered, not looking up from the map.

Denis looked around, noticing that his friend was right, and that the near constant background sounds of nature had hushed. The boat gave a sudden lurch, the bottom scraping against the ground as the prow caught in a thick, snaky tree root that stuck out from a grassy embankment.

"My fault," Denis announced, regaining his balance and adjusting the oars. "There goes my hat again! Sorry, I didn't see us drifting into this little cove...are you all right, Fred?"

"I'm fine," the bearded man grumbled, tucking the map into his coat and shifting so he was kneeling, rather than sitting in the bottom of the boat. "We should be nearly there. Are we stuck?"

"Oh, no," Denis reassured him. "One good push will get us loose. I'm more worried about how shallow it's gotten."

They were moored with the prow wedged into the tree root and the embankment around them formed a makeshift harbor for the little boat.

"It should be an open area," Fred said, peering around. "Almost a small pond."

"I'll go have a scout around," Denis said, unsteadily making his way to the prow. He used the roots sticking out of the dirt as steps and grabbed hold of clumps of tall grass to pull himself up.

"Just mind your step," Fred warned. "And don't wander too far. It's easy to get lost."

"I won't be a moment," Denis said, and pushed through the tall grass.

The ground was uneven, but firmer than the rest of the surrounding marsh. It seemed to stretch out for a ways, a sort of peninsula of safe ground. The grass and bushes gave way after several yards for a strand of skeletal trees. Denis walked slowly and cautiously amongst the trees, hoping to find their watery destination without falling into it. He didn't think his hat could survive another dunking. Fred's earlier comment had made him especially aware of how quiet the marsh had become. Even with the full moon, his surroundings were almost oppressively dark and hushed.

Which meant the gently whiney of a horse sounded to his anxious ears like a lion's roar.

Denis bit his lip to keep from yelping in surprise and alarm. He huddled behind a trio of trees grown close together and peered out anxiously. The landscape, which, before, had appeared quiet and full of wonder, was now shadowy, full of menace... The stories told by local tavern dwellers seemed all too plausible.

Denis caught a bit of movement, as a clump of darkness separated itself from a larger shadowy area. He took a second to catch his breath and calm his thoughts. Horses meant riders, and most vengeful spirits were able to get around without the aid of steeds, he surmised.

"Smugglers," Denis muttered, crouching down lower, as he nervously scouted the nearby shadows.

There was no other hint of movement or out of place sound. He crept forward, torn between his need to find their destination and wanting to avoid any smugglers. Getting down on his belly, he crawled through some bushes to get closer to the source of the noise.

It was a horse, black as the night; its bridle and saddle were also black, so, at first glance, Denis thought it wore neither. The animal shook its head and gave a snort.

Denis' forehead wrinkled in thought and he had the sudden, fearful realization that the only place its rider could be was right behind him.

Quickly looking over his shoulder, while praying his was wrong, Denis was startled to see the figure standing behind him.

The figure of a scarecrow.

Dressed all in ragged black, its eerie white cloth face seemed to glow.

Its arms were stretched out and its head cocked slightly to one side, giving the impression that it had been hung on a pole, and there the entire time Denis had been crawling through the undergrowth.

Denis slowly, anxiously got to his feet and leaned in to peer at the strange figure.

"Have ye not been warned?" it rasped, in a gravely sing song. "After dark, any soul that dwells within the marsh is mine!"

Denis flinched back, bumping against one of the trees he had recently used for a hiding spot.

"I didn't...we just wanted... uh... to go home!"

The scarecrow took a step forward, one long black clad arm reaching towards Denis. Both man and night creature halted, as a strange warbling sound drifted through the marsh and a ball of light could be seen in the distance, moving towards them.

"How many creatures lurk in this swamp?" Denis muttered, scooting around the tree.

The light grew brighter, the noise shriller; then, a second noise rent the night.

"Denis lad?" it called. "Where are you?"

Fred stepped into the clearing, a lantern held high and the temporal amplifier tucked under one arm. Several lights on it were blinking green and yellow, and it appeared to be the source the warbling sound.

Denis dashed from the trees and past the mysterious scarecrow to join his companion. He reached Fred, fear and exertion leaving him breathless.

"Th-thank goodness!" he gasped. 'We need... must... go... it'll find us!"

"What are you nattering on about?" Fred asked. "Of course, we have to go. It'll be here in minutes. What will find us?"

"I will," the scarecrow said, stepping into the cone of light formed by the lantern. It held a black flintlock pistol in its gloved hand.

All three stood locked in place, taking in the others and making their own mental calculations concerning what to do next.

The two stranded time travelers' eyes were wide with fear and disbelief, while those of the scarecrow were cold and seemed almost alive, staring directly into the young violinist's and the bearded handyman's souls.

Any plans or further talk were stalled, as the amplifier began to beep and a bright light appeared overhead.

All three looked upwards in amazement. The object arced downwards with a sound like a massive ocean wave rushing towards the shore.

Fred and Denis bolted through the bushes and trees, racing for their boat. They skidded to a halt at the edge and Fred held out the lantern, as they looked for where they had moored it.

Finding it, Fred handed Denis the lantern and scrambled down the steep embankment. Once in the boat, he adjusted the temporal amplifier. Denis shifted the lantern and was about to begin his descent when a gloved hand with a grip like iron clamped onto his shoulder. He turned his head and found himself inches away from the ghastly face of the scarecrow.

"What have you summoned?" he demanded in an angry growl. "What is that thing?"

"I... don't know," Denis stammered desperately. "We don't think it's a danger... are just... uh... trying to... trying... so desperately to go home!"

Denis' mind reeled, thoughts colliding, as he tried to muddle through all that was happening around him: the need to hurry if they were to have any hope of using the "meteor" to end their exile, the observation that this scarecrow may not be a supernatural being at all and that he seemed more concerned with protection, rather than frightening off, and the realization that he kept referring to the space-time vessel *Cosmos* as "home."

Something in either Denis' tone or expression reached the scarecrow and he released his grip and nodded to the young violinist.

"Do what you must," the scarecrow said. "I shall keep the British away."

Puzzled, Denis looked past the scarecrow and saw several other forms moving among the nearby trees. A trio all dressed in dark colors.

"Go," the scarecrow said. "Before I come to my senses."

Denis, still confused, nodded in reply turned and stumbled down the embankment, landing in an ungraceful heap in the boat. It rocked dangerously for a moment, but Fred, already at the oars was able to wrestle it back into balance.

Once Denis was in, Fred started vigorously rowing away from the little cove and toward the increasingly brighter light.

"He let you go?" Fred asked, intently.

"For some reason," Denis said, struggling to sit up. "He is willing to trust us. If this doesn't work, and the meteor causes any damage, I have a feeling we are in a great deal of danger..."

"Take the oars," Fred snapped, getting up.

He adjusted the cylindrical device, which was now blinking like a set of erratic Christmas lights. Wincing after his tumble, Denis struggled to keep the boat moving, Fred stood in the prow and held the temporal amplifier out, adjusting switches as it beeped and flickered. The light from the approaching object grew brighter and the rush of its descent louder.

Denis winced at the roar, too timid to look upwards and see how close it was. The light was soon bright enough to read by and as it moved closer it appeared almost like the boat was caught in a spotlight.

"Um…Fred…?" he asked, nervously. Then had to shout to be heard. "We seem to be right below the meteor! Isn't that ill-advised if it's just a meteor?"

Fred's answer was drowned out. The bearded man looked up and Denis' last clear view of his friend before the light grew painfully bright was Fred driving towards him. Fred tackled the younger man. The duo lay, huddled in the bottom of the boat while the light and sound swirled around them in a maddening maelstrom.

Minutes passed, then the two men, coming to the realization that they had not been crushed to death by a hunk of rock from the stratosphere, raised their heads.

The meteor was a perfect sphere, with a surface like polished marble. It shown like a light bulb: a light bulb large enough to house a family of four. It hovered several feel above the boat. Getting to his feet, Fred bumped his head against the underside.

Awkwardly and with much haste, they moved the boat til was no longer beneath it, but floating several feet away.

"What is it…?" Denis breathed, wide-eyed.

"No idea," Fred replied, in an equally hushed tone. "There was something similar looking in this village on an island, but not that big…!"

Suddenly, a line formed on the surface of the sphere. It traced across until it was an oval. The shape slid away, revealing an opening in the sphere. There was a light inside, not as bright as the exterior and a figure stepped into the opening.

"I thought I'd find you here," it said.

"Denis!" Fred exclaimed. "It's… It looks like…!"

"Me!" Denis added. "How'd I get there?"

It was indeed Denis Borel standing in the opening, but an older Denis, sporting a thin beard, streaked with grey. He was dressed in a frock coat, waistcoat and trousers of blue. Just past his right shoulder, the younger Denis could make out a second figure, a young woman in a skintight bodysuit.

Older Denis kneeled down and offered his hand to his younger self.

"You need to pay attention," he said. "From here, it's going to get complicated…"

Younger Denis, still feeling a bit shell shocked, stood up to basically shake hands with himself.

Their hands were mere inches apart when the boat rocked and the water around it began to bubble and steam. Leaning over the edge, Fred and Denis could see a light, shining up from the depths of the murky water. Even before they could puzzle over these strange events, a half dozen forms burst through the surface of the marsh water and began to lurch towards the small rowboat.

They were naked with skin red and shiny, like lobsters. They had malevolent, human-ish features: snub noses, tiny holes for ears, a black gash mouth and eyes that were no more than orbs of black. They sputtered and screeched as they reached for the boat's occupants with stubby red fingers.

"Lectroids!" the older Denis exclaimed, clutching the edge of the opening in the sphere. "We arrived too late!"

He and the young woman behind him ducked back into the interior of the glowing sphere.

Fred and Denis both grabbed up an oar with the intent of fighting off the strange beings. Denis made a clumsy swing and a red Lectroid grabbed the oar and snapped it like a twig. Fred hit his target and knocked one of the aliens back.

"Grab the lantern!" Fred yelled as he swung again.

As the half dozen creatures were about to climb into the rowboat, a voice rang out across the marsh.

"Denis!" it shouted. "Take shelter!"

The young violinist dove to the bottom of the boat, grabbing hold of Fred's waistcoat and dragging him down, seconds before a volley of shots echoed across the muddy pond.

Anxiously, Denis peered up and saw the Scarecrow and a trio of other men or creatures, each dressed in ragged dark colors and each bearing either the face of a monstrous bird or scarecrow. They held a variety of flintlock pistols and rifles and were all firing intently at the vicious red creatures.

The Lectroids screeched and growled, as the Scarecrow's followers placed their shots with deadly accuracy. The duo in the rowboat got back up just in time to see the dead and dying Lectroids sink into the marsh.

"Um...thank you," Denis said, with a wave towards the mysterious band on the embankment.

"There are more than enough unearthly creatures in Romany marsh," the Scarecrow declared, making a salute with his pistol before melting back into the night.

"Dear me," Older Denis announced, reappearing in the doorway. He and the young woman held bulky, white plastic pistols. "Well, that's sorted, I suppose, but we still have work to do."

"What is going on?" Denis asked.

"The radioactive turbulence striking the *Cosmos* was no accident," Older Denis explained, "but rather an attack. The Lectroids are attempting to enter this dimension in several spots in the time stream. Miss Bauer recruited me to help her find Doctor Omega..."

"We can talk on the way," the young woman snapped. "Two of the dimensional entry points have been dealt with, but that still leaves two more and we still haven't found Doctor Omega. All aboard!"

With that she ducked back inside.

"She's actually quite a charming young woman," Older Denis said, holding a hand out to the men in the boat. "But, she has a point. *Allons-y!*"

Fred and Younger Denis awkwardly climbed from the unsteady boat to the floating sphere.

"Talk about 'Be careful what you wish for'," Fred grumbled.

"Nice hat, by the way," Older Denis said, as he pulled his younger counterpart aboard. "Looks quite jaunty."

In Paul Hugli's latest tale, we find Doctor Omega embroiled in yet another saga, this time trying to recover his shi,p lost during the turmoil of World War II. Paul, who previously penned an Egyptian adventure in Tales of the Shadowmen *7, returns to the Land of the Pharaohs for a new time-hopping saga, in which the mysterious Doctor visits the most famous* Café Américain *of all and challenges the might of the Nazi empire...*

Paul Hugli: *As Time Goes By...*

Casablanca, Morocco, 1942

"With a burning spear and a horse *of air, to the wilderness I wander."*
Tom Brown's Song

The bluish-gray nimbus of the contraband Lucky cigarette haze drifted lazily, circling endlessly, blurring the ruggedly handsome features of the smoker, marred only by a scar on his lower lip. Absently, he took a sip of gin as he studied the man seated before his desk. He was giving him a song-and-dance story, but Rick wasn't buying it. *Not that it matter,* he thought, *Rick Blaine sticks his neck out for no one.* Still he agreed to listen to *this* Frenchman as a favor to Ferrari. Never a good idea. Even in the best of times.

The melody of an old standard by *Bobby Rose and the Rosettas* drifted into the room from Sam and his piano outside, in the gaming area of Rick's *Café Américain,* and Blaine tried to filter it out as he continue to study the man before him. He was elderly, tall and willowy, with long whitish hair, slicked back save for an errant shock of hair which played about his brow. Even in Casablanca's humidity, the man was decked out in black velvet frock coat, scarf (decorated in a motif of whorls and vortexes), dark pants, and highly polished black shoes. In his lap was a triangular fur hat, his agile long fingers absently stroking it as if it were a kitten.

Doctor Omega was, himself, studying the American dressed in a white dinner jacket and black tie. He desperately wanted to trust him. He knew from the histodiscs that Blaine had run guns to the Ethiopians in 1935, and in the next year, fought on the Loyalists side in Spain. Yet, the Doctor couldn't fess up and say: *I was traveling through the aether when, suddenly, there was a breach in the* mufkuzt *collector... Ah, no that would never do...* At the moment Omega had only a faint idea where his craft, the *Cosmos,* was; in fact, that was the reason he was here in the office of the owner of this café.

"I don't see how I can help you, Doctor," Blaine said, calmly firing up another Lucky. "I have no influence here. I'm just an ordinary saloon owner who came here for the waters. And stayed."

"I am not seeking special treatment, young man."

"And you will receive none. Not here. Not from the Vichy French or the Nazis. Major Strasser will see to that."

"I only require an exit visa."

"You require a *letter-of-transit*, and Captain Renault doesn't just hand them out to anybody." Blaine crushed out his cigarette in the overflowing ash tray. "Nor do you have the legs."

"Excuse me?"

"Never mind. I can't..." Blaine began, then suddenly stopped, bolting to his feet. "It can't be..."

The Doctor didn't understand. All he heard was Sam crooning: "*...you must remember this...*"

"Of all the gin joints..." Blaine mumbled as he hurried out of the office.

When he returned to his office, an hour later, he discovered that Doctor Omega had gone--not that he had actually thought about him in the interval. He hurried to his desk and unlocked his bottom right drawer, withdrawing two documents, two transit visas which could not be revoked.

Relieved, he sank into his chair. He had to find a better hiding place for the visas. A piano interlude from Sam filtered into the room, giving Rick Blaine an idea...

Converted Krupp Factory on the Danube, Black Forest, South-West Germany

The elderly man was stoic in his wood-frame wheel-chair, the burnt scar on his forehead itching and throbbing; but he resisted the temptation to scratch it, having gotten use to the irritation during the past three years. In fact, he had survived many trial and tribulations in the past decade: the actions of *that* masked vigilante had been just a minor set-back.

Rolling across the room, he stopped at a long display table, and studied the object nestled on a cushion of red velvet, within a exquisitely carved cedar box: a broken wooden shaft with a twenty-inch long blacken iron spear point split vertically, with an iron Crucifixion Nail placed in the divide, and held together by weathered leather straps; with the neck of the spear wrapped in gold and silver bands.

It was the object of myth... of legend ... of *Destiny*!

According to the Gospel of John, a crucified man could not remain hanging during the Jewish Passover, so the order was given to break the legs of Jesus, to hasten his death due to apoplectic trauma. But when a soldier was about to carry out the order, he had found the self-proclaimed Christ already dead. To verify this fact, the soldier's spear had pierced the side of Jesus, which had spouted water and blood.

For the rest of the story, one had to refer to non-Canonized sources, such as the *Apocrypha*. They claimed that that soldier was aged and almost completely blind; that the blood and water spouting from Christ's wound had sprayed his eyes, restoring his sight, cleansing his sins. He, in turn, had lovingly proclaimed Christ's divinity; and, with spear in hand, he preached the Good Word along the dusty roads of the Roman Empire for the next 28 years. But the Romans weren't buying what this ex-soldier was preaching. He was tortured, his teeth removed, then his tongue, and, lastly, he lost his head. This dutiful Angel of the Gospel was named Longinus , and his spear, or lance, became known as *Longinus' Lance* or the *Holy Lance* or, more appropriately, the *Spear of Destiny*.

The Spear had been said to have passed through many hands since the beheading of Longinus, including those of the Third Century C.E. co-ruler of the Holy Roman Empire, Maximianus Herculius, whose daughter, Fausta, married the world's first "Christian" emperor, Constantine. At the First Ecumenical Council of the Church, in Nicaea, to iron-out biblical canon, the Spear was ever-present, representing the conquest of Christianity over paganism and, more notably, the Jews.

It then passed through many and powerful hands, including Emperor Theodosius; Visigoth King Alaric; Justinian I; Charlemagne; Henry I, First King of the distinctly Pan-Germanic State and, to Hitler, the First Reich; his son, Otto I, and so on, down to Henry IV, whose daughter's grandson, King Frederick I, carried it into the Third Crusade. Then history lost it for 150 year, until Charles IV found it, and it passed through five centuries of subsequent monarchs. When Napoleon came looking for it, the Spear was hidden in Vienna. Though it had lost some of its mythical aura, replaced in medieval times by the Holy Grail, it still resonated with the Nazis trying to build a "Thousand Year Reich" around their "Black Camelot" at Himmler's Dahlem Castle, with the Fuhrer as King Arthur, the SS as the Knights of the Round Table, and the Holy Lance as Excalibur.

The Spear had been "liberated" from Austria in 1939, along with the Crown Jewels of the Holy Roman Empire, and hidden in a bunker beneath Nuremberg Castle, after temporary storage in the Kohn Bank's vault. Then, the RAF began bombing Germany in the Summer of 1940... So, Major Liebel of the SS would arrive soon to take possession of the Spear, to be re-united with the Crown Jewels in the re-enforced bunker.

Before joining the Nazi party and becoming leader of the SS in 1929, the *Reichfuhrer* Heinrich Himmler had been a fertilizer salesman. And with all of the nonsense he believed in, such as the Ark of the Covenant, the Holy Grail, Atlantis, and endless other fantasies, he appeared to still be in the bullshit business! But all this meant nothing to the old man... it was all mystical nonsense to him. He was a man of science, not a believer in fairy tales. And, as expected, this man of science found nothing extra-ordinary about the Spear, whether metallically, spiritually, magically, or metaphysically. It was an ordinary iron spear or lance point. Period. Of course, his report would be filled with pseudo-scientific arcana to justify the *Reichfuhrer*'s Black Sun cult, and its research branch, the *Deutsche Ahnenerbe* (the German Ancestral Heritage Research and Teaching Society), whose ranking members wore specially created uniforms, ceremonial daggers, and "Death's Head" signet rings.

The old scientist even snickered at the thought of the signet rings and the mythical nonsense surrounding theirs designs: skull and crossbones, and a row of Germanic runes, created in honor of the great Aryan god of thunder, Thor, who possessed a similar ring to which his warriors sworn allegiance. The ring was presented to officers after three years of dedicated service, and retired with the death of each owner.

The man who had just entered the old man's lab wore just such a ring, having just become a proud member of the SS Elite. This new recruit into the Himmler's Black Sun was the old man's own son, Frank Drexler.

An ex-cop, the former owner of and chief investigator for the Drexler Protection Agency, in New York City, he had been brave and courageous and honest, until he snapped. It was all due to the meddling of a self-proclaimed vigilante, a man who dressed in a silly get-up of a slouch hat and hunchback, with fright-wig and fangs, calling himself the Spider. The creature had brought down the last of Frank Drexler's father's *Ironmen*, and destroyed the old man's misguided dream of using giant robots to cure all the ills of the world. He had even used his cigarette lighter to burn his mark—that of the Spider—on the forehead of Professor Drexler, thinking him dead. But the Professor had lived, and his son had cracked, raving about vigilantes who dressed like spiders, bats, cats, or wrapped themselves in the Red, White and Blue of America, or, the Union Jack colors of Great Britain. This lawlessness was worse than democracy, itself a losing cause. *En masse*, the people were incredibly stupid, believing in equality. Absurd! Only the Master Race, the law and order provided by the Nazi Party, could save humanity *and* the Earth, from themselves.

Drexler's father had befriended Nicola Tesla in the past and knew where the inventor kept his papers, so Frank had raided the Manhattan warehouse, microfilming hundreds of pages among the twelve metal boxes, 35 metal cans, five barrels, and eight trunks: the secrets to rotating magnetic fields, frictionless induction motors, AC polyphase power distribution system, charged particle beam, bladeless turbine, VOTL aircraft, and dozens more blueprints were handed over to a Nazi cell in America. This was in 1939. By 1942, father and son had relocated to Germany. The father was a top scientist, and the son had become a proud member of the SS, in charge of the Nazi's *Wunderwaffle* ["Wonder Weapons"] division. All because of the interference of a madman who called himself the Spider!

"Come, Father," Major Drexler said, "the item from the desert awaits your inspection."

Herr Doktor Drexler, as he was now known, glanced at his personally autographed picture from Marlene Dietrich, smiled, and allowed his son to wheel him from the room, and into Krupp's converted factory floor, where, today, he was overseeing the research being conducted on an object recovered in the Egyptian desert, across the Nile from *Tel el-Amarna*, just south of Hermopolis. The converted factory had many projects in the works—a V-rocket, heavy-water experiments, giant robotic weaponry, etc., but the two Nazi were, at the moment, concentrating on the object occupying the center of the factory: a cylindrical, missile-like craft, thirteen meters long and three meters wide, bolted to the bed of a truck by nine large disc-shaped magnetic hooks. To Doktor Drexler the craft reminded him of something out of Jules Verne's *From the Earth to the Moon*, and, perhaps, it was indeed some sort of space craft. He smiled: *First, Europe. Next... the world. Then... the Moon? The Fuhrer would like that...*

Drexler's jackboots echoed through the open space as he paraded around the artifact, his hands clasped together behind his back, wondering out loud to his father what the vehicle—for surely, it was some type of vehicle—was doing, seemingly abandoned, in the Egyptian desert.

"Perhaps it's from the future... a time machine, like the one H.G. Wells mentioned..."

"Hmmm," Doktor Drexler mumbled. "Perhaps it's a space craft? Yes, it's cylindrical... Shell-shaped... A craft from Mars?"

The two freshly-minted Nazis would have been surprised to learn that both their musings were correct: that craft had, indeed, traveled through the aether, including to and from Mars, and had utilized a temporal bubble to traverse time. For the ship was Doctor Omega's *Cosmos*. Its designer, builder and captain was presently cooling his heels, hidden behind a heap of strange exotic electrical equipment tucked in the corner of the gigantic factory. To his right was Fred, his mechanic. The amiable bearded, hulking assistant was fumbling with a transparent cube, six-inches wide, containing what appeared to be an ionized cloud.

Doctor Omega sighed and grabbed the cube from the gentle giant's hands, and was about to replace it on the work-table, yet, for a moment—just a tiny moment—he felt an eerie, tingling sensation surging through his body, inflaming his every pore. It took most of his will-power to put the cube back in its lead container, its glow dying even before he closed the lid.

"Keep your hands in your pockets," he whispered to Fred.

"Sorry, Doctor."

Doctor Omega then turned his attention back to his ship, watching Drexler and his son pace around the *Cosmos*. If it had wheels, the Nazis would probably have kicked the tires. The two Nazis continued to speculate wildly as they tried to discover an access to the craft's interior.

"Good," the Doctor said. "They are stumped. We need to get my ship back."

But at the moment, that was wishful thinking. The Doctor settled behind a wooden crate and pondered how he and Fred had arrived at their present predicament.

Two Months Before

The *Cosmos* had been in the future, in 1986, researching some space-time anomalies. After taking in a "flicker" entitled *Star Trek IV: The Voyage Home*, and foregoing a second feature starring the latest starlet, Christy Canyon, the Doctor and Fred had boarded their craft and began *their* voyage home... to 1904 Normandy, France. Throwing switches and pulling levers, they shot into the temporal void. Then, suddenly, there had been a *pop* and a release of steam and radiometric gases. Quickly Fred reacted, shutting down the chronotron-flux power, causing the *Cosmos*'s stellite shell to shake violently, threatening to rip the craft apart. They had no choice but to drop out of the aether.

The chronometer read: *May 14, 1942*. They would need a new power supply. And the best source was meteor-impact sites. The substance had been called by many names: *t'cam, res mehit,* and *mufkuzt* and *hydrozite*. It has many properties of *vril* energy. Some believe the meteorites originated from an exploding planet, and since they had traces of solidified krypton gas, some referred to it as *k-metal*. It sometime radiated a non-radiometric green glow, caused by bio-illumination created by microbes attached to it, after it had crashed to Earth.

The substance was quite rare, but it emitted a distinct chronal signature, which the ship's temporal meter had picked up. Following the Doctor's instructions, Fred had set the *Cosmos* down amongst swirling dust and sand, just south of the ruins at el-Ashmunein. In ancient times, the place had been known to the Egyptians as *Khmunu*, and was dominated by the temple of Thoth, god of wisdom and writing. In antiquity, on this primeval hill, the Sun God Ra had created the world out of chaos. The Greek Ptolemy had equated Thoth with their god Hermes and thus dubbed the city... Hermopolis.

Though *mufkuzt* itself wasn't radioactive, the collection and processing of it was. But first they had to find a source. While out of the ship, the Doctor and his companion were caught in a menacing sandstorm, a *simoon*. Fortunately, they had brought a portable electro-shield, which provided them with shelter to outlast the storm. At first, the Doctor regaled Fred with stories of vanishing armies, disappearing in *simoon*s, and how many had dreamed of finding the legendary treasures lost in history; especially a certain Persian expedition during Egypt's 27th Dynasty.

Later, while Fred waited out the storm, dreaming of treasures, the Doctor took the time to get some work done: correcting the errors in Noel Essaillor's

Revue de Mathématiques, a crippled Frenchman who claimed to understand the mechanics of time-travel. *The fool!*

Once the storm had abated, they had made their way back to the *Cosmos.* But it wasn't there!

"Where is it?" the Doctor pondered.

"It couldn't just get up and move itself? Could it?" asked Fred.

"*E pur si muove.*"

"Huh?"

"Never mind," the Doctor replied, not explaining Galileo's alleged response after recanting his heretic, heliocentric theory.

Gigantic, deep tracks in the sand soon told the Doctor the story: the *Cosmos* had been loaded aboard a flat-bed truck and driven north.

"Hmph," was all he said as he pondered the situation. The logical option was to follow the *Cosmos*; the truck's tracks were heavy enough in the sand to make it easy. Perhaps, hire a *dahabiya* and motor up the Nile? But the north was occupied by the so-called "Desert Fox," Field Marshall Erwin Johannes Eugen Rommel, and his Afrika Korps' Panzer Division, based at el Alamein, less than 165 kilometers from the Pyramids. *No*, the Doctor thought, *that would not do.* Since the *Cosmos* was destined, no doubt, for Germany, he and Fred would have to go there.

But how?

When they had first become stranded the Doctor had his chronospectrometer with him. It was used to track down non-radiometric decay emissions, indicating the presence of stellite; fortunately, the hand-held device could also detect the quantum-signature wave of the *Cosmos*' leaking Chronotron-Flux generator. Yet, there was still one problem: the signature wave could only be picked up within a relatively small distance radius.

The Doctor was pondering these facts, and a thousand more, when Fred asked:

"Now what?"

"Well, the French Foreign Legion have a motto: *Marche ou crève.*"

"*Oui.*"

In the near distance, they saw—if it wasn't a mirage—three men on camels, with three donkeys in tow. They were Bedouins, dressed in *kaftans* and *khafiyas* tied with twisted *agabs*. They looked like extras from some T.E. Lawrence epic or, perhaps, the Three Wise Men, though they didn't seem to be laden with frankincense, myrrh and gold.

"*Habib,*" the Doctor intoned as the trio neared.

"*Aleman? Inglizi?*" the oldest of the trio asked.

"*Merci, Monsieur,* but we're French!" the Doctor replied, slightly peeved at being taken for German, let alone English!

148

"*Allah yisallimak, habib,*" replied the older of the trio, seemingly satisfied. He introduced himself as Mohammed, and his companions as Mustafa and Daoud.

"*Allah isabbekhum bilkheir,*" the Doctor replied in kind, introducing himself and Fred. After some discussion and bartering, and a fist-full of *baksheesh*, the two Frenchmen were given robes and *khafiyas* to wear, and a donkey each. And thus, they set out across the Libyan Desert.

Skirting Rommel's forces, which controlled most of Northern Egypt and Libya, they proceeded north-westward, through the Bahariya and Faiyum Oases, up to the Siwah Oasis. It seemed to take forever, and Fred kept inquiring when they would arrive at their destination. Mohammed replied softly each time with: *bokra.* That is, *tomorrow.* Anything could happen—*tomorrow.* Plus the Bedouins kept calling Omega *hakim,* even after he constantly told them he was, indeed, a doctor but not a physician.

At the Siwah Oasis, they rested for a day. Doctor Omega and Fred explored the famous site, best known for the Temple of Ammon, which, in 332 B.C.E., had been visited by Alexander the Great. Alexander had asked three questions of the Oracle, and though no one knew what the questions or answers were, the Macedonian King seemed satisfied that he was, indeed, divine and had a special relationship with Ammon, perhaps even that the god was his father and not Philip. According to Arrianof Nicomeda, Alexander "put his questions to the Oracle and received the answers his soul desired." Then again, it was said that Alexander had made it across the Libyan Desert on the guidance of the cawing of ravens and, according to Ptolemy, the advice of two talking snakes.

Here the Bedouins and the Frenchmen parted way. After more *baksheesh* exchanged hands the Doctor and Fred had acquired two camels, date wine, dates, water and other supplies. They set out westward. With the swaying of the camels, Fred came down with a bad case of motion-sickness, discovering why the creatures were referred to as "ships of the desert."

A week later, Doctor Omega and Fred reached Tripoli, former headquarters of the Barbary States. The term *Barbary* was derived from the *barbarians*, who occupied Northern Africa after the fall of the Roman Empire. Now, another band of "barbarians" ruled the region: the "Huns" via their Fascist lackeys, Mussolini's Italy.

In Tripoli, the Doctor, via more *baksheesh* and some mesmerism, managed to get himself and Fred on a plane. Unfortunately, they could only make it as far as *ad-Dar al-Bayda*, better known as Casablanca.

There, discreetly, Doctor Omega asked around, and the answers had landed him in the office of Rick Blaine at the latter's *Café Américain.* But he got nowhere fast—he had to try something else. The opportunity came when Blaine stormed out of his office after mumbling: "Of all the gin joints…"

The Doctor glanced around, decided he was alone, and shrugged. He went around Blaine's desk, picked the lock on the bottom right hand drawer and, finding an unfolded letter-of-transit, he laid it out on the desk. From his jacket, he removed an electronic device about the size of a deck of Chesterfields—a *facsimilulator*—and photographed the document. Later, when alone, save for Fred, the Doctor pressed a button on the side of the machine and, with a slight hum, the device unfolded itself twice, before quadrupling and octupling its size, creating a flat-bed printer. With the press of a couple more buttons, the Doctor created two perfect letters-of-transit to Lisbon. After forging the official signature, he and Fred were ready to seek out the *Cosmos*.

From Lisbon, the Doctor and Fred, with help from the French Underground, smuggled themselves into war-torn Germany, through the Black Forest, to the old Krupp's factory on the Danube. Then, with the aid of mesmerism, the Doctor managed to get Fred and himself inside factory.

Now, as they watched the Drexlers ponder the wonderments of the space-time ship, the Doctor's eyes fell upon the means of their deliverance. Its schematics and operation manual were sitting on an abandon workbench. He snatched up the data and quickly scanned it, nodding here and there, with an occasional "*hmmm*" to accent his thoughts. Satisfied that he understood the mechanism—which wasn't that difficult for him—, the Doctor set down the manual, and whispered to Fred:

"Let's go."

"Where?"

"There, my man!"

The Doctor pointed to a twenty-foot tall mechanical man standing against the far wall. Its arms hung from ponderous shoulders. A helmet-like head had a glass-plate for eyes, and a mouth full of teeth like a steam-shovel. Its joints were steel plates overhanging flexible rubber. Its chest was embossed with a giant swastika.

"According to the schematics, it's one of Drexler's *Ironmen*."

"Huh?"

"A back-up plan in case things turn badly for the Nazis. They plan to bury these *Ironmen*, to be awakened when the Fatherland has regrouped."

"Ah, sleeper agents?"

"Yes."

"I don't think I want to be around when one of these Sleepers awakens."

"Well, that is exactly what we are going to do."

"Wait a minute..."

"Shhhh...."

Stealthily, they inched their way along, behind stacked crates, towards the robot. A quick look told the Doctor that the Nazis were still thrashing out the design of the *Cosmos,* pondering how to get into the damn thing. Satisfied, he began climbing up the metal ladder attached to the concrete wall next to the *Ironman*, reluctantly followed by Fred.

The Doctor pushed a button on the side of the robot's head, just under the "jaw" line, and saw the tempered-glass face-plate rose with an audible hiss. He and Fred scrambled inside, with the Doctor commandeering the only control chair, forcing Fred to stand behind him, amongst a cornucopia of wires, vacuum tubes, levers and switches. The Doctor then made a quick survey of the control panels before starting to push buttons, pull levers, and switch switches.

The *Ironman*'s hydrogen/nitrogen power furnace fired up. The Doctor discovered that the robot had been updated since the prototypes had wrecked New York three years before. Unfortunately, the racket drew the attention of the Nazis and their flunkies. Drexler drew his Luger and pointed it at the awakened "Sleeper" and yelled:

"Fire!"

His men complied. Shells from Lugers and sub-machine guns pelted the *Ironman*, but to no effect against the tempered steel/titanium alloyed body,

As the Doctor became more familiar and comfortable with the controls, the *Ironman* jerked and creaked and took a practice step forward, then another, and another, until it moved like a well-oiled machine. Bullet ricocheted off its metal body, not even leaving a dent. though becoming a danger to the Nazis goons. They were killing themselves with the ricochets.

Despite the chaos, Drexler continued to demand action!

A robotic hand came down and snatched up the Nazi in its claw, raising the struggling SS agent, until he was facing the thermo-glass faceplate of the *Ironman*. He beat his fists against the metallic fingers gripping him, while screaming obscene insults.

Tired of the madman's ravings the Doctor casually flung him aside, sending him crashing into a group of stormtroopers, who tumbled like so many bowling pins. The Doctor then pulled a lever and, with a hum, the potential energy charge stored into the face plate became accessible. The *Ironman*'s eyes glowed, before unleashing a Teslan particle beam, creating a disruptive gash in the floor, and sending chunks of concrete flying into the air, falling back on the Nazis, burying them under the debris.

Next, the Doctor had the robot look upward as he charged the polyphase electronic generator. Suddenly, the entire face-plate of the *Ironman* began to glow as the energy potential built up, ionizing the air, causing it to crackle. A concentrated blast erupted forth from the machine, melting through the ceiling like a hot knife through butter. To finish the job, the Doctor instructed the robot's hands to reach up and grab the sagging girders. With a metallic groan, the girders pulled free, sending steel and concrete crashing down on the Drexlers and their horde.

Turning his attention to the *Cosmos*, the Doctor commanded the mechanical hands to slither under the belly of the ship. With a groan, the giant robot lifted the ship, snapping the circular magnetic braces with had held it to the flatbed, leaving the top crescent-shaped halves of the braces still attached the hull.

Quickly, the Doctor and Fred slid down the robot's arm and landed feet-first on the flat-bed of the truck, just beneath the spot where the robot had the *Cosmos* suspended. After taking his key from his jacket pocket, the Doctor pushed a button on the ship's underbelly, activating the lock to the ventral hatch.

It irised open.

Fred boosted the Doctor through the hatch, then followed him, securing the door as Omega rushed to sit in front of the control panel, turning dials and pulling levers.

Within a whirlwind of dust, the *Cosmos* began to lift, rising slowly before picking up speed and attitude. Once they cleared the hole in the ceiling created by the *Ironman*'s rampage, the ship tilted up, and, with the pull of two more levers, shot skywards like a rocket.

They had just shot out of Earth's atmosphere when the *Cosmos*'s stellite hull began to violently shake and rattle—space began to warp around the ship. The Chronotron-Flux power-drive was still ruptured, and threatened to burst through the quick-fix mending job Fred had done earlier—the breach that had caused their present predicament in the first place.

"Fred," Omega yelled, sweat pouring down his brow, "the Tesla-Flux Compensator is... is, er, well... over-compensating for the added weight. We need to lose what's left of those magnetic locks."

He tossed a few more switches, and Fred pulled more levers as the *Cosmos* traversed billions of possible time lines. Popping out of the aether five years in the future, in June 1947, the *Cosmos* shot west across the United States of America.

At last, Doctor Omega was able to gain some control over his ship.

Degaussing the ship's hull caused the nine crescent-shaped metal magnetic anchors to fall away over the Pacific Northwest, where their momentum sent them skipping across the skies, over Mt. Rainer and Mt. Adams, in Washington State. The pilot of a CalAir A-Z, Kenneth Arnold, just a few minutes before 3:00 p.m., at approximately 9200 feet, observed these highly reflected crescent discards. He reported these "half-moon shaped, oval in the front and convex in the rear" objects "flying like a saucer would if you skipped it across water." The newspaper carrying the story dubbed them: *flying saucers.*

With the extra weight now discarded, the *Cosmos* once again shot forward, zooming through the Van Allen belt, rocketing like a speeding fireball into the aether. The Doctor continued fooling with dials, switches and levers, but the temporal rotor was over-reacting, smoking, and unable to maintain the chronal signature bubble and keep the chronotronic flux under control.

"We're losing coherence," Omega shouted. "We still need to repair the time rotor and find additional fuel."

"How about ionizing the dilithium crystals?" Fred exclaimed.

"This isn't a 'flicker,' Fred! This is reality!"

"Then I guess a sling-shot around the Sun is out?"

Doctor Omega ignored him, pulling more levers, tossing more switches in order to effect an emergency landing.

Again they popped out of the aether, right over a source of meteoric *mufkuzt,* according to ship's detectors.

The *Cosmos* descended like a falling leaf, and landed onto the desert sands, kicking up a miniature sandstorm.

The Doctor glanced at the chrono-meter. It read: *May 14, 1357 B.C.E.* The astrogator gave the location: *mid-Egypt, west of the Nile.*

He smiled; time was like the tide—it always returned you to your starting place. Give or take 3300 years!

The area was, however, completely different from what it had been a mere two *relative* months ago. The Temple of Thoth at Khmunu was a glorious sight of magnificent engineering, not the ruins it would become when future genera-tions would label it Hermopolis or el-Ashmunein. But the Doctor and Fred had no time to enjoy any sightseeing; they had work to do if they ever hoped for their own *Voyage Home* back to 1904 France.

Since mining meteoric *mufkuzt* used radiometric elements to process the ore and to refine it, the Doctor and Fred were forced to don special protective overalls, gloves, boots and hoods. From the *Cosmos,* they carried a translucent glob of tempered-glass, three meters in diameter, mounted on a tripod of lead legs. They positioned it carefully over a meteor impact crater. The Doctor ad-justed some dials on its base, and, satisfied that the device was working proper-ly, set it on "automatic" so that it could process the ore without their constant supervision. Then, he joined Fred in the *Cosmos* to make repairs to the ship's navigational system.

Unseen by the two time travelers a twelve-year old native prince, Naphuria, was napping against a pillar dedicated to the God of Wisdom, near the Shrine of Thoth, in the 15th Nome of Kemet, some 240 miles north of Oper—modern-day Thebes. He awoke to the gentle humming of the *mufkuzt* accumula-tor over the sand hill, and, out of curiosity, wandered towards it as if the sound was beckoning him. And, perhaps, it was.

In the East, the skies began to darken, as if Ra was slowly being devoured by a serpent; but how was that possible? Ra's Solar Barge should be no more than half-way across the skies... The young prince was frightened as more and more of the sun disc disappeared, plunging the land in darkness.

But then he saw it. On the ground before him: *A glowing globe.*

Its eerie light illuminated the darkness of the solar eclipse. Its legs radiated beneath it like out-stretched arms. Set in bas-reliefs on the globe were the sym-bols of its manufacturer, Sol-Hill Oscillators: a circle with a dot in the center a half-circle facing up, and a wavy line. The young prince recognized the symbols as the sun, or the deity, a half-loaf of bread, and water: *Creator, "T"* and *"N."* Since the Ancient Egyptians used no vowels in their hieroglyphs the young prince interpreted the symbols as *God the Aten*, the non-anthropomorphic, amorphous Solar deity, sometimes favored by his father and mother.

The prince fell to his knees, genuflecting before the globe, mumbling an ancient incantation. Then, daring life itself, the young man reached out his hand and touched the embodiment of the Aten, and, for a full minute, absorbed the gamma radiation caused by the mining process, a transcendental glow engulfing his body. Every hair on his body, including his princely side-lock, stood on end. Then, he was violently repelled, and landed in a daze on his back. Foggy-headed, he crawled away as the light returned to sky—as the eclipse waned and Ra resumed his normal journey across the Heavens.

The effect of this encounter would stay with him for the rest of his life.

An hour later, having finished the repairs on the *Cosmos*, Doctor Omega and Fred re-donned their protective suits, went outside and switched off the ac-cumulator. Between them, they carried it back to their ship. They attached it to the chronogenerator, and replaced the lead shielding.

With everything in place, and the gauges reading normal, Fred tossed a couple switches and pulled a couple levers. The *Cosmos* began to rise. At first, the ship shook and sputtered before humming with electronic proficiency as more levers were pulled. It began to send up a whirlwind of sand dust.

"Where to, Doctor?" Fred said as he checked a couple gauges.

"1904...Home—for the time being" the Doctor replied, with a tear in his eye, writing a few notes on his clipboard as the chronal signature bubble en-gulfed the *Cosmos*.

And the *Cosmos* left the Ancient Egyptian skies with a *"poof!"*

On the ground, Prince Naphuria watched the space-time ship vanish, and swore an allegiance to this god of the skies. Within two years, his older brother, Tuthmosis V, Crown Prince, High Priest of Ptah, and Overseer of the Prophets of Upper and Lower Egypt, would die in a hunting accident, thus leaving Amenhotep III and Queen Tiye's only surviving son, Naphuria, as Crown Prince and co-regent under his coronation name of Amenhotep IV ("Amen is Satis-fied").

During the intervening years, the radiometric effects of the *mufkuzt* accu-mulator, which the young co-regent, in the darkness of the eclipse, had mistaken for the earthly manifestation of the Aten, had taken their toll, mutating his body: elongating his face, thickening his thighs, reducing his arms to spindles, and making his chest and stomach pendulous.

He married the enigmatic beauty Nefertiti ("The Beauty Has Come") and, in Year Four of their reign, he changed his name to Akhenaten ("Effective Spirit of the Aten") and moved his capitol to the newly-erected Akhataten ("Horizon of the Aten"), the present-day ruins of el-Amarna, across the Nile from where he had first had his Vision of the Aten. Like Ra at Khmunu (Hermopolis), Akhena-ten created his city out of the chaos of his times, hoping to bring order to the world. Alas, it was all for naught.

Afterword

Though Doctor Omega and Fred may well have been the first Frenchmen to visit Egypt, they were not the last.

The Land of the Pharaohs was most notably exploded by Jesuit priest Claude Sicard, who, in 1708, found ten open tombs in the "Place of Truth" (the Valley of the Kings). Then, in the Summer of 1798, under the pretence of stemming the oppressive rule of the *Mamluks*, and to deny the British access to the Red Sea, thus India, Napoleon set sail for Egypt with some 335 ship, including his flag ship, *L'Orient*. Aboard these ships were 40,000 troops, 1200 horses, 171 field guns, and 167 hand-picked scholars, including engineers, surgeons, chemists, botanists, zoologists, and architects, collectively known as the *Commission des Sciences et Arts d'Egypte*.

After the defeat of Napoleon by the British, his scientists were allowed to retain their scientific works, but had to surrender all their finds, including the Rosetta Stone, which became so instrumental in decoding the Ancient Egyptian language, mainly through the efforts of the Frenchman Champollion and his 1924 translation/publication.

Yet, for obvious reasons, the history books are mute about certain events connected to Napoleon and his team.

Alas, that story must wait for another time…

Our regular contributor Rick Lai has become the de facto *chronicler of the secret history of the Black Coats. In this tale, which focuses on the early exploits of the enigmatic Colonel Bozzo-Corona, the All-Father of the sinister brotherhood, Rick expands his research in order to bring in yet another criminal mastermind, the notorious Vautrin, the creation of Honoré de Balzac. The large shadow of the real-life Eugène-François Vidocq, the rogue responsible for the founding of the French Sûreté, influenced all the founding fathers of the detective novel, from Edgar Allan Poe to Paul Féval, from Alexandre Dumas to Balzac, Gaboriau and Ponson du Terrail...*

Rick Lai: *Gods of the Underworld*

France, 1808-10

The young boy rested face downward on the straw-covered floor. His hands were tied behind his back. He was only three years old. Unless a miracle happened, his life would be snuffed out in a cell underneath the Convent de la Merci in 1808.

He looked at his fellow prisoners. On his right, his brother, only two years older was bound as he was. So was his father. On the left, was an old man whom he had never seen before, struggling with the ropes around his wrists. He ceased his exertions upon hearing the cell door open.

A handsome man with a mustache loomed over the captives.

"So, Colonel, you will soon pay the price for your constant refusal to divide the Treasure of the Black Coats with the rest of the High Council."

"You swore an oath of loyalty to me, Draco," said the old man.

"Loyalty is a two-way street. You promised to share the Treasure. Yet you guard it like a miser." Draco's foot rested on the neck of the father of the two young boys. "Your servant here may believe your empty promises. I don't."

"If you must slay me because of my loyalty to the Colonel, then do so," pleaded the captive. "Just spare my sons."

Draco removed his foot from the prisoner's neck.

"Have you forgotten, Lecoq, that this is Corsica. Here, we live and die by the rules of the *vendetta*. If I let your children live, they'll eventually seek vengeance as adults. Let them be consoled by the knowledge that they shall soon be reunited with their late mother."

"If you kill us, you'll never find the Treasure," predicted the Colonel.

"Perhaps. But I, Marcel Draco, shall command the Black Coats as the new All-Father. They shall create a new Treasure for me."

"The other Masters on the High Council will never follow you!"

"You're wrong, Colonel. Six of the Masters currently in Corsica already have. Only Anne needs to be persuaded to accept my supremacy. Once she falls into line, the other four Masters in Paris shall soon follow. My six fellow rebels and I are going to play a game of cards. The winner gets to kill you, Colonel."

Leaving the prison cell, Draco locked the door,

After 10 minutes, the prisoners heard rejoicing.

"You've won, Doctor Lerne!" yelled Draco. "Kill the Colonel!"

"There's no need," protested Lerne. "The Colonel has a weak constitution. In my professional opinion, the physical strain of his imprisonment will cause heart failure. What's the point of killing a dying man? Leave him tied up in the straw and I'll guarantee he'll be dead in the morning."

"Yes, *there will be daylight tomorrow*," joked Draco.

He and his comrades left the Convent.

Shortly after dawn, Draco and his accomplices returned to the prison cell. Unlocking the door, they peered inside. The Lecoqs were still there, but the Colonel was gone.

"He broke out of his bonds during the night!" yelled Lerne. "He picked the lock!"

"He'll go to Anne and promise her a larger share of the Treasure!" said Draco. She'll come here with..."

Draco never finished his sentence. A hail of gunfire exploded in the corridor outside the doorway. In a matter of seconds, Draco and the other conspirators were dead.

A group of men armed with pistols entered the cell. They were followed by an attractive woman of thirty-four. Her hair was auburn. She reached down and untied the ropes around the wrists of Lecoq's younger son. She raised the boy to his feet.

For a moment, he thought the woman was his mother, but then he remembered visiting her grave with his father.

"Who are you, Milady?"

"I am your salvation," she replied, kissing him on the forehead.

A year later, two men had an argument at the Callyx Bar in Paris.

"You need me to dispose of Josephine's necklace, Bibi-Lupin," whispered the man with close-cropped red hair. "Only I can protect you from being fleeced by the Black Coats."

"The Black Coats are a myth, Trompe-la-Mort," professed the dark-haired man. "The All-Father is merely a bogeyman to frighten children."

"No, he isn't. He's belonged to both the Camorra and the Corsican Brotherhood. As Fra Diavolo, he used the former to plunder Naples and Sicily. His exploits accumulated a huge hoard, known as the Treasure of the Scapular. He then used his Corsicans minions in Ajaccio to move it. Some say it's in Sartene, at the Convent of La Merci. Others believe the Treasure's here in Paris. He adds to it by robbing thieves like you and me."

What a ridiculous fairy tale!" exclaimed Bibi-Lupin.

"You'll soon pay a price for dismissing my warning," predicted Trompe-la-Mort as he rose from the table.

After paying for his drink, the red-haired man departed. Ten minutes later, a squad of policeman arrived to arrest Bibi-Lupin. A search of his clothing disclosed an emerald necklace.

In the autumn of 1809, the most feared man in Paris was Joseph Fouché, Duc d'Otrante, Napoleon's Minister of Police. In his private office, Fouché was conferring with Jean Henry, the chief of the Paris police. Seated at his desk, he examined the emerald necklace.

"You did well, Henry. This bauble could have easily caused the Emperor's downfall."

"Surely your Grace jests. Public knowledge of Empress Josephine's loss would have only been a minor embarrassment."

"The Emperor intends to divorce his wife and marry a foreign princess. Most likely, the new Empress will be Austrian. He gave this valuable necklace to Josephine in happier times. If it had remained stolen, a rumor would have circulated that the Emperor arranged the theft in order to give the necklace to his future bride. Not only would our master's reputation be sullied, but so would that of his new consort."

"Surely the public would never be so gullible, your Grace."

"Have you forgotten our recent history, Henry? In 1785, another Austrian became the wife of a French king. The theft of a similar necklace led to the widely accepted libel that she was the mastermind behind the crime. The ultimate consequence of that calumny was the execution of Queen Marie Antoinette and her husband eight years later. Do you have the thief in custody?"

"Yes, your Grace. His name is Bibi-Lupin. Do you wish to see his file?"

Fouché indicated his assent by extending his hand. Jean Henry gave him one of three folders that he had brought to the meeting.

The Duc read aloud as he flipped through the papers. "Alias Louis Gondureau and Albert Lupin... arrested for treason in 1793 by Citizen Chauvelin... escaped before his execution... fled to England... became a coachman employed by Sir Percy Blakeney..." Fouché paused thoughtfully before resuming. "I met Blakeney once. He married an alluring actress who was one of Saint-Just's cousins. I never understood what she saw in him. The man's an absolute dunce."

"No doubt, Mademoiselle Saint-Just was attracted by his title and wealth."

"Perhaps," stated Fouché before continuing his perusal. "Bibi-Lupin took advantage of the amnesty for émigrés to return to France in 1802. He served loyally in the French army until committing this robbery during his last leave.

We can't afford to have this man tried for the theft of Josephine's necklace. He must have committed other crimes before striking at the Emperor. Let him remain in custody until another charge can be levied against him."

"That may take weeks, even months, your Grace."

"It doesn't matter whether he is sentenced to the galleys this year or next. Are you sure that Bibi-Lupin's crime wasn't politically motivated ?"

"Monsieur Jackal assures me that Bibi-Lupin only acted from greed."

"Jackal? Who is Jackal?"

"A former criminal recently recruited as an informer. He identified Bibi-Lupin as the culprit. Bibi-Lupin considers Jackal a close friend."

"Jackal is the English word for *chacal*. Is this modern-day Judas an Englishman?"

"No, he's French. Jackal is a *nom de guerre* used solely to protect his true identity. If his criminal comrades learned that he was betraying them, his corpse would soon be floating in the Seine. Would you like to see his file too?"

Fouché accepted a bulky file from Henry.

"Born in 1775.... the son of a baker..." he murmured, impatiently flipping through the pages. "I hope this man never writes his memoirs. His entire life is a boring repetition of arrests and escapes. Henry, give me the abridged version. When did you coerce this thief into becoming your pawn?"

"I didn't coerce him. He volunteered."

"What? This man was a hardened felon. I find his sudden appearance at an opportune time suspicious."

"Jackal underwent a religious conversion through the efforts of a well-known philanthropist, your Grace."

"Who?"

"Colonel Bozzo-Corona. Would you like to see his file as well?"

"There is no need, Henry. I've met the man. The Colonel may be a Corsican, like our Emperor, but he's little more than a simpleton who believes in the innate goodness of mankind. He lacks the sophistication to recognize that our race is composed primarily of selfish brutes. He is no more a threat to the French state than Percy Blakeney."

"Are you mad, All-Father?" said Anne. "You had no right to arrange the return of Josephine's necklace without consulting the rest of the High Council. It should have been added to the Treasure before arranging Bibi-Lupin's arrest."

"I will not have my authority questioned, Madame de Breuil," asserted Colonel Bozzo-Corona. "You may have inherited the beauty of your namesake, but you lack her judgment. She would never have dared challenge me."

"Cardinal Richelieu would never have squandered such an opportunity to manipulate the destiny of France," interjected Claude Verdier. "Napoleon betrayed you, All-Father. As a youth, he swore eternal allegiance to your Brotherhood in Corsica. Upon achieving power, he broke that oath and fought them."

"Buonaparte never had any direct dealing with me, my lad. He dealt solely with my two main subordinates. Now that they've been slain by one of his officers, the Emperor does not suspect my role in his rise to power. The Brotherhood served its purpose. They diverted Napoleon while I gathered my own organization."

"You imply that events are somehow following a plan of your own design?" asked Verdier.

"They are, my boy. Maître Portal-Giraud, please remind everyone of the doctrine that your keen legal mind fashioned at my command."

"Yes, All-Father," replied a jovial man of considerable girth. "Give the courts a *guilty party* for every crime committed."

"You see the advantages of earning a Doctorate of Law, my children," stated the Colonel. "How have we been implementing this doctrine of *paying the law*, Claude?"

"We spy on other criminals. We let them commit robberies, and then betray them to the authorities. Once the original perpetrators are in police custody, we steal their loot for ourselves."

"A rather simplistic implementation of Portal-Giraud's concept, my boy. I intend to expand this policy on a more sophisticated scale. We shall inaugurate the crimes directly, but evidence will be planted to implicate the innocent."

"Your plan is missing a key ingredient," argued Anne. "You need agents inside the police."

"Daylight is finally illuminating your mind, my dove. I have just planted the first agent in the form of Monsieur Jackal. Eventually he will influence the police to hire other criminals. The police will become riddled with our operatives."

"But Jackal's merely a lowly informant!" protested Anne.

"For the moment. Now understand the full extent of my plan. I supported Napoleon in order to fashion a European Empire with France at its center. Imperial expansion inevitably leads to the establishment of police authority. Joseph Fouché has fashioned a formidable instrument as Minister of Police. However, his apparatus has largely ignored criminals in order to neutralize political threats. Fouché's focus will now change due to Bibi-Lupin's brazen theft. If the possessions of the Imperial family are in jeopardy, the Emperor will make it a priority to suppress crime. He will realize that Fouché lacks the necessary experience so the Minister will be instructed to promote someone with an intimate knowledge of the underworld. Who better than our Monsieur Jackal? After allm he has already gained the Emperor's favor by returning Josephine's necklace!"

"You expect Napoleon and Fouché to be blinded by the old adage that it takes a thief to catch a thief?" declared Verdier.

"Precisely, my bright boy! As the Empire consolidates its power, French police will evolve into a European police. Our puppet will control the criminal investigation division of this new colossus. He will allow us to fill our coffers by transferring blame for our crimes to others. The Treasure will grow in leaps and bounds. When it is finally divided amongst us, each of you will be wealthier than Croesus."

"I would be placated by your assurances," said Anne, "if you shared the location of the Treasure with us. You aren't getting any younger, All-Father."

"I'm a healthy 60."

"Your age is closer to 80," corrected Anne.

"Allow an old man the indulgence of lying about his age, my dove. Don't worry, my children. The secret of the Treasure shall not perish with me." He pointed to a locket around his neck. "Hidden in this Scapular is the Treasure's location. If I perish prematurely, any of you will be able to locate it by examining the Scapular. Claude, you are our host. Please provide glasses for a toast with that wonderful vintage of La Frenaie that I brought from my private wine cellar."

Verdier poured wine for himself and the other twelve conspirators. Raising his glass, the Colonel shouted: "To the Treasure!"

The other members of the High Council echoed his cry.

The High Council had assembled at a remote retreat, the Villa Brossard that Claude Verdier owned on the edge of the forest of Chevilly. As the other members were preparing to leave in their coaches, Portal-Giraud took the Colonel aside. Verdier was outside making farewells to his guests.

"The defiance of Anne and Claude was intolerable, All-Father. Shouldn't they be eliminated?"

"Both are valuable assets to be preserved. Anne is outspoken, but she's loyal. She proved that last year. She's also the only member of the Council whose knowledge of poisons matches my own. Similarly, Claude is probably the most dangerous swordsman in France. Where else would I find such a formidable bodyguard? I am touched by your loyalty, my boy. When I die, you shall be my successor."

Once Portal-Giraud had left, Verdier re-entered the Villa. Removing the Scapular, the Colonel placed it inside a small iron chest. Carved on the lid were seven skulls and a dragon. The claws of the monstrous reptile held a golden sphere.

Verdier contemplated slaying the Colonel right now and stealing the Scapular. However, he remembered that the last attempt to slay the Colonel had led seven former Council members to their death only a year ago. Verdier had filled one of the very vacancies caused by that revolt. The Colonel was never to be underestimated. The duelist felt it prudent to make peace with his superior.

"All-Father, I apologize for my earlier imprudence. I should never have questioned your decisions."

"Your sincere repentance moves me deeply, my lad. Don't tell the others, but you have always been my favorite. I shall make you my heir. Now let us depart discreetly. I don't want any of our colleagues being tempted to purloin the Scapular."

Approaching the massive fireplace, Verdier touched a panel on the sculptured wood. The fireplace turned sideways and disclosed a stairway that led underground. Holding a sword-cane, Verdier descended, followed by the Colonel carrying the metal box. Behind them, the fireplace returned to its former position.

The duo navigated through a maze of ancient quarries. Eventually they reached the exit, a crevice inside a formation of ivy-covered rocks. In the moonlight, they spied a coach on a distant road that could only be reached by walking across an open field.

"Come, Claude," commanded the Colonel, "Lecoq is waiting with my coach."

"Surrender the Scapular!" shouted a man with a sword.

He lunged at Verdier, but the master duelist easily dodged the blow. Drawing his sword out of the cane, Claude went on the offensive. The Council member was clearly the superior swordsman.

Watching on the sidelines, the Colonel was expecting the demise of the unknown assailant when the unthinkable transpired. The intruder delivered a spectacular thrust that imbedded his blade right in the center of Verdier's forehead.

The victor disengaged the blade from the vanquished. The lifeless body collapsed at the Colonel's feet. The All-Father of the Black Coats viewed the wound between Verdier's eyes.

"The *Botte de Nevers*... The mark of Lagardère," he said with a shudder. "Who are you?"

"I am called *Trompe-la-Mort*, the Death-Cheater." The man extended his sword in a threatening manner. "If you don't wish to share your friend's fate, you'll hand me the Scapular."

"It's inside this locked box. Let me open it for you."

"Do you think that I'm a child, All-Father? You probably have a pistol inside. Hand me the box!"

Seizing the box with his left hand, Trompe-la-Mort pressed the tip of his blade gently against the Colonel's forehead.

"And now, how do I unlock it?"

"Press the dragon's head and the sphere simultaneously."

Withdrawing his sword from the Colonel's brow, Trompe-la-Mort did as instructed. He winced in annoyance as he pricked his thumb on a sharp carving inside the dragon's mouth. He lifted the lid. Inside was the Scapular alongside a pistol.

Suddenly, Trompe-la-Mort felt dizzy. He dropped his sword.

"You touched the dragon's fang," saidf the Colonel, softly. "It's coated with a poison derived from the black scorpion of India. This is one death that you won't cheat, Trompe-la-Mort!"

The bandit collapsed.

Jean Henry, the chief of the Paris police, had reassigned Monsieur Jackal to La Force prison, Supposedly incarcerated under his real name, Jackal's assignment was to gather information from his fellow prisoners.

One of the Colonel's phony charities was the Fraternity of the Merciful Redeemer. Its ostensible purpose was to preach Christian virtues to incarcerated felons. Its actual function was to allow the Colonel access to prisons under the guise of a lay preacher.

The Colonel conferred with Jackal in a private meeting room provided by the warden.

"Have you ever heard of a man called Trompe-la-Mort?" he asked.

"Yes. His real name is Jacques Collin. He's about 30. He earned his nick-name due to a talent for getting out of deadly scrapes. The man's a consummate egotist who lives for the admiration of his criminal peers. He fled France last year when he was falsely accused of forgery."

"Did someone make him *pay the law*?"

"In a strange way, he made himself *pay the law*."

"How so?"

"Collin is intensely loyal to his friends. One of his comrades, Franchessir_, was the actual forger. Collin pretended that he was the real culprit in order to protect his friend."

"Did he have any accomplices?"

"His aunt. Her name is Jacqueline. In her youth, she was Marat's mistress during the Terror. After his death, she romanced a chemist who was later exe-cuted for counterfeiting. She's only five years older than her nephew. They say she was very pretty in the 1790's, but now she's as ugly as an ape. In fact, I've never seen a more homely woman in my life! In 1806, she was sentenced to prison for two years for leading a prostitution ring."

"Where does she live?"

"No one knows. She just appears at opportune times to sell her wares."

"Which are...?"

"Poisons."

The Colonel laughed. "Forgive me, my boy, but I find that ironic since I just poisoned her nephew."

"Is he dead?"

"More or less."

When Trompe-la-Mort opened his eyes, his wrists encased in shackles high above his head. He hung suspended from his arms, with a gap of four feet separating his toes from the ground.

"So you're alive, my dear Jacques," observed the Colonel. "The venom of the black scorpion is quite unreliable. Sometimes, it produces a quick death. Other times, it throws the victim into a cataleptic trance. My last subject expired after two days in a coma. However, one other person was as lucky as you and awakened after three days. Actually, that was rather unlucky, since I slowly tortured him to death. I'm seriously considering replacinf that venom with a Brazilian drug called the 'Mato Grosso Pestilence.' Its cataleptic properties are more reliable, but it has the disadvantage of making its victims look like mummies. At the very least, I would want to remove that side effect. Perhaps I should experiment on you?"

"Are you trying to intimidate me with words?" replied Trompe-la-Mort.

"Yes, but clearly actions will speak louder." The Colonel signaled to a massive man holding a whip. "Toussac, teach this young lad to respect his elders. Five lashes will suffice for now."

Taking a position behind the prisoner, Toussac savaged the prisoner's back with the whip.

"Now, my sweet Jacques, let's talk business. How did you learn about the Scapular?"

"Marcel Draco recruited me a year ago. I was ordered to spy upon the Masters of the High Council still in Paris when he launched his revolt in Corsica. He told me about the Treasure. After his death, I swore to steal the Scapular. I would have tried last year, but a forgery investigation forced me to take a vacation in Spain."

"How did you discover the secret passage from the Villa Brossard?"

"Draco had identified you as the All-Father. I followed your coach on horseback. I saw you and your bodyguard leave the coach near a field at Chevilly. The two of you then entered the crevice. I guessed it was a subterranean entrance. I hid my horse, and waited for you and your friend to return through the same underground passage. It's a pity that I had to kill him. He was a decent swordsman."

"I'm more interested in another swordsman. About 100 years ago, there lived a rogue named Henri de Lagardère. He mastered a thrust invented by the great fencing master Delapalme. Lagardère had learned it from his friend the Duc de Nevers. It's been known since as the *Botte de Nevers*. That thrust slays its opponent by stabbing him in the center of its forehead. Legend has it that Lagardère documented that killing technique in a notebook. My poor dear Verdier was dispatched by you employing that *Botte*. You must have found Lagardère's notebook. Where is it?"

"You're wrong, All-Father. I invented that thrust myself."

"Liar! You were an obviously inferior fencer when you fought Verdier. Toussac, loosen his tongue with 20 more lashes!"

The brute followed the Colonel's orders.

"Why... do... you... want... the... notebook?" asked the prisoner,

"Finally, you admit its existence! Very well. I intend to recruit a bodyguard to replace Verdier. I want this replacement to be thoroughly schooled in the *Botte de Nevers*. Now, since I was kind enough to answer your question, my darling Jacques, answer mine. Where's the notebook?"

Slowly the captive muttered the address of an apartment in the Rue St. Claude. He indicated that the notebook was in a desk drawer.

"Lecoq will take me to the Rue St. Claude, Toussac," informed the Colonel. "I should be back in a few hours. You may amuse yourself with our guest in the interim. Play with him as much as you like, but don't kill him. I reserve that pleasure for myself. Know this, Jacques Collin, there are two supreme forces in the universe. One is God. He is good. The other is myself. I am evil."

"If you are the Devil, then your inevitable defeat has been preordained by God."

"You may wonder why, if God is omnipotent, he hasn't destroyed me long ago. You will learn the answer to that eternal riddle when I return."

After the Colonel's departure, Trompe-la-Mort's eyes focused on a ring of keys that dangled from Toussac's belt.

"I once knew a man named Toussac in Calais," revealed Trompe-la-Mort. "He was as strong as an ox. It took three men to kill him."

"He was my brother. I was serving as a quartermaster in the army when he died."

"Your brother once knocked me clear across a room."

Toussac chuckled. "I can do the same. Let me show you."

Toussac punched Trompe-La-Mort in the stomach. The captive swung backward.

"Your brother hit harder."

Toussac replied with another blow. Trompe-La-Mort swung further back.

"Your brother's punch was still harder."

After another blow, Trompe-la-Mort swung an even greater distance backwards. When the trajectory caused him to swing forward, he extended his legs upwards. They gripped Toussac's neck. The former quartermaster was unable to break the stranglehold,

"If I wasn't so weakened, Toussac, I would simply break your neck. As it is, I have no choice but to slowly throttle you."

Within a few minutes, Toussac expired. Trompe-La Mort's steadied the deceased giant with his right leg as his left hooked downward. Ensnaring the ring of keys, the prisoner's foot ripped it off the corpse's belt. Then, Trompe-La-Mort allowed the dead body to slump to the floor. The captive's foot flipped the ring backwards into the air. The keys landed in his hands. It didn't take long for Jacques Colin to unlock his shackles.

At the Rue St. Claude, the Colonel searched through a batch of skeleton keys. Eventually, he found one that unlocked the door to Trompe-la-Mort's apartment. Once inside, he quickly located the notebook. The pages stuck to each other. It was necessary to constantly lick his forefinger with his tongue. His moist forefinger was used to separate the pages. This method of reading left a bitter taste in his mouth.

The notebook was clearly genuine. It was filled with diagrams detailing the secrets of the *Botte de Nevers*. The last page was filled with a boldly drawn name in a different hand writing: "Charles IX."

The Colonel gasped. In 1574, King Charles IX of France has been fatally poisoned by a book, the pages of which had been coated with arsenic. They had been difficult to turn, forcing the monarch to lick his finger. The pages of Lagardère's notebook must have been doctored by Trompe-la-Mort with a virulent poison!

The Colonel felt weak. Vertigo began to overcome him. Through sheer force of will, he managed to reach his coach. There was only one person who could help him now. He had to go to the only member of the Black Coats with a knowledge of toxicology.

"Drive me to Anne de Breuil's house!" he yelled at Lecoq. "It's a matter of life and death."

The Colonel was in the bed of the guest room at Anne's house.

"I've given you drugs to increase your stamina, All-Father, but I fear that they are only delaying the effects of the poison. If only I knew what it was. It clearly wasn't arsenic."

"Trompe-la-Mort knows," gasped the Colonel. "Send Lecoq to Toussac's."

"Lecoq's already been there. Toussac is dead. Trompe-la-Mort is gone."

"Can't you examine the pages to identify the poison?."

"I would need to perform tests that might render the notebook unreadable."

"Do it! My life is more important than Lagardère's secrets."

Leaving the Colonel, Anne went downstairs to her laboratory. Inside were Lecoq and a shirtless man. The coachman was rubbing a salve into his companion's back.

"Do you feel better, my nephew?" asked Anne.

"Yes, your husband is an effective nurse," replied Trompe-la-Mort. "How is the Colonel?"

"I'm keeping him at death's door until we locate the Scapular."

"He's too dangerous to let him live. He called me Jacques Collin. He must know that I have a formidable aunt."

"What does it matter? I paid an ugly woman to go to jail for two years under my real name. Now I only call myself Jacqueline Collin when wearing a disguise that makes me resemble that she-ape."

"The Colonel isn't as perceptive as he imagines. For the last seven years, Jacqueline and I have been secretly married," interjected Lecoq. "The Colonel never suspected the truth. He thinks my wife was some poor peasant who died two years ago. False gravestones certainly have their uses."

"It was necessary to shed the skins of both Madame Lecoq and Jacqueline Collin in order to join the High Council," claimed Anne. "The name of my ancestor, Cardinal Richelieu's most accomplished agent, was an appropriate alias."

"I still think that you should have used our illustrious forebear's title of Milady de Winter," argued Trompe-la-Mort.

"Calling myself Anne de Breuil is more subtle, and it takes subtlety to outwit the All-Father. Our initial plan of a direct assault on the Scapular failed. Luckily, we had arranged a contingency plan involving Lagardère's notebook. That has succeeded more brilliantly than we had hoped."

"The late Marcel Draco was a convenient scapegoat, Aunt Jacqueline. The Colonel totally swallowed my lie about being employed by the Corsican. The old goat still views you and Uncle Aubert as his loyal supporters. He doesn't realize that you're really my accomplices in a scheme to steal the Treasure."

Anne was ecstatic. "The Colonel is at our mercy. We know that the Scapular is hidden in an iron box. We know the secret of safely opening it. The box must be hidden at his mansion. With the Colonel a bedridden invalid here, my dear husband is free to locate the Scapular without interference."

"When all the other servants are asleep tonight, I shall search the Colonel's house," promised Lecoq.

"I wish you could give my love to our sons," said Anne, "but it still remains necessary that they believe me dead."

That evening, Aubert Lecoq implemented the search. Touching a wall panel in the Colonel's bedroom, the coachman discovered a concealed alcove. Inside was the iron box adjacent to an old book entitled *Les Chroniques de Nemedea*. Perusing the book, he saw an illustration that resembled the iron box. It was next to an account of a bloodthirsty criminal who butchered his way across the ancient world. Doubtlessly, the Colonel modeled his iron box on the one encountered by this legendary killer.

Wearing heavy gloves, Lecoq touched the dragon's head and the sphere on the lid. His fingers scrupulously avoided the dragon's mouth. Opening the box, he grabbed the Scapular. He needed to remove his gloves to pry open the two halves of the locket. After examining the writing inside for ten minutes, Lecoq was consumed with disgust. He closed the locket.

"Papa, what are you doing in the Master's room?" interrupted a young boy in a nightshirt. It was Lecoq's four-year old son.

"Why aren't you in bed, my child?" asked his father.

"I had a bad dream. I dreamt Mama was in Hell. I went to wake you up. You weren't in your bed."

"So you wandered through the house to find me. Your mother is in Heaven with the angels. Where's your brother?"

"He's is still sleeping. Can I see that locket, Papa?"

Lecoq handed the Scapular to the younger of his two sons. Seated on his father's lap, the boy played with the Scapular. He opened the locket.

"What do these letters mean, Papa?"

"You see this word, my son. It's Hebrew."

"Is it the name of God, Papa?"

"That was what I thought until I saw this other word in Arabic. I don't know the language, but I've seen the Arabic script for Allah, the Islamic name for God. This Arabic word isn't Allah. Look at these other words: the Latin *nihil*, the German *nicht*, the English *nothing*, the Italian *niente*, the Spanish *nada*, and words in several other languages. Eventually we come to our own language. The word is *rien*. What does that tell you my son?"

"Nothing. All the words mean *nothing*."

"Exactly, my son. You must never breathe a word of this locket to anyone else during my lifetime. It shall be our secret. Promise."

"I promise."

"Now let me put this locket away, and then tuck you back into bed."

"Nothing!" screamed Anne de Breuil at her husband and her nephew.

"The Colonel has been lying to the High Council from the beginning," concluded Trompe-la-Mort. "He has no intention of sharing the Treasure with anyone. The Scapular is a sham. We are no closer to discovering the Treasure's whereabouts."

"Then, if we can't have the Treasure, we shall have revenge!" swore Anne. "I'll let the Colonel die from the poison eating inside him!"

"That would be foolish, Aunt Jacqueline. Let him live."

"Are you mad, Jacques? What good will that do?"

"It will allow us to build our own Treasure. I know the answer to the eternal riddle of God and the Devil."

"You're not making any sense," said Lecoq.

"Let me explain, Uncle. Your lovely wife here will provide me with details of all the criminals sentenced to the Toulon galleys due to the intervention of the Black Coats. Then, once the Colonel has recovered, she will…"

Two days later, a fully reinvigorated Colonel prepared to depart Anne's house.

"I shall never forget your successful treatment of my illness, Anne. Don't fret about the damage to the notebook. The *Botte de Nevers* is not essential to my plans. When I depart this world, my secret testament shall be read before the

High Council. You shall be proclaimed my successor. You will become the All-Mother."

"Let us worry about the here and now rather the hereafter, Master. There remains the matter of Trompe-la-Mort. He must be aptly punished for his attempt to kill you. May I make a suggestion?"

"Please do, my precious."

"Use Trompe-la-Mort as a stepping stone to advance the career of your protégé, Monsieur Jackal. As you mentioned earlier, your would-be assassin is wanted for the Franchessini forgery. Have Jackal use his sources at La Force prison to locate Trompe-la-Mort. The police will then arrest him. A threat will be removed, and Jackal's prestige will increase in the eyes of the authorities."

"Your proposal has merit, but merely sentencing Trompe-la-Mort to the galleys seems an inadequate revenge."

"Not if you make his life a living hell. It is within your power to drive Trompe-la-Mort mad. Jackal told you that this egotist lives for the admiration of his fellow criminals. Transform that admiration into ridicule. Let our agents in the underworld spread the news that Trompe-La-Mort allowed himself to be sentenced for another man's crime. Then, the other prisoners will view him as a fool. They will ostracize him. He'll become an isolated pariah in the galleys. Trompe-la-Mort shall descend into the depths of insanity."

"An incredibly subtle revenge, my love."

At La Force prison in early 1810, the Colonel conferred with Monsieur Jackal.

"Any progress in locating Trompe-la-Mort?" asked the leader of the Black Coats.

"Normally I follow the maxim of *cherchez la femme,* to trace a felon through the woman he favors. Our quarry, however, is different. He's a misogynist. He prefers male company. Therefore, I must look for a man."

"Did you find such a man?"

"Yes. A new prisoner told me that Trompe-la-Mort is currently infatuated with a youth named Alexis Ladeau. The police have placed Ladeau under surveillance."

"Excellent, my boy. If you continue to be so productive, you shall soon be in charge of all criminal investigations in Paris."

In response to the Colonel's praise, a smile appeared on the face of Monsieur Jackal, alias Eugène-François Vidocq.

The Colonel's prediction proved accurate. After his undercover operations at La Force concluded, the Ministry of Police allowed Vidocq to form a brigade of plainclothes detectives. In December 1813, the Emperor signed a decree transforming the brigade into a national police force henceforth known as the Sûreté Nationale, and placed under Vidocq's supervision.

A few days after the Colonel's visit to Vidocq, the police arrested Trompe-la-Mort at Ladeau's apartment. Under his real name of Jacques Collin, he was sentenced to the galleys at Toulon.

About three months after his arrival, Trompe-la-Mort met with six fellow convicts on the beach during a work break.

"I have revealed to each of you privately the details of your betrayal by the Black Coats. If anyone doubts my veracity, then let him speak up now."

The other convicts remained silent.

"We must band together to defeat the All-Father," said Trompe-la-Mort.

"That would be suicide," argued a convict called Fil-de-Soie. "The All-Father is as dangerous as a wild boar."

"Even a wild boar can be defeated by a pack of hounds," retorted Trompe-la-Mort.

"I have heard of such hounds," noted a prisoner nicknamed Le Biffon. "They are called *vautres*."

"We can be as formidable as a *vautre*," continued Trompe-la-Mort. "I earned my reputation as a death-cheater from being able to escape dangerous situations. Over the next year, I shall help each of you escape from this prison. Once outside, you shall commit the same sort of daring crimes that landed you here. You will be given instructions on how to contact my aunt. You will turn over your loot to her. For a small fee, she'll become your banker. You will be able to withdraw your money at any time."

"How small a fee?" asked Le Biffon.

"Ten percent of the deposit. That's not unreasonable."

Le Biffon grudgingly nodded.

"How do we know that you can and your aunt can be trusted?" objected another convict. "You could swindle us just as the Colonel cheats the other Black Coats."

"You know my story, Auguste," declared Trompe-la-Mort. "I'm here solely because I placed a friend's needs above my own."

"Some people would call you a fool," coldly observed Fil-de-Soie.

"Perhaps I am a fool, but all of you need someone incapable of betraying you in order to flourish."

"Let me understand this," interrupted Le Biffon. "We're on the outside, and you're in Toulon. What will you be doing here?"

"Recruiting other members for our Society. Once I've built up an organization, I'll escape myself. After all of you escape, I'll recruit others, men like La Pouraille and Bibi-Lupin."

"Don't recruit Bibi-Lupin." advised Auguste.

"Why not?"

"He hates you, Trompe-la-Mort. Bibi-Lupin thinks you, rather than the Black Coats, sold him to the police. He's been trying to turn the other convicts against you. His hatred is so intense that he might even inform the guards about our escape plans."

"Thanks for the warning, Auguste. I'll avoid Bibi-Lupin."

"If we're going to be a secret society, we'll need a name," suggested Le Biffon. "We're all men who aim high. I intend to deposit 10,000 francs with Trompe-la-Mort's aunt. If we all pledge to do that, we can be the Society of the Ten Thousand."

The name of the new alliance was approved unanimously.

That night in his cell, Trompe-la-Mort scratched the word *vautre* in the dust on the floor. He then wrote the name *Vautrin*.

"A fitting alias," muttered the man who would later become feared under that name. "You posed an eternal riddle to me, Bozzo-Corona. Why doesn't God destroy the Devil? I know the answer. God permits the Devil to exist in order to ensure an endless supply of worshippers. So long as the Devil endures, mankind will always seek God's protection against evil. Therefore, it's in God's interest to be locked in an endless conflict.

"There are now two competing forces in the criminal underworld. One seeks to cheat his adherents while the other protects his loyal followers. If you are the Devil, Bozzo-Corona, then I am God. Let our eternal stalemate begin."

We beg the reader's indulgence with this next story, a short-short that doesn't quite belong in Tales of the Shadowmen, *but is a crossover of sorts. The reason for its existence came from a discussion during which the undersigned expressed his desire to see more unexpected, even "oddball," crossovers, bringing together virtually incompatible characters, such as the one between Doc Ardan and the Little Prince that appeared in our Volume 2. As an example of such outrageous encounters, I mentioned, off the top of my head, without any forethought, Richard Matheson's classic horror short story "Born of Man and Woman" (published in* F&SF *in 1950 and reprinted many times since) and* The Wizard of Oz. *Once the challenge had been issued, I had to prove it could be met, and this is the result...*

Jean-Marc Lofficier: *Dad*

Bobo says, I must kill Dad. Dad, he brings another hoe today. That's how he says, but I don't know what a hoe is. Dad, it makes him laugh. He put her in the pit, like the others. I'm the one who dug the pit in the cellar. The walls are smooth. Once inside, you cannot get out. I am five, but Dad, he says I look fifteen. I am very strong.

I went to see the hoe in the pit. She is not like the others. She has pretty red hair. She looks like Mom. Mom, I did not know her because she died when I was born. But I've seen her pictures. Dad, he keeps a big book with pictures of the hoes and the results of his speriments. It is in a locked drawer, but I found the key. I am also very smart.

Bobo, he is my monkey. He is my best friend. Dad began his speriments on Bobo before the hores. It was full of tubes with blue, green and red liquids that he sinks into their belly with a needle, and after, he put his sausage in their bellies, and the hoes, they scream a lot. Dad, he goes, han-han-han, but he loves it. Sometimes I wonder if his speriments are not an escuse to dip his sausage. Once, after, Dad looked at me funny, he laughed and asked me if I wanted to dip my sausage too, but I started squealing. Because I can't talk.

The hoes, they all die after Dad's speriments. Except one who got all big. Dad was very excited. And then, little brother broke her belly with his claws and teeth, and she died too, and Dad eutanazed little brother. He was not pretty with all his scales. Except his eyes. He had blue eyes like the hoe. Later, Dad asked me to take the body to the Rock. Because I have a Gift.

It came when I was two. I went to the Rock. It's like a little island of black rock, lost in a sea of red liquid fire red. Dad, he says he don't know where the rock is, elsewhere or in my head, but it's useful to get rid of the bodies. He says that, with the Rock, the fuckincops won't find anything. And he laughs. I told Bobo of the Rock. He says it can't be the only place I can go. There must be other rocks but prettier. Where we could go and live, me and him. Because I suffer.

The new hoe who looks like Mom, she is nice. She begs me to get her out. All the hoes, they do the same, but I dare not disobey Dad, because he beats me with the electric thing that hurts. I squeal loudly when he beats me, it's like he go crazy. He calls me names I don't know, like mongolide, mutant... So I hide or I go to the Rock but I can't stay long because the air there, it feels like what Dad use to clean everything, and it's very hot. And I really hurt and I cry.

Glinda is the name of the new hoe. Yesterday, Dad pushed a new bright green liquid in her head and belly. Then he dipped his sausage. I cried a lot. I don't know why.

Glinda, she saw the Rock. Since yesterday, she sees like noodles of colors that twist around me. The one that goes to the Rock is a red. I can't see them too, but Glinda, she can. Bobo, he says that with her, we can find other places to go, Glinda, me and him. Bobo, he says that we don't need Dad. Bobo, he says to kill Dad. Glinda puts her hand on mine and looked at me. Now, her eyes are very blue and they shine. She's very pretty. I'm happy.

Tonight, I grabbed Dad and took him to the Rock and threw him into the sea of fire, like all the other hoes. Then Glinda, Bobo and I, we follow another noodle, all blue, all pretty. I take Glinda's hand, and Bobo take mine, and I push really really hard. And we got there. The soil is full of rose petals and the sky is very blue. And in the distance, there is a yellow brick road and a city made of green glass. It's very pretty and I'm sure people will be very nice. Now I am happy.

Nigel Malcolm is a new contributor to Tales of the Shadowmen. *His story is a suspenseful World War II vignette that brings together Harry Dickson (already encountered in Nicholas Boving's tale earlier in this volume) and Nigel Kneale's famous Professor Bernard Quatermass. The title is a line from the hymn "Come Down O Love Devine" written by Bianco of Siena...*

Nigel Malcolm: *To Dust and Ashes, in its Heat Consuming*

London, September 1944

Another moonlit night. London was apprehensive. Blackout was observed. The only people who were out were those who really had to be. Everyone knew where the nearest shelters were.

Then, there was a bolt of sheet lightning. A flying saucer appeared. And another. And three more. Gliding and whirring. Making a sound like a firework noise played on a crackling record. It sounded unhealthy. The six discs started in an incomplete "V" formation, and began to spread out.

Below them, urgent police and Air Raid Warden whistles started blowing. Warnings were shouted. Soon after, the air raid siren groaned into life.

The saucers started firing missiles onto buildings. They looked like conventional missiles, but often the only sign of a hit was a pile of metallic dust. They caused hardly any damage at all. Sometimes missiles would explode just after they were fired, causing a dust cloud into which the saucer would literally disappear.

This happened to the first saucer. It fired, a dust bomb exploded, and the saucer flew into it, never emerging. Fine metal grains snowed over New Oxford Street.

Nearby, Royal Air Force spitfires were taxiing along airfields, gaining speed. There were five airplanes, one of which was flown by Group Captain Victor Carroon. And elsewhere, in mission control, the five leading members of the Flying Saucers Investigation Unit (FSIU) were arriving to see what was going on.

The saucers continued their swift progress over the London skyline. One severed its way through one of the ropes mooring a barrage balloon. It fired at buildings, causing big explosions. Then it seemed to wobble off course and crash into the dome of St Paul's Cathedral, vanishing in a puff of dust. It left not even a dent in the roof of the building.

Flight Lieutenant Carrington, known to the others as Tug, flew after another saucer.

"Right, here you are," he said, as he aimed and fired.

He was a good shot. His missile flew over to the saucer and tapped it. The saucer exploded. It was strange, but these freak occurrences did occasionally happen.

"Sierra to Mission Control, target destroyed. Repeat: target destroyed. Over."

In Mission Control, the five investigators exchanged baffled looks.

"That shouldn't have happened," said Captain Boothroyd. Air Commodore Beltham unconsciously clenched his fists.

Tug flew towards another saucer, whirring over Shoreditch. It was taking pot-shots at the streets below, seemingly at random.

"Sierra to Mission Control, another target sighted. Over."

"Make sure you only clip this target. Over."

"Will do."

Tug fired at the saucer. It exploded.

"Now, that is peculiar. How can there be two lucky hits in one sortie?" he said.

Back at Mission Control, Beltham became agitated.

"Clip them I said! Not destroy them completely!"

"But the missiles are low in explosives. This makes no sense," said Boothroyd.

"Well, the instructions went wrong somewhere," growled Beltham, before being struck by a thought. "One of you is an enemy agent!"

"Oh, don't be..." Quatermass stopped himself from saying something insubordinate. "Boothroyd's right. We're virtually firing wooden logs at those saucers."

"It's one of you!" Beltham glanced wildly at the two scientists. "You're both German spies!"

The room froze. Everyone in the room was looking at Boothroyd and Quatermass.

Harry Dickson broke the tension.

"Steady on, Air Commodore. Remember that you selected these men yourself. Their references are impeccable," he said, calmly but firmly. "Besides, if they were enemy agents, they'd sabotage the spitfires, not destroy the saucers."

Beltham looked round at the rest of the room, realizing it was bad form to behave as he had done.

"Yes of course," he conceded, before glancing at Boothroyd and Quatermass and murmuring, "I'm sorry."

He was about to act on an impulse to leave the room, when the radio operator said:

"Group Captain Carroon reports one saucer left, sir."

"Where?" Beltham said.

"It's just over Vauxhall and heading towards Deptford. They're both flying rather low, sir."

Beltham looked at the others.

"Carroon's a good shot. He should be able to bring it down in one piece."

Over the rooftops of south east London, the last saucer raced along, nearly clipping the chimneys. Carroon, in his spitfire, was close behind, as low as he'd dare go.

"It's going to crash into a railway station. Over."

The saucer dipped downwards, and sliced into a Victorian School building.

"Target has crashed. Repeat, target has crashed. It is in one piece, over."

Moments later, Carroon was returning to base.

July 1944.

To the Prime Minister's office staff, reports of Unidentified Flying Objects appearing over Britain made for a sobering repost to the D-day landings.

There were Spitfire pilots encountering saucer-shaped flying craft over the English Channel. There were sightings over Aberdeen, Skegness, Hull, Cornwall and, increasingly, London.

One or two of these sightings could be dismissed as tricks of the light, or even as Battle Fatigue. But to senior staff in the British government, comprehensive sightings from reliable witnesses of flying disc-shaped machines could not be dismissed. In a top level meeting, the Prime Minister himself expressed concern at these possible visitations from aliens. He ordered the sightings to be classified as top secret. After all, public knowledge of aliens and their interest in Earth, and its war, could seriously undermine public morale and their Christian beliefs.

The others in the meeting quietly thought to themselves that this was quite a generous gesture from a one-time practicing Druid.

However, some eyewitnesses reported that these flying craft bore the mark of the German Iron Cross. This was what disturbed the military chiefs of staff most.

It was decided that a unit would be set up to investigate these "flying saucers." Air Commodore Lord George Beltham, fresh from D-day maneuvers (where he had been more active than most, to the point where his superiors virtually had to restrain him), was put in charge of the unit. He set about recruiting for it.

At the FSIU's top level, he recruited Captain Simpkins to act as his Chief of Staff, and Captain Boothroyd from the army's engineering division, where he'd gained a reputation for being a technical genius. He also recruited Professor Quatermass, a physicist from Cambridge University and an expert in rocketry and explosives. Finally, he brought in the retired consulting detective Harry Dickson, who was an expert in strange crimes and incidents.

Dickson insisted on drafting in a young protégé of his; a sergeant seconded from the Marine Police called Stanley Bulman. He seemed to think he showed a

176

lot of promise. As far as Beltham was concerned, Bulman was a young dreamer with little common sense, but he retained him to keep Dickson happy.

September 1944.

Half an hour after the crash, Beltham, Simpkins, Dickson, Bulman, Boothroyd and Quatermass were all driven to the site. The building was on Stanley Street. The saucer had just missed New Cross railway station and hit Mornington School, on the other side of the road.

The craft could not be seen from outside the building. The only sign of its presence was the short, wide hole in the front.

Simpkins talked to one of the firemen outside, who reluctantly allowed them to go in, providing it was for a short time, and they all wore their helmets. This concession met, and armed with torches, they all went in.

There, wedged into the floor at a forty-five degree angle, was a seemingly intact saucer. It was surprisingly small; about the size of two cars welded together.

"My nephew George would love one of these in his classroom," murmured Bulman, but nobody took any notice of him.

Beltham clambered over the stray rubble, stone and miniature wooden animals scattered on the floor, past the children's paintings pinned to the walls. He walked up to the side stabbed into the ground. He looked like he was squaring up to an opponent, even an arch-enemy.

He kicked it, savagely.

His foot went straight through the rim. It was as though the saucer were made of cardboard. If it weren't for the quick reactions of Simpkins and Bulman, who were standing just behind him, Beltham would have fallen straight in.

As the Air Commodore wrestled their arms off his, Boothroyd and Quatermass both crouched down and shone their torches on the hole left by Beltham's foot.

"This metal is so brittle, and yet it must be, what, aluminum?" said Quatermass, with a trace of excitement in his voice.

"It must be as light as aluminum, certainly. The hull of the craft is quite thick too," said Boothroyd, equally fascinated.

Dickson walked round to the other side, shining his torch onto the ground. There was a beach of silver dust spread across the floor. It was difficult to tell where the saucer ended and the dust beach began. Then he realized what it was.

"The dust is the decomposed saucer. They don't emit the dust, they *are* the dust," he exclaimed.

"Well, they vanish into it," said Bulman. "But what about the flash of light when they disappear?"

"*Spark* of light," Quatermass corrected him. "It is the discharge of energy as it dissolves. However they appear, it clearly doesn't do them any good."

Dickson pointed his torch at the saucer's body.

"There are burn marks all over. This craft has been through extraordinary heat," he observed.

"It would have to be going implausibly fast to get those," said Boothroyd.

"And yet, it wasn't going so fast that a spitfire could not chase it," murmured Dickson.

"It looks like it's based on a whole new method of sp..." said Bulman, stopping himself from saying something that would have been too fanciful in front of this group of rationalists. But Dickson knew what Bulman had meant to say, and responded to that remark:

"Space travel, indeed."

The pause that came after it gave Bulman the idea, or maybe the encouragement, to express it:

"Of course. If it were capable of space travel, it could be capable of space-warp. It would get here much quicker. That's how they appear out of nowhere."

"Space-warp travel... yes..." said Quatermass, thoughtfully.

"That's preposterous," said Boothroyd.

"No, no, I think Sergeant Bulman is on to something," said Quatermass, as plaster began to crumble around them.

"Later—Run!" shouted Dickson, and everyone scrambled out of the Mornington School as its roof collapsed and the walls gave way.

Moments later, the building was just another bombsite.

Within an hour, the six men were sitting around the table in the FSIU's makeshift meeting room, drinking mugs of tea and trying to stop shaking, either from nerves or the cold night.

"So, Professor, what were you saying earlier about 'space-warp travel'?" Beltham asked.

"Space-warp travel. It wasn't my suggestion, it was the Sergeant's," replied the professor, who then turned to Bulman. "Where did you get the idea from? Do you read science journals?"

"No, actually," said Bulman, rather shyly, "I read it in a science fiction story by Isaac Asimov."

There was an awkward silence, broken by Quatermass.

"It's only a theory. At least, the scientific community knows of it only as a theory. Maybe the Nazis have made it a practical reality."

"What exactly is it?" asked Beltham, more testily.

"Yes, how can I explain it?" replied Quatermass. "Imagine a spider crawling along a blanket. It would take that spider a long time to get from one side of the blanket to the other. Now, if someone were to come along and fold the blanket so that the end that the spider's on met the opposite corner, then the spider

178

could simply climb from one edge to the other. Then, when the blanket is un-folded again, the spider has traveled from one end to the other. It has only walked a small way itself, but it has traveled a vast distance."

"But that's not possible," argued Boothroyd.

"Oh, it is, according to Einstein's theories. Space is warped, you see. One could travel from one place, disappear from there, and reappear in another place entirely."

"So," said Dickson, "space does not 'fold over' exactly like a blanket, there are some... holes where the saucers go in, and then they come out of another hole in an entirely different place, many miles away?"

"Yes."

"Or maybe the spider would just get squashed by the blanket," said Boothroyd, drily.

But in the split-second pause, realization dawned on everyone in the room, including Boothroyd, whose eyes widened.

"Folding the blanket *does* squash the spider," said Bulman, with wonder

"Yes. The metal is so traumatized by space-warp travel that it turns metal to dust," said Dickson. "And no doubt does the same thing to the unfortunate pilot. They leave their base, presumably somewhere in Germany. The craft pass-es through a threshold and ends up in London. That may also explain why sau-cers were sighted over other parts of Britain, but are now exclusively over Lon-don. The Germans are refining the process, learning how to aim it more accu-rately. However, it is sheer fluke that flying saucers have survived the journey at all, and they don't survive for long. Hence the erratic flying and shooting. Hence also their total destruction when our pilots give them a glancing blow with a low-explosive content missile."

"Yes, I see now," said Boothroyd, reluctantly.

Quatermass' mind was on other things.

"Imagine if the technology could be made successful. Why, a space craft could make impossibly long journeys within moments. It could reach the Moon, or any planet in the Solar System. It could even go beyond!"

Beltham, who had remained silent through all this, listening, struggling to keep up, finally spoke to rein in the professor.

"Now steady on, Quatermass. We're still on planet Earth, and we need to study this technology for this war," he said, sharply.

Quatermass fumed. "A stupid, idiotic war," he growled.

"But it's still a war and we've got to win it," said Beltham. "From now on, we will develop our own version of space-warp aircraft. I'll get on to the Air Ministry first thing tomorrow."

"But sir, space-warp technology doesn't work safely," said Boothroyd.

"Then *make* it work safely, Captain Boothroyd. Then, when we've con-quered space-warp travel, and Germany, then the professor and the sergeant can indulge their... science fiction fantasies. Dismissed," said Beltham, getting up and leaving the meeting.

Quatermass managed to restrain himself until the Air Commodore was out of the room.

October

Quatermass used his university contacts to find and talk to experts in space-warp technology. There weren't that many in Britain. However, he drove up to Oxford to talk to a young man with a beard that had never been trimmed, who gave him one or two bits of useful advice.

The rest of Boothroyd's team got to work putting this (mostly theoretical) information into practice. They assembled what Beltham decided should be three machines.

Supplies were scarce. Boothroyd acquired bits of equipment by calling in favors, bartering, and even cannibalizing other machines, including a couple of radars that he bought off a spiv in Shoreditch who told him that they were "army surplus." The Captain wasn't convinced, but he bought them anyway after a brief examination. "After all, Needs must when the Devil drives." he later grumbled to his staff.

Quatermass developed a new respect for the captain. His practical skills, not to mention his talent for converting ordinary and—from a military point of view, mundane—objects into something that had an entirely different purpose. He even once joked that Boothroyd "could turn an ordinary wristwatch into a transistor radio." Boothroyd, without any irony, just seemed to think that was a very good idea.

Meanwhile, Dickson and Bulman used army intelligence and police sources to pinpoint the precise timings of the appearances and disappearances of the flying saucers, in search of any discernible pattern. In the end, though, they concluded that there was no pattern, and the saucers came on moonlit nights when their development was right.

"Either they will develop a method of making the saucers space-warp-proofed, or they'll abandon the project," said Dickson, in a staff meeting.

"Then we must develop a way to make 'space-warp-proofed' saucers first," replied Beltham.

Work progressed over the next few weeks. The Air Commodore pushed his team further and further, driving them all relentlessly.

November

Dickson was making his way to the workshop having just returned from a meeting at Scotland Yard. He passed Beltham's office.

"Dickson!"

Harry stopped. He retraced his steps to the office, where the door was open, and the Air Commodore was shouting down the phone.

"I don't care about El Alemein. We won't win the war with that sort of complacency. We've got to crush the enemy. Just get on with it!"

He slammed the phone down.

Dickson started filling his pipe, whilst looking at the phone. It got slammed down quite a lot.

"That Bulman of yours," said Beltham to Dickson, "I heard him saying insubordinate things about me behind my back. I want him out of the FSIU. I'm informing you first."

"What *insubordinate things* has he said, precisely?"

"Something about calling me *Captain Ahab,* or some such nonsense. I want him off the premises."

Dickson lit his pipe, thoughtfully. "Captain Ahab, eh? Why do you think he called you that?"

"It doesn't matter, Dickson. It's insubordination. It's a bad show."

"Because...?"

Beltham paused for a moment. "Alright, I know I may push the team quite hard sometimes, but there is a war on."

"And you want justice."

"I want respect from my juniors."

"You want justice," repeated Dickson. "From what I have seen of you since I joined this unit, I deduce that your war with Jerry is personal. That's what drives you, isn't it?"

"Not wanting to live under a Nazi regime is what drives me."

Dickson puffed on his pipe. "You have lost at least one person dear to you in this war. Maybe others in the last one too.?"

"Don't use your observation and deduction nonsense on me!"

"But I am right though."

This seemed to stop Beltham. He sat down. For a moment, his hard features softened and he looked tired.

"Yes. Yes you're right. I lost a brother in the Somme. And my son, Alexander, died in the Battle of Britain."

"I'm sorry."

"I have no other children. It's just me now. I am the last of a long, noble line of Belthams going back to William the Conqueror."

Dickson hoped that his sympathetic silence showed enough respect. However, he also quietly reflected that George's father hadn't been considered very noble amongst those who'd met him.

"All right. Bulman has one last chance," Beltham conceded.

Dickson nodded, gratefully. "I'll have a word with him, but he is an asset to this unit. I firmly believe that he'll go on to greater things. And someone will need to pick up the pieces after the war."

He made for the door.

"Where on Earth did you find him?"

"Read the *Verner* file at the Admiralty," said Dickson at the door, "Bulman was very helpful during what Tom Wills likes to call *The Incident of the London Bridge dynamite, the miniature submarine and the trained monkey.*"

The three machines, christened "warp-closers" by Boothroyd, were assembled and stood side by side on the floor of the hangar. The team of engineers were clearing away the tools and preparing for the arrival of trucks to take the three warp closers to their respective destinations.

Boothroyd, meanwhile, stood by the middle machine, which looked like a radar dish mounted onto a bulky tripod and with what looked like a cumbersome aeroplane dashboard fixed to the opposite side to the dish, with knobs and switches on it. They had thick cables attaching them to motor generators. The three contraptions looked like a mad scientist had become a rogue RAF engineer and had tried to build some sort of "radar gun" or three. That wasn't too far from the truth.

In front of him were the five principle members of FSIU, and a troupe of army soldiers.

Boothroyd began his crash course in how to actually work these contraptions: "Now pay attention, men. To activate the warp closer, press this switch here. The knob and dial next to it here controls the strength of the ray. Begin on minimum and work your way up *gradually* if you judge that more output is needed. This big dial here reverses the process. That may be extremely important. All the machines are pre-set to the same frequency. Any questions? Good, off you go!"

The three warp-closers were distributed to strategic parts of the city. These were north, south and east of central London, where flying saucers were most expected to come. Fortunately, Regent's Park, Hyde Park and Greenwich Park were convenient open spaces in which to set up the machines

Beltham split the FSIU into three teams. Captain Boothroyd led a small team in Greenwich Park; Professor Quatermass lead another, similar team in Regent's Park; Bulman led the team in Hyde Park, overseen by Dickson when he wasn't busy with other work commitments.

Beltham and Simpkins generally oversaw the whole operation, shuttling between the three parks, the FSIU HQ, and the War Office.

All they had to do now was to wait for the next fleet of saucers.

January 1945

In more or less the middle of Hyde Park was the river Serpentine, part of which was a boating lake. On one of its banks stood the wooden clubhouse. A barrage balloon was tethered 50 yards away. About 150 yards further away, a large army tent was standing on higher ground.

On such a crisp day, the park was only populated by a small number of dog walkers and exercisers. Meanwhile, Bulman's team; including the Sergeant himself, were pacing up and down. They were all stamping their feet and rubbing their hands in an effort to keep warm.

Suddenly, there was a crackle of lightening over the clubhouse. The cold was forgotten about.

The saucers came.

The team, including Bulman, hesitated for a moment, surprised. No one expected the invaders to appear quite this close. But then they sprang into action. Four men pulled back the covers of the tent to reveal the warp-closer machine. Bulman rushed to the controls and switched it on.

He pointed the machine in the direction of the sheet lightening. By this time, four saucers had appeared and were gliding over the Serpentine.

As the machine hummed into life and gradually powered up, Bulman took a moment to stare at these new saucers. They were different this time. The previous saucers had looked like they'd been built in this world. These new ones seemed to have been made out of an entirely new material with an unfamiliar bright red shiny texture. They were unearthly.

He realized that, whether these were Nazis or aliens, or even both, they had perfected space-warp travel, and would more dangerous than ever.

The ray from the warp-closer made the lightening in the sky rip open with a piercing scream of nature. A fifth saucer had just emerged. It seemed to stop in mid-air, wobble and then be dragged back into the white tear.

A sudden gust of wind seemed to blow all the trees and plants in the direction of the white tear. But then Bulman realized, as his colleagues staggered to stay standing, that the gust was *sucking* them towards the tear.

He realized he had to reverse the ray's effects. He powered down the machine and twisted the reverse dial.

Starlings, sparrows, pigeons, ducks, geese, evergreen tree leaves, twigs and dead branches were getting sucked in. The river Serpentine stretched upwards into a reverse-waterfall.

Bulman switched on the machine again and continued to point it at the tear. He wondered why it wasn't powering up. He glanced frantically at the motor generator, which was dead. A fuse had blown.

He knew all was lost. He admitted defeat as his feet left the ground. He was reminded of a boyhood dream of flying as he travelled towards the infinite white.

As the reverse waterfall turned into a stream, the clubhouse broke up and scattered upwards.

Four red saucers were enough. And their missiles, also shiny red, were far more effective. One saucer destroyed Victoria Railway Station in four shots.

Meanwhile, nearby, amid the air raid sirens and civilians running for cover, Beltham and Dickson were being driven to the War Office. They saw the red saucers up in the sky.

"Why hasn't that blasted idiot fired at them?" murmured Beltham, pensively.

They watched the new saucers. Their movements in the sky were more assured than the previous steel ones. But he saw the answer to his question in the streaks of cloud and smog in the sky, centering on Hyde Park.

"We'll have to leave the saucers to the RAF. We need Quatermass' machine. Go straight to Regent's Park, driver."

"Yes sir."

The driver immediately turned the car round in a single, swift movement and sped into the nearby road.

A saucer fired at a tall building in full sight of Beltham and Dickson. It blew up in a spectacular fireball reaching through its windows.

"These ones are clearly more effective," said Dickson.

Meanwhile, the Air Force was mobilized. Spitfires approached the saucers and began firing at them. But the new red discs seemed almost impervious to ammunition. Captain Carroon and his men realized very quickly that they had a much more difficult fight on their hands than before. Especially when one of the planes was shot by a clean missile, causing it to crash into Harrod's.

It was Dickson who spotted a truck with Quatermass' warp-closer coming in the opposite direction. Evidently, it was on its way to Hyde Park on the professor's orders.

With his own unique genius he'd mounted both the warp-closer and the motor generator onto the back of an army truck, bolted down to prevent them coming off. This way, the warp closer could work whilst moving. Boothroyd had reacted first with apoplectic dismay; then with horrified fascination and finally quiet enthusiasm as his mind seemed to be designing an improved version of a mobile warp-closer.

Unfortunately, Boothroyd, and his warp-closer, were too far away across London to be of any help now.

Beltham and Dickson flagged down the truck, and everyone got out to talk to each other. The white tear was about half a mile away. Everyone could feel its pull, like a strong gale. They were all just in time to see a spitfire and a red saucer, both wobbling around each other in a dogfight, get sucked in.

The professor gasped. "It's appalling... and..."

"Concentrate man!" shouted Beltham, above the sound of the wind. "What's happening? You're the expert."

"The threshold has become a void. It's sucking everything into it... the air... everything is being sucked into oblivion."

"Yes, well we can all see that," said Beltham.

"Will it die down, Professor?" asked Dickson.

"There's no way of knowing," said Quatermass. "It could get bigger. It could suck in the whole planet," he repeated, horrified.

"Don't talk rubbish, that's impossible," said Beltham, trying to convince himself more than anything else.

This turned Quatermass from horror to anger.

"Look at it with your own eyes. Does that look impossible to you?" he roared "You see what your obsession with warfare has done? Nobody ever *wins* a war. Won't you ever get that into your thick head? Nobody."

Dickson interjected: "Save the recriminations until later, gentlemen. Now, Bulman used..." he was suddenly hit by the notion that Bulman was almost certainly dead now. "Bulman used the setting you and Boothroyd gave him, didn't he. What if the process were reversed?"

"Yes. Yes I see," said Quatermass. "Well there's no other solution available. It's our only hope."

Beltham, on hearing this, left his two colleagues and struggled through the strong winds over to the truck.

"Once I'm on the back, start driving towards the void," he ordered the bewildered NCO.

Dickson and Quatermass hurried over to follow him, but Beltham was on the back of the truck, banging on its roof. It sped off, past them and their protests.

Beltham stood astride on the back of the truck, balancing himself perfectly on the rattling vehicle. He reversed the dial, switched on and powered up the warp-closer. It hummed into life. At least the wind was behind him rather than against him.

Soon the truck went into Hyde Park itself, with little effort from the driver, who was just trying to keep it steady under these conditions. By now, the driver's foot was mainly on the brake pedal.

Beltham continued to point the machine straight at the void. His peaked cap had been dislodged and gone on ahead of him, but he used all of his strength and physical dexterity to keep the warp-closer pointing directly at the tear.

The truck was now sliding over the grass. The white tear was shrinking. The stream stopped flowing upwards.

As both he and the machine were ripped off the truck and up into the air, Beltham felt peace. Oneness. This was the place where his troubles seemed to evaporate. He'd always known he would die in the air.

As Beltham and the warp-closer flew into the tear, it was about half the size of a car.

Of the three remaining saucers, Tugg Carrington managed to shoot one down over Buckinghamshire. It crashed, but it remained solid and the pilot survived. The other two evidently tried to fly back to Germany the conventional way. One saucer was shot down over Kent. That pilot also survived. The other saucer was discovered in Dieppe, where evidently its pilot had made a forced landing, before trying to sabotage the craft and disappearing into hiding somewhere in the local area.

Over the next few hours, the tear healed up completely. All the city smog and smoke was gone. The air in London had not been this clean since the first Roman settlers. And all that remained of Hyde Park was grass. Every tree, plant and living creature had gone. However, the river Serpentine was slowly refilling from its underground source. It was already a shallow pool.

And on the dip of earth where the clubhouse had once stood, Dickson, Quatermass and Boothroyd were now standing. Reflecting on what had happened, and that many members of the FSIU had perished, not just its leader. They'd all liked Bulman, and mourned him each in their own private thoughts. They'd also begun to see Beltham in a new light, now that he'd sacrificed himself.

"Of course it's highly feasible that the void was sucking in objects from the other end to," said Boothroyd, breaking the silence.

"Yes, it's highly likely," said Dickson. "Their equipment would have perished. We've probably seen the last of those saucers."

"Good," said Quatermass decisively. "When this war is over, and I develop rockets for space travel, they'll go to the stars the long way—through space. No short cuts. Space-warp technology is far more trouble than it's worth."

With that, he walked briskly away. He was soon followed by his two weary colleagues.

Australian writer David McDonald has taken to chronicling the adventures of Harry Paget Flashman's son, whom he introduced in "Catspaw," published in Tales of the Shadowmen 8, *and reused in "The Girl from Odessa," in* Night of the Nyctalope. *In the latter, Harry met Leo Saint-Clair, the Nyctalope, and in the former, his father, Jean Saint-Clair. After being in the French Navy, Jean became a Foreign Office diplomat and, quite possibly, a secret agent. Here, Harry teams up with Jean again to investigate the strange events originally narrated in Charles Derennes' ground-breaking 1907 "lost world" science fiction novel,* The People of the Pole *(also available from Black Coat Press), hence the title of the story...*

David McDonald: *Diplomatic Freeze*

Somewhere over the Arctic Circle, January, 1907

Clouds of sleet and snow howled far below, causing Jean Saint-Clair to shiver despite the warmth of the cabin. He stood on a sheet of perfectly clear glass which took up an entire wall and stretched along the floor a good six feet into the room, giving him a far better view of what lay beneath than he might have wished for. It had taken a considerable amount of time to get over the feeling that he could fall at any moment, but he was not the sort of man to give in to any challenge, and he had steeled himself to stay there until the sensation passed. Now, he found the view almost soothing, patterns of cloud forming and dissolving as they raced by beneath him.

"Dammit!" A loud voice rang out behind him, and Jean turned, his relaxed mood evaporating.

"What is the matter now, Monsieur Flashman?" Jean asked, trying not to let his exasperation show.

His cabin was spacious and well appointed, all leather and brass fittings, designed for comfort. A large four-poster bed nestled against one wall, while at the end, furthest away from the window, was a cluster of comfortable chairs and a long bar set up to entertain the occupant's guests.

"That appears to be the last of the brandy! What sort of bar is this?"

The speaker was a study in contrasts with Jean. Where Jean was of average height, with a compact build, Flashman was tall and broad-shouldered. Instead of a neatly trimmed goatee, the younger man had luxurious whiskers, moustache and sideburns with a clean shaven chin. His pale skin had a slightly ruddy hue, which went some way to explaining where the brandy had gone.

"It's not a bar. It's a diplomatic mission," Jean said. "But I do seem to recall that they stocked a generous amount of brandy, amongst other things. I don't think that they were expecting someone of your," he paused, "appetites."

"Bah," Flashman scoffed. "I've never been on a diplomatic mission where there wasn't more than enough booze to go around. Political types like their victuals; it's a well known fact." He took another sip. "Speaking of facts, I am still a little shaky on why I am here, old chap."

"As our governments are allies, my superiors felt it was only appropriate to invite someone to represent His Majesty on this little expedition, and they trusted my discretion. You were my first choice." Jean smiled. "After all, we worked together very well during that business in Afghanistan, no?"

"Very flattering, I'm sure," Flashman said. "But, that isn't what I meant. What is the point of this expedition? I've been looking out the windows and all I can see is snow and ice. What embassy could we be visiting this far north?"

"*Sacrebleu!*" Jean exclaimed. "You cannot be serious! Were you not listening during the briefing?"

The other man stared at his glass, as if to avoid meeting Jean's eyes.

"To be honest, I wasn't paying attention; all these diplomatic missions blend into one another after a while. Anyway, there was a young lady who wanted to know about my adventures in Congo last year," Flashman said. "So, I was a little distracted."

Jean shook his head. "Well, this is like no other diplomatic mission I have been on."

"How so?"

"It is no human government that we have been sent to treat with."

Flashman coughed and spluttered, choking on the last mouthful of brandy.

"Not human?" he asked when he had caught his breath. "I have seen enough strange things in the past few years to know that all sorts of misbegotten creatures walk the Earth, but I have never seen anything capable of forming its own government."

"Neither have I, *mon ami*, but when Professor Valenton speaks, my superiors listen. And, when my superiors speak..."

"Yes, I know, ours is but to do or die," Flashman snapped. "But..."

Whatever Flashman had been about to say died on his lips as the cabin lurched and the floor dropped out from beneath their feet, sending them stumbling and bottles crashing from the bar. Flashman managed to throw out a hand and grab the edge of the bar for balance, but Jean was left teetering, what had been a level floor now a treacherous slope. Just as he fell, he felt a fingers like iron pincers take his upper arm in a vice-like grip, steadying him.

"There you are, sir, I've got you."

Jean swore under his breath, startled. He could never get understand how such a big man could stand so quietly and unobtrusively that his presence could be forgotten, or move so quickly and silently.

"*Merci*, Monsieur Ballantine."

"Ballantine is fine, sir, and it's my pleasure. Can't have you getting injured before we even get there!"

There was still more than a hint of the Highlands in the big man's voice. He stood a good head taller than Flashman, and his massive shoulders spoke of vast strength. He had a bluff, good-natured face, but Jean had seen the Scot in action and knew what he was capable of. Memories of a desperate fight against monstrous foes were cut short by another lurch as the cabin righted itself.

"Well, Ballantine, Monsieur Flashman, let us see what is happening."

Jean strode purposefully to the cabin door and threw it open. There was a muffled squeak and fluttering cloud of papers, as a shadowy figure recoiled in shock.

"Marcel! *Excusez-moi, s'il-vous-plait!*" Jean said, kneeling to help gather up the scattered documents. "I was in a hurry."

Marcel combed a greasy fringe of hair off his forehead with his fingers and blinked watery eyes.

"*C'est de ma faute, Monsieur Saint-Clair!*" Marcel said, then noticed the other men. "Oh, I am sorry! English is better, no? It was entirely my fault, Monsieur, I was concentrating on the reports you asked for."

Jean smiled. The young man might not look like he had ever set foot outside of a library, with pale skin and hunched, narrow shoulders, but he was conscientious to a fault and worked hard. To Jean, that covered a multitude of sins.

"No harm done! Now let us see what is causing all this fuss," Jean said.

As the four men walked down the corridor, Jean could not help but admire the craftsmanship that had gone into building the immense vessel in which they found themselves. No expense had been spared: the walls were lined with rich wood paneling and trimmed with gleaming brass. The air was a perfect temperature, reminiscent of a glorious summer's day in Paris. It was hard to believe that the winds outside were cold enough to freeze a man's flesh solid in seconds.

At the end of the passage was a set of doors made from riveted steel, a guard to either side, carbines held at the ready. At the sight of Jean, the right-hand guard pressed a button and the doors slid open, revealing a flight of stairs leading down. Even the stairs were opulent, with a brass handrail and lush carpet to prevent anything as bourgeoisie as slipping and falling. Soon, though, they were through the upper level and the stairs became more functional, a cage of bare metal that spiraled down to the floor of a vast hangar. As they descended, they could look out over the three huge turbines, each the size of a small cottage, which provided both thrust and the power that kept the lights burning and air warm.

As he reached the floor, Jean moved out towards the starboard turbine where a group of men had gathered around and were busy removing the paneling. One of the men looked up and hurried over.

"Monsieur Saint-Clair! What brings you down here?" Sweat shone on the man's brow, and he hurriedly wiped it off with a greasy cloth, unmindful of the streaks it left behind. "I assure you, we have everything under control."

"Relax, Foreman Gasson, I have the utmost faith in your abilities," Jean said. "I merely wanted to see what had caused the problem, but I am certain that you are already dealing with it. I am not one of those men who try and tell those more qualified how to do their jobs."

"It is simply one of the couplings, perhaps half an hour to repair. The other two turbines can compensate indefinitely, we built in a large margin of redundancy."

Despite his reassuring words, the foreman seemed uneasy. Making an excuse about wanting to see how the gauges on the far wall worked, Jean drew him aside.

"Is there something else bothering you. Monsieur Gasson?" Jean asked.

"Well, Monsieur, the coupling... it could have perhaps been wear and tear, but I checked them myself before we left."

Jean felt a chill. "You mean... We might have a saboteur on board?"

The look on Gasson's face was answer enough.

When it came, the landing was so simple as to be an anticlimax. As the airship had approached the coordinates Professor Valenton had provided, Jean had moved to the control room, watching through the window and making conversation with the pilots. Gradually, the light had begun to change color, shifting to a soft violet glow that suffused the cabin, giving it an unearthly appearance. Slowly, the vessel began to descend, the clouds parting to reveal a circular clearing in the snow, perhaps half a mile in diameter. It appeared to be made of some dull, grey metal and despite the blustering winds it was completely bare. Any snow that fell would simply disappear a foot above the surface.

The chief pilot, a veteran of many years, coaxed the airship into position, fighting the winds until they were hovering directly in the centre of the circle. Jean could feel it shuddering beneath him, like some great nervous beast ready to stampede. There was a soft clunk that echoed through the hull, and the motion stopped as everything went completely still.

"What happened?" Jean asked.

"I am not sure, Monsieur," the senior pilot answered. "Something seems to be holding us steady. Should I abort the landing?"

"No, please continue," Jean said. "I believe that we are expected."

The airship settled down with barely a jolt, and the pilot sounded the siren that signified that they had landed. Jean hurried down to the landing platform where he found Marcel, Flashman and Ballantine waiting for him alongside a company of soldiers bearing the distinctive green epaulettes and flaming grenade badge of the Foreign Legion.

"Thank you, corporal, but you won't be required," Jean said.

"Monsieur?"

Jean gestured at the other three men. "The four of us will be sufficient."

"*Sauf votre respect,* Monsieur, you can't go out there alone. Who knows what is out there waiting?"

Flashman stepped forward.

"Jean, surely it won't hurt to have them along."

Jean shook his head.

"This is a diplomatic mission, remember? What sort of message would it send to bring along troops?" He smiled at Flashman. "Besides, with you and the good Sergeant by my side, there is nothing to fear!"

Flashman muttered something under his breath, but Jean chose to ignore it.

"Shall we, gentlemen?"

Jean led them to a set of lockers, and they began to prepare themselves for the harsh environment they knew they find outside. There were thick woolen pants and jackets, with the latest in innovations, copper bands woven through the fibers that were warmed by a light electric current. Knee-high boots with snow spikes that could be retracted or extruded by the flick of switch rounded off their ensemble and once they were all fully dressed Jean pulled down on a lever and the doors slid open, a ramp extending to the cold ground. Without hesitation, he marched down, the others following behind him.

Even with the thick woolen clothing, the wind had a chill bite to it, tendrils of air trying to worm their way through the layers of clothing to the flesh beneath. Jean had expected the metal to be slick and treacherous beneath their feet, but instead, it provided surprisingly sure footing. He paused for a moment, unsure of which way to go, unable to find his bearings through the dense flurries of snow all around them. As if sensing his hesitation, the metal surface began to emit a low hum and a glowing red arrow appearing, pointing away from them. Beyond it another appeared, then another, creating a path that led out into the snow where, even as they watched, a path of the same metal was rising from the drifts.

"It appears we were expected," Flashman said. "Let's just hope that they are friends."

Jean felt a flicker of fear at the thought of what might lie ahead, but then took a look back at the airship that had transported them to northernmost part of the world. It was the biggest vessel that had ever been built by mankind, larger than the greatest passenger liner, and just as luxurious. It had transported them in warmth and comfort over the most inhospitable and deadly of terrain, following a route that had claimed the lives of countless explorers. It represented the culmination of the finest technology and the greatest minds of his land, and there at the prow fluttered the tricolor. Jean felt a swell of pride that it had been France who achieved this marvel, and a fresh resolve. How could he fail his nation now?

He straightened his shoulders and led on, the others trailing just behind. They followed the path for a little over a mile before it came to an end, melding seamlessly into the base of a sheer cliff of black volcanic rock. Some ancient glacier had scrubbed it clean of soil and vegetation, leaving it bleak and lifeless. Flashman walked up and placed his hands against the rock, pushing.

"Well, that was a waste of a walk," he said. "What do you say we head back and see if I haven't overlooked a crate of cognac?"

Before Jean could answer, there was a muted rumble and a seam appeared in the cliff face. Slowly, a huge piece of rock slid across revealing an archway easily the height of three men, and twice the width. The four men looked at each other, and then stepped through into wonder. The whole mountain must have been hollowed out and carved into a veritable city of platforms and walkways. Vast pillars of stone reached up, their tops fading into darkness before they reached the ceiling.

As far as the eye could see, they teemed with white figures going about inscrutable errands. It reminded Jean of some great nest of insects, scurrying about as they fulfilled whatever imperative drove them. The travelers has not gone unnoticed though, as Jean watched a party of about a score broke free from the mass and headed towards them. Soon, they were close enough to make out their features.

"By Jove, they are hideous. What in blazes are they?" Flashman said, far too loudly.

Jean shushed him. "If you had been paying attention to our briefing you would know. They are the lizard people of the Pole and, our governments hope, soon to be our allies."

"Lizard people, sir?" Ballantine asked.

"Just like we are of mammalian descent, evolved into thinking, rational beings, these are the descendants of the great lizards that once roamed the Earth." Marcel's voice had a strange intensity to it. "Another intelligent race, with their own government and their own secrets…"

"Marcel is our resident expert. He is the Sorbonne's foremost linguist, and has studied the papers that Professor Valenton discovered. I hope that he will allow us to communicate and come to an understanding with our new friends," Jean said.

The creatures were almost upon them and Jean had to fight to keep his face composed. The lizard-men stood on two legs, more like a thicker version of those of the ostriches he has seen in his time in Africa than those of a man's, with three toes that sprouted vicious looking claws. A long thick tail thrust out behind them as if for balance, while two strangely jointed arms seemed to protrude directly from their chest with no need for shoulders, ending in three delicate fingers. It was their faces, though, that had given Jean pause. The same pallid white shade as the rest of their body, they had no discernible ears or nose, merely holes in the skin that flared at odd intervals. A lipless mouth extended almost from ear hole to ear hole, opening to reveal razor sharp teeth and a forked, flickering tongue. Folds of skin bunched at their throat, in some cases hanging down to their chests.

The two groups stood staring at each for a moment, neither moving. Then, to Jean's surprise, Marcel stepped forward, palms extended in a peaceful gesture. He began to make strange hissing sounds, punctuated by low grunts.

"We appreciate the courtesy, but we are fluent in both English and French." The voice was strange, but not unpleasant, with odd sibilants. "What would you prefer we used?"

Marcel seemed frozen in shock at their unexpected knowledge, so Jean shook of his own surprise and stepped forward.

"English, if you please," he said. "Sadly, not all our party speak French as well as Marcel and I speak English. But, how is it you speak our tongue so well?"

The creature let out a low, gurgling hiss as the skin at his throat ballooned in and out, and Jean wondered if it might be laughing at him.

"Please, follow me and all your questions will be answered."

Jean Saint-Clair had served his country with distinction for almost three decades, and had traveled to the four corners of globe on sensitive mission after sensitive mission. He had lost count of the throne rooms and audience chambers in which he had found himself. He had seen all manner of sights, from the Peacock Throne of Persia to a keep in the depths of Mongolia where a war chief had sat on the contorted bodies of his conquered foes. But nothing he had seen could have prepared him for this.

The audience hall was easily the size of the airship, and could have held hundreds, if not thousands, of the lizard-men. But, for the moment, it was deserted save for the four humans and a mere handful of the reptiles. Jean and his companions stood in front of a raised dais, warily watching the lizard-men standing before, six to either side of a vast throne. They were bigger than the other lizard-men they had seen so far, and held weapons that, despite their strangely curved design, were obviously guns of some type.

Even though they were deep inside the mountain, there was no shortage of light. Dotted at perfectly intervals along the walls were white domes the size of a soup tureen that emitted a soft white light. Normally, Jean would have been wondering what its source was, but instead he was trying to take in the amazing sight that surrounded him.

The soft light was caught and thrown back a hundredfold by the gems that encrusted every surface of the chamber. Rubies the size of his fist jostled for space with diamonds worthy of royalty, while pearls and sapphires cascaded in abstract patterns. That much wealth should have been garish, but what at first seemed mere random placement was perfectly designed to show off each stone to its best advantage and capture the eye in a soothing whole.

"By Jove, would you look at that," Flashman whispered in Jean's ear. "I have never seen the like, not even in the Raj's palace."

"It is beautiful, *n'est-ce-pas*?" Jean replied.

"Beautiful? Perhaps," Flashman said. "But, I was thinking if a man could grab even a few of those stones he would be richer than Croesus, and set up for life."

Jean looked at him aghast, hoping he was joking. How could anyone be unmoved by such a sight? His thoughts were interrupted by the guards on the platform stiffening, standing to attention and bringing their guns across their chests in what looked like a salute. A door opened in the wall behind and the left of the throne and three figures emerged and made their way to the throne. The middle took a seat, while the others took position to either side.

The three figures had nothing in common, each with their own disticnt appearance. The one to the right was taller even than the guards and wearing black, velvety robes that were inscribed with strange silvery runes that made Jean slightly queasy to read. As Jean watched, the figure reached up and pulled back the hood that had covered its face. While still reptilian, it resembled a snake far more than a lizard, even to the cobra-like hood that flared to either side of its head. Glittering eyes fixed on the humans, and a forked tongue flicked out as if tasting the air.

The figure seated on the throne was one of the lizard-men, but wizened and bowed under the weight of years. The folds of skin under its chin had drooped almost to where a man's navel would have been, and the pallid white of its flesh was streaked with veins of green. Upon its brow rested a light circlet of gold in the shape of a lizard curled around to bite its own tail, while the throne on which it sat was carved from a massive chunk of black obsidian into the shape of a monstrous reptile. Outstretched wings cast shadows across his silk robes, and the statue's mouth roared in frozen rage.

But, it was not these bizarre figures that were the centre of the men's attention. Instead, it was the one on the left. He, too, was clad in silken robes but that was where the resemblance ended. He was no lizard, but a man of average build and perhaps the same age as Jean. Before Jean could say anything, one of the guards stepped forward, and puffed up the folds of skin beneath his chin.

"All hail King Vendrak!" The skin must have acted as a natural amplifier, because the words boomed out, echoing from the walls. "Son of Gendrak who was son of Varlar who was son..."

"Enough." The figure on the throne waved its hand wearily and the guard subsided with an almost sulky look, moving back into formation. "I am sure our guests do not need to hear my full lineage. Let us dispense with the formalities quickly, please, make your introductions."

It seemed that the audience would be conducted in English, but Jean was more than fluent and at least Flashman would be able to contribute if needed. Jean hoped that would be a good thing.

He stepped forward and cleared his throat. "Thank you, your majesty. I am Jean Saint-Clair, and these are my companions Marcel Gioja, Major Flashman and Sergeant Ballantine. I am empowered to speak on behalf of the Republic of France, while Major Flashman speaks for the British Empire. We are here to discuss a possible alliance between our peoples."

"I see. This is my vizier, Bal'sa'zar," the snake like figure nodded, but did speak, "And my advisor on human affairs, de Venasque."

"I am glad to hear rumors of your demise were unfounded, Monsieur de Venasque," Jean said.

"You found my documents, I presume?" de Venasque asked. "I wondered whether they would ever find their way back to what used to be home."

Jean noted the past tense, but decided to ignore it.

"They did, but the ending, well… It left us thinking that the writer was no longer with us."

"It was a close call in the end. I had been wandering in the snow for days," de Venasque said. "I had given up hope. The last thing I remember was thinking I would close my eyes for a moment before I pushed on. The next thing I knew, I was warm and lying in a bed covered in blankets. The fact I was in a cell didn't register for quite a while."

"A cell?" Flashman asked. "They locked a man who had nearly frozen to death in a cell?" His moustache was quivering with outrage and he didn't seem to care what the lizard-men thought. "Hardly seems civilized to me!"

"Monsieur Flashman, all things considered, I would not have blamed them if they had put me down like a mad dog." At Flashman's incredulous look, he went on. "My companion, Ceintras, there was something about this place, or something that already festered within him, it drove him crazy. He did some terrible things."

"Yes, unlike Monsieur Flashman, I read your account," Jean said. "It was no wonder they locked you in a cell."

"I've been to many so called civilized nations that would have tarred me with the same sins as my companion, and held me accountable for his actions," de Venasque said, "but the lizard people showed mercy, and nursed me back to health. To show my gratitude I offered King Vendrak my services as an advisor on human affairs."

"And he has been a loyal servant, though he does have a tendency to talk too much," Vendrak noted drily. "What brings you to my kingdom, humans?"

"After the discovery of Monsieur de Venasque's papers, my government, along with those of our British friends, with whom we share the *Entente Cardiale*, resolved that we would extend the hand of friendship so that humans and, er, lizards might mutually benefit through the sharing of technology and resources," Jean said. "We are empowered to reach agreements in principle in matters of trade."

"By which you mean that you hope to make us allies against the German Empire and discover if our technology might be used to develop new weapons?" The vizier's voice was sibilant and cold.

Jean opened his mouth to speak, but the king cut him off.

"Do not take me for one of the savages you are used to treating with, Monsieur Saint-Clair. Our civilization was ancient when your ancestors were still wearing stinking furs and painting on cave walls," Vendrak said. "Monsieur de Venasque has told me much of the political realities of the human world, and we have our own methods for discovering more of what we need to know."

"Your Majesty, you mistake our purpose," Jean said. "We are here to seal a bond of friendship between our peoples, a relationship from which we both stand to gain."

"That remains to be seen. It would be premature of me, and an ill service to my people, to sign an agreement with the first humans to arrive, especially as we only need to wait."

Jean felt his heart sink. "What do you mean?"

The vizier stretched its lips in what Jean assume was a smile.

"Even now, the humans who call themselves the *Deutsches Kaiserreich* are on their way, and the Russian Empire will not be far behind," it hissed. "His Majesty will wish to hear their offers too."

Jean fought to hide his anger. He was not overly concerned by the news of the Russians; they had long been on good terms with France, and he had even heard rumors of an approaching agreement between them and their old foes, the British. But, the Germans were another matter entirely. They had been rattling their sabers for years, and seeking a military advantage. So far the *Entente Cordiale* had matched them gun for gun and ship for ship, but the lizard people would throw a dangerous unpredictability into the equations.

"Your Majesty, surely Monsieur de Venasque has told you of the militarism of the Germans, and championed the cause of his homeland?"

De Venasque stirred at his name. "I have taken no sides, merely given impartial facts. The lizard people have my loyalty now, not any human nation."

"He's gone native, what?" Flashman whispered. "Jolly bad show."

Jeans shushed him and continued. "Let me explain why we are your natural allies, Your Majesty, please."

"No, I am sorry. I will hear your terms when the other nations are represented," the king said. "I have spoken. You will be shown to your quarters. They are well stocked with every necessity and you may remain there, or wander the lower levels as you please."

Jean opened his mouth to argue, but, before he could, the detachment of soldiers stepped down from the dais and surrounded them.

"Follow me if you would, sirs," one of the soldiers said. It was marked out from the others by a more ornate weapon, which Jean presumed was a symbol of rank.

For a moment, Jean thought Flashman might refuse, but instead, he only muttered under his moustache, and fell in behind Marcel and Jean, the sergeant following him as the humans were led from the chamber.

Jean woke with a start, stifling a cry at the terrible, hairy visage that hovered over his face. He realized he was staring at the whiskered face of Flashman.

"Jean, are you awake?"

"*Oui*, I am awake," Jean yawned. "But why? It cannot be morning already!"

"It's Marcel, sir, he is gone." Ballantine was standing by the door, a concerned look on his face. "I woke just as the door was swinging shut. We need to go after him now if we are going to at all."

"But what could he be up to?" Jean asked. "He has many fine qualities, but I would not have picked him as the adventurous type."

When they opened the door, Jean realized that he might have been wrong about Marcel. The two guards that had been posted at their door were lying in slowly growing pools of blood, their throats neatly and expertly cut.

"Looks like they bleed just as red as we do, Jean," Flashman said. "Guess we have something in common after all."

Ballantine had already started moving down the corridor. "This way, sirs, he is leaving tracks."

They hurried after him, moving deeper and deeper into the building. Every few hundred feet or so, they would come across another slumped body. Jean shook his head. How could he have been so blind? Marcel had seemed so mild-mannered, as far from a man of violence as Jean could imagine. Jean wondered who he was working for. The Germans? The Russians? The Japanese? He shrugged; it could be anyone, but right now, they had to stop him before did any more damage.

As they followed hot on Marcel's heels, Jean noticed that tunnels they were traveling through were growing steadily more ornate. Rich tapestries woven from thick fur or glossy scales cascaded down the walls, while sculptures of pure gold or silver perched on intricately carved pedestals. Jean wished they had time to stop and admire them, their inhuman beauty enthralling to even the most casual glance.

Jean was so distracted that he almost crashed into Flashman as the Englishman came to a sudden halt. Ahead of them the passageway formed a t-shape, ending in a massive reinforced metal door. At its base were the corpses of two guards in rich ceremonial armor, clutching clubs gilded with gold and silver leaf. Jean realized what had been niggling at his mind: all the guards had been armed with clubs.

"Why aren't they carrying those guns we saw in the audience chamber?" Jean asked, not really expecting an answer.

"Well, sir, I can think of two reasons," Ballantine said. "First, this place is stuff-full of a king's ransom and I'd hate to be the poor soldier that put a hole in some priceless bit of loot. Secondly, and more importantly, I wouldn't want to be firing off shots in an enclosed place like this, miss and the ricochet might kill you or chum instead. Remember that battle in the caves under the Khyber Pass, Major Flashman?"

Flashman shuddered. "I've been trying to forget that for years now, Sergeant."

"Well, it certainly made Marcel's job easier," Jean said sadly. "I dread to think what we will find behind the door, but waiting around won't help."

Just as he lifted a hand to push the door open, the sound of footsteps echoed from the right hand passage. A crowd of lizard-men came hurrying towards them, at least twenty, clubs clutched in their trifurcated hands.

"I think we might be in a spot of bother, old chap," Flashman said. "But, whatever Marcel is planning can't be good, you have to stop him."

"What about you?"

"We will do our best to keep them off you until you can deal with Marcel, and hopefully convince them that we have nothing to do with his insanity." Flashman's face had gone red, and Jean knew that meant he was working himself up to something.

"You are a brave man, Monsieur Flashman," Jean said, placing his hand on the Englishman's shoulder. "I hate to abandon you like this, but you are right, Marcel must be stopped."

Flashman smiled and went to draw his sword, but Jean placed his hand over the hilt.

"You must not kill any of them. Too much blood has already been spilled."

For a moment, Jean thought Flashman would argue, but then he nodded his head.

"Hear that, Ballantine? We somehow have to stop these bunch of lizards without hurting them too badly," he paused and grinned, "and without letting them kill us, of course."

"Right you are, sir." Ballantine picked up a club and tossed it to Flashman, who gave it a few experimental swings.

"It's not quite a cricket bat, but it will serve. Did I ever tell you that I taught Ranji how to play the leg glance?" Seeing the look of incomprehension on Jean's face he hurriedly went on. "Ballantine, are you going to grab a club?"

Ballantine shook his head and held up his hands. As he clenched them into fists, they cracked and popped. Jean started at them; they looked almost as big as his head.

"I don't need the club, sir," the big sergeant said. "Especially not since the formula."

Jean remembered the change he had seen the huge man go through years ago in Afghanistan and shuddered. Twenty lizards would not be enough, he actually felt sorry for them. He patted the other men on the shoulder and walked to the door, stopping briefly for one more look.

"Once more into the breach, eh, Ballantine?" Flashman shouted as the pair waded into the crowd.

Despite knowing the urgency, Jean could not help but spend a moment watching the other men fight. It was a study in contrasts, their styles complementing each other perfectly. Flashman was a born swordsman and he wielded his club like a wand, getting inside his opponents swings or diverting their blows with a flick of his wrist. Instead of wild swings of his own, he struck out with delicate jabs, striking at vulnerable places like the midriff or knees.

Where Flashman radiated a sense of control, Ballantine was simply terrifying, more like an avalanche than a man. His muscles had swelled unnaturally, ripping his shirt and jacket open at the seams, and he was roaring unintelligibly. As Jean watched, the sergeant simply picked up two of the lizards, one in each hand and threw them effortlessly back into the ranks of the lizard soldiers, sending them scattering like skittles.

Flashman looked over his shoulder and saw Jean still standing there.

"For God's sake, Jean, go! We will hold them as long as we can."

Jean turned and pushed open the door revealing a scene from nightmares. It was obviously a bedchamber, with a huge bed like structure at the far end. Between there and the door, though, were several bodies and the wreckage of furniture. The king stood at the end of the bed, watching unflinchingly as Marcel advanced on him, a wicked looking knife held in each hand.

"Very brave of your servants to give their lives for you, your majesty," Marcel said. "Such a pity it was in vain."

"Not if I can help it, Marcel."

Jean had barely finished his sentence by the time Marcel had whirled to face him, throwing one of his knifes in one fluid motion. Fast as he had reacted, it was not fast enough, Marcel's eyes widening in surprise as Jean's cane flicked up, sending the knife clattering into one of the stone walls with a shower of sparks.

"Not bad for a man of your age," Marcel said, a mocking sneer in his voice. "Never mind, this should be fun. For me, not you, of course."

He drew another knife and, quick as a snake, launched himself at Jean. Jean back-pedaled, trying to keep the knives away from him, but the assassin seemed to be everywhere at once. His knifes wove intricate patterns in the air and, and, despite the superior reach of his cane, Jean could barely block Marcel's darting strikes. Questions of how and why and who went unasked as Jean focused all his attention and energy on simply staying alive. Marcel could see the desperation on Jean's face and his smile grew wider as he pressed his advantage. Suddenly, he stumbled, the smile draining from his face.

In his overconfidence, Marcel had forgotten to be aware of his surroundings and, as his foot came down near one of his victims, the dying lizard had latched on to the human's calf, jagged teeth cutting through sinew and flesh. As Marcel screamed, Jean took his opportunity. Faster than the eye could follow, his cane cracked into Marcel's right wrist, sending the knife flying. With an extravagant twirl, Jean sent the cane spinning back the other way, smashing into the fingers of Marcel's left hand. Before the knife had even hit the floor, Jean jabbed the cane into the other man's temple, sending him crashing to the ground.

He had no time to savor his victory, though, before there was a commotion behind him. Jean turned just in time to see Flashman and Ballantine come tumbling through the door, slamming it shut behind them. The sergeant immediately began to toss furniture in a messy pile against it.

"Jean, we are in trouble! Reinforcements have arrived, along with that cursed snake-man, and there are too many for us to fight with being forced kill someone," Flash gasped. "I hope you are in a   particularly persuasive mood today as this is going to take a lot of talking to get out of."

Catching his breath he looked around, and seemed to notice the wreckage for the first time.

"Gods. What happened here?" His eyes widened as he noticed the king. "Your Majesty! Are you alright? Please, accept our assurances that we knew nothing of this."

The king walked past him, towards the door. "Fortunately, Monsieur Saint-Clair has proven that in the most convincing fashion. However, too many of my people died first, and I will get to the bottom of this and find out who is to blame." He reached Ballantine and waved him away from the door. "I should call off my troops before there is any more death, and then we will deal with the murderer."

"You are wasting your time. There is nothing you can do to me that will make me talk."

Marcel was sitting in one the few chairs that had survived the struggle in the king's bedchamber, securely fastened with strips torn from the sheets. They had not wanted to take any risks so he was almost completely cocooned in the material, only his head uncovered. The vizier had joined them and, along with the other humans and the king, stood staring down at the would-be regicide. Despite the fact he had no chance of escaping and could expect no mercy, Marcel appeared unconcerned and had not shown a trace of fear.

"Oh, I don't know about that," Flashman said. "Ballantine and I picked up some nasty tricks in the jungles of Borneo. There was this particularly painful thing you could do with bamboo. I don't suppose you have any bamboo handy, Your Majesty?" He trailed off, perhaps realizing the absurdity of what he had just asked.

"Torture will not be necessary."

Jean felt a rush of relief at the vizier's words. He had no stomach for torture, nor, he suspected, did Flashman; the Englishman's words mere bluster.

Bal'sa'zar stepped forward, and stared directly at Marcel who returned his gaze unflinchingly.

"You will not get any information out of me, snake," he said. "Whether you torture me or not."

"Snake? You say that if that is an insult, human, but my lineage stretches back further than you can imagine. When your ancestors were rodents shivering in the shadows of the dinosaurs, we had built a civilization greater than any of these so called nations. We ruled Valusia until the coming of Kull and his people. I am ten thousand-years old and an initiate of the Serpent God." He reached out and placed a hand on either side of Marcel's head. "You will answer our questions and answer them truthfully."

Bal'sa'zar stepped back as Marcel let out a high-pitched scream and slumped forward. When he looked back up, his eyes had a slight green glow.

"I will answer your questions."

"Why, Marcel? Why would you kill all these people?" Jean shouted. "Who sent you? Why are you here?"

"I serve the Black Coats. They sent me to ensure that no treaty would be signed with the lizard people."

"The Black Coats? Who are they?" Flashman asked.

"We are the ones who work in the shadows. We are the greatest criminals the world has ever known, and our reach knows no limits."

Despite his mind-altered state there was still a note of pride in his voice.

"But why did you wish to prevent an alliance?" Jean asked.

"My master knows there is a war coming, a war the likes of which the world has never known. In the chaos, there will be many opportunities for the Black Coats. My master does not wish any side to possess an advantage that might end it quickly," Marcel said. "He instructed me to try and delay your expedition until the other nations could catch up."

"The sabotage!" Jean said. "But why all this murder? Why try and kill the king?"

"I was to wait until the other delegations were here if I could, but I decided I could not risk you coming to an agreement first. Either way, I knew you would have been blamed and the alliance would never happen, not with any human."

"And, who is your master?" Flashman asked. When Marcel didn't answer immediately, he repeated himself. "Your master, I command you to tell us!"

Marcel moaned and began to shiver. Slowly, the capillaries on his face began to burst, painting red lines on his skin. As they watched, horrified, blood began to ooze from his pores, until finally blood began to spurt from his eyes and nose and ears. He let out one last gurgling scream and then collapsed against his bond. They didn't need to check for a pulse to see that he was dead.

"A spell to prevent him saying too much," Bal'sa'zar said. "I knew that might happen, but his life was forfeit anyway."

Jean wrenched his eyes away from the gory sight.

"What happens now, Your Majesty? Shall we wait for the other delegations?"

"No, you will leave tonight."

"What?" Jean asked.

"I want you gone from my kingdom before the sun rises." The king's voice was heavy, but full of authority and resolve. "The other delegations will be turned away. We want nothing to do humans, any humans. All they do is bring death with them."

"Now, look here!" Flashman's moustache was quivering with barely suppressed rage. "We just saved your life!"

"I know. That is the only reason I am letting you leave alive." He turned his back on the humans. "Now, go, before I change my mind."

Jean watched the snow and sleet far below, just as he had on the way to the realm of the lizard people. That time had been different, though; he had been full of high hopes of forming an alliance. Now, he was headed home having failed his mission.

"Cheer up, Jean, the mission wasn't a complete failure." Flashman's cheery voice drifted from the bar at the other end of the cabin.

"How so, Monsieur Flashman?" Jean struggled not snap at the other man. "I can't think of much else that could have gone wrong."

"Think about it. We may not have gotten an alliance with the lizard people, but nor will anyone else," Flashman said. "It's simply back to the status quo. And we know now of the Black Coats, and we can work on eliminating them as a threat."

Jean was surprised that he actually felt a little better; the Englishman was right.

"Very true, Monsieur Flashman," he said. "But, I am afraid this mysterious master of Marcel's is correct, there is a war coming and I think it will be a long and terrible one."

"I am not much of a God botherer, Jean, but there are two Biblical truths that spring to mind."

Jean was intrigued at the thought of Flashman quoting Bible verses.

"Yes, Monsieur Flashman?"

"The first is 'Sufficient to the day is the evil thereof' and the second is "Eat, drink and be merry for tomorrow we die'" Flashman said. "Yes, there is a war coming, I can feel it. But, all we can do is worry about today, and try and enjoy it. Speaking of which, I did find some more brandy. You should have some."

Jean laughed and walked towards his friend. They would need to deal with the Black Coats someday soon, but today was not that day. Today, he was with friends, and he would make sure he enjoyed it, and store up that feeling against the dark days ahead.

Chris Nigro picks up the challenge of the Treasure of the Black Coats; but his story is also a sequel to Kim Newman's "Angels of Music" series (from Tales *of the* Shadowmen 2 *and* 4*) and Chris' own tale, "Patricide," from* Tales *of the* Shadowmen 8*. In a clever set-up devised by Kim, the Phantom of the Opera is shown to secretly control an agency not unlike a proto-*Charlie's Angels, *always using three lovely "Angels of Music" as his operatives—but never the same girls twice. Previous "Angels" have included Elizabeth Doolittle, Rima the Jungle Girl, Gigi, Trilby, Irene Adler, Brianna Warren, Helene the Daughter of Fantômas, etc…*

Christofer Nigro: *Death of a Dream*

Paris, 1931

The tramp known to many in the seedy neighborhoods bordering the Right Bank of Paris as Bouzille, after his similarly iniquitous father, leaned against the side of a severely dilapidated building, awaiting an important arrival. In his left hand was a sealed envelope that he concealed within a pocket of his untidy stolen jacket; in his right hand was a small dagger that he was prepared to use to the best of his ability to kill anyone who may attempt to take the envelope. The contents were too valuable not to risk life and limb to prevent it from being stolen, as the fate he would suffer were he to lose the information it contained before the proper messenger arrived was utterly unthinkable. The severe beating, or relative quick death, he might suffer in an attempt to defend the envelope from common street thugs was but a pleasant dream compared to what Erik would do to him—and slowly—should he be unfortunate enough to survive losing the letter. This degree of fear and loyalty to the personage known in terrified whispers as the Phantom of the Opera, one of the deadliest assassins in Europe, was soon to be put to the test.

"*Excusez-moi,* Monsieur," came a young-sounding voice from the open end of the alley, startling Bouzille. "*Pardonnez-moi* for noticing, but you appear to be standing in a way that suggests you have something of value. Let me see what it is."

Bouzille turned to confront three menacing looking young men wearing the distinctive jackets of the Sons of the Red Hand, a brutal street gang of younger men who modeled themselves on the infamous Red Hand criminal organization, in the hope that their activities would lead to their being welcomed into its official ranks. The leader brandished a razor-sharp stiletto at Bouzille, while his two confederates displayed a long chain and a bludgeon.

This is wonderful, the tramp thought with fearful irony.

"I have nothing of value to you," he defiantly replied to the gang leader, letting him see the dagger in his hand so they would know that he would not be easy prey. "You play at being one of the real contenders in this great city; yet the true Red Hand regularly overlooks your existence due to its sheer insignificance." He gave them a rough laugh, followed by an involuntary cough. "But know that I am here on business for the *Angel of Music* himself. Interfere with that, and you will spend the last few hours of your miserable lives in his torture chamber."

The leader of the gang looked at his two partners, and all three erupted in laughter.

"Is this a fact, you filthy little bum?" the leader asked as he inched closer to Bouzille. "You truly expect us to believe your obvious lies? That *you* are of any significance to the likes of... *him*? A disgusting excuse for a man like yourself, who cannot even afford his own coat?"

Bouzille smiled, exposing a mouth full of yellowed teeth.

"You, my young friend, are just too naïve to consider the possibility that much of how I present myself to the world is a ruse to cover my true importance."

The gang leader laughed again.

"Oh for sure you are! Now, show me what is in your pocket or I will cut you open like a raw fish..."

As Bouzille stiffened and prepared for the fight of his life, the gang leader's threat was suddenly cut off as the business end of a large dagger was suddenly plunged into the back of his neck and clear through the front of his throat. He spewed a torrent of blood all over Bouzille's coat before collapsing into a bloody heap on the ground.

"*Sacrebleu!*" one of the other gang members shouted as he raised his bludgeon.

He turned to find himself standing eye-to-eye with a tall young blonde girl clothed in a leather outfit wrapped tightly around her shapely figure. Her expression was one of great anger as she eyed the wooden weapon he had raised.

"Drop the weapon and flee, or share the same fate as that pathetic leader of yours," she said in a soft but stern voice.

Reacting more from instinct than anything else, the young man attempted to club the young lady before him, only to suffer great agony as she effortlessly blocked his arm, dislocated his jaw with a vicious elbow thrust to the side of his chin, and kicked him in the solar plexus, sending him flying several feet backwards into the side of the alley, where he landed at Bouzille's feet.

Ever so efficient, these lady warriors of Erik! Bouzille thought with a satisfied smile. *And they do arrive right when they are needed, too. He trains them so well in the combat arts that I wonder what other skills of theirs he nurtures...*

The uncouthly-clothed tramp beamed again as he watched the fallen body of the young ruffian writhe in agony at his feet, blood dripping from his mouth.

"You little bitch!" the remaining gang member shouted as he lifted his chain and began whirling it in preparation for cracking the skull of the blonde vixen standing before him.

Before the young woman could act to dispatch this last opponent, a slender hand grabbed the gangster's wrist and thrust a syringe into his head, just behind his left ear. The young man's eyes rolled back into his head, and he collapsed, his consciousness taken away by the chemical just introduced into his blood-stream.

"Now, now, that wasn't a very nice thing you wanted to do to Mizzeia," said another, even younger blonde woman, with a surprisingly well-endowed bust for her age, who spoke in a distinctly American accent.

She was attired in a white outfit clearly designed to highlight her assets as a distraction for any male—and doubtlessly, a few appreciative female— opponents she may encounter.

"Trust me, it's in your best interests that I sent you to visit that Nemo kid in his Slumberland than to let you face Mizzeia directly on."

"Damn you a thousand painful impalements, Ellen!" Mizzeia shouted at her fellow blonde companion. "That fool threatened me; he was mine to deal with!"

"Oh, cease your complaints, *mes amies*," said a third woman with long, wavy strawberry blonde hair who stepped into the alley. She was dressed in a gray outfit reminiscent of a female cat thief. "You got more than your share of fun by dispatching two of these miscreants, whereas I didn't get to neutralize even one of them. Ah, *c'est la vie,* I suppose."

"You be silent too, Josephine Balsamo!" shouted Mizzeia, pointing her index finger at the new comer. "Did Erik tell us that we each get to take one down, or simply to accomplish our objective as efficiently as possible?"

"Not to sound rude, Mizzeia, because that uncivilized kingdom you once ruled obviously left you with some serious power issues, but you do not put your finger in my face like that ever again, *compris*?"

As the angry Amazon of a hidden kingdom in the Himalayas gritted her teeth, Ellen stepped in and defueled the growing metaphorical flames.

"Ladies, I know girls will be girls and all that, but we have a job to do here, and ripping each other to shreds isn't part of it," the buxom young blonde said as she lowered Mizzeia's hand and stood between the two.

She then turned towards Bouzille, kicking aside the still flailing body of the injured gang member.

"Greetings, Monsieur Bouzille," Ellen said, holding out her hand. "The envelope, please? And also, be a dear and keep your eyes pointed towards my face and not my chest, or I may have to adjust your posture for you."

Grinning impishly, Bouzille excused himself as he placed the envelope in her hands.

"Like you girls, I am nothing but efficient in the service of Erik."

"Then you had best hope that the information in this letter is accurate, or you will see exactly how efficient he can be in the art of blood-letting."

"That, I already know," Bouzille replied, "and rest assured that the sources from which I acquire this information haven't failed me yet, just as I have never failed the Phantom."

"You had best keep things that way," Ellen said with a smile, as she handed a wad of banknotes to the tramp as payment for the info.

A second later, she and her two partners-in-carnage turned and disappeared into the darkness of the streets.

Deep within his comfortable living quarters ensconced in a hidden tunnel far beneath the Paris Opera, the man known and feared by many as the legendary Phantom of the Opera sat on a lavishly decorated velvet chaiselongue assimilating the fantastic information from the message brought to him by his Angels of Music.

Dressed in an outfit and cape as black as his soul, his hideous visage hidden under a mask of the type worn by opera performers, Erik discussed the implications of this information with his servant and confidante known traditionally as the "Daroga," even though the current incarnation of the role did not have a drop of Persian blood in him, nor had he ever stepped foot in Asia. The man's ruddy face looked down upon Erik with a concerned expression upon hearing the news that envelope contained.

"Do you not understand what this means to me, *mon ami?*" Erik asked his companion in solitude. "This makes nothing less than my fondest dream not only possible, but within my very grasp!"

Taken aback for a moment by Erik's intensity, the Daroga quietly replied:

"But the Treasure of the Black Coats may not truly exist. Some say it is nothing more than a metaphor of some kind. It may have no material basis, especially when one considers the different descriptions of its appearance given in the various accounts."

"Do not forget, my loyal Daroga, that I am privy to much that is said throughout the underground of Paris, and even far beyond that. I have no doubt that the Treasure exists in some concrete form, as there are too many reports to fully discount. Besides, Bouzille knows better than to provide me with faulty information, particularly something of such inestimable value. This letter reveals that the Treasure is currently in the form of a stack of paper bills that is presently concealed in a vault inside a large apartment in the 16th Arrondissement That building is secretly used to house the Masters of the High Council of the Black Coats."

"But the risk of taking such a prize, even for you and the Angels, is extraordinary, Monsieur. Is the wealth you now have not sufficient to finance the surgery you seek?"

"No, such a procedure would require more money than even I can currently offer—and I can no longer wait! It's been my dream to have a normal human face for longer than I can remember! The technique of building an entirely new body out of available organic material by Doctor Ambrose Vollmer has been confirmed by my investigations! Only he can help me achieve my dream of having a normal, handsome appearance, while still retaining all of the unearthly attributes I inherited from my progenitor. Is not any risk worth achieving one's most fondly desired dream, *mon ami*?"

"I would rather not provide you with an answer to that question now, Monsieur. But are you certain that there is no other method available to you to compensate Doctor Vollmer for his services?"

"I'm afraid not. He needs that vast amount of money to create his own kingdom in the Pacific. Besides, it would be very useful indeed to have a man such as him beholden to me at a later date."

"I see. But what of the apartment you mentioned, where the Treasure is supposedly hidden?"

"This is what I have learned. The leader of this infamous cartel, Colonel Bozzo-Corona, for whom I have performed assassinations in the past, is said to be residing there at this time, so it's likely to be well guarded. The report says that not only is the apartment protected by the Colonel's legendary bodyguard, the fearsome Marchef, but also by an animated mummy taken by the Black Coats from its tomb in Egypt. It is unliving, and thus is not likely to be stopped by anything save for fire. Unfortunately, that avenue of attack is unavailable to me, because the Colonel has installed a new system of automated sprinklers into the ceiling and walls, designed to detect great sources of heat, and to activate at once upon such detection."

The Daroga frowned. "Is such a thing even possible, Monsieur?"

"I have no doubt that such an innovation is possible, and will likely be put into widespread use in the future. If anyone could acquire a prototype of such a flame-suppressing device, it would be the Colonel. We ignore such reports at our peril. We must be nothing less than fully prepared to deal with the Mummy upon entering that room."

"What can we use to dispatch such a being if we can't use fire?"

"That, my dear Daroga, is to be found in the Arabic exhibit currently on display at the Louvre. While in the midst of a drunken binge financed by one of my minions, a street soldier of the Black Coats foolishly dropped information about an enchanted scimitar said to have been forged by Aladdin himself. Its enchantment enables it to exude etheric vibrations that will paralyze the cursed human spirit entrapped within the mummified body if it's plunged directly into its sternum. This will cause the Mummy to be rendered immobile for months."

"But the Louvre has enhanced its security since that golden ankh was purloined from the Egyptian exhibit a few months back. Rumor has it that their new guards have been trained by the best combat instructors sent from America as part of a program initiated by a number of governments to stop those who would attempt to steal ancient artifacts."

"But like many others who have regarded themselves as the 'best' in their field, they, too, will fall before my Angels of Music. Dispatch them to the Louvre tonight to acquire the scimitar."

"*Très bien,* Monsieur Erik. It will be done."

Soon after midnight, the three deadly damsels, now attired in charcoal gray stealth outfits, made their way through the quiet streets of the Right Bank. Sticking to the shadows, the Angels approached the entrance of the Louvre. Ellen Patrick held out her arms, motioning for her two companions to stop just behind her.

"Alright, ladies, remember what Erik said about the locks on those doors," the blonde-trussed leader reminded her teammates. "We need to hit precisely the right tempo, and we all have to do it simultaneously. Are you ready?"

"As I shall ever be, *mon intrépide amie,*" Josephine Balsamo (the latest in that infamous lineage) replied enthusiastically.

"I am well aware of what to do, Ellen," Mizzeia Khali hissed.

Ellen glowered at the amazon for a quick moment before continuing:

"OK, then. Take a few breaths, concentrate, and let us do the great Verdi proud with our shattering rendition of *La donna e mobile.*"

I love this choice! Josephine mused to herself. *Ironic and apropos librettos always get my blood flowing.*

"After the third breath, let's start," Ellen commanded.

Following this, the tempestuous trio began singing in unison at such a low pitch that one would have to be less than six feet away to hear them:

"*Qual piuma al vento, muta d'accento e di pensiero...*"

From there, the trio's mini-chorale lowered even further, at almost too scant a pitch for the human ear to detect. The air in front of them quivered as vibrations of penetrating sound emanating from their larynxes hit the locking mechanisms behind the doors.

Beads of perspiration formed on the girls' brows as they concentrated intensely, projecting their waves of sound at a very specific frequency. A single false note and the mission would be botched before it truly began. Roughly two minutes later, as all three were desperately fighting the urge to stop singing and gasp for air, they heard a click within the doors, indicating they had succeeded!

Stopping instantly, the three successful women took the luxury of several precious inhalations.

"*Doux Jesus,*" muttered Josephine, straining to recover from the effort.

"Buck up and be a warrior, girl," Mizzeia spat at her colleague.

"Enough, Mizzi," Ellen interceded. "That was a very trying song; yet we were successful. Cheers to us! Now remember, we have to be careful upon approaching the Arabic exhibit. Erik's reports indicate these are no ordinary

French guards, so we'll need to each have a weapon in hand and be alert at all times, or our lives could end in a snap."

"The only thing that will end in a 'snap' is the sound of a guard's spine breaking by my hand," Mizzeia boldly declared.

"One must love her incessant bravado, *n'est-ce-pas*?" said Josephine with a grin.

"Hush, Josie!" Ellen intervened. "Now stay quiet, let's move, and don't forget what I just said, no matter how high your confidence—or ego—may be."

The three lovelies cautiously made their way through the labyrinthine corridors of the vast museum, avoiding distraction by keeping their eyes away from the incredible displays of art culled from the entire fulcrum of human history. Unable to use an artificial source of light, they relied on their training to navigate through pitch darkness and steer towards the Arabic exhibit.

If only my Leo was here right now, Mizzeia thought, as she realized how useful the Nyctalope's vision would have been in their situation.

Ellen carried her signature hypodermic needle in her right hand, ready for anything. Mizzeia brandished two long Tibetan daggers in each hand. Josephine followed up with a Punjab lasso in her right hand and a French Army *poignard* in the other.

Within moments, however, a dark-clad sentinel appeared from a corridor directly behind Ellen. His right arm held a hardwood baton that he planned to bring down on her skull. Before he could strike, the loop of Josephine's lasso suddenly entwined his neck, choking him into immobility long enough for her to end his career by plunging her dagger into his body.

"From India with love," she remarked as she yanked the Punjab lasso from his neck.

"*Merci beaucoup,*" Ellen said to her teammate.

Just then, four other guards rushed out of various corridors, obviously alerted to the robbery in progress. The first swung his baton at Ellen, only to have her duck under it with blinding quickness and plunge her hypo needle into his chest; the man made a gagging sound as his eyes went white, and he fell to the floor unconscious.

"Sleep well," she told him with a snicker.

Two other guards hurried towards Mizzeia, apparently deciding that her twin daggers made her the most dangerous of the intruders. With a few fast and graceful motions, almost as if going through a series of dance movements, the amazon whirled her blades in a spinning motion, skillfully slicing open the neck of one of her assailants, and adroitly disemboweling the second. With two loud simultaneous thuds, the dead men hit the ground, gallons of blood and guts gushing onto the floor.

Let us see you top that, leader-lady, Mizzeia thought to herself proudly.

The final guard sped towards Josephine, wielding what looked like an electrical prod. She taunted him by making a 'come here' motion via a wave of her finger. Angrily reacting to the taunt, the man ran closer to her than he should have. When he clicked his device to electrocute her into submission, she suddenly kicked him in the diaphragm.

Reflexively, he dropped the prod. In a quick series of movements, Josephine kicked it in the air, dropped her own weapons, caught the prod by its rubber hilt, and shoved its electrified end into the guard's face. The man promptly emptied both his bladder and his bowels as high voltages of electricity coruscated through his body. After two seconds of contact with the prod, the hapless man fell to the floor, his body being subjected to extreme spasms.

"I am certain the realization that a mere lass could do this to a strapping male such as yourself has proven quite *shocking, n'est-ce-pas*?" Josephine commented, with a mischievous giggle.

Suddenly, all three Angels jumped to attention as they heard footsteps approaching from a nearby corridor. They were curiously calm, too calm to be an oncoming attack.

From the darkness emerged Erik, casually dragging the bloodied corpse of yet another guard with him.

"You must take better care in the future, my fair ladies," he lectured them. "This guard here was in the process of sounding an alarm when I sent him on his bloody way to God's domain."

"*Toutes mes excuses,*" Josephine apologized solemnly. "I should have been aware of that."

"Yes, you should have," Erik retorted with even greater firmness.

"You followed us here?" asked Mizzeia. "You were secretly monitoring our mission?"

"*Oui,*" Erik confirmed. "I do that at times, and this explains why. But needless to say, this mission proved a success, for I secured the scimitar when you ladies were showing these foppish guards who is better trained." He held up the purloined silvery blade to emphasize their triumph.

"They were indeed skilled," Mizzeia said, "but we were better."

"Of course," Erik responded proudly, his stiff mask making it impossible to determine if the grotesque visage beneath was smiling. "Now, let us make haste back to our quarters so we can plan the even more important—and even more difficult—mission two nights hence."

Early the following evening, during the planning session, Erik explained to his agents precisely what he expected of them. The three Angels of Music sat on a large velvet sofa eagerly listening to his instructions, while the Daroga was standing in the corner of the room in rapt attention.

"Each of you must understand the level of importance of this mission," concluded Erik. "The successful capture of the Treasure is nothing less than the culmination of my fondest dream, one that will give me my heart's desire: To experience the unadulterated joy of having an appearance that is pleasurable to behold, and not one I must shamefully hide beneath a mask. The visage of my birth has blackened my soul and tarnished my heart over the decades of what has passed for my life. I was spawned from the loins of a monster, and was fated in turn to become one myself. But it does not have to be that way any longer.

"Rumors say that Colonel Bozzo-Corona will be leaving Paris in the morning. No doubt, the Treasure will be leaving with him. Hence, we must act to-night, or our chance—*my* chance at true salvation—may forever be lost. Because of the importance of this mission, greater than any other I have ever embarked upon, both I and the Daroga will be accompanying you."

Regaining the composure he had nearly lost in his speech, Erik gave the word to his team to head out into the night.

Never have I seen him like this before, Ellen thought. *This mission must be of great importance to him. I have tolerated him being what he is to take advantage of his marvelous training, which I will require if I ever want to take on the criminal element of California in the near future. If this Treasure enables him to be normal and transcend the decades of pain that led to him to becoming what he is, then it decreases the odds that he and I will someday end up knocking heads. I truly sympathize with him, and I owe him so much. I could have become just like him after the murder of my father—and that may still happen if I'm not careful...*

Less than an hour later, the Phantom led his team into the *hotel particulier* of the 16th arrondissement owned by the Black Coats.

Picking the locks were child's play for one with his proficiency. The next step was taking advantage of his superior memory, with which he had mastered the map of the interior layout, secured by another of his agents.

Each member of his team had ample opportunities to exercise their craft as they stealthily climbed the multistoried building and dispatched the security guards hired by the Black Coats.

Within a short period, three guards laid on the floor in slumber, courtesy of Ellen's hypo; five others lay dead, their viscera spattered about after running afoul of Mizzeia's twin daggers; four were hanging from the ceiling by way of Erik's deadly Punjab lasso; two had gaping holes in their throats and stomachs caused by Josephine's *poignard*; and one had been thrown down a flight of stairs by the Daroga, his neck breaking upon reaching the bottom.

Following the aforementioned bedlam, they found themselves beholding a seven-foot-high vault door.

"Finally!" Erik exclaimed. "Hand me the explosive, *Daroga.*"

Complying with his master's order, the Daroga reached into a pocket of his tunic and handed Erik a tightly-sealed metal container holding a highly incendiary powder that the Phantom had developed himself.

Carefully affixing the six-inch cylinder to the locking handle of the vault with a handful of adhesive putty, Erik motioned for his team to quickly take cover.

Within seconds, all were briefly deafened by a massive explosion that knocked the vault door off of its hinges.

Rushing back into the room, they entered the huge safe behind the vault to find themselves confronted by exactly who their reports had said they would: A huge, brawny man dressed in a traditional French Foreign Legion uniform, wielding a deadly antique sword in his right hand—this individual clearly being the fearsome assassin known as Le Marchef;—the second personage was even taller, shambling and rotting, but obviously powerful. It was a mummy with withered grayish facial skin exposed through swaths of bandages. It was known by the name of Pha-ho-tep.

Standing behind these two was an elderly but seemingly quite spry man, with flowing white hair, dressed in an immaculate black suit It was none other than the dreaded Colonel Bozzo-Corona, who had ruled the Black Coats for well over a century. He was holding a golden ankh with a mirror in its center that enabled him to control the Mummy. At his side, her arm affectionately wrapped around his, was a sultry girl with shoulder-length blonde hair, who held a pistol at her side.

"Ah, if it isn't the vaunted Phantom of the Opera, along with his triad of wenches and his foolish lapdog," the Colonel said in his strong but raspy voice. "You must be here for my treasure, which, incidentally, is in this container." He pointed at a metal box on the floor beside him. Then, turning to the young woman at his side, he added: "Don't they make a rather sorry sight, my dear Miss La Verne?"

"I dare say they do, darling," Jo Jo La Verne replied with a grin. "It would seem this is the day the exalted Phantom and his overrated little Angels finally bit off more than even they can chew—despite what big mouths they have."

"Colonel Bozzo-Corona," the Phantom said, holding his Punjab lasso between his two hands with menacing intent. "We finally meet for the first time... and the last."

"We shall see," the Colonel laughed, turning towards the Marchef and holding the ankh in the direction of the Mummy. "Tear them to pieces, my darlings."

Hearing that, Ellen rushed towards the Marchef, attempting to thrust her hypo into his neck. However, he skillfully blocked the needle with his blade, which he then swung at his smaller opponent's mid-driff, a move she deftly evaded by somersaulting over it.

Landing on her feet, she then executed a back kick to the bend behind the Marchef's right knee, causing him to lose his balance and stumble to the floor. She then initiated a side kick to his face, but he intercepted her foot with his left arm.

Pushing himself back up to his feet, he swung his massive fist, striking the blonde *femme fatale* in the side of her face, knocking her to the ground, where she almost lost consciousness. As he raised his sword to cut her in half, he was stopped dead when a choking noose was flung over his throat, strangling him.

"*Pardonnez-moi, brave homme,*" Josephine said from behind him, "but I cannot allow you to bisect my little Ellen; she still owes me ten *sous* I loaned her so she could purchase of one of her oversized bras."

Josephine began pulling the lasso with all her might, hoping to at least choke the Marchef into immobility until she could reach him with her knife. However, the mighty warrior shrugged off the debilitating choking rope long enough to swing his sword back, neatly severing the lasso.

The backlash resulted in Josephine falling backwards onto her *derrière*.

On the other side of the room, both the Daroga and Mezzeia Khali moved to confront the advancing Mummy.

Pulling out a Luger from under his Persian-style tunic, Erik's assistant, who had once been a skilled officer of the law, shot the bandaged creature directly in the forehead.

The Mummy's head shook with the force of the bullet entry, but no other effect was evident; the walking corpse continued to advance.

Damn this to Hell, the Daroga thought. *I had heard that some walking dead can be taken down if their brains are destroyed. But it seems that this creature is not of that type...*

Meanwhile, Mizzeia lunged at the Mummy, slashing its decaying body with both of her daggers several times, albeit to no discernible effect. Luckily for her, the amazon's speed and fluidity of movement exceeded that of the Mummy, enabling her to dodge every swing of the silent creature's pile driver fists.

Rolling into a classic combat stance, she thrust one of her daggers directly into the Mummy's heart. Reacting as if nothing at all had happened, the bandaged monster grabbed the blade, extracted it from his chest, and bent it in half as if to emphasize his might. The creature then again reached for the amazon, who evaded his crushing grip by back flipping out of reach.

"Mizzeia!" the Daroga bellowed from a few feet away. "Go and aid your sisters against the Marchef! I will deal with the Mummy!"

"But your weapon is no more effective than mine!" she hollered back.

"Just do it!" he spat.

Reluctantly following the order, she grabbed her remaining dagger and ran to another of the three battles that were ensuing in the spacious safe room.

Lifting his sword above him, the Marchef ran towards Josephine, intending to swipe his blade clear through her body. Bracing herself, the Angel thrust both of her legs forward, causing her feet to hit the herculean man's groin.

Barely stifling the urge to bawl in agony, the Marchef bit his lip and went down to his knees.

"The family jewels may be a little bruised, *hein, mon gros*?" Josephine said with a smirk.

She then spun around and attempted a follow-up kick to his face, but the Marchef surprised her by catching her leg. Despite the pain he felt after having his testicles kicked inwards, he lifted her into the air as if she were no more than a rag doll. He then retrieved his weapon. As he raised his sword to sever Josephine's head from her body, Mizzeia entered the fray, slashing the back of his legs with her dagger.

Again falling to his knees, the Marchef nevertheless stood his ground and stopped the amazon's next strike by catching her wrist with his left hand. He then swiftly punched her in the face, causing her to fly several feet before landing on her back.

With trickles of blood streaming out of each nostril, Mizzeia gritted her teeth and said: "You will die for this!"

Forcing himself back to his feet once more, the Marchef observed the now-recovered Ellen motioning both of her fellow Angels to do likewise.

"Before he can make another move, let's give him a complimentary performance of Offenbach's finest!" she shouted.

Taking a moment to recover his sword, the Marchef had inadvertently given the Angels time to prepare themselves for the aria they were about to unleash.

Upon Ellen giving the signal, the three women began their concerto: "*Les oiseaux dans la charmille...*"

Buffeted by the waves of deadly sound released by the girls, the Marchef flew backwards against the far wall as if struck by the impact wave of a TNT explosion. He slowly slid to the floor as blood trickled out of every orifice on his face, including his eyes.

"I love it when my voice knocks a man off of his feet!" Josephine quipped as she caught her breath, garnering a rolling of the eyes from both her teammates.

Meanwhile, a few feet away, the Daroga barely ducked a fist swipe by the Mummy, which went several inches into the wall behind him. He knew he would be a dead man if he was struck by the creature. He also knew that he had to keep it at bay until the mission was completed

Unfortunately, the Phantom was the one holding the enchanted scimitar that was able to take down Pha-ho-tep.

Dodging another swing from the Mummy, the Daroga quickly aimed his Luger and shot the walking dead man several times in the chest, the impacts barely slowing down his advance. Suddenly displaying more speed than Erik's assistant would have believed possible, the Mummy grabbed his right wrist, subjecting it to a crushing grip that caused him to drop his weapon.

The Mummy then lifted him into the air by the limb and made a fist with his free hand, preparing to pummel the Daroga's head into a bloody pulp.

Just before that could occur, however, he heard the Phantom call his name, which distracted the Mummy also.

"Here, take this!" Erik yelled as he hurled the silver scimitar towards his assistant before turning back to face the Colonel and Miss La Verne.

With expert alacrity, the Daroga caught the scimitar by its hilt with his left hand and shoved it directly into the Mummy's sternum.

Releasing his grip, the Mummy's movements suddenly became erratic, as if it was beset by waves of electrical force. The seven foot dead thing looked more like a true corpse when its now insensate body crashed on to the ground, kicking up a cloud of dust upon impact. This paralytic state would last for months even after the blade was withdrawn.

Having narrowly avoided death, the Daroga leaned against the wall to nurse his crushed wrist and pain-wracked right arm.

Meanwhile, the Phantom of the Opera was confronting the mysterious Colonel Bozzo-Corona. The two men, whose names were synonymous with death and terror, looked at each other contemptuously.

"Stand aside, you liver-spotted old man, or you will not live to see another day," the Phantom threatened as he held out his lasso, his eyes on the metal box on the floor, which was guarded by Jo Jo.

"You truly think you can possess the Treasure of the Black Coats, you hideous freak of nature?" the Colonel asked with a vile sneer.

"Nothing will keep me from it, not even you," Erik replied icily. "I shall choke the life from you and take the Treasure from your very heel!"

Erik rushed forward to attack the Colonel while evading a gunshot from Miss La Verne, but the Phantom found, to his surprise, that the old man was able to move much faster than a man of even half his apparent years should be able to! Then, to the Phantom's further surprise, the Colonel entwined his arm around Erik's neck, exerting a vice-like grip he was unable to break.

"Who shall choke the life from whom, now?" the Colonel asked his opponent as Miss La Verne pointed her gun at the Phantom.

"No need, my dove," the Colonel told her. "I've got this. We don't want our guest to maneuver you into shooting me now, do we?"

"Perish the thought, dearest," Jo Jo La Verne replied with a devilish grin as she lowered her weapon.

Suddenly, performing a skillful move despite the Colonel's choking grip, Erik managed to swing his lasso backwards around the old man's neck. He then pulled on the lasso, causing the crime lord to gasp for air.

"It would appear we're at an impasse now, Colonel," the Phantom said.

"We... shall... see," the Colonel replied, hurling the Phantom against the wall with astounding strength for one who resembled a decrepit old man.

But Erik shrugged off the impact and rolled into a somersault, after which he jumped back to his feet in front of Miss La Verne. As she raised her pistol, Erik backhanded her clear off of her feet with one mighty blow. He then

215

grabbed the metal box with its invaluable prize inside, and quickly ran to the other side of the room, his escape now secure.

"The Treasure is mine!" Erik shouted victoriously as his team assembled around him. "And with it, my dream will be fulfilled!"

"Will it, fool?" the Colonel asked as he helped Jo Jo back to her feet. "Take a look inside that box, if you will..."

Unable to resist the suggestion, Erik opened the box, only to find nothing but dried leaves inside.

"This must be a trick!" he shouted in horror.

"Oh no, my dear freakish one, it most certainly isn't," the Colonel replied with an evil gleam in his eye. "Don't you understand what the Treasure of the Black Coats truly is? It is far, far more than mere money, or a pile of gold, or priceless jewels. Whatever physical form it takes at any given time, it is nothing less than the embodiment of Wealth itself, the epitome of Avarice— a manifest essence of what makes the world run. It is the source of my power, it is that which the majority of men accept as the natural way of human existence, it is the personified quintessence of the system for which so many fight and die for, yet which enriches a mere handful—a system of which I am the Master! As long as this system exists, so shall the power embodied by the Treasure. And only those few such as myself shall prosper from it. As for those who take hold of it and are not empowered by unbridled greed and lust for power over others, it shall turn to dead leaves, like the legendary crock of gold owned by the leprechauns. Why, I can already sense it manifesting elsewhere in my empire."

"You're lying!" Erik bellowed.

"Am I?" the Colonel replied. "Needless to say, you shall never know."

"No..." Erik said to himself as he angrily threw the box of dead leaves to the floor.

"Oh, before I depart, I must thank you," the Colonel said as he moved towards the far door with his latest paramour.

"What...?"

"Why, for acquiring *this* for me," the Colonel replied, showing him the scimitar he had retrieved from the still body of the Mummy. "You see, this enchanted blade has the power to confer extended longevity to anyone who wields it and learns how to tap into its power. It can not only extend life, but has great restorative powers. It could conceivably bequeath attractive features even to a monster such as you. I didn't want to risk my own men breaking into the Louvre and taking it as they did with the Ankh for me months earlier; not with the enhanced security. Thus, I saw to it that the information about my Treasure would convincingly fall into your hands. And like the unwitting lackey you were, you brought the scimitar to me on a futile quest to get something you not only could never possess, but which you didn't even need if you had simply known enough to keep the scimitar. Beautifully and tragically ironic, *non*?"

The Colonel then released a sadistic cackle, and reached out to his attractive companion.

"Come now, Miss La Verne, let us take our leave."

Without further ado, they sped out the entrance way and slammed the door shut behind them, the sound of an elaborate locking system activating to guarantee their escape.

Falling to his knees in an emotional breakdown, feeling used and betrayed by the cruel whims of Fate like never before, Erik shed tears profusely as he pounded on the floor repeatedly in abject rage and despair. The Angels and the Daroga approached him and put their hands on his shoulders, hoping to offer as much comfort as they possibly could to a terribly embittered man who had his fondest dream within his grasp, only to watch it die a tortured death.

In addition to being a regular contributor to Tales of the Shadowmen *and a distinguished sf/fantasy writer, John Peel likes to pen amusing little capers featuring characters such as Biggles, Rouletabille, etc. In this tale, he takes great delight in depicting an elaborate game of cat-and-mouse in which both cops and robbers are drawn to the Treasure of the Black Coats like moths to the flame...*

John Peel: *The Benevolent Burglar*

Paris & London, 1930

It was one of those beautiful days that made one glad to be French and in Paris. The sky was a cheery blue, flecked only by fleeting soft clouds, allowing the sun to cast a pleasant warmth on the city. It was still early, so the streets weren't crowded with the inevitable tourists, nor workers heading to and from their jobs. It was the rare kind of day that Maigret enjoyed too infrequently.

He doubted that he'd enjoy this one for much longer, so he walked at a slower pace than normal, dragging out the time he had virtually alone. The streets here wound rather vaguely in the direction of the river and there was the far-off sound of the boatmen mingled with the rumbles of traffic. He had grown up with the motor car, but he still cast nostalgic thoughts back to the days when horses and not internal combustion engines roamed the cobbled streets. It was foolish, he knew, but days like this made one a trifle foolish.

Maigret found himself approaching the small café where the rendezvous was slated and he sighed a trifle in regret; his pleasant walk was ending and work was about to commence. Honoré was already there, slouching a little in his seat outside, the inevitable croissant thickly buttered and half-eaten on a small plate in front of him. He was sipping at a thick, Turkish coffee and fumes rose from the omnipresent Gauloise loosely held between his lips. He looked up and nodded as Maigret approached and then took the other chair at the small table. The waiter, who had been somnolently lounging in the door-frame, approached. Maigret quietly ordered a coffee of his own, though he doubted he'd actually drink it. But Honoré always seemed vaguely insulted if Maigret ordered nothing, and it was important to keep the bulky man happy.

"You're a good man, Maigret," Honoré said, staring off into the air, "for a policeman."

"Detective," Maigret corrected him, automatically. "Or Commissaire, if you want to be technical."

"I don't," Honoré replied, blowing smoke. "Policeman is quite close enough for my sensibilities. But either way, I find I like you, Maigret. You're not dull or plodding, like so many policemen. You're more interested in justice than mere laws."

Maigret might have been offended, but he knew the other man was not being insulting intentionally. If the truth be told, quite a lot of his time *was* dull and plodding, because that was the nature of police work. It was only in fiction that leaps of intuition and deduction worked; in real life it was generally boring leg-work that paid off. But all he said was: "I try to do the best I can."

"I know," Honoré said. "And it is because of this that I feel I can talk frankly with you." He glanced around them. "Is it safe to talk, do you think?"

Like many an informer, Honoré was worried about being seen and heard passing along information; it was a fear that Maigret understood, because if an informant was uncovered, his life expectancy would have alarmed any insurance salesman. Maigret glanced about also, but saw nothing to alarm him. There was an Englishman two tables over—quite unmistakable by his refusal to alter his lifestyle in any way to accommodate a foreign country; he was dressed in a suit and tie, despite the warmth of the morning, with highly polished shoes, perusing his copy of *The Times* of London and sipping from time to time at the inevitable cup of tea. In the other direction was a pair of young lovers, murmuring gentle endearments to one another and ignoring the rest of the world entirely. Maigret envied them, remembering his own days of courtship.

"I can think of no place safer," he finally announced.

Honoré shrugged. "Nor I," he admitted. "Why should two friends not meet at a small café to share coffee and conversation?" As if on cue, the waiter appeared with Maigret's drink. When he had placed it on the table, he returned to leaning on the door frame. He would be able to hear nothing from that distance if Honoré continued to speak in hushed tones. The large man seemed to be in no hurry to divulge what he had called Maigret here to hear, however. He blew more smoke, and then crushed his cigarette out. Instead of speaking, however, he promptly lit another. As he extinguished his match, he finally looked Maigret directly in the eyes.

"You have heard of the Black Coats, of course," he stated.

"Which policeman has not?" Maigret answered. "That criminal organization is blamed for a great many crimes—though it is hard to say how much of that credit is truly due them."

Honoré smiled. "And they are *not* credited with a great many more crimes that they *have* committed."

"You are not a member." Of this Maigret was certain—In all of his memory of all of the cases he had conducted or read about, not a single person had claimed to ever belong to the gang. Especially not the ones who did.

"I am not the sort of man that they would recruit," Honoré answered. "I am a thief when it suits me, that is true. But it is a hobby rather than a vocation, and I do not do well when given orders. I do not join gangs, and gangs do not ask for the dubious pleasure of my company. But they do, from time to time, ask for the loan of my skills. If they ask on the right day and in the right way and with the right remuneration... Sometimes I say yes."

"You said yes recently, I take it?"

"Off the record, I did." Honoré trusted that Maigret would not insist on being accompanied to the CID to research the matter and Maigret knew that he would get more in return for being discrete. "In the Third Arrondissment. I doubt you'll have heard of the work. It was not the sort of job that would be reported, so you are not neglecting your duty by not questioning me on it. But in the course of the... work I met a few members of the Black Coats." He glanced around the street again, but there were no new intruders in their space save a distant pedestrian carrying groceries home. "Generally speaking, if they do not bother me, I do not bother them. But these men were not like you, my friend—they were cold and cruel and arrogant, and I did not take to them. They treated me as if I were a cheap hireling and not a skilled craftsman and I tell you—this kind of treatment I do not like."

"No man would," Maigret answered carefully. It seemed that Honoré's pride might be quite useful, so it didn't hurt to feed it a little. "It is painful when one's abilities are looked down upon."

"Quite so." The informer beamed. "I knew that you would understand, Maigret—you're a good man. So I resolved to pay their insults back, and I do so to you. These arrogant men, these Black Coats—they spoke of their Treasure..."

Maigret took out his pipe and fussed with it. "Their Treasure?" he asked. "What might that be?"

Honore shrugged. "It might be anything—I do not know. But they spoke of it with reverence and some awe. If it is money, then it must be a lot of it. But it may be something that simply has great value to them. I did not ask questions, which would have drawn their attention to me, and one does not wish to be noticed by such men. Needless to say, they do not trust their Treasure to a bank; after all, they are responsible for breaking into more banks than the rest of the Parisian underworld added together. Instead, I gather, they move this Treasure of theirs around from place to place at seemingly random intervals in order that nobody should know where it is at any moment." He beamed. "But I know. At least," he amended, "I know where it *will* be on a given date. It will remain there for one day only before moving on again to a place I do not know. But for this one day—its location is known." He looked earnestly at Maigret. "My friend, I will tell you where it will be and when. It seems to me that you may be able to pay back the insult these men have given me by taking their Treasure and inconveniencing them. And it will do you no harm if you are the sole officer who can bring about such a devastating strike against the Black Coats, will it?"

"No," Maigret said slowly. "It would do me a great service."

"And you, my friend, are one man who knows how to repay a kindness," Honoré said. "Which is why I tell you these things. I know you will not forget poor Honoré, or fail to treat him with respect."

"I should certainly not forget such a deed," Maigret replied. "To strike a blow like that against the Black Coats—there is not a man on the force who would not give his right arm for such an opportunity."

"There is, however, a complication," Honoré admitted. "It is one that is not beyond your powers to resolve. But the Treasure will not be in France—it will be in England. Ebbington House, just outside the town of Turley, to be precise." He looked over the rim of his coffee cup at Maigret. "But you are a pleasant companion; I am certain you must have friends in England who would be willing to help you."

Maigret wasn't quite as certain as his informant. There was no formal accord between his department and Scotland Yard, nor, indeed, between their two countries. A man might be wanted for a crime in England, but be completely free to walk the streets of Paris unmolested by the police, or vice versa. The English police, then, might consider the fact that the Black Coats were not wanted in England as leaving them out of any possible course of action. The Treasure undoubtedly consisted of the outcome of many crimes—but if none of those crimes had been committed on English ground, then Scotland Yard could not become involved.

Officially.

He had met one or two officers from the Yard in the past few years that he had found amiable enough. There was a certain Detective Inspector by the name of Teal who had been hunting an English criminal by the name of Simon Templar... Templar had been wanted for murder in England, but living the high life in Paris, as he recalled. Teal had been quite frustrated that he could not arrest the miscreant, but there had been nothing that could be done about it as long as Templar was on French soil and committed no crimes in Paris. Maigret had been apologetic and wished the Inspector well... Would Teal hold that unavoidable failure against him, or would he be willing to try and aid him? It was impossible to know in advance. But, still, that was his problem, and one he would do his best to resolve.

He placed the pipe back in his pocket without lighting it. "And the date the Treasure will be there?" he asked.

Honore smiled...

There had been a faint noise in the background that now grew louder. Maigret had dismissed it, but now it was getting intrusive. He glanced around to see a motorcycle heading toward the café down the otherwise quiet street. It looked to be one of the German DKW models, quite modern. The rider was bundled up, in cap, scarf and heavy coat. Oddly, he did not wear gloves. Maigret noticed this all in passing and then turned his attention back to Honoré. As long as the rider obeyed the speed limit, Maigret had no interest in him. He always felt that motorcycles were noisy, unpleasant devices and preferred an automobile for travel.

Honoré, however, seemed to be fascinated by the machine. He had still not spoken, but his mouth was open.

There was a bang from behind, presumably the noisy motorcycle backfiring, and then Honoré had two open mouths, the newer of which was filled with blood. Time seemed to have slowed for Maigret as he started to stand and turn, looking over his shoulder toward the rider.

The man had a large pistol in his hand, and the barrel of it was moving away from pointing at Honoré to aim in Maigret's direction. Maigret was unbalanced and knew he would not be able to dive out of the line of fire in time. His only hope was that the bumpy ride over the cobblestones would make it difficult for the assassin to shoot straight.

It was not much of a hope, considering the accuracy of the man's first shot. He was a professional killer, that was quite clear, and the gun was almost centered upon Maigret's head.

Out of the corner of his eye Maigret saw the English gentleman two tables away jump to his feet, clearly startled by the shot. His foot caught the chair opposite him as he did so, sending the cast-iron seat clattering into the road.

The assassin, concentrating on the difficult shot at Maigret, did not allow himself to be distracted by this movement. It was an understandable response, but quite the wrong decision. The chair landed in front of the DKW's wheel, and the bike hit the iron chair at a good fifty miles an hour.

The bike upended, flinging the startled rider into the air. The gun went off again, the bullet narrowly missing the two lovers. The man had leaped to cover the pretty girl, keeping her safe, but the bullet missed them by several feet.

Maigret was on his feet now and already moving toward the falling killer. The motorbike hit the cobbles and slid across the road, finishing up on the far curb, still spinning its wheels and making its horrible racket. The rider hit the stones face-first, bounced and then slammed down harder. The snap of his neck was audible even over the row from his machine. No need to worry about further trouble from him, then. Maigret turned to Honoré as the Englishman hurried to join him.

"Is your friend...?" the man asked, clearly concerned. He had turned quite pale—obviously these sort of things were not a part of his daily life.

"We shall see," Maigret said.

Honoré had fallen, sprawling, from his chair. Blood was still flowing sluggishly from the hole in his cheek. There was no exit wound, so the bullet had probably remained within the skull. His eyes flickered slightly, and his arm moved feebly. "Twenty-third," he managed to croak, and then he died.

Maigret sighed; the man had been a crook and an informant, but he had been a likeable rogue. He had never in his life been violent, nor committed any crime that injured anyone. It might not be much of an epitaph, but Maigret was sorry that he was dead.

"My condolences," the Englishman said gently. "He was a friend?"

"Only in business," Maigret admitted. He glanced around and saw the waiter. The man had ceased lounging casually against the door jamb and was now flattened on the ground, shaking. "You!" he called. "Telephone the police immediately! Tell them to send men here." The waiter nodded, glad of the chance to rush inside the café. Maigret looked at the Englishman. "Thank you," he said. "Your actions saved my life."

The man looked embarrassed. "Well, I'd love to take the credit, but it was a pure accident. When I jumped at that shot, I knocked the chair over. You should be thanking the furniture, not me."

Maigret smiled slightly—a typically modest Englishman. "Nevertheless, it is you I thank, Mr...?"

"Tombs," he replied. "Sebastian Tombs."

A short while later, the modest Englishman ran into the two young lovers. "Brother," he murmured gently, "you may unhand Pat now. Your role is over."

The male "lover" smiled. "I was merely doing what any good thespian would, Simon," he replied. "I was throwing myself into the part."

"If you don't detach yourself immediately," Simon warned him, "I shall throw you into the river."

"I thought we were very convincing," Patricia Holm commented, making a slight adjustment to the way her golden hair flowed. "That policeman wasn't at all suspicious of us. It was almost as much fun as teasing Claud Eustace."

Simon lit a cigarette thoughtfully. "This Maigret is no fool," he warned her. "He wasn't expecting to be observed at this meeting with Honoré, which is the only reason he didn't detain us all for questioning."

"Did you hear enough, Simon?" Roger Conway asked. "We managed to catch some of it, but we were too far away for the man's last words."

"The twenty-third," Simon replied. He blew a smoke ring and watched it evaporate. "Children, this one could earn us a bundle of boodle. It is time for us to smite the ungodly..."

Mr. J.G. Reeder was a quiet, respectable man of very definite and mild habits, but he had three vices. Two of these were reasonably public, but the third—as far as he knew—was still a secret. The secret vice was that he read fairy stories. If booksellers looked at him oddly when he bought his latest volume he would invent some totally fictitious niece or nephew to explain his purchase – in truth, Mr. Reeder had no close relatives. Quite why he enjoyed fairy tales so much he was at a loss to explain, unless it was that their innocence and their firm grasp of good and evil was in distinct contrast with the everyday world he occupied.

Of his more public vices, the first was a tendency toward secrecy. Partly this was because he worked in a business where secrecy was considered a virtue, but it was mostly because Mr. Reeder rather enjoyed springing surprises on people. He knew this was an unworthy motive, but he acknowledged it because it was true.

His final and most public vice was the one he was indulging in at this moment in time. He had a predilection for smoking very cheap cigarettes when he was thinking. Almost everyone who worked with him had complained of their foulness at one time or another. Mr. Reeder apologized. He apologized most sincerely, because he knew that it irritated others. But the truth was that he needed those odiferous objects to help him think. He had experimented from time to time with smoother, more expensive cigarettes, but discovered that they were too distracting – he spent his time noticing the subtle flavors and the tastes of the various additives to the blends. Rather than help him think, they detracted from his studious ways. He knew that he needed the terrible smokes he employed precisely because they were cheap and easy to ignore.

At least, for *him* to ignore.

His visitor was attempting to be polite, but Mr. Reeder could see that the cigarette was bothering him. Mr. Reeder could hardly fault the Frenchman for that—the cigarettes bothered almost everyone who knew him. With a hidden sigh, he crushed the life from it in the overflowing ashtray on his desk and resolved to conclude the conversation unaided.

"You do seem to have a bit of a, ah, problem, Commissaire Maigret," he said, politely. "But I am not sure why you came to see me."

"It is a shame that we police cannot cooperate more fully between national borders," Maigret answered carefully. "The International Criminal Police Commission[1] is a step in the right direction, but your country has only recently joined it and..."

"The left hand still doesn't know what the right hand is doing," Mr. Reeder finished for him. "Yes, that much, um , I can see. But what do you expect me to do?"

"Expect? Nothing. Hope? Ah, well, that is another matter." Maigret shook his head. "I know that the Black Coats are a criminal organization almost beyond belief in their efficiency and income. But proving this knowledge is harder, and proving it to the point where Scotland Yard might make arrests on my behalf is beyond my small powers. Though I have information that some of their ill-gotten gains will be in Ebbington House in Turley on the twenty-third, I cannot establish this sufficiently for the law to act."

Mr. Reeder sighed. "Yes, I have often thought it a great shame that while we are handicapped by, ah, a need to follow the law, criminals are not. So, Scotland Yard cannot help you, and thus you come to me—to do what?"

"To be honest, I do not know." Maigret spread his hands. "I can do nothing; your police can do nothing... But it seems to me that it would be a greater crime for *everyone* to do nothing and that these Black Coats should get away with the proceeds from their illegal activities."

---

[1] The forerunner to Interpol.

"I find myself compelled to agree with that assessment," Mr. Reeder admitted. "But if the police cannot act, neither can the Public Prosecutor's office."

"But can Mr. J.G. Reeder?" Maigret asked. "Chief Inspector Teal mentioned that you sometimes…" He searched for the correct English word. "Circumnavigate the problem."

Mr. Reeder sighed a second time. "It is true that I possess a criminal mind," he admitted. "And I am often tempted to, ah, bend the law a trifle to get things done. Sometimes the temptation is virtually overwhelming. But I do not think it a matter I should be, er, discussing with a policeman. Even one who cannot actually arrest me for my thoughts."

Maigret smiled. "Then perhaps, my friend, I should leave you alone with your thoughts. I am sorry to have troubled you."

"I am used to trouble," Mr. Reeder said, with a final sigh. "It is my lot in life." But he noted that the French policeman looked distinctly hopeful. He could only wish that this faith could be repaid.

Mr. J.G. Reeder did not possess many friends. In fact, one might count them on the fingers of a single hand and still find several fingers out of work. It was considered somewhat strange, then, that his one real friend was a man nobody would have expected him to have had anything to do with, and that on two counts.

Firstly, Mr. Larry O'Ryan was rumored to be a thief—or, more accurately—a safe-cracker. He had been arrested and tried once for this crime, but had somehow managed to evade being sent to jail due to a technicality. Mr. J.G. Reeder was morally certain that Larry had in fact committed two further thefts that also involved gaining entry to safes, but his moral certainty and his ability to prove the same were at quite opposite ends of the spectrum. Mr. Reeder, however, knew that the thefts in question were in fact from men who were more larcenous than Larry and far more deserving of punishment. Again, he could not prove this, but his moral sense was, once more, assuaged.

Secondly, Larry O'Ryan was a millionaire—twice over. Mr. Reeder lived very modestly in the Brockley Road; Larry's residence was immodest and in the country. Mr. Reeder was a confirmed bachelor, whilst Larry was happily married to the beautiful one-time Lane Leonard (who had contributed the second million to their joint account). Their life-styles were far apart, but, despite this, they met quite regularly for tea—which they both enjoyed—or classical music concerts—which Larry did not like, but endured for the sake of both Mr. Reeder and his adored wife.

It was over tea at the O'Ryan mansion that Mr. Reeder broached the reason for this particular visit. "Did you know," he said, as if reciting a fact he had discovered on the back of a packet of corn flakes, "that Ebbington House has recently installed a Monarch Security Steel safe?"

"I did not," Larry replied honestly. His interest in the company had declined since he had left their employ more than a year earlier, along with a set of duplicate keys that could open many of their safes. "More profits for Monarch, eh?"

"I imagine," Mr. Reeder agreed. "As you know, their installations are not, um, cheap."

"Nor as impregnable as they might wish," Larry agreed, catching the drift of his friend's conversation. "Did you know," he added, "that Ebbington House is actually little more than a hop, skip and a jump from here?"

"The fact has been brought to my recent attention," Mr. Reeder confessed. "And that brings me to a, ah, somewhat embarrassing question." He eyed the beauteous Mrs. O'Ryan but knew them both better than to suggest the rest of the conversation might best be continued with her absent. "I am reluctant to ask it, but ask it I must. Are you free on the night of the twenty-third?"

Lane glowered at him. "Mr. Reeder, I am ashamed of you!"

Mr. Reeder lowered his head. "I am ashamed of myself," he said. "Frequently. I should not have asked..."

"That is not why I am ashamed of you," she snapped. "I am ashamed that you think so little of our friendship and the debt we owe to you for our happiness together that you feel reluctant to ask a favor of us!"

"But this is not a little favor!" Mr. Reeder exclaimed. "If things go amiss, there is a distinct prospect that I might be forced to arrest myself for breaking and entering. And anyone else who accompanies me. Also, um, there is the possibility that the people I am planning on... visiting may have hostile tendencies."

Larry looked distinctly cheerful. "Life has been rather quiet of late," he observed. "No reflection upon you, my love," he added quickly to his wife. "But there are days when I sometimes pine for a little excitement again."

"Do you think you're the only one who likes to feel alive?" Lane growled. "I wouldn't miss this for the world."

Mr. Reeder was appalled. "I had not planned on asking for your aid!" he protested. "It would trouble my conscience greatly if anything were to happen to your husband as a result of my request – but should anything befall you..."

"Anything worse than my uncle had planned for me?" she asked drily, alluding to her relative's attempt to rob and murder her. "That you and Larry saved me from? How could you even think I would not be there to help you both? Mr. Reeder, I am sorely tempted to blacken your eye." She made a fist and shook it in his general direction.

"And she'd do it, too," Larry said, proudly. "That's my girl."

Mr. Reeder was a realist, and he knew when he was facing a foe he could not defeat. "Very well," he agreed. "But you must undertake to do *exactly* as I instruct."

"You can tell you're not married," Larry muttered, "if you think *any* woman will do exactly as she is instructed."

"When you two children are *quite* finished..." Lane said, glaring at each in turn. "Mr. Reeder, I assume you have some sort of a plan?"

"It's rather vague at the moment," he confessed. "I have not yet reconnoitered the ground, so to speak and until I have, I would not, um, venture a fixed plan."

"But with my skills and my keys," Larry observed, "I am assuming a little burglary is being planned."

"Strictly in the name of justice," Mr. Reeder added, hastily. "The proceeds will be turned over to the French police to see if they can match them up with any known missing property. I doubt the current owners will file a complaint about the, ah, robbery."

"About the house," Larry said. "I'm assuming there are guards."

"One or two," Mr. Reeder replied. "The Black Coats do not wish to draw the attention of other, um, criminals to the place. I suspect there will be some sort of security system in place, so we will have to scope out the lay of the land first. We have three days until the twenty-third, when the treasure will arrive.'

"How certain are you of this information?" Lane asked thoughtfully.

"You have, sadly, put your finger on the main problem we face," Mr. Reeder admitted. "The information comes via an informant who was murdered, presumably in a vain attempt to stop him talking. But I cannot help thinking that he may have been murdered *after* he talked in an attempt to underline his testimony, so to speak."

"In other words, that the information is false, but that the Black Coats wish us to believe it to be true." Larry rubbed his chin. "It would be a clever diversion if the treasure was really going to be somewhere else instead. But how can we know?"

"Only by going ahead as if the information is correct," Mr. Reeder said. "I have little other choice."

"Well," Lane said, in a far-off voice, "I for one am quite intrigued to see what this treasure might possibly be." She smiled at Mr. Reeder. "I just hope it isn't so fascinating that I'm tempted to keep any of it for myself." Seeing his aghast expression, she added: "Oh, don't worry, I'm pretty certain I can restrain any larcenous impulses I might feel. At least, you'd better hope so..."

Mr. Reeder and Larry were both flat out in the grass, elbows down and binoculars propped up in their hands when Lane slipped in beside them. They were studying Ebbington House carefully, and Lane noted an air of frustration. She glanced at the edifice herself: early Elizabethan, obviously, with a lot of additions in varying styles seemingly attached to the main part of the house at random. It was a quaint, early English mess.

"So," she asked cheerfully, "what have you boys decided?" Not many people would have used the word *boy* to describe Mr. Reeder, who was distinctly middle-aged.

"This is a tough one," her husband answered. "There would appear to be three guards at all times, one of whom has a dog with large teeth and an unpleasant attitude. They patrol the grounds about the house. According to the delivery records, the safe was installed in the main study. It is some twenty feet deep, eight high and eight across. Whatever the treasure is, it sounds to be fairly large."

"Quite," Mr. Reeder agreed. "So we somehow have to navigate the open grounds in front of the house, avoid raising the suspicions of the guards and their canine assistants, break into the house, make our way to the study and then break into the safe. After which we, er, have to carry half a ton or so of treasure back out without being observed."

"We'd need a lorry of some sort parked nearby," Larry added, "but not so close it would be spotted." He shook his head. "It all sounds perilously close to being impossible."

"Nonsense," Lane said, firmly. "I'm quite sure that is what these Black Coat people are counting upon to dissuade anyone from attempting what we shall manage." She looked at her husband. "Are you sure you can break into the safe?"

"In all modesty, yes," he replied. "I helped build the things, so I know a few tricks that the average safecracker wouldn't. It'll probably take me an hour, but I know I can manage it."

Lane smiled. "I'm so proud of you, my darling," she murmured. "How many wives have husbands like you?"

"Thankfully few," Mr. Reeder interrupted. "Or else my job would be considerably harder than it already is. But breaking into the safe is, um, the simplest part of the problem."

"Well, it's the only part I can't assist with," Lane informed him. "I've already worked out the rest of it." She rather enjoyed the look of pure astonishment on Mr. Reeder's face.

"But you haven't even studied the place!" he protested.

"Oh yes I have," she retorted. "Where do you think I've been? I was in the village taking tea with Mrs. Oswald Murphy."

"I wonder what they slipped into the tea to make you so sure of yourself," her husband muttered.

"It wasn't the tea that matters," she informed him, "but the conversation. Mrs. Murphy is the head of the local Conservation Society. She has been pressing for the preservation of Ebbington House as a national monument. It seems it is an excellently-preserved example of the builders' arts dating from the Elizabethan period. The Society did a thorough survey of the house five years ago and have been struggling to raise funds for its purchase ever since. I am strongly tempted to send them a cheque to aid them in their work."

"That's all very noble," Larry replied, "and I certainly have no objections if they really wish to preserve that monstrosity. But are you going to get to the point of your brilliance?"

"During the Elizabethan age," Lane explained, "people got very upset over whether you were Catholic or Protestant. The upper hand went from one to another at the drop of a monarch. Most of the nobility were Catholic, and it was sometimes very dangerous to be identified as such. Having a priest about the house tended to get you labeled as a traitor. But the nobles liked having their pet priests about to say Mass in their private chapels, so they built bolt-holes and secret passages in order to smuggle said priests in and out of the house unobserved." She saw the light dawn on her companions.

"And Ebbington House has such a bolt-hole," Mr. Reeder ventured.

"It does indeed," she agreed. "Mrs. Murphy was quite specific about it. She helped to clean the mechanisms to open and close it during that survey five years ago. It starts in the study where the safe is and comes out in the stables."

"And you got the information from her," Larry said, grinning cheekily. "My love, you are a wonder." He gave her a quick kiss. "Well, now we can get in and out without being seen. But we still have the problems of transporting the treasure."

"No," Mr. Reeder said thoughtfully. "We don't have to transport it at all." Lane and her husband stared at him in complete confusion. He smiled. "All we have to do is to move it into the bolt-hole. The Black Coats have the lease for only three days, and they must vacate. We can simply wait until they are gone before bringing in the necessary lorry and then removing the loot."

"What about the dogs?" Larry asked. "We can dodge the guards to get to the stables, but the dogs will most likely sniff us out."

"Aniseed," Mr. Reeder said, promptly.

"I beg your pardon?"

"Dogs love aniseed," Mr. Reeder explained. "They go crazy for it. All we need to do is to spill some on the far side of the house and, ah, the dogs will go for it. They will ignore us completely."

Lane smiled in satisfaction. "Then I do believe, gentlemen, that we are ready for our burglary tomorrow night."

Mr. Reeder was pleased that the night had turned out to be rather overcast. From the same vantage point he had used to initially survey Ebbington House he could now see only the lights of the house and beyond that merely shadows and vague shapes. It would make slipping into the stables a lot easier for them.

Beside him, dressed all in black, Lane fidgeted nervously. "Where's Larry?" she muttered. "Shouldn't he be back by now?"

"Patience, my dear," Mr. Reeder advised. "It is better that he doesn't rush and perhaps stumble and break a bone or, ah, two." Larry was off planting the aniseed lure to attract the dogs to the side of the house they would not be approaching. "Once he returns, we can make our way down." Mr. Reeder knew that in this kind of mission waiting was almost as important as acting. One premature move could spoil an elaborate plan. Lane, not having been raised with a strain of larceny in her soul, could not quite grasp this. He could only hope her eagerness to be a part of this venture wouldn't put them all in jeopardy.

There was no more than a slight rustle in the grass—any casual observer would have put it down to a vague gust of wind—and Larry was back with them, grinning. "Once the dogs get around that side of the house, they won't be returning in a hurry," he promised.

"Then we shall allow them ten minutes," Mr. Reeder decided. Lane looked as if she might be wanting to say something, but then she wisely snapped her mouth shut. Mr. Reeder liked and admired her more the longer he knew her.

Once the ten minutes had passed—Mr. Reeder timed it precisely on his pocket watch—they moved cautiously out and down the hillside toward the house below. There were lights ablaze outside the front and rear of the house, and he could see two guards in place. There was no sign of the one with the dog. With luck, he was off on his rounds and not close to the stables. There was, after all, no reason why the guards should be concerned with the outer buildings on the estate when the treasure was ensconced in the main house. The stables were as old as the house, but had been rebuilt a number of times over the centuries. The last owner had evidently used them, but now they appeared to be mainly applied to the storage of landscaping tools. That was a stroke of luck, as it meant nobody was likely to be in need of a rake at this time of night.

"This way," Lane said, confidently. "Mrs. Murphy was quite detailed in her descriptions." She entered the third stall, which now was clear of hay or tackle, and held only a wheelbarrow and tarpaulins neatly stacked. There was a feed bin attached to the end wall, and Lane felt beneath it with a grin. A moment later there was the sound of a catch being released, and the entire wall swung gently toward them. Larry gripped the edge and pulled it open. There was just sufficient light to see a tunnel sloping downwards away from them.

"Come on," Lane whispered, and started down the way. Larry gestured for Mr. Reeder to follow her, and then he pulled the wall closed behind them. There was a moment of utter blackness before Mr. Reeder switched on his electric torch. Two pale, excited faces blinked back at him.

"Excellent work," he complimented the young woman. "Now, let us perambulate."

They walked down the passageway, which had been constructed of ancient bricks and which dropped about ten feet under the earth. It had a musty, earthy stench to it—not pleasant, but bearable. There were no side passages and no turns; it was arrow-straight to the house. Whoever had built this had chosen the simplest, straightest way. They reached the end of the passage inside of five minutes. Like the entrance, this end was simply a section of wall on a hidden pivot, with a catch holding it in place.

"Plenty of room in here to hide any amount of treasure," Larry observed. "So far, so good."

"This was the simple part of the plan," Mr. Reeder replied. "Now comes the most difficult part." He clicked off the torch as Lane triggered the catch to open the wall. With barely a sound, the section swung out and they slipped through into the study.

The lights were on in here and the curtains drawn open. If any of the guards walked past, they were bound to be able to see straight to the safe, which stood alone in the center of the room. It was twenty feet by eight by eight, and had obviously been installed in sections as none of the doors in the house were large enough to bring it in constructed. The walls were of steel and the door had a heavy, impenetrable looking lock.

"Nice," Larry murmured in appreciation. "They've spared no expense on this. It's almost unbreakable."

"But only almost?" Lane asked.

"Yes, my love—only almost." He pulled his bag of tools from his knapsack and glanced at Mr. Reeder. "I estimate it will take me about an hour to get into this. You'd better keep watch at the window and call out if you see any guards coming this way on their rounds."

"Of course." It was what Mr. Reeder had planned to do all along.

"And what can I do?" Lane asked.

"Apart from telling me how wonderful I am?" Larry grinned. "Take the bag and go around the side of the safe. If any guard looks in, you and the tools will be out of his line of sight. I'll tell you what I need and you pass it to me. That way, if I have to hide, I'll be unencumbered."

"Righto," Lane said, with a grin. She was clearly enjoying her first foray into a life of almost-crime. Mr. Reeder sighed silently and went to his position by the window. He could only hope that she wouldn't be cured of her mistaken belief by an influx of armed men. He hadn't mentioned it to his companions, but there was a loaded revolver in his coat pocket. Mr. Reeder disliked using guns almost as much as he disliked being shot at.

For a while there were no sounds in the room save for the noises that Larry made working on the lock. Mr. Reeder glanced at his companion from time to time and could see the furious look of concentration on the young man's face and the sympathetic glances cast at him by his wife. For the most part, though, he focused all of his attention on the grounds beyond the windows.

Twice he gave a low call to alert the others to the presence of patrolling guards. Both time they all ducked from sight and waited until the patrols had passed on. Thankfully there was no sign of the dog handler—hopefully, he was entangled in deep brambles right now with his animal seeking the intoxicating taste of aniseed.

The thought made Mr. Reeder wish he'd brought along some humbugs to suck. It might have helped him pass the time with less strain. Instead he could only think of all the possible things that could go wrong with their plan. Most of these thoughts led to guards shooting the three of them to death. The rest led to his being brought up before the beak on burglary charges and being sent to prison for the rest of his life. None of them were in the slightest bit comforting.

"Almost there," Larry said, softly. He chuckled. "I have to hand it to the development boys—they've come up with a winner in this design." There was a soft click, and then he turned the handle, without any effort. Mr. Reeder took a final look for guards, but the coast was clear. He slipped over to the vault.

Larry looked at him, a slight grin on his face. Lane beamed proudly at her husband. Mr. Reeder gave a polite smile. With a flourish, Larry opened the door and the three of them stared inside.

"I don't believe it," Larry finally said.

"I'm afraid I do," Mr. Reeder murmured.

The vault was completely empty. The only thing marring the polished metal walls was a large, crude stick figure in chalk opposite the door. It showed a man with a slightly-tilted halo above his head.

"Simon Templar..." Mr. Reeder breathed.

Neil Penswick has written a morality fable composed of several "playlets," the theme of which is the eternal dance of good and evil, using the character of Fantomas as his medium. This is not the usual kind of story we publish in Tales of the Shadowmen, but then, from time to time, as was the case with our own, earlier story, we like to challenge our readers with odd tales that don't really fit comfortably into any specific category...

Neil Penswick: *The Conspiracy of Silence*

1913

In the early years of the 20th century, the Parisian newspaper Le Temps *published puzzles called Detectograms for the amusement of its readers. These stopped in 1913 after a series of five were published, only to be met by confusion and bafflement by the general public. None of the stories apparently had a solution, leading the Editor to print an apology and subsequently to resign. The destruction of the newspaper archives in the Great War unfortunately left no further clues to one of the more mysterious events in the history of puzzle fiction. We are printing these stories exactly as they were printed then.*

Editor.

The body was found hanging from the ceiling of Notre Dame Cathedral. The skin had been peeled from it and its sexual organs had been removed. The doors were locked. There was a scent of tobacco permeating the Cathedral.

The first detective, whose name we do not know, said that it could only have been caused by a ghost. The second detective, Juve, said that he did not know the name of the victim, but did know who had killed him. He said that the first detective should be arrested for the murder.

Would you have the courage to report one of your colleagues?

(Published 11 January 1913)

Lions wandered outside the compound, hungry for prey.

"Even miles away, when they roar, you feel your chest vibrating. They are the dominant species, and they only need to occasionally make their presence felt." The politician smiled showing off his gold teeth.

Juve replied: "You know why I am here. People have come to the police in the French capital and reported that you were responsible for murdering hundreds."

"I murdered no one," said the politician. "My work is about coordinating the administration of our African colonies."

The policeman stood, removing papers from his pocket.

"Look at these!"

The politician glanced at the papers and shook his head.

"These prove your involvement in a massacre," said the detective. "Because of these, several hundred people died in the most horrific and inhuman manner."

The politician smiled.

"It is like the lion. I don't deny my involvement. But the victims were of no consideration. Hardly human."

Would you be able to stand up to politicians?

(Published 18 January 1913)

Juve held the decapitated head of the woman in his hands. He looked around the ballroom. At the great-and-good of the Paris scene. Bejewelled, well-turned out, but completely disinterested.

Someone laughed: "Caviar?"

Juve stared at them. They were all expressionless. Blank-faced.

"Does anyone know who she might be?" he shouted.

"She? Doesn't look like a woman to me."

"How do you know that it isn't a department store mannequin?"

"They're dashed prettier."

General laughter. *And not nervous*, he thought. *They have nothing to be frightened of. The so-called 'elite.'* His mind thought fast, trying to keep those strange thoughts away.

"One of you isn't who they claim to be," he stated.

"None of us is who we claim to be," replied a wit.

They all laughed louder.

"This is a very serious matter. Have a sense of occasion," Juve spoke firmly.

A man started to bark like a dog. Another fell on all fours and started to crawl around. The wit moved forward and said:

"You should remember where you are."

"I do. And someone here is not who you think they are. They are in disguise. Look around you."

"Say please," a woman said.

"I am investigating a murder," he shouted.

The wit continued: "Tidy that thing up. And don't bother us with your idle thoughts."

The pretty woman laughed.

Can you stand up to corruption and the petite bourgeoisie?

(Published 25 January 1913)

The train had come off the tracks and had continued to travel for hundreds of yards, throwing passengers and luggage across the French countryside.

Bodies were mangled. Horribly mangled.

Juve walked through the catastrophic scene, occasionally stopping to search through the scattered belongings. He stopped, seeing a masked man in black apparently pilfering the pockets of a mutilated body.

"Stop that," said Juve.

"Who are you?" responded the man in black.

"I am Juve."

The man in black looked shocked.

"I see. Then you will have noticed that this is a terrorist attack. Explosions on the track and, it appears, simultaneously on the train. See the flash marks on these bodies."

It was Juve's turn to be shocked.

"How do you know this?"

"The terrorists, or should I say terrorist, has created an event, maiming and killing hundreds to divert attention."

Juve focused his attention on the man in black, who looked like a common criminal. But appearances could be deceptive.

"From what?" asked Juve.

"The murder of many of our leading politicians," said the man in black.

"I have read nothing in the press," replied Juve.

"There are many terrible things that you won't find written about in the press. There has been a conspiracy of silence. We must find other ways to directly communicate with the public."

"How fanciful!" Juve laughed.

"Dreadful villainy and vile corruption is rife in French society. There is a spiders' web leading around one man."

"What you say is madness," said Juve.

"Yes it is madness. But the madness of one man," the man in black said. "And let us not carry with on this charade, you are not Juve!"

"You seem to have gone insane," said Juve.

"You are the devil at the heart of this matter. You are Fantomas!"

"I am Juve," said the policeman.

"No," said the man in black, "*I* am Juve!"

The policeman didn't react immediately. Then, then his mouth curled and his face seemed to transform into a devilish mask.

"There are many dead bodies here," said Fantomas. He pulled out a gun and aimed it at the heart of the man in black. "One more would not go amiss, Juve."

Fantomas pulled the trigger. And a loud bang sounded across the country-side.

Would you be prepared to put your own life at risk?

(Published 1 February 1913)

The psychiatrist stared at the man being led from his cell. The man was sat in front of him. The two guards stepped back. The man stared ahead, blankly.

"What is your name?" asked the psychiatrist.

'"He is drugged," replied the guard, "for our safety."

"What sort of drugs?"

The guard shook his head.

"I have been asked to interview you," said the psychiatrist. "The board of this asylum are recommending that you be locked up for the rest of your life. But they need the authorization of an independent psychiatrist."

The man continued to stare.

"They say you are extremely dangerous."

The man stared.

"I cannot agree. This man is catatonic." The psychiatrist stood up. "You may take him away."

The guards nervously looked at each other.

"He frightens us," said one of them.

"Why?" asked the psychiatrist, "he doesn't speak."

The psychiatrist started to walk away.

"He did," said a guard.

The psychiatrist stopped. "Then tell me what he said."

One of the guards shook his head. The other guard thought for a moment and said:

"He said that his name was Fantomas."

"And he sings," interrupted the other guard.

"He said that he was responsible for tortures, murders and massacres across the colonies and France."

"And he sings," repeated the other guard.

"He is insane" said the psychiatrist. "Many people believe their mad views are real. They may believe they are the Head of State. That does not make them dangerous."

"He killed the guards."

"And he sings. Continually sings."

The psychiatrist repeated: "He killed the guards?"

"He sings all-the-time."

"What do you mean, 'He killed the guards?' You are the guards!" said the psychiatrist.

"Said the spider to the fly," sang a guard. "Said the spider to the fly!"

"We are not the guards. We are patients. Some of the few that he hasn't killed."

The psychiatrist focused on the staring man. "This man's name is Fantomas?"

The guard shook his head.

"Fantomas escaped. This is a policeman, Juve, from the Sûreté, who was sent to interview him."

"And you are going to sign a form to keep him locked up forever," said the second guard.

"Why should I do that?" asked the psychiatrist.

"Fantomas said that you will take part in a conspiracy of silence."

"Everybody does," said a guard.

The psychiatrist pointed at the staring man, and said:

"Not everybody."

What would you have done?

(Published 8 February 1913)

Note: *The Paris Sûreté was formally disbanded in 1913, for "corrupt and aggressive practices not commensurate with the good name of the French police." There are no further records of these events. We would also like to note that there is nothing in any existing records from the time about a master villain named Fantomas.*

Editor.

Pete Rawlik has chosen to throw his hat into the ring with a Black Coats-themed story that focuses not only on the intense rivalry that has always torn the murderous brotherhood apart, but on the fate of another item, one of great interest to all Wold Newton devotees...

Pete Rawlik: *Professor Peaslee Plays Paris*

Near the Podkamennaya Tunguska River, 6 March 1910

Even in March, the wind that whipped out of the north across the plains and down the river chilled men to the bone, but the two men who stood on the hill ignored it. Not too long ago, this had been an ancient forest, now for miles around them the trees lay scattered like matchsticks, the victims of an explosion that had less than two years earlier cracked open the sky and set fire to the world. The inferno had burned for weeks, the light of which could be seen for thousands of miles. No one had dared to investigate the disaster, and for that the two men who stood on the hill overseeing the excavation were grateful. It was not the first time that they and their minions had worked to salvage fragments of meteorites, and it wouldn't be the last, though their prior operations had not always met with success.

Below, in the pit that had been dug, the men, the eunuchs, suddenly grew loud and excited. An object, a stone about the size of a man's fist and dripping with mud was raised up into the air. A cry of achievement moved through the crowd as the stone was passed from the center of the pit out, and then up the hill. The last man wrenched himself out of the mud and scrambled up the slope, wiping the stone clean with his shirt. He knelt before the well-dressed man with the fur lined coat.

"Count Ferenczy," the mud-covered man spoke meekly, almost apologetically. "Master, we have found it, the stone, the chondrite, it is ours!"

The aristocrat reached for the stone, but then cautiously withdrew. The mud covered servant was confused for a moment, and then shifted his offering to the second of the two men. He was taller, thinner with glasses beneath his wind whipped hair.

"Professor Peaslee, would you please take this from me?" The man was practically begging. Peaslee took the stone. Even through the mud, he could see the crystalline structure of the treasure they had unearthed. He wiped the last of the muck off and rolled the gem about letting it catch the sun. The servant inched back down the hill and rejoined his brothers in the pit.

The man called Ferenczy spoke for the first time in hours:

"You will do what must be done?"

Peaslee wrapped the jewel in a cloth and tucked it into the pocket of his coat.

"I will do what you failed to do in 1795. Because of you, we must now deal with men who are more than they should be, who think like we do, who are developing technologies they shouldn't even have thought of. If you had done what was needed of you, I would not have to have come to this time, and live amongst these filth." There was no malice in his voice, no emotion at all as he turned and stared at the dozens of men who struggled below. "These men, you have made sure that they are all castrati?"

Count Ferenczy nodded.

"I have. They are unable to procreate, whatever the stone has done to them here, it will not enter the gene line of humanity."

"The risk is too great. We cannot allow another Holmes, or Nemo." Peaslee turned and walked toward the river and the waiting boat. "Liquidate them all."

Paris, 22 August 1911

The painter Louis Beroud struggled up the stairs of the Louvre, his case of brushes and paints banging against every stray object that happened to get in his way. He wasn't normally clumsy, but last night's revelry had left him hung over and stiff. Neither were ideal conditions for working, but he was a creature of habit, and the sketches for his own piece, *Mona Lisa au Louvre*, were nearly complete.

As he came through the entrance, a young man with blonde hair and a fore-lock curl held the door for him. He smiled at Beroud as they passed, and, for a brief moment. Beroud thought that the boy might make a decent model; he was tempted to stop him and ask him to come round his studio. But that thought was fleeting, and, as he made his way into the galleries, all other thoughts except one left his mind.

The gallery was empty, as it usually was at this hour. The richly-colored walls and gilt molding accented the ornate frames that, themselves, served to complement the masterpieces that decorated the walls. For weeks now, Beroud had come to this museum, to this gallery, to this very spot, and sketched. He had come for the light; it was only right for a few minutes every day, when the sun hit the window through the tree and cast itself through the halls, and about the wall in a just so manner. He had grown to love the light, and the shadows, how they played out across the gallery, making the gold and copper hues rich and deeply luxurious.

It had taken him weeks to prepare the right mixture of paints to reproduce that color, weeks and scouring the shops of Paris for the right ingredients. But it had all been worth it. Just a few more days, a few more sketches, and he would have everything he needed to complete his own painting, his study of the Mona Lisa in its place in the gallery at the Louvre.

As he settled into place, he set his case in its usual spot, unpacked a handful of pencils, and settled back onto the bench that he had come to think of as his own. The pages of his notebook fluttered in the light and cast wistful shadows splaying against the wall where his beloved subject hung. Except—the wall was bare! Where Leonardo da Vinci's masterpiece had once rested, there were instead four iron pegs that held nothing but empty space.

The master's masterpiece was gone!

23 August 911

The statuesque Gascon who went by the name of Flambeau, "The Torch," stared at the little American who was sitting across from him. All around them the other patrons of the Moulin Rouge were lost in the wild debauchery of absinthe, song and the wiles of beautiful and willing women. Flambeau did not like the American; the little man had a dead face, slack, his eyes were empty and soulless. The women of the Moulin Rouge did not like the look of the man either. He made the girls uneasy, which made Flambeau uneasy. If anyone knew how to judge a man, it was surely these women.

Flambeau took a sip from his brandy.

"It is an interesting proposition Professor Peaslee. Is there a reason you bring it to Flambeau?"

The little man with the dead face did not smile. He should have, but he did not. When his mouth moved to compliment Flambeau, there was no hint of any emotion at all.

"You are Flambeau. Your physical stature and prowess is unmatched. Your flair for the dramatic, the ingenious, the bloodless, is legendary. It was you who created the Tyrolean Dairy Company, with no cows or carts, yet served thousands in the city of London. Your trick of a fake portable pillar-box was ingenious. The renumbering of an entire street so that you could divert a courier and intercept a single package was sublime. The theft of a shipment of precious metals by sinking them in the harbor channel was simply inspired. I plan on tricking the *Habits Noirs*, one of the most notorious and dangerous criminal organizations in all of human history. You ask why I come to you, why I wish to engage your services? I ask you, who else can I possibly turn to?"

Flambeau nodded.

"This incident at the Louvre, it has stirred up the police. This will make things more difficult, not impossible though. We will need some help. I know a girl, she is very good at what she does; she does not like to take risks. It may be necessary to pay them more than what is usual."

"I have told you, Monsieur, money is not an issue." The strange little man with dead eyes paused. "You have a plan then?"

The master thief smiled broadly.

"I have an idea Professor Peaslee, I have an idea."

24 August 1911

Inspector Romaine found what he was about to do distasteful, but he felt he had little choice. The Louvre was in a shambles, Paris was in chaos, all the roads out of the city had been closed, but to no avail. His colleagues had found nothing, and were now grasping at straws. They had arrested the poet Guillaume Apollinaire, who had once called for Louvre to be set afire. There was talk that Apollinaire had implicated the artist Pablo Picasso. Romaine found the whole affair ridiculous, and was sure that, had he still been in charge, Aristide Valentin would have better organized and directed the investigation and manhunt.

But Chief Valentin was dead, a victim of his own hand. His successor was no detective, but merely an administrator, a counter of pennies and fanatic for forms and procedures. Crime had suddenly exploded in Paris. The best and the brightest, Broquet, Guichard, Maigret and the like, were doing what they could. But under the current leadership, there was to be no chance at recovering the lost painting. Which is why Romaine had taken his own initiative, and come to this place, this temple to crime.

The nervous inspector did not have to wait long before he was ushered from the entry hall and into a dimly lit study. His escort was a young woman, dressed in a provocative leather corset and carrying a matching riding crop, both ends of which were tipped with silver studs. She motioned to a simple wooden chair and Romaine took a seat. She continued to walk and took up a position behind a figure that sat in an ornately carved black mahogany throne.

He was an imposing figure, not overly large or muscular, but his shoulders were wide and his and sat as if the world was his. Whoever he was, Romaine would never know, for his face, and indeed his entire head, was covered with a heavy iron mask. Five slits accommodated his eyes, nose and mouth, and Romaine saw what seemed to be grates where his ears should be. In an ironic touch, a crown of short iron spikes lined the brow in mockery of the crowns worn by true monarchs. Between the horns etched into the metal was the symbol of the man who had founded the criminal syndicate so many years earlier.

He motioned with his hand and the woman in black leather spoke for him.

"You took a great risk coming here Inspector Romaine. We normally kill policemen who come to our house."

"I'm honored," Romaine stammered out.

She smiled.

"The night is still young. What do you want?"

He fumbled his hands, and his words.

"It was suggested that I come here about the theft of the Mona Lisa. We wish to recover it, undamaged."

241

She shook her and gestured with her hands.

"We do not have it, nor do we know where it is."

"I know; it is not your style." He paused and caught his breath. "I am not here to accuse you; I am here to ask for your help."

The man in the iron mask stood up and crossed the space between them in majestic steps befitting the monarch he pretended to be. He knelt down beside the nervous policeman. Romaine could hear him breathing, a heavy, thick sound, like an animal.

"You want us, the *Habits Noirs*, to help you find the men who committed the most audacious crime to occur in Paris in the last twenty years?"

Romaine nodded.

The room filled with deep, cackling laughter from both the iron king and his assistant. The king stood up and spun round, his silken robe catching the air.

"Imagine it Josephine, us working with the police! If he weren't already dead, the Colonel would have keeled over by now." He came back at Romaine like a cat ready to pounce. "What do we get in return?"

25 August 1911

Professor Peaslee sat in the cafe sipping his coffee and watching as the little girl ate her pastry. She was a child, but it was with this creature that Flambeau had arranged for him a meeting. Though she was but six, the girl called Nardi, with flowing black curls, carried herself with a pride rarely seen in women of any age. As she finished she spoke.

"You have the money?"

He nodded.

"Half now, half when you deliver the package outside of the city." He paused and then leaned forward to whisper the lines that Flambeau had made him memorize. "You understand, this stone, the Tear of Azathoth, is more valuable than the Heart of the Ocean, more beautiful than the Pink Panther, more sought after than the infamous Maltese Falcon. That if you fail, my agents will find you, they will kill you, and all those you hold dear."

Nardi took the small bundle of bills and made it vanish into her dress.

"I understand. I will see you tomorrow at the agreed upon place." She looked up at the sky. "There is a storm brewing."

As she left, she caught the eye of Flambeau who indicated his satisfaction with her performance.

Neither Nardi nor Peaslee noticed the statuesque woman with the riding crop rise up from her table, daintily dab at her lips with a napkin, and then rush out of the cafe.

Nardi and Peaslee did not see this happen, but Flambeau had, and he smiled as another piece of his plan fell into place.

Vincenzo Peruggia hurried through the streets of Paris as the rain came down in sheets. He had hoped that the storm would have cooled things off, but instead it just made the heat wet, and the streets steam. It didn't help that the driving rain had found its way between the seams of his coat and beneath the brim of his slouch hat. Despite the fact that the storm had cleared the streets, it had also slowed his pace. He kept his head down, watching his feet, moving as fast as he could, dodging puddles and swollen ditches full of dingy, grey water rushing toward swirling drains. One wrong step and he would be soaked; five more minutes and it wouldn't matter either way. Through it all he clutched the painting, the poplar panel and its frame close to his chest.

Peruggia never saw the man with the umbrella until he plowed into him. He was impeccably dressed, with thick black hair sculpted with pommade, dark olive skin and a hawkish nose. He cursed in Italian as he brushed the rain from his coat. Peruggia recognized the sicilian dialect and apologized in kind, though he felt somewhat ashamed of his own northern accent.

The man with the umbrella looked him up and down.

"You are Vincenzo Peruggia are you not?"

Peruggia was startled.

"Yes. Do I know you?"

The dapper man smiled slyly.

"My name is Stromboli, Baron Cesare Stromboli. I am a dealer in unusual merchandise. I have a proposition for you. I have clients who would be interested in acquiring what you have hidden within your coat. They would pay you quite nicely."

Vincenzo Peruggia laughed at the suggestion.

"I am sorry, Signore, but I have little interest in money. I have done what you think out of national pride, for my countrymen."

As he turned to walk away, Stromboli stopped him.

"We will pay you, Vincenzo. We will pay you handsomely."

The Italian janitor turned to face the Sicilian, there was a gun in his hand.

"I think not Baron Stromboli." And with that Vincenzo Peruggia faded into the storm.

"What do you mean he refused our offer?"

The Iron King was furious, and he stalked about the room circling Stromboli like a rabid dog. In the shadows, the High Council of the Masters of the *Habits Noirs* sat watching in silence, but the Iron King could sense their displeasure, hear in his mind the things they would say to each other when he was gone.

"Did you tell him how much we were offering?" he asked.

Stromboli flailed about.

"He is mad, mad with nationalism and pride. No amount would have swayed him. I cannot tell you how afflicted he was. I have never seen anything like it."

The Iron King roared and started after Stromboli, but a hand reached out and touched his shoulder. Josephine's touch was all that it took to restrain him.

"My Lord, the *Mona Lisa* may have escaped us, but there are other treasures that move through the streets of Paris, and other ways to prove your worth to us."

She leaned in close and whispered through his mask. In the shadows, the High Council withdrew and whispered amongst themselves.

26 August, 1911

The little girl named Nardi, and she moved through the sewers as if she owned them. She was six, and had been running the tunnels since she could walk. She was a courier, a very specialized courier, transporting things that other people didn't want to have seen in the light of day. Today it was a box, small, heavy, wooden, wrapped in paper so she couldn't even see what she was carrying. It was the only thing in her bag. Her client had paid extra for exclusivity. She had one job, move the package through the tunnels that led outside the city and beyond the road blocks.

The tunnels ran for miles, and in the smaller ones, she had to worry about the buildup of poisonous and explosive gasses, but in the main galleries, with their towering ceilings, she had no such fears, and lit her torch with impunity. The flickering flame cast weird shadows across the pillars and arches, and only served to make the strange sounds that echoed through the tunnels even stranger. But Nardi had no fear of the haunting music that leaked through the underground, nor of the dark shapes that slithered in the black waters. There were places she would not go, culverts that led deeper and radiated a wicked green light that arced like lightning between misty clouds. She would not go down those tunnels, not because she was afraid, but because she knew better.

As she moved from the city center, the tunnels grew smaller; it was the way of things. At some points, the sewer was so tight that only someone of her size could have fit through. It meant that she was safe, that no one could get at her while she moved through the pipes, but it also put her at risk. When the pipes connected to the larger central galleries, they did so in a manner that left her blind. It was the one place she was vulnerable, where anyone was vulnerable, she knew it, and so did the men who were waiting for her.

They grabbed her by the collar of her coat as she came out of the pipe.

"Look what we I've caught," said the one as he held the kicking child up into the light.

The other looked her up and down.

"Rats are getting bigger it seems. Regular Sumatra down here." He grabbed her bag, the one with the box inside and ripped it open. "What do we have here?"

Nardi twisted and slipped the short blade she kept at her wrist into her hand. She slashed at the man who held her, slicing his coat and causing him to dodge backwards. His grip broken Nardi twisted free, hit the hard rock of the floor and rolled back into the pipe. The man lunged a hand in after her, but it was to no avail. He pulled back empty handed and cursed."

His partner whistled.

"Jean-Marc would you look at this?"

He had torn the paper from the box away and revealed a dark mahogany box, polished smooth save for a symbol burned into the lid. A symbol the two thugs knew very well. A symbol that they had never expected to find on a box in a sewer beneath the streets of Paris, the symbol of the *Habits Noirs*!

The Iron King turned the box in his hands over and over again while Josephine went through the catalog. She slammed the thing shut and sneered.

"The catalog number on the box doesn't match anything in our books. But the mark, and the style of the numbers, the orientation, these are consistent with other cases commissioned from 1876 through 1892."

"Well, let's open it up shall we?"

The lid slid off and revealed the treasure inside. It was a lump of crystal, larger than a man's fist. It caught the light and radiated it back in an eerie, abnormal spectrum that was at once beautiful and terrifying.

The King stared into it. It was not diamond, not a ruby, or an emerald. There was some resemblance to an opal, but only in its ability to catch the fire. In shape it was not unlike an egg, but with irregular facets and protruding shards. There was a glow about it, that in itself made it unusual, but many of the treasures in the vault were radiant, it was nothing special.

Josephine slammed the lid back down, and the King winced and grabbed at it, but only for a second.

From the shadows a figure stepped forward.

"That," said the figure, "is quite enough."

A gasp of awe escaped the Iron King as he recognized the voice and visage of Colonel Bozzo-Corona.

"Josephine, my dove, enter the stone into the catalog. Place it in the vault with the rest of the treasure. There may come a day when we want to figure this little thing out, but that is not today. We have other things to attend to."

"You are supposed to be dead!" mumbled the Iron King.

Another shadow emerged and grabbed the Iron King by the arm. The fallen monarch tried to pull away, but the man's grip tightened.

"It's not possible, you're supposed to be dead!" he whimpered.

As the Iron King was marched out, the Colonel picked up his cane, assumed his rightful place and smiled at the High Council, who once more paid fealty to the true leader of the Black Coats.

27 August 1911

Flambeau sat in the café in the shadow of the Louvre, sipping coffee and watching his niece, Nardi, hungrily devour a plate full of madeleines. Across from them sat Professor Peaslee, drinking tea and adding up the expenses Flambeau had incurred.

The tall Frenchman put down his cup and leaned in to talk to Peaslee.

"What was it? The thing in the box what was it? What was so valuable that you needed to get it into the vault, a vault surrounded by some of the most dangerous people in the world?"

Peaslee stared blankly back.

"Why not tell me? It is not as if I am foolish enough to try and steal it back."

Professor Peaslee stood up, and placed an envelope full of bills on the table.

"Three years ago, in the wilds of Siberia, a stone fell from the sky, a stone with the power to make men more than what they are. I have done my best to keep it contained, but my time is running short, and I need a more permanent solution. The *Habits Noirs* are fanatics. You, Flambeau, you steal for the art, to show that it can be done. Nardi, for the thrill. But they steal for simple greed. The insane desire to simply take what others have, and what they steal, they keep, forever. It is the only motivation that they and their Colonel have."

"The Colonel is dead," commented Flambeau, "killed by his own many years ago."

Peaslee put on his hat and shook his head.

"The *Habits Noirs* have always been led by the Colonel, and they always will be. There must always be a Colonel"

And as the strange little man with the dead face walked away, Flambeau saw Inspector Romaine find a seat at a table across away.

He wasn't alone, and Flambeau did not recognize the regal old man with the cane that he sat with. But the more he watched, the more he realized that if there were men like that in the world, men who could make even police inspectors look ill, then perhaps it was time to find a new line of work, for him and for his Nardi.

What Sam Spade is to the American hard-boiled thriller, and Lemmy Caution to its British cousin, Nestor Burma is to its French equivalent. The pugnacious and sarcastic director of the Fiat Lux detective Agency has not graced our pages since Win Scott Eckert's "Les Lèvres Rouges" in our Volume 3 (which is briefly referenced in the story below). Josh Reynolds's contribution to the saga of the unflappable and quintessentially French Monsieur Burma is therefore most welcome, especially since it involves uncovering the secrets of yet another genealogy of evil...

Josh Reynolds: *Nestor Burma Goes West*

Arizona, 1954

Dust congealed on the car's windows, baked into the glass by the heat of the sun overhead. Nestor Burma took another drag on his pipe, his third bowlful since the last gas station, and squinted against the bright light seeping through the streaks of dust on the glass. He twisted the knob on the radio, scanning the dial for anything without a twang or a choir.

"*...so-called devil-girl claiming to be from Mars terrorized the guests at a country inn in Scotland for...*"

He twisted the knob again, wincing at the burst of static.

"*...Ellinson's daughter was found unharmed. Doctor Harold Medford, an entomologist with the Department of Agriculture and Agent Robert Graham of the FBI could not be reached for...*"

Burma flicked the radio off. He was too far out in the middle of nowhere to get anything but AM news stations. Burma wasn't a fan of the news, especially when he could only follow two words in three. His English was rusty. He'd tried practicing on the air hostess on the flight over, but she hadn't been buying it.

He expelled smoke through the corner of his mouth, gnawing slightly on the end of the pipe. The sun made the horizon look like water. It was all sand and rock, and great, vast expanses of nothing. Apparently, that was why his quarry had come out here. He glanced at the files tossed haphazardly across the Ford's passenger seat.

He then thought of Jim Anthony.

He was a recluse now, but he had been a detective, back when Burma himself had been more idealistic and criminally inclined. Back before the War, and before Hitler's jackboot had set its print on Paris, Anthony had been a frequent visitor. He'd tangled with the 'mask and menace' set in the 30s, when Burma had still been espousing the tenets of anarchy with a straight face.

The Frenchman grunted with bitter amusement. Doctor Cornelius and his lot had been more anarchic than Burma and his friends on their best day. There weren't many of them running around these days, though. The War had hit them hard. Replacing bell-clappers with body-parts was kids' stuff compared to herding a third of your population into crematoriums.

He frowned. He wasn't amused any more.

The woman had called herself Pam Rive, but that name had been as fake as her tan. The case was a runaway girl, gone hunting a runaway *père*, a father long gone, and during the war, according to Rive. Not so strange. Plenty of Yankee and Limey daddies had come and gone with the Nazis. Only this Yankee daddy was a prize catch.

Burma had been at it long enough to know there was always a hook, especially if the bait was as tantalizing as Pam Rive had been. Hélène had hated her at first sight, as she leaned against the doorframe of the Fiat Lux Agency in a pose she'd picked up from the *femme fatales* from the films. She was a beauty, no two ways there, but there was beauty and then there was beauty, and hers was the former. There was a feral sharpness in her, like a street apache dressed up in a fancy suit. A killer in fine clothes was still a killer; and Pam Rive reeked of blood, in the spiritual sense.

Still, it was hard to resist a face like that. So now, he was tooling across the Sonoran Desert in a beat-up rental, listening to lay-preachers scream about the rapture and monotone newsmen bark about the twin dangers of communism and nuclear gigantism in insects.

Something heavy and fast scuttled across the road in front of him, and he spun the wheel hard, nearly biting the stem of his pipe in half. A tarantula the size of an elephant paused in the watery glare of the sun and the red hairs on its abdomen looked like blood. It gazed at the car for a moment, eight eyes oscillating weirdly and then it was gone, moving south. Burma watched it go and released a shaky breath. He realized that his pipe had fallen into his lap when he smelled his trousers begin to burn and he yelped and cursed. Angrily, he stuffed the pipe back in his mouth and re-filled and re-lit the bowl.

Shaking his head, he re-started the engine and continued on. Overhead, something dark and far away banked and turned. He'd seen it twice before since he'd entered the desert, though he wasn't certain that it was the same shape. Perhaps it was a giant bird, hunting for the giant spider. Everything was bigger in America and it was a land of gods and monsters, with emphasis on the latter.

It was another hour of driving through the heat and the dust before he saw the pueblo. It looked a little different from the grainy, distance photo in *Time* magazine, but that was only to be expected. Burma himself looked a lot different from the photos taken a decade ago, and if people could change, why not buildings? It looked like the drawings he'd seen of pueblos, like a series of children's blocks made from adobe and stacked one atop another in a semi-circle around a large stone well. But the similarities ended there. On the roof were flat metal structures that reminded him of mirrors and something like a tarp made from linen and canvas stretched from the edges of the rooftops past the well, pulled taut by heavy poles driven into the ground at the corners.

He knew what it was without really knowing, because he'd seen enough camouflage to recognize it no matter the shape it came in. Someone was scared of being seen from the air. Maybe the paparazzi had taken to buzzing Anthony's hideaway? Or maybe it was something else. Burma leaned forward, peering up through the windshield, squinting. He drove under the tarp. He tapped the brake and the rental slid to a halt in a cloud of dust beside the well.

Burma got out. He considered calling out, but decided that whoever was in residence had likely seen him coming a mile out. It had taken him weeks to locate this place. Weeks spent poring over mouldy magazines in libraries that still showed signs of the war. Jim Anthony hadn't been one for sitting still for interviews or photo opportunities. He had been a private man, despite having his face splashed across the front pages of a dozen different newspapers. Burma had read them all, trying to get a feeling for the man Pam Rives' daughter had gone hunting for.

He'd even contacted Ardan, who owed him for that thing with Adelaide Lupin back in '46. Ardan and Anthony had crossed paths several times, and the American press had attributed more than one of the former's adventures to the latter and vice-versa. But Ardan hadn't had much in the way of information. Anthony had tangled with a bad lot in Vienna close to the beginning of the war, and done a round or six with some Nazi *ubermensch* calling himself Sun Koh off and on throughout the Forties. And he'd had a daughter, apparently.

Vera was the girl's name. Vera Pima, last name with the south-western twang, the name her father had used. That was what Rive had said, only that rang false the longer Burma was on the trail. If Anthony had used an assumed name, that was one thing, but why had Rive never tried to find him? And if she had been intent on raising the girl alone, why let her know who her father had been in the first place? No, something stank here.

He looked at the sky again, the sun drizzling down through the frayed patches in the canvas, but the sun was still too high and he saw no sign of the flying thing. Hands in his pockets, he strode towards the pueblo, trailing a twitching tail of pipe smoke. The doors were open, letting in the heat. Brightly coloured rugs were on the adobe floor but no pictures on the walls, no sign of habitation, other than the faint smell of bread cooking in vegetable oil. Burma took his pipe out of his mouth and, leaning against the door frame, tapped out the bowl on the sole of his shoe. He refilled it, looking around. He stepped back and relit it, looking up at the next level. No ladders leading up, like he'd seen in the drawings, but stairs.

Something clattered, above him. Instantly alert, his hand found the butt of the *Modele* 1935A semi-automatic pistol holstered in his armpit and he drew it. The weight was comforting, though he'd rather not use it, if he didn't have to. It had been easy enough to get it into the country, and his documents were up to date, something that was necessary in his line. Anthony hadn't been one for guns, according to those yellowed column inches he'd scrounged. He was a knife and fingers sort of guy, the Super-Detective. A gun put you even, in most cases, but hands meant skill. Burma had fought stranglers and brawlers before and it was never pleasant.

He sucked on his pipe, debating the merits of going upstairs to investigate. He felt eyes on him. Ardan had said that Anthony was a bit of a savage, and not in the *le bon sauvage* sense. A man like that might not take kindly to visitors, especially armed ones.

Something moved in the front room, just out of the corner of his eye. The pistol swung around, but there was nothing to aim at, just a clicking beaded curtain. But he could hear something, something that might have been footsteps. The canvas rustled and he saw a blotch of darkness and then it was gone, even as he spun, cursing. He turned back as he heard a scrape of bare flesh on wood.

The poles at the far end of the pueblo's front expanse rattled, and then the roof of his rental gave a groan. He turned back, but too slowly. There were two of them, he was sure of that much. The canvas bowed as more dark splotches appeared.

"Maybe more than two," he muttered, looking up. Rocks rattled. His eyes swivelled down. Something dark, with two great blazing eyes, lunged at him, impossibly close. Metal flashed and the wide flop of his tie was sacrificed as he stumbled back against the adobe, his semi-automatic giving a bark. The black shape twisted with a cry and staggered. It was a man, he realized, clad in a black bodysuit, his head hidden in a black mask, a pair of odd goggles covering his eyes. A long knife fell to the ground as the man in black fell back, blood pumping from the wound in his chest.

Burma touched his own chest. The knife had sliced through his tie and shirt, but only barely kissed the flesh beneath, leaving a seeping trail of red. He heard the sounds of canvas tearing above him. More knives shredded the canvas, cutting ragged gaps. Through one such gap, the black muzzle of a Sterling submachine gun was thrust and it gave a savage burp.

Burma felt himself hauled inside, out of the path of the swarm of lead hornets. He hit the floor and rolled as a large, tawny shape tossed something outside and kicked the door shut.

"Up, detective," the shape growled.

It grabbed the crook of his arm and jerked him to his feet. Through the thin window, Burma saw brightly coloured smoke filling the empty space beneath the canvas.

"What?" he said.

"You got here right on time, Mr. Burma," Jim Anthony said—and it was him, older, but large, broad and rangy.

Burma recognized him, despite the addition of a decade to the face on his pictures. Shirtless and shoeless, wearing only a pair of linen trousers, Anthony looked more dangerous half-naked than most men looked fully-clothed.

"Any later, and I'd have had to go out and look for you."

"There was a tarantula," Burma said, jerking his arm free of Anthony's grip.

"Is he still out and about?" Anthony murmured, peering out the window. "We'll add it to the to-do list, I suppose."

"What the Devil is going on?" Burma said, touching his chest again.

"*Les Vampires*," said a young woman who'd stepped out from behind the curtain, clutching a battered looking Sten gun in two hands. She was as pretty as her mother, but she had her father's eyes.

"*Merde*," Burma said. The name was like a stone in his belly. He looked at the girl. "You're Vera Pima," he said.

"And you're the patsy my mother hired to lead her here, when she lost my trail," Vera said.

She was tall with a figure that put him in mind of an acrobat he'd known once. Dark hair, chopped short and dark eyes that gazed out hungrily from a Mediterranean face. Burma thought if being the daughter of a murderess and a millionaire didn't suit her, she'd be right at home in the pictures. She wore black like a second skin and carried style like the Sten she cradled in a sure grip. There was something feral about her too, that set Burma's hackles to saluting.

"You weren't hard to find," he said defensively even as he cursed silently. He'd known something was up, just not what...his eyes widened. "Oh, Hell," he said. "Pam Rive... Vampire!"

He looked at Anthony, who nodded.

"Irma Vep," he said.

"She can't be! Irma Vep has to be, what, seventy by now? Not to mention dead!" Burma said.

"She is, but her daughter isn't. And her granddaughter," Anthony said, glancing at Vera.

A look passed between them, and Burma felt a flush of guilt for having interrupted what was quite likely a very intense bit of soap opera. The guilt was replaced a moment later by annoyance and he threw up his hands in frustration.

"Vera Pima? No wonder I couldn't find any record of that surname," he said, disgusted with his own idiocy.

Anthony chuckled.

"They're clever. You have to know that the pattern is there before you can spot it," he said, hiking a thumb over one shoulder to indicate the door.

A moment later, the door shuddered in its frame, as if struck by a dozen fists, rapidly.

Anthony's grin turned feral. "Armor plated."

"I hope that goes for the walls. There must be a dozen of them out there," Burma said.

"More than that," Vera said. "Mother doesn't believe in half-measures."

"The pueblo was built to withstand an invasion. Granted, I didn't think it'd be them doing the invading, but one gang of murderous ideologues is as good as another," Anthony said. He looked up, eyes narrowing. "Of course, eventually they'll get in. Vermin always does one way or another."

"What was that you threw out there?" Burma said.

"A concoction of mine," Anthony said.

He reached into the pocket of his trousers and pulled out a handful of what looked like marbles of varying hues and shades.

"Hard jelly spheres. Each contains a different ingredient that, when you mash two or more together with enough force, creates a specific chemical reaction." He smiled thinly. "Such as that cloud of chilli gas out there now. It burns the eyes and lungs."

"Ardan told me you were smart," Burma said.

Anthony's eyebrows went up in an expression of mild surprise. "High praise," he said. "Of course, if I was so smart, I'd have figured out who Pam Rive was before I…" He hesitated and looked suddenly downcast. "Dolores is never going to let me hear the end of this."

"Your wife," Burma said, recalling the name from Ardan's files. Dolores Colquitt-Anthony, the daughter of an American senator and Anthony's wife. As formidable a woman in her own way as Irma Vep was in hers. "I think you'll have a bit of explaining to do, yes."

"How did you track me?" the girl said. "I was taught to hide by the best!"

"You obviously didn't listen then," Burma said. "I lost your trail in Cannes, for a bit, but picked it up in Bruges, and then again in London. You went all over the map, but once I had your scent, I saw the pattern."

"There was no pattern!" Vera protested.

"That was the pattern," Anthony said, and Burma nodded.

"It…" he began.

"My mother is here," Vera said suddenly.

The girl was sitting easily on her haunches, mimicking her father, the Sten gun across her knees. She cocked her head, listening. So did Anthony. Burma strained to hear whatever it was the pair had caught. All he heard was a brief, faint whine of thin sound.

"What is that?" he said.

"Battlefield whistles. The Vampires use them like signal drums these days, or so I'm given to understand." He nodded to Vera. "She's pulling them back until the cloud dissipates, which should be in twelve seconds, if the breeze holds."

Anthony rose and peered out the window. He didn't flinch when a bullet flattened itself against the glass.

252

"The windows are holding. That's something at least," he said mildly.

"I can't believe I didn't see them," Burma said, pounding his fist into his knee.

Anthony craned his neck, looking up.

"Something is up there. Looks like one of Mayen's atomic vessels, but it's painted in reflective paint. No idea how it's hovering there though. I'd give a finger to study it up close. Mayen destroyed most of his vessels after the fall of Berlin, and the Russians snapped up the last one. Or what I thought was the last one," he mused.

"I should have asked for triple my fee," Burma said, chewing on the stem of his pipe. "Reflective airships and assassins in black are out of my league."

"I'm feeling *déjà vu* myself," Anthony said. He looked at his daughter. "Your mother is sparing no expense, it seems. Then, from what I recall, she did seem to enjoy the grand gesture."

Vera made a face.

"She enjoys a good many things," she said, her fingers tapping the barrel of the Sten. Burma could see more than one story in her eyes, and none of them particularly happy. What must it have been like to grow up as the daughter of the Great Vampire? Burma didn't like to think about it. It was bad enough knowing your father was a master thief, and bad as he could be, Arsène Lupin was no patch on Irma Vep.

"Yes, well," Anthony said. He held up a hand. "It's gone quiet. That's almost never a good sign."

The pueblo suddenly shook, again and again, as if struck by the hand of a giant. Dust sifted down.

"What the Devil was that?" Burma said.

Flames roared up around the window and metal screeched as one of the reflectors toppled from the roof to crash through the now burning canvas.

Anthony crab-walked towards one of the large rugs and hauled it aside.

"Our hint that it's time to go, I'd say."

"Go where?" Burma said, coughing. Smoke was boiling into the room from above and the pueblo shook again.

"Down and over," Anthony said, looking around.

He placed his fingers into a set of five depressions, evenly spaced, and rotated his wrist. Burma's eyes widened as dust puffed and a trapdoor rose on weighted hinges.

"It'll take them a few minutes to figure that we're not coming out. By the time they do, we'll be in the garage."

"How does that help us?" Burma said.

"There are cars in the garage," Anthony said, as if bewildered at the question.

"Yes, but there's an invisible jet out there," Burma said.

"Argue later. Run now," Vera said, dropping with cat-like grace through the trapdoor.

Burma clambered after her, and Anthony came last, pulling the stone trap door shut as he descended. It shut with a thump, and for a moment they were cast into utter darkness. Then, with an insect hum, harsh lights sparked to life along the walls. Burma turned and saw that Anthony had pressed a switch on the wall. In the light, he could see ancient drawings marking the rough walls.

"These tunnels were here long before I moved in," Anthony said by way of explanation. "I simply re-purposed them. According to a friend of mine—a fellow named Harley Warren—there was an entire civilization down here, stretching across the width and breadth of the American Southwest, and they were an unpleasant people, by all accounts. Harley and a gentleman named Ravenwood had a nasty encounter with the inhabitants of one of their cities—K'n-Yan, I think he called it. They were snake worshippers, apparently."

The corridor shook around them. Anthony grinned and glanced up as Burma made a strangled sound.

"We're safe enough, Mr. Burma. I designed the pueblo to collapse in on itself in the event of this sort of bombardment. The debris will shelter the tunnel better than reinforced concrete."

"I still don't understand why they hired me in the first place," Burma said, lighting his pipe. He peered at Vera. "What did you take?"

The girl blinked. "What?"

"What did you take? People like *Les Vampires* don't go to war over wayward daughters."

"And what do you know about them, Mr. Detective?" she said.

"Enough," he said. "I've run across and skirted the edge of a scheme or three, and felt lucky not to do more than that!"

"It's not what she took. It's what she has," Anthony said. "We were in the process of discussing just that when you showed up, Mr. Burma."

Vera frowned at her father, who grinned insouciantly.

"Eidetic memory," she said finally, tapping the side of her head. "Names, dates, amounts, locations, everything mother never wanted me to see until the right time. I have it all up here."

"You stole their entire organization," Burma said, comprehension dawning slowly.

"For all intents and purposes," Anthony said. "Imagine, Mr. Burma, what Interpol could do with that, eh? Or SNIF, or even an old coyote like me." He grinned again, and the expression this time was positively vulpine. "We should continue this in the car. Let's go."

The corridor sloped down and then rose again in an uneven, silent rhythm, like fossilized waves. The scrawled atavisms on the walls seemed to pursue them, and the faintly ophidian nature of their design set Burma's guts to squirming. Anthony led the way and when they came to what looked like a deck hatch, he opened it with barely a grunt of effort, throwing it wide and bounding into the cavern beyond.

Lights came on, revealing a wide, deep cavern. The walls were lined with workbenches and bulky machinery, the purposes of which escaped Burma. There was also a pool of dark, oily looking water and a cylinder of metal descending from the roof of the cavern into its center. Burma nodded to it.

"The well," he said. "That's not water, is it?"

"Very observant," Anthony said. "It's oil, actually. A natural reservoir, I believe."

More lights flickered to life, illuminating several drop-cloth covered automobiles resting on what looked to be hydraulic lifts, like one might find in a mechanic's garage. Burma whistled.

"Yes, it is quite impressive, in a sort of brute chic way, I suppose," a woman's voice said.

Shapes rose from behind a car, weapons flashing. Anthony's hand sent Burma tumbling as gunfire ripped through the hollow silence of the cavern. As he hit the ground, Burma clawed for his pistol. He saw Vera brace her legs and let loose with the Sten, stitching shots across the cars. A man screamed in pain as more men, more vampires, leapt from atop the banks of machinery, blades in their hands. These were not the malignant street apaches of earlier decades, but instead, lean, black-clad killers, looking like something out of an Italian comic book.

Anthony slapped aside a thrust blade and spun, stealing his opponent's momentum, rolling with the blow, his elbow snapping down like a trip-hammer, into the small of the vampire's back. Burma heard bone crack and then he was up, the semi-automatic in his hand spitting lead. A body staggered and flopped at his feet. Then, all at once, something sharp tickled his carotid artery and everything fell quiet.

"Stop, please," a woman said, her voice carrying easily across the cavern.

Vera had taken cover behind a bullet-riddled Studebaker, and Anthony dropped the vampire he'd been throttling.

"I will kill Mr. Burma, unless you stop."

Anthony raised his hands.

"Hello Pam. Or is it Irma?"

"Either will do. The letters mean the same thing, no matter their order," Pam Rive—Irma Vep—said, her breath tickling Burma's ear. "You are quite the bloodhound, Mr. Burma. You accomplished in one week what it would have taken my people months to do."

"Maybe you should get new people," Burma said.

The tip of the blade dug into his neck and he fell silent.

"Maybe so, eh? Still, they did well enough getting me in here," Vep said. "A secret garage, really?" she said, sounding faintly disappointed. "I expected better."

"You're flying around in an invisible jet," Anthony said. "Those went out of fashion with consulting detectives and rubies filched from Asian idols."

"Touché," Vep said. "*Bonjour,* my sweet girl," she continued, twisting Burma towards Vera. "You have led me on quite the merry chase, my child. And all for what, to meet the brood stallion who provided a few errant chromosomes?"

"I'll admit that wasn't my finest night, but really now—brood stallion?" Anthony said. He was tensed, legs spread and bent, arms raised, but not in an attitude of surrender.

"Oh, quite," Vep purred. "You were a means to an end, Mr. Anthony."

"Me?" Vera said, her word tinged with bitterness.

"But of course, my poppet," Vep said. "Every queen must have her heir, even a Queen of Vampires. My mother sought out a dangerous man, and her mother before her. Only the strong survive in this cruel world, and Irma Vep will be the strongest there is, even if we must design her to be such..."

"Eugenics dropped out of fashion a few years ago," Anthony said.

"The results speak for themselves," Vep said.

Burma could feel her heartbeat through his coat. She was excited. The thought made him queasy.

"My father's name was synonymous with terror in his time, as mine is now. But terror isn't enough, anymore. Survival is the key to the future. And you, Mr. Anthony, are a survivor. You play idealist, but my father knew you for what you are and my mother as well. Why else would she have sent me to you? You are a savage, as brutal as any Cimmerian or Pict from the *Nemedian Chronicles.*"

Burma felt her shift and he winced as the blade scored his throat.

"You're also a bad influence."

"No worse than you," Vera said, rising slowly, despite Anthony's gesture for her to stay put.

"When I was five, you shot my piano tutor."

"I'm not a fan of Brahms," Vep said. Burma felt her shrug.

"When I was eight, you had my nanny strangled," Vera said.

"I got you a better one right after," Vep said.

"You kept me locked away. You trained me to steal and kill and seduce."

"Would any mother do less?" Vep said. She clucked her tongue. "I've spoiled you, really."

Burma saw the Sten come up. The look in Vera's eyes said that he had become an obstacle rather than a person, and she wouldn't hesitate to shoot through him to get to her mother. Vep chuckled, and he knew she'd seen the same thing. Maybe that was what she wanted. Maybe that was how the myth was kept alive, one Irma Vep replacing the next down the long dark line of vampire queens.

It was quite mythic, after a fashion. Burma, however, wanted no part of myths. His elbow jabbed back, catching Vep in her leather-clad midsection, eliciting a surprised exhalation and then he was diving aside. The Sten spat seventeen years worth of repressed hostility, but Vep wasn't going easily. The bullets chewed the stone floor and Vep caromed off of a '36 Ford and sprang for her daughter like a bat out of hell, hair streaming behind her, teeth bared, her eyes hidden behind dark goggles. The throat-slitters in her hands scraped streamers of sparks off the Sten's barrel as Vera hastily interposed the weapon. Her mother's boot caught her in the belly, knocking her sprawling.

"Ungrateful whelp," Vep hissed. "Spare the rod, I suppose. From here on out it'll be more beatings, fewer kisses."

Her blades slashed down. And then Anthony caught her wrists. For a moment, they strained over their daughter. Then the girl was rolling aside and Anthony flung Vep backwards with a heave of his shoulders.

The vampires swarmed the Super-Detective, black-clad shapes folding over and covering a bronze one like oil on metal. Even as the thought occurred to Burma, a second shoved its way to the fore.

"Ha!" he said, scrambling to retrieve his pistol. He snatched it up and spun, his eyes finding the bullet-riddled cars and the fluid leaking from them. He fired. The bullet struck the rock, trailing sparks. The gasoline caught, and quickly.

The oil caught even quicker.

In the hazy light, Burma saw Anthony rise to the top of his particular heap, manhandling the vampires with simian ease. He moved quicker than a snake, all piston fists and jabbing fingers. There was a tiger's grin on his face, a rapturous look that chilled Burma to the bone, and made him very glad not to be the one on the other end of it.

"Get to the car," Vera said, coughing, grabbing his arm. He almost shook her off, but she had inherited her father's strength, and held him tight. "He'll be fine, Mr. Detective! Get to the car!"

Burma allowed the girl to shove him into an Aston Martin DB2. He didn't complain when she slid behind the wheel. He was too busy putting a bullet into an overeager vampire's chest as the man grabbed for the door, a Mauser clutched in one gloved hand. The straight-6 engine grumbled to life and then they were moving and quickly, shoving two other cars aside with dual screeches of chrome-on-chrome. The Aston Martin shot forward, nothing but fire in the rearview mirror.

Something thumped onto the roof and then they were charging up a ramp, around a tight corner and out through a heavy drop-cloth that had been painted to look like rock. They hit light, and skidded through flames. The vampires had been busy upstairs; they'd flattened the pueblo, wiping it off the map. What they hadn't flattened was now shuddering with internal explosions as something deep in the heart of the complex went off like a roman candle.

Burma gazed mournfully at his rental as it skipped, twisted and burned in the explosion, before finally tumbling into the growing sinkhole spreading outward from the pueblo. Sighting the latter, he turned to Vera.

"Faster, please, *mademoiselle*," he said.

Vera's only reply was a snarl. The car bumped and swerved, and then hit the road, riding straight and flat out of a cloud of dust. Vera spun the wheel with the flair of a Grand Prix winner, spinning the Aston Martin around, so that the front faced the way they had just come. Dust swept over them and dispersed. Burma yelped as a grimy, soot-stained hand swatted the windshield.

He got out even as Anthony rolled off of the top of the car. Even blistered and slightly baked, Anthony looked cheerful. He stretched and swatted at a flicker of flame on his trouser leg.

"Well, that's the deductible done for," he said.

Burma shook his head and sat down on the Aston Martin's hood. "Did they...?"

"Get out? Probably," Anthony said, "Some of them, at least."

He looked at his daughter over the roof of the car. She frowned. For a moment, Burma considered asking what secret communication had passed between father and daughter, but then thought better of it.

"I don't think I am getting paid," Burma said.

"Probably not," Anthony said. "Still, if you're interested, I might have a job for you." Burma looked at him. Anthony slapped the roof of the car. "Someone needs to cover her trail," he said, gesturing to Vera. "I think the best man for the job is the one who tracked her in the first place."

Burma grunted and scrubbed the heels of his hands across his head.

"Change her name," he said. "That's the first thing I'd suggest."

Anthony looked at Vera, who grinned suddenly, in an expression eerily similar to her father's own.

"I've always been partial to the name Gemini," she said.

"Vera Gemini," Burma said, rolling it around on his tongue. "Sounds like something from a comic strip."

"I think it suits me," Vera said, leaning against the Aston Martin.

Burma looked at Anthony and then back at Vera, all in black, leaning against the sports car. He got an image in his head, not quite a premonition, of what she might become, and what sort of world the Vampires and Super-Detectives were leaving her, of black-clad killers and masks and menaces.

"Maybe it does at that," he said.

One more tale in our ongoing series devoted to the Treasure of the Black Coats. This time, our regular contributor Frank Schildiner explores the fundamental power that lies at the very core of the Treasure: that of absolute corruption. Here, Frank shows that even one as evil and powerful as the notorious Mr. Big can succumb to its fatal attraction...

Frank Schildiner: *The True Cost of Doing Business*

Paris, 1952

Buonaparte Ignace Gallia stepped out of the Rolls Royce Silver Shark and looked about the Paris street. He was a tall, powerfully built man with dark skin, and hair and eyes, dressed in an expensive suit freshly tailored from one of the most exclusive shops on Saville Row. Glancing about again, he couldn't see the purpose of this meeting with the infamous Colonel Bozzo-Corona of BlackSpear Holdings. His new, powerful organization, sponsored by SMERSH, was rising in power in France and the United States, not to mention a small island he would soon control.

But he had agreed to a meeting with the Colonel as a way to prevent open warfare that would have been detrimental to all concerned. But why here? Before an elderly English banking house? Perhaps his belief that the Colonel was losing his grip and should be replaced as the premier criminal leader in the Old World was proving true.

"The street's clear, boss," Tee Hee Johnson said, with a giggle, his bald, bullet head swiveling about slowly and carefully, searching for any enemy who might take out his leader.

Tee Hee, so named because of his habit of giggling for no reason, was as tall as his boss, but broader and possessing the physique of a wrestler.

"How's your arm?" Gallia asked, checking his new Rolex.

The diamonds twinkled in the bright sunlight and he smiled at his affluence.

Tee Hee laughed briefly and flexed his right arm slowly.

"Just fine, sir. Albert almost got me this time!"

Gallia shook his head.

"You spend too much time with those alligators. Someday, one of them will bite your arm off."

Tee Hee cackled again.

"And you'll buy me a new one, boss. Sorry about Baron Samedi. That big dude won't be easy to replace! Who knew those Union Corse gangsters would come out shooting? The poor Baron didn't stand a chance!"

Gallia shook his head.

"Those were not Draco's men; they belonged to the Matarese group. And the Baron is the man who cannot die. He will return."

Before Tee Hee could respond, the Baron himself stepped out of a nearby alley and gave them both a wide shark-like grin. He towered above both men, long and lean, dressed in a white tuxedo jacket with tails and a long white top hat. He moved with the smooth grace of a jungle cat and the left side of his face was painted white.

Before Tee Hee could register his shock, Baron Samedi whipped out a long flute and began playing *Peter and the Wolf.* He nodded towards the bank's door and continued to play as the legendary Colonel of the Black Coats strode out of the bank.

The Colonel resembled an elderly banker, his gray hair perfectly brushed into place, his suit quietly elegant. But there was an air of power about the man, a calm control that made Gallia think of a tiger.

The Colonel gave a respectful bow to Baron Samedi and raised an eyebrow as he examined Gallia and Tee Hee.

"You must be Colonel Bozzo-Corona," Gallia spat out. "They say you're immortal and the son of the Devil."

He wished he could pull out the pistol from his waist and shoot this man dead. But that would merely start a war that the Black Coats would continue to the death. Gallia planned on taking them apart, one piece at a time.

"You are Buonaparte Ignace Gallia, or should I call you 'Mr. Big?' Or Doctor Kananga, soon master of the island of San Monique? Your slow liquidation of the treasure of Captain Morgan was quite enjoyable to witness."

The Colonel placed his hands behind his back as he looked up at Gallia. Mr. Big smiled slightly and responded:

"Your once-proud but now dwindling organization was my inspiration. Now my people are about to control all of your holdings in France and Italy."

The Colonel nodded and continued:

"I could simply start a war between us, and let the chips fall where they may, but I have a proposal for you. You have heard of the legendary treasure of the Black Coats? Good! Follow me."

He turned back towards the bank. Gallia started and asked:

"Here? This is the Pilaster Bank! Is this where you hide your treasure?"

The Colonel smiled enigmatically and led them through the bank, Baron Samedi's flute still playing as he trotted behind. The bank employees bowed and stepped aside as the Colonel took them through the main floor and into the Chairman's chambers.

Entering a private elevator, they rode downward for several minutes. Then, the doors opened upon a room that streetched as far as the eye could see.

But the size of the room was unimportant compared to the contents before their eyes. Even the hoard of the mythical dragon Fafnir could not have compared to the fabled treasure of the Black Coats. Stacks of gold bars lined the walls; chests full of sparkling jewels and chalices lay about in various spots around the room. There were huge columns of gold coins. There were ancient books and manuscripts, stacks as far as the eye could see of paper money from England, the United States, China, France, Switzerland and Germany... bags full of ancient coins made from silver and platinum... safes filled with stocks and bonds and warrants and IOU's...

Gallia and Tee Hee could barely breathe at the sheer magnitude of the treasure...

"All the contents in this room will be yours," the Colonel stated with a broad smile, "but in exchange, you will give me all of your agents in Europe and your growing interests in South America."

"That will take several days to gather," Gallia explained, putting his hand under his jacket and on his pistol. "What is there to prevent me from simply ordering my men to kill you here and now?"

The Colonel continued to smile and raised his hand, showing a small box in his fist.

"The building is wired to explode and this is a dead man switch. I am not the master of the foremost criminal organization in the history of the world for nothing! I am wealth incarnate. Kings and Emperors are lesser beings to me, and none equal me on this Earth. I have one rival, and only he can view the world such as I do."

Leading them upstairs back to the board room, the Colonel pointed to a telephone and said:

"We both know your statement about needing more time is a poor lie at best. A man such as yourself knows the name of every single member of your organization. Tell everything you know to the person at the other end of this telephone, and your men will be dealt with summarily. I will know if you are holding something back. And I will respond poorly if you lie..."

Gallia stood and stared at the Colonel for several moments, but the thought of the sheer volume of treasure was overwhelming. Sighing and shrugging, Mr. Big strode off to the telephone, lifted it, but heard no dial tone. There was only the sound of breathing at the other end of the line...

A second later, Gallia began reciting the names of all of his agents in Europe and South America. He knew that, with the treasure, he could rebuild his organization in a short time, and this time, destroy the Colonel and his pathetic, gang.

The Colonel nodded and handed a key to Tee Hee.

"A wise decision, my friend. Now I will leave you to your riches. May we never meet again."

Gallia led Tee Hee and Baron Samedi to the elevator, the doors closing as the Colonel vanished from sight.

A moment later, the elevator dropped several floors and opened on the same sub-basement level they had visited earlier.

But it was empty!

Nnothing was there... the room echoed with the footsteps of Gallia and Tee Hee as they strode around, looking with disbelief.

Gallia spun in a circle and yelled:

"Empty! This is not possible! I counted the time it took us to drop! It was the same! What happened to the treasure?!"

"Hey, boss!" Tee Hee called out, lifting a small leather bag up and handing it to Gallia.

The bag contained thirty identical silver denarius coins, the likeness of Emperor Tiberius visible to their eyes. Also within the bag was a tiny piece of paper, which Tee Hee unfolded and read aloud:

"*The price of doing business.* What's that supposed to mean, boss?"

Baron Samedi threw back his head and laughed aloud, his voice echoing through the walls of the empty room...

Bradley Sinor already used Jules Verne's intrepid Michel Ardan in his story "Where the Shadows Began" published in Tales of the Shadowmen 6. *Whereas the previous tale took place in Paris, and pit Ardan against otherworldly horrors, this yarn happens in Baltimore, where our cosmic traveler faces a much more earthly threat...*

Bradley H. Sinor: *The Silence*

Baltimore, 1889

Michael Ardan knelt by the edge of the lake and picked up two round smooth stones. He weighed them in his hand, reminded of the days in his youth at his grandfather's farm when the two of them would have contests to see who could skip a stone the most times across the water and try to get one farther.

Along the shore there were several dozen others, children and adults, all enjoying an early Saturday morning; picnicking, laughing and watching the several dozen ducks who skimmed their way across the clear blue surface of the lake.

Coming out here, just letting his mind wander back to his childhood, was one of the things that Ardan enjoyed. Sometimes he needed to get away from all the demands of his life. Not that he didn't enjoy the things he did, but sometimes he just needed to get away to some place far, far away.

Ardan knew he had not gotten far enough away when he heard the sound of footsteps behind him. Without much conscious thought, his hand slipped inside his coat, reaching for the colt peacemaker he wore in a shoulder holster. He stopped in mid-movement and didn't draw the weapon when he saw who the stranger was: Officer Jonas Drake of the Baltimore Police department.

A thin scarecrow of a man, who looked like a good stiff wind would send him flying off into the inner harbor, Drake had recently been assigned the Homicide squad and was known for being willing to shake up things if it was necessary to solve a case.

"Well, hello, Drake. I would hardly have expected to see you out here. Taking a walk to clear your head?" said Ardan, standing up and brushing loose grass from his trousers.

"Not really. I came looking for you," said the policeman.

"Me?"

"Yes, we've had a bit of an odd case, and I need the opinion of someone who knows his firearms."

From his coat pocket, Drake produced a small envelope that he offered to Ardan.

Inside was a soft-nosed revolver bullet, the end blunted from impact to form a little metal mushroom. Ardan couldn't be sure, but there looked to be some sort of scratch marks on the sides, no doubt from someone taking a pocket knife and digging it free from whatever—or whoever—the projectile had ended up in.

"Who was the victim and where's the body?" asked Ardan.

"That's the interesting part," said Drake. "There is no body; the shooter missed. The victim will be waiting for us at his office."

The law offices of Santee & Dickson were located in a recently completed building overlooking the docks of the Inner Harbor. Ardan watched bricklayers and other workmen moving around on scaffolding that wrapped itself around a building just across the street. Two men sat at the end of one scaffold, apparently deep in a conversation while eating sandwiches, and quite at home nearly thirty feet in the air.

"Nice view," he said.

Drake looked up and nodded.

"I talked with one of my cousins who just came back from New York City. He said he saw buildings ten and fifteen stories, and men building them like they were working down on the ground. The future is coming at us full blast."

"Indeed it is," said Ardan.

The suite of law offices took up most of the floor. There was a young man sitting behind a desk when they walked in and he nodded and pointed toward a large oak door.

"If you gentleman will wait in the conference room, I'll fetch Mr. Santee. He said to let him know the minute you arrived," the younger man said.

Like most lawyers' establishments that Ardan had been in, and he had frequented his fair share over the last few decades, the conference room was dominated by a large wooden table and a half dozen leather upholstered chairs.

"It looks to me like the legal profession has been very good to the partners here," he said.

An ornate oriental vase stood on a table beneath an oil painting of a man dressed in clothing from the founding of America. There were five other such paintings on the walls of the conference room.

"Indeed it has, and for well over a hundred years."

The voice belonged to a man in his fifties, who came through the door that Ardan and Drake had used mere minutes before.

"Mr. Santee," said Drake. "It's good to see you again."

The lawyer stood in the doorway for a moment, eyeing both men, before coming into the room. He seemed momentarily reluctant, which puzzled Ardan, though that passed quickly.

"Gentlemen, welcome." Santee extended his hand to Drake and then turned to Ardan.

"This is the man that I spoke to you about, Mr. Santee," said the policeman. "May I present Michael Ardan of the Baltimore Gun Club."

"I'm hoping, sir, that you can supply some answers and help officer Drake find out who the Devil is trying to kill me, and why."

Santee walked across the room to a curtained window and pulled it open. The window looked out over the waters of the bay. There were several ships working their way toward the distant docks. A single glass pane bore a small bullet hole, the breakage lines radiating out from the hole like an unholy spider's web.

Ardan nodded to himself as he put his face within inches of the hole. Then he turned, using his finger to trace a line in the air across the room to a single discolored spot in the dark paneling. It was there that he found the hole, the edges of it enlarged with a pen knife; no doubt Drake's work, since it had been done carefully to not distort the impact point.

"When did this happen?" he asked.

"Early this morning, at just past seven," Santee replied. "I had come in early to go over some papers before a meeting at ten. I stepped in here because the morning light is excellent. Alexander, my assistant, was preparing tea. Suddenly the glass shattered and I heard something hit the wall."

Ardan paced the distance from the window to the wall and then moved to various points in the room.

"And you heard nothing? No sound of a shot?" he asked.

"Just the glass breaking and the bullet hitting the wall," he said. "When I realized what had happened, I sent for the police right away."

"Could it have been a disgruntled client?" asked Ardan. "Or a family member of one of your clients who perhaps thought they should not have ended up in jail?"

Santee shrugged. "I wish it were that simple. I'm not a criminal attorney. I do mostly real estate law and wills. My partner, Mr. Dickson, handles the criminal matters for the firm. *He* has had any number of death threats. In fact, last week, several men jumped him on his way home."

Drake nodded. "He's quite good, one of the best that I've ever seen. I've been on the receiving end of his cross examinations on more than one occasion."

"Yes, and he's never been able to break you or refute your testimony. Just so you know, that irritates him to no end," said Santee.

"Happy to be of service," said Drake.

Ardan walked to the window and looked out over the street. There was plenty of construction going on, not to mention plenty of commerce passing below them. The addition of a new face could easily pass unnoticed among the daily throngs that moved through these streets.

He studied the various buildings for a few minutes, trying to imagine himself in the mind of the assassin. As he scanned the area, Ardan noticed a man in a dark suit who seemed to be staring straight up at the window. After a moment, he touched the edge of his hat, nodded at Ardan and walked off down the street.

The problem was, this was a soft-nosed pistol bullet; given the angle involved and the distance to the nearest building, even the ones under construction, it would have required a rifle for that shot to have had any chance of hitting as it did.

"So, if you are a member of the Gun Club, then it is a fair bet that you know your way around weapons, and by that logic, perhaps the people who use them. Why did someone try to kill me? Whoever it is could come at me again, this time with a knife or a garrote," said Santee.

The older man had seemed calm and correct when he had entered the room, but now Ardan noticed a slight tremor in his hands, a slight sheen of sweet across his forehead. He was frightened, but was good at hiding it.

"I really don't think you have too much to be worried about, sir. I sincerely doubt that our shooter was trying to kill you," Ardan said. "Frighten you, yes, kill you, I rather doubt that."

"What do you mean?"

"Look at the wall and the hole in the window. In order for it to hit there, it had to come from a very limited number of places, and they are some distance away. Whoever made that shot had more than a modicum of skill, I should say. I know a few marksmen who could make it, but damn few. So I think I am not wrong to say that if he had wanted to kill you, he would have," said Ardan.

Santee walked over to the cabinet next to one of the paintings, opened it and poured himself several fingers of what Ardan presumed was whiskey. He emptied the glass in two swallows, followed almost immanently by a coughing fit.

"I am not the bravest of men, gentlemen; what does this all mean?"

"I'm not certain, yet," said Ardan. "Have you had any of your clients who seemed out of sorts with you? Or perhaps were not pleased with your services?

Santee shrugged. "Not really; my life is very pedestrian. Frankly, when it comes to the legal profession, my practice is probably one of the most boring around. And according to my wife, I match my work."

"It's the silence; that explains it," said Ardan. "The problem is, I cannot explain the silence."

The drawing room of the Baltimore Gun Club was quiet enough right then to have heard a pin drop. Ardan had seen only a few of his fellow members when he had walked in. Being just after four in the afternoon, most of the members were out and about dealing with their various businesses and assorted family matters. Within an hour the room would begin to fill up as they drifted in and the evening began.

"All right, it's the silence; mayhap I can offer an explanation," said McDonald Boothroyd. "Tell me again what happened."

Boothroyd and Ardan had been friends for nearly five years, meeting during an uprising in Southeast Asia, where the two of them had barely made it out alive. Boothroyd, though he was English, had come to America to study weapons design and engineering. Over the course of several incidents, under the auspices of the gun club and its members, the two men had become fast friends.

Ardan took the envelope with the bullet out of his pocket and handed it over to his companion. The Englishman was smaller than Ardan, with large hands; but the American had seen those hands move with such style and delicacy with the smallest details of a weapon.

"Someone tried to kill a lawyer with this, or at least to frighten him, a deed he seems to have succeeded at quite well. The problem is, the man didn't hear the shot being fired, only the glass breaking and the impact in the wall. True, there was construction close by and that could have masked the sound of the shot. But I have a gut feeling that is not the explanation."

Boothroyd held the cartridge up to the light and studied it for some time, at one point extracting a pocket magnifier to look at it in more detail.

"I will say the idea of shooting lawyers is not a bad one, when you get down to it. I would suggest that it be on a seasonal basis and there be a limit to how many you can take. We wouldn't want the species to go extinct. In fact, you people here in America have far too many of them."

"Wasn't it Shakespeare who said 'The first thing we do, let's kill all the lawyers'?" said Ardan.

"True, it was in *Henry the Sixth*, Part 2, Act 4 scene 2; too many lawyers is but one of the reasons I have been giving serious consideration to returning to England," said Boothroyd..

"You would be bored inside of six months," said Ardan.

"Perhaps, but I do have a wife and children to think of," he said, holding the bullet up toward the window. "There's something about this that is familiar. A soft-nosed revolver fired from a distance that should have required a rifle. You say that the lawyer fellow heard nothing?"

"Correct; only the glass shattering and it impacting the wall just over his shoulder."

"Damn it, I wish Barbicane were here. He's the one who would be able to tell you without a doubt what kind of weapon fired this," said Boothroyd.

Impey Barbicane was one of the most flamboyant members of the Gun Club. It was said that he had forgotten more about weapons then many of the members who were at the top of their profession had known. He and a number of members had departed Baltimore some weeks before for Tampa Town, Florida, to investigate the place as a possible site for a secret project that the club had under development.

"What about that Gordon fellow?" asked Ardan.

"Artemus? He headed out west several years ago, something about helping to design a very special train," said the Englishman. He paused for a moment and then his eyes went wide and he began to laugh. "I'm an idiot! I should have remembered."

"What?" asked Ardan.

Boothroyd held up the bullet, displaying it like a miniature mushroom.

"A soft core bullet fired with no noise. The answer is bloody simple, if I care to use my brain. Von Herder."

Ardan smiled. "Simple for you, not so simple for me. Who or what is a Von Herder?"

"A German mechanic who, to put it lightly, is a bloody miracle worker when it comes to weapons design. I've corresponded with him for several years. He's blind now, but what has lost in sight, he more than made up for in genius. The reason there was no shot heard was because it was fired by an air gun."

"Well, good evening, Boothroyd. I didn't think I would be seeing you so soon."

The speaker was a heavy-set man with a neatly trimmed goatee, who moved with a sense of confidence and had the look of someone that no one would want to go up against in any sort of a confrontation.

Delmonico's restaurant was abuzz with people. It was filled with a cross section of upper class Baltimore; everyone from businessmen to judges to politicians and even a few newspaper men.

"Well, Colonel Moran, it is a surprise to see you, as well," said Boothroyd. "I had thought you had decamped for England last week."

"That was the plan; unfortunately I could not conclude my business as swiftly as I had hoped. With luck, and the steam ship schedule's cooperation, I hope to be returning to Britain within the week."

"Well, may the gods of travel smile on you. Allow me to introduce my friend Michael Ardan. We're fellow members of the Gun Club."

Ardan felt like Moran was staring at him like a big cat studying its prey. He returned the look, but saw no reaction on the British man's face.

"A pleasure, sir," he said finally, extending his hand. "Colonel Sebastian Moran, formally of Her Majesty's Indian Army."

"It's very nice to meet you," said Ardan.

"I look forward to a chance to chat with you but now, gentlemen, if you will excuse me I need to speak with someone about a small real estate matter," said Moran, with a slight smile, one that Ardan suspected had sent shivers through those of lower rank. "About a very small, but important piece of real estate that if I am correct will justify my trip to America."

Ardan watched with interest as Moran walked away from their table. The man moved with the even pace of a hunting animal.

When he was well gone, Ardan looked at Boothroyd and said:

"So what does this fellow have to do with the air gun you mentioned?"

Boothroyd signaled for the waiter to refresh the coffee in front of them.

"Even after he lost his sight, Von Herder was known as a master craftsman when it came to firearms," he replied. "In a letter dictated to his daughter he told me how he had been commissioned to create a very special rifle, an air powered one that could fire upward of several dozen shots without reloading; you only had to re-pump up the compressor portion of the weapon. It was to be a secret commission, for which he was very well paid; the person ordering the weapons even supplied the blueprints for them. It was designed to use several types of ammunition, including soft-nosed revolver bullets."

"Well, well, well, things become clearer," said Ardan.

"Von Herder's weapons, in the hands of the right person, would have no problem doing just exactly that," said Boothroyd.

"How did you know that this Moran fellow was the one behind it, if it was a secret commission?"

Boothroyd leaned back in his chair. He seemed to be weighing his words carefully.

"When he delivered the weapon, it never occurred to the person he handed it over to just how sharp a blind man's hearing was. Von Herder overheard one of the fellows' companions address him as Colonel Moran and later as Sebastian. When I met this fellow, and he introduced himself, I recognized the name. Apparently, he retired from the British Army several years ago. From a few things he said, I suspect he served for some time in India, although he was reluctant to give any details beyond recounting his various tiger hunting expeditions. I have little doubt he is the same man that Von Herder wrote me about."

Across the room, he saw the soldier retrieving his hat from the coat check room. No more than three or four seconds later, Ardan was out of his chair and heading toward the door.

A light fog had rolled in with the sunset. Moran hailed a cab from the line of transports that waited down the street. Ardan leisurely walked in the same direction, holding himself back a dozen yards, swiftly stepping into one, though, as his quarry pulled away from the curb.

"See that dark blue hansom pulling away right now?" he asked the driver.

"Ole Fritish's rig? I surely do, and I know those horses of his; no way can he beat me and my Maida," said the driver in an accent thick with the tone of the Deep South.

"Follow him. There's a double eagle for you beyond your normal fare, if you don't lose him, and don't let him know you're there."

The cab was soon mixing in with a rush of other cabs, wagons and bicycles that filled the Baltimore streets. As they traveled, the gas lights began to flicker into life creating small islands of light in the darkness, with an odd yellowish dusk mixed between.

A half an hour later, the cab pulled to a halt.

"There he is, boss. I told you there was no way he could lose me, not with those two brown nags of Fritish's," said the driver.

Ardan's driver had pulled over a full block away from the other vehicle. For nearly ten minutes, the two cabs sat unmoving. Whatever it was that Moran had in mind, he seemed to be taking his own sweet time about it.

"Ya think he's waiting for someone, boss?" said the driver. "That's Jock for you, he could sit and smoke for hours and barely twitch an eye."

"Wait for me," Ardan said as he stepped out of the cab. "But be prepared to go to the whip on your horses if circumstances demand."

The driver reached under his seat and produced a small sawed off shotgun, holding it up for Ardan to see.

There were times when stealth was called for and this seemed to be one of them, so Ardan moved as carefully as he could. The neighborhood was not actually a bad one, mostly middle class homes that seemed like they could have been in any one of a half dozen cities around the country.

The fog added to the highly distinctive sound of a pistol being cocked. Ardan didn't have to see it to know that it was more than likely a derringer.

"Really, Mr. Ardan, if you needed a lift, you could just as easily have asked to ride with me," said Colonel Sebastian Moran.

A number of possibilities ran through Michael Ardan's mind as he stood there. They all centered on dodging out of the way of the gun that the retired British officer had in his hand. Ardan considered it possible, but it could be just as possible he could end up with a bullet blasting through his head. The odds seemed to favor the latter rather than the former.

"Colonel Moran, where did you come from? I was just going to the driver of that cab where we are. I'm afraid my driver has had more than a few swallows of old barley corn and has gotten turned around."

"You're lost?" said Moran. "I have to admit I admire your chutzpah! You are lying, sir. I know that, as do you. Turn around and face me."

Given the gun that Moran held, Ardan opted to do as he had been ordered.

"I think that you are either a copper or you work for my boss," said Moran, slipping his pistol back inside his waist coat, and producing two large gold coins from the pocket. "If you're a copper, then these are for you, just forget everything and whoever you report to…Well, all they need to know is that you lost me in the fog. You don't even have to mention the money, that's up to you. If you're working for my boss, you may tell him that just because that detective fellow has christened him The Napoleon of Crime, I will carry out my mission. He can count on that."

"What if I'm neither?" Ardan asked.

"Then it won't bother me in the slightest to make sure you turn up face down in the harbor tomorrow without his interference. So if you aren't either of the things I've mentioned, then you, my friend, should make damn sure not to cross my path again, under any circumstances, because I will crush you beneath my heel. Do you understand?"

"Indeed, Colonel, I understand fully."

"Good man," he said. "Now, I would be very disappointed if you weren't armed. But think of this, if you draw whatever weapon you have on you, I would hope you can kill me with that first shot. Because, as God is my witness, you will not get a second one."

Ardan pursed his lips for a moment, and then gave a half smile.

"You have no cause to worry about anything like that happening" he said.

"Why, yes, I have met Colonel Moran; a most unpleasant man, if I do say so myself," said George Santee.

"How do you mean?" asked Ardan.

The lawyer picked up the thick file of papers that lay on the desk in front of him. He shuffled several of them around with the dexterity of a knight of the green velvet preparing to deal a round of poker. Ardan had known people like this, who were so much a part of what they did for a living that the whole concept of being away from it, having a personal life, just didn't seem to exist. It was such an alien idea.

"As I mentioned, I do a great deal of real estate work, also work preparing wills and property transfers following the deaths of clients. Over the last few months, I have received a number of inquiries about the estate of one of my clients, its status, if there are heirs, all from the same gentleman: Sebastian Moran of London. He was rather displeased with me when I refused to cooperate with him. Is he the man who tried to kill me?" asked Santee.

After meeting Moran, Ardan was convinced that he had been right. If Moran had wanted Santee dead, the lawyer would be laying on a slab at the morgue

"I believe that he did pull the trigger, using a very unique weapon in the process," he replied.

Santee began to drum his fingers on his desk. "It doesn't matter how unique a weapon is; if what it fires hits you, you can be just as dead!"

"Tell me about the estate that Moran was asking about."

"Yes," nodded Santee. "It was the estate of a client who this firm has been associated with for many years, the late Captain John Carter of Virginia."

The name was common enough that Ardan didn't recognize it. He personally knew of a half dozen Carter families, and only two of them were related to each other.

"A ship's captain, perhaps?"

"No, Captain Carter was a Calvary officer in the service of the Confederacy. He fought in a number of battles; I believe he was highly decorated. After the war, he spent more than a decade out west, mining gold. That was what Moran wanted to know, where Carter's money came from. Naturally, I couldn't tell him, for the simple fact that I don't know. The captain was very secretive about his affairs. Even if I did know, lawyer-client confidentiality would prevent me from saying. Captain Carter died some years ago, but I still represent his heir, Ed Burroughs," said Santee.

Ardan templed his fingers and thought for a moment. There was obviously much going on here, but the question was, what?

"Obviously, Moran hasn't gotten what he came after, otherwise I suspect he would be long gone," mused Ardan. ."Do you have any ideas, Mr. Santee?"

The lawyer thought for a moment. "I am at a total loss on that matter. The captain was always very secretive, dealt in strictly cash. So, indeed, it may be the source of his money. Moran did ask a lot of questions."

"Most of it went into trusts, with the interest being paid to his nephew Edgar. The house and grounds passed to him, as well, though with some odd provisos in the will about them."

"Odd? How so?"

"The house cannot be sold for thirty years. He set up a trust to cover its upkeep and maintenance. But even if the place is eventually sold, a small portion must always remain in his nephew's family, the piece that contains the mausoleum."

"Mausoleum?"

"Yes. Captain Carter designed it himself; he had, as I mentioned, a number of talents. He even set up a separate trust for its continued maintenance. The strange coincidence is that less than a month after the construction was completed, it was put to use."

Ardan cocked an eyebrow. "Really?"

"It was in the middle of winter and they found Captain Carter lying dead in the snow."

"Murdered?"

Santee shrugged and leaned back in his chair. "If so, it was the most cunning death I have ever seen. There were no wounds on the body and no signs that he might have taken his own life. For as old a man as he was, he hardly looked older than thirty or thirty-five. I would say for whatever reason his heart just gave out. I always had a feeling that he was a lonely man. It seemed like he had just given up on life and wanted to be somewhere else. Perhaps in a better world than this one."

"We all hope for that," said Ardan.

Keeping watch on a mausoleum was not on Ardan's normal itinerary and certainly not his main choice of places to be. However, over the years, he had to admit that he had been in some stranger places.

Santee had been able to supply directions to the Carter estate. It was some distance from the city and shrouded in trees covered by Spanish moss, marked on two sides by a small creek.

On the trip out, Ardan had had the distinct feeling that he was being followed. He had hidden his horse in an outbuilding a quarter mile from the mausoleum, then found himself a rather large tree that had bent its trunk into a niche that made a perfect observation point.

"Now, we wait."

The mausoleum was not the largest that he had ever seen. A few of the older southern families had built resting places for their dead that would have put a number of family homes to shame. This one was the size of a small horse stable, yet as far as Ardan knew; it had been intended to house only one body on its way to eternity.

For nearly two hours, Ardan watched the place. His only companions an owl, a couple of rabbits and a bobcat. The feline stared at him for a few moments, and then moved on in search of different prey.

At midnight, he decided it was time to reconnoiter the area. He'd brought a small lamp; the shutter was only a sliver, but it was more than enough to let him make his way to the tomb.

The entrance to the mausoleum was an intricate design that at first seemed like some sort of artistic rendering. Then he realized that it was the solar system that had been carved into the stone, each planet in its proper place around the sun, although the fourth planet seemed a bit bigger than her sister worlds.

"Mars?" muttered Ardan.

A bronze metal plate had been attached to the door, bearing only the words *John Carter, Captain. Confederate States of America.* No date of birth or death. Santee had briefed Ardan on several major oddities about the mausoleum: there was no way to open the door, except from the inside. Carter had had the complicated locking mechanism custom made by the best locksmith in town.

"There is also excellent ventilation, although what the dead would want with fresh air, Heaven only knows. Personally, I suspect that Captain Carter spent far too much time out in the western sun."

Ardan wondered if there were other reasons, deeper secrets in the tomb. As he stared at the building, he could almost see the man pouring over the blueprints, making certain that every time point was correct. The whole idea of hiding the key to a secret fortune inside a mausoleum sounded more like something in the pages of one of Ned Buntlines yellow novels.

"Carter, you were a strange one. But those are the ones that make the world interesting," muttered Ardan.

There was a slight puff of air and almost at the same moment something slammed into the rock that made up the mausoleum's east wall. Ardan dodged to his left, rolling into the darkness, wrapping it around him as his colt peacemaker came into his hand. The problem with a pistol or any sort of gun remains the same: you have to know where your enemy is in order to make any shots you take worth the trouble.

No additional bullets followed Ardan, which didn't surprise him. If it was Von Holder's air rifle it would take a minute or so to re-pump up the firing mechanism. It had its advantages, and its disadvantages.

"Laddie-buck, you are so, so predictable," said the gravelly voice of Colonel Sebastian Moran.

The man stood a few yards away, a rather large pistol aimed at Ardan..

Ardan glanced around but didn't see any sign that Moran was accompanied by anyone, which was an advantage. He just had to find a way to exploit it.

"Well, fancy meeting you here, Colonel! I suppose you came to admire the architecture," said Ardan.

"Let's have no preposterous twaddle-cock from you, boy. I would as soon put a bullet in your gut and spend the next half hour watching you bleed out," he said. "The first thing that I want you to do is to drop any weapons you might have on the ground. Use two fingers to take them out and then give them a good swift kick. I have five bullets that will ensure your cooperation. If I see any lack of enthusiasm in what you are doing, I will start off with a shot to your left kneecap, followed by one to your right and then I will work on your elbows."

"That makes only four," said Ardan.

"I'll leave it to you to figure out where the fifth will go; just recall that you will be alive afterward."

Ardan nodded; the retired army officer was being careful and not coming closer to him than was absolutely necessary.

"Perhaps, we can come to an understanding, Colonel," said Ardan.

He began to remove his weapons, per the instructions; laying his pistol on the ground and kicking it off onto the grass. A knife and two derringers followed.

"That's the smart way to go, me bucko. You may end up walking away from this whole situation with your body parts reasonably intact."

Ardan kicked the derringers and the knife away, though noting exactly where they landed.

"Now, I know you're here to find where old Captain Carter stashed directions to his mine. From what my employer has told me, he brought at least five million American dollars out of it with a steady flow ever since. That nephew of his has no idea just how rich he actually was."

That explained a lot of things. Ardan had faced down thieves with guns and lawyers with brief cases over amounts far less than Colonel Moran was talking about.

"So you're looking for some kind of map? Does X really mark the spot on it?" he said.

This time the shot struck the ground a half dozen inches to Ardan's left; kicking up a small cloud of dirt. He fancied he had felt the lead projectile as it passed close.

"Did Von Herder make the pistol like he did your rifle?"

Moran arched an eye brow and smiled.

"So we are a bit in the know, are we laddie-buck? That might be the determining factor in this evening's conversation."

Just then, a deer came crashing through the underbrush, the animal seemingly terrified. For a moment, Ardan found himself expecting to see a bobcat giving chase.

Moran turned toward the sound. That was when a figure leaped from atop the mausoleum and came down on top of the ex army man. The newcomer landed a solid blow to Moran and the big man lay still. The stranger knelt by the prone form of Colonel Moran, rifling through the man's pockets. He dropped several items into his own.

He got to his feet and went over to Ardan.

"I'm John Carter," he said. "We don't have much time. That Moran character is tough. I've fought tougher men, but they were damn few and far between. He won't stay down for long. We need to be out of sight."

This was the first chance that Ardan had to look at the man. He was tall, well over six feet, with steely grey eyes. Confidence exuded from every move he made. There was something familiar about him.

"Wait a minute," Ardan said. "You're the man I saw on the street that day, outside the lawyer's office."

"You have good eyes."

He led Ardan up along the hill to a spot a hundred yards distant. The mausoleum was still visible, as was the prone form of Moran. They settled in beside a large eucalyptus tree and waited. From a spot on the ground Carter produced a pair of field glasses with a CSA emblem engraved on them and handed them to Ardan.

"Army issue?" asked Ardan.

"Yes, they have been useful on any number of occasions," said the man, "Now, keep your eye on that fellow. By the way, what the Devil is his full name?"

"Colonel Sebastian Moran, formally of the British Indian Army."

"From what I overheard, I would say he was just the sort that does not give officers a good name."

"That would be a fairly accurate assessment."

Ardan watched as Moran struggled to his feet. He heard him mutter a few explicit words, ones that he had no doubt put to good use on the Indian frontier.

"Come out and fight like a man," Moran yelled into the darkness. Carter put his hand on Ardan's shoulder, shaking his head.

When no one appeared to answer his challenge, Moran turned back toward the mausoleum.

"Now he gets his chance at what he things is the key to the gold, or at least he thinks he will," said Carter.

Ardan cocked an eyebrow at his companion. "A good trick, since the door is locked and can only be opened from the inside. No way in short of blasting," said Ardan.

"No need to blast; I left the door open. Things should get interesting very quickly."

Moran saw the open door and walked up to it. Ardan guessed him as an experienced campaigner, a little too cagy to just walk into the small building. So instead he circled the place twice, surveying it from all angles. When he seemed satisfied, he grabbed several pebbles and tossed them through the door into the darkness. There was no reaction, so he advanced, his pistol drawn, and moved warily through the door.

"What's in that mausoleum besides bones and fading memories?"

The other man smiled and then sighed.

"I suppose it's a matter of perspective. One man's treasure might be something else entirely for another. What might bring ultimate happiness for one person, the same thing could show terror and fear to another."

As if on cue the most terrifying scream that Ardan had ever heard came from inside the small structure, a sound that he hoped to never hear again in this life or the next. In the distance the call of a scavenger bird and several animals echoed in response.

Moran staggered out, his face ashen white, grabbing the side of a nearby tree to help support himself.

"I think that our friend Colonel Moran found... something. Maybe not what he expected, but something," Carter said.

Ardan walked up to Moran and waved his hand in front of eyes. He responded, but only with the slowest blink that Ardan had ever seen a man do.

"What the Hell just happened?"

"Many years ago, after the 'recent misunderstanding' between the states, a former soldier who was feeling disillusioned with life went prospecting out west. He nearly lost his life, but in the process, in a cave lost in the dreams of the west, he found a door that led him to the place of his heart. When he was forced to return to this land, making himself rich when he did, he brought the thing in the cave to him so that, if he were very, very lucky, it might once again open the door for him."

"A door to his heart and dreams?" repeated Ardan. "If he was lucky. Was he?"

"He was, and has returned only on occasions to see the only family he has remaining." He gestured at Moran. "For our friend Colonel Moran, it was not his heart's happiness, but something else he saw. Would you care to take a look, Mr. Ardan?"

"How do you know me and that I would be here tonight?"

"My lawyer told me; although, thanks to a few tricks I learned while I was 'abroad,' I seriously doubt he will remember the visit." Carter passed over the items he had taken from Moran. "I think you will find that if you take Colonel Moran back to his hotel, he will awake, remember very little and hopefully try to make the nearest steam ship for England. I suspect his mind will manufacture its own explanation for what happened here tonight. Oh, you will find that very bizarre rifle of his, along with his other supplies hidden beside one of the outbuildings about two hundred yards to the southeast"

Carter gestured toward the door and into the mausoleum.

"Are you sure you don't want to have a look? Who can say what door may open for you, my friend? Perhaps your heart's desire, or, then again, perhaps not a thing will happen."

Ardan shook his head.

He would say nothing about what he had seen this night. He wasn't even sure exactly what *had* happened.

"Then I must bid you good evening, sir."

Carter turned and went into the mausoleum, the door swinging shut behind him, the sound of the locking mechanism echoing into the night.

Ardan looked up into the night sky. His eyes settled on a single red star. He felt a distant pull in the very heart of his soul.

"Safe voyages, Captain Carter."

The novel Vipère au poing *(Viper in the Fist) is considered a classic of French literature. Published in 1948, it is a thinly-veiled account of the miserable child-hood of its author, writer Hervé Bazin who, in the book, is represented by Jean, the second of three sons. Michel Stéphan uses the character of the eldest son, Ferdinand, to tell a moving story about that wretched household...*

Michel Stéphan: *Vampire in the Fist*

Near Angers, 1923

It had been another uneventful spring at the Belle Angerie. I say "uneventful," but that obviously ignores the "good treatments" that our mother inflicted on us daily; every kind of physical and verbal abuse, which my brother described so well in his memoirs.

It is said that we choose our friends, but not our family. This cliché is both profoundly true and, unfortunately, still relevant. That is why the little book that my brother Jean wrote quickly turned into a cry of hatred and rebellion for more than a generation.

The last thing I want to do is cast a shadow on his undisputed masterpiece; I would only add a chapter.Nothing big; I just want to reveal an event which passed unnoticed, because there was already too much to say. Also, it was *my* event. Now that time has passed, I'm certain that it only happened to me. This was my adventure, my only happy memory in this dismal period.

Since the beginning of the last century we had lived in a house near Angers, called the Belle Angerie, which had been the Rézeau family estate for more than two hundred years. It had thirty-two furnished rooms, not counting the chapel. (We had a religious upbringing.) The region, which bordered the provinces of Maine, Brittany and Anjou, had to be one of the most backward parts of France.

When our parents went to Shanghai, we were left in the care of our grand-mother. By "we," I mean my brother Jean, nicknamed "Brasse-Bouillon" be-cause of his terrible fits of anger, and I, Ferdinand, the quieter and more sensi-tive younger brother. We truly enjoyed these days with our grandmother. In hindsight, I think of them as the sweetest times of my childhood. We didn't complain about our education, even though it was very demanding—especially our religious training. We worshipped the Lord's ways in our hearts as part of our happy childhood.

Our third brother, Marcel, was born in China where our parents were living at the time. My father, Jacques Rezeau, a law professor, had married the wealthy Paule Pluvignec, the daughter of Senator Pluvignec, who had a dowry of three hundred thousand francs. I didn't know anything about Marcel's childhood. While we were temporarily separated, we lived a happy life.

Then Grandma died. My parents returned from Shanghai, with Marcel, the little brother we had never known. My mother, by her own admission, kept us under her thumb. Our father was very meek, and didn't challenge her. We thought we had regained a mother, but that was actually the moment when hatred was planted in our hearts.

We were three brothers, living under the same roof; three children at the mercy of that woman, whom we called "Folcoche," a nickname created by combining the French words "mad" and "sow." There are children who are lucky enough to know the love of a mother. Ours only grudgingly acknowledged our existence. In return, the same hatred inexorably rose in our young bodies like bubbling sap, ready burst forth at any moment, filling us with a lust to murder. To strangle the viper! To strangle the beast who had come to live with us!

Madame Leon, the housekeeper, nearly always took our side. It disgusted her that someone could be so tyrannical toward three children. Even little Marcel, though not bullied as badly as we were, did not have things much better. The poor boy was just another tool in our mother's hands.

Because we liked Madame Leon, and she loved us, Folcoche fired her. She couldn't allow us even a little love and happiness; it was unbearable to her. So we lost her and all the affection she had for us.

It didn't stop there. Our mother then hired Georgette Le Lourec to replace Madame Leon in the thankless task of watching over our little world. Georgette arrived from Morlaix one morning. Just by looking at her, I could see that Folcoche had finally made what she would consider the right choice. Georgette's gaze was even sterner than my viper-mother's. No doubt Folcoche had taken meticulous care in choosing her. As soon as we saw her, we regretted losing our dear old Madame Leon.

I watched her on the sly. She wore a prim uniform and had the strict attitude of a prison guard. Underneath this, I thought she was very beautiful, though she took pains to hide it. I felt a curious mix of attraction and repulsion for her. This was largely because she was very young and did not—at least in my eyes—fit the traditional image of a governess.

As the days passed I grew more and more intrigued. Even Folcoche—usually stingy with compliments—said that our new governess was doing her job perfectly. We had absolutely no complaints, though she never showed us any trace of compassion, regardless of the treatment we suffered at our mother's hands. I began to hate her for her indifference. Yet, if she had, just once, removed her fussy hat, undone her severe hairstyle, and revealed the woman under the mask, I would certainly have forgiven her.

Occasionally, I found her alone in the kitchen. As she stood, ramrod straight, Georgette seemed completely absorbed in her chores. I tried in vain to engage her in conversation, as only eight years old children can, but she merely nodded coldly, or gave single-syllable replies, never offering the slightest hint of a smile. Could it be that the world was filled with people as hard as my mother? Sometimes, these brief interviews with Georgette made me wonder, though I never forgot that Folcoche had selected her to satisfy her own agenda. That meant that any happiness in our young lives was nothing more than a distant fantasy.

My brothers and I had been waiting impatiently for months for a weekend trip to the cinema in Nantes. Our father had been promising to take us for a long time, and a break from the stifling environment of the Belle Angerie seemed almost miraculous. Just the thought of spending two days away from our mother was gratifying, but the prospect of going to the cinema delighted us even more. Everything had been organized for several weeks, the film had been chosen, and our cousins were waiting for us to arrive in Nantes. What happened next should have been obvious, but we were so blinded by joyful anticipation that we didn't see it coming.

At the last minute, Folcoche found an excuse to deny us our weekend away from her. We hadn't done anything wrong; she just decided she wasn't feeling well, and didn't want us to go. Our father, accustomed to obeying her, looked unhappy, but said nothing. Despite our strongest protests, we knew the game was over.

That evening found all three of us cursing Folcoche, as we did so often. We wished the torments of the damned on her and hoped that she wouldn't drive the Devil out of Hell when she arrived there.

It was nearly nine in the evening, after the confession session our mother imposed on us. We did this daily, rattling off the same nonsense each time. My mother had graciously allowed me a half hour in the salon, but I decided to go to bed, preferring the comfort and warmth of my single blanket. Folcoche only allowed her children one cover whether summer or winter, claiming this would toughen us, but it was spring now, so it was enough.

That's when *she* arrived, not Folcoche, but Georgette. She had entered my room as quietly as a ghost. She did not smile as she stood by my bed with her usual cold-as-marble expression, but her presence calmed me. Finally, she knelt and put her face close to mine and whispered:

"There is a full moon tonight, Ferdinand. It will illuminate the garden. Try not to fall asleep too quickly."

That was all. She rose and disappeared as silently as she had come. It had been so brief, so magical, that it filled my mind with confusion. Had she stroked my forehead affectionately—the kind of gesture my mother had never given me? Or was it my delirious imagination? A kind of numbness came over me and, totally disregarding her advice, I fell asleep.

I could not tell how many hours had passed when I woke, but the moon was high in the sky. I don't know what had disturbed my sleep, but I felt a kind of agitation that rose all around me, or rather came from outside. My mind still hovered in that confused state between dream and reality. I rose hurriedly, like an automaton, and walked to the open window, which seemed to be the source of the surreal excitement.

And there I saw... I saw the garden beneath the moon, which, in its fullest phase, lit our estate almost like daylight. To my left stood the gigantic eastern façade of the Belle Angerie, four stories high. Five black silhouettes climbed this wall, clinging to its crevices like huge human spiders. The scene was fascinating. The moon, like a movie projector, made the vision even more beautiful; a show that seemed to have been staged just for me.

I knew these men. They were wanted through all of France. Before me was the gang known as *the Vampires*, and one of the five silhouettes was that of a woman. She was the closest to me; so close I could almost touch her. She was agile as a cat, and wore a black jumpsuit that hugged her perfect figure in a way that unsettled me. Her body seemed to move in slow motion. Her face was hidden. Only her eyes remained uncovered. I recognized her at once, of course.

That night, Folcoche's jewels were stolen. My father wanted to call the police, but she stopped him; I still don't know why. She preferred to languish for three days on the couch, imposing on us the grotesque spectacle of a woman in despair at having suffered a great loss.

My brothers were sleeping; no one had seen anything. The matter rested there. No one had ever heard of Georgette Le Lourec.

As for me, I have the vision of the eyes I saw that night. The eyes that belonged to the most beautiful woman in the world: Irma Vep, Queen of the Vampires.

I like to think that it wasn't just jewelry that motivated the gang to climb the façade of our rather ordinary provincial estate. Irma Vep had probably wanted to console me in my grief over having a leisurely day stolen by my mother. She must have been appalled by the wickedness Folcoche showed us, and had a touch of compassion for me. That's why she had decided to give a performance, just for me, a thousand times more beautiful than I could have seen in any film.

In the end, this is what I prefer to believe. I can't imagine that her only motive was to steal my mother's jewels, even though Folcoche claimed they were quite valuable.

I know about Irma Vep's tragic end. I read about it in the newspapers like everyone else. But I also knew her humanity. I read it in her eyes when she looked at me that night, hanging from the gutter just two meters from me. I saw in her eyes a smile I will never forget. It was a motherly smile. At least, it seemed so to me. I don't really know what a mother's smile is.

(Translation by Matthew Baugh)

Maigret
(ill. by Fernando Calvi)

Credits

The Tournament of the Treasure

Starring:	**Created by:**
Steve Costigan	Robert E. Howard
Ned Dargan	Frederick Clyde Davis
Virginia Harper	Edgar Rice Burroughs
Bill O'Brien	Robert E. Howard
Sven Larson	Robert E. Howard
Seaman Pallant	Sax Rohmer
Bebert	Marcel Allain
Fatala	Marcel Allain
Townsend Harper (Bulan)	Edgar Rice Burroughs
Kaspar Gutman	Dashiell Hammett
Cairo	Dashiell Hammett
Madame Ingomar	Sax Rohmer
Cadwiller Oden	Lester Dent
Mullargan	Edgar Rice Burroughs
Butch "Slug" O'Leary	Norman Daniels
	and Otto Binder
Jack Holligan	Paul Alfred Müller
Rayt Marius	Leslie Charteris
Captain Bull Dawson	Roy Crane
Sing-Lee	Sax Rohmer
Co-Starring:	
Colonel Bozzo-Corona	Paul Féval
Ace Jessel	Robert E. Howard
Fantômas	Pierre Souvestre
	& Marcel Allain
Professor Maxon	Edgar Rice Burroughs
Also Starring:	
Jack Johnson	

Matthew BAUGH is an ordained minister who lives and works in the Chicago area. He is a longtime fan of pulp fiction, cliffhanger serials and old time radio. He has written a number of articles on characters like Zorro, Doctor Syn, Jules de Grandin and Sailor Steve Costigan. He has had stories published in *The Green Hornet Chronicles, More Tales of Zorro, Six Guns Straight From Hell,*

The Avenger Chronicles and *The Phantom Chronicles*. He is a regular contributor to *Tales of the Shadowmen*.

Wings of Fear

Starring:	Created by:
Hugh "Bulldog" Drummond	H.C.McNeile
Harry Dickson	Anonymous
Carl Peterson	H.C.McNeile
Irma Peterson	H.C.McNeile
Richard Hannay	John Buchan
Sir Walter Bullivant	John Buchan
Doctor Lerne	Maurice Renard
Archie Roylance	John Buchan
And:	
The Dinosaurs of Gambertin	Maurice Renard

Nicholas BOVING lives in Toronto. He was formerly a mining engineer and traveled the world widely. He also worked from time to time as a docker, fruit inspector and forester. His books and screenplays draw on these experiences to provide characters, backgrounds and scenes. He is the author and publisher of the *Maxim Gunn* series of action/adventure books. He has also written some fifteen other novels and screenplays which follow the central character to countries and places where the forces of nature as much as people provide the conflict. He is a regular contributor to *Tales of the Shadowmen*.

The Man With the Double Heart

Starring:	Created by:
Léo Saint-Clair	Jean de La Hire
Kephal Clavigny de Chambrun	Robert Darvel
Niyadi	Robert Darvel

Robert DARVEL was born in 1958 and chose his nom-de-plume as a memento to his discovery, at age 10, of Gustave Le Rouge's *The Vampires of Mars*. After working in bookstores and visual communication, in 2005, he founded the French small press publishing house Le Carnoplaste, dedicated to the publication of new texts of popular literature in their original formats. He is the author of new adventures of Harry Dickson, Joan of Arc and the Great Psychagogue, and has contributed articles and stories to the Jean Ray Society, Malpertuis, Imajn'ère and The Eye of the Sphinx. He doesn't yet live on Mars, (the psychic powers of 10,000 fakirs would not suffice to move him and his books), but in the Yonne. This is his first contribution to *Tales of the Shadowmen*.

The Treasure of Everlasting Life

Starring:	Created by:
Allan Quatermain	H. Rider Haggard
Hans	H. Rider Haggard
Doctor Miguelito Loveless	John Kneubuhl
Voltaire	John Kneubuhl
The Black Coats	Paul Féval
Colonel Bozzo-Corona	Paul Féval
Ayesha	H. Rider Haggard
The Waziri	Edgar Rice Burroughs
The Marchef	Paul Féval
Doctor Dolittle	Hugh Lofting
The King of the Elephants	Jean de Brunhoff
Cornelius the Elephant	Jean de Brunhoff
Co-Starring:	
The Phantom	Lee Falk
Solomon Kane	Robert E. Howard
Nakari	Robert E. Howard
And:	
The Steam-Powered House	Jules Verne
Kor	H. Rider Haggard

Matthew DENNION lives in South Jersey with his beautiful wife and daughter. He currently works as a teacher of autistic students at a Special Services School. Matt has been a huge fan of the works of Edgar Rice Burroughs ever since he first picked up *A Princess of Mars*; he is also a big follower of Sherlock Holmes, Doc Savage, Spider-Man, Batman, and James Bond. He is a regular contributor to *Tales of the Shadowmen*.

Violet's Lament

Starring:	Created by:
Siger Holmes	based on Arthur Conan Doyle
Violet Blakeney	Win Scott Eckert based on John Montagu Orczy Barstow
Ziska	Alexandre Dumas
The Giaour	Lord Byron
Lecoq	based on Paul Féval
Durand	Jean-Marc Lofficier based on P.A. Ponson du Terrail
Thénardier	based on Victor Hugo
Mondego	based on Alexandre Dumas

Count Aubri	Peter Josef von Lindpaintner and Cäsar Max Heige
Countess Nadine Carody	Jaime Chávarri, Anne Settimó & Jesus Franco
Count Yorga	Bob Kelljan
Colonel Bozzo Corona	Paul Féval

Co-Starring:

Sir Percy Blakeney	Emmuska Orczy
Armand Tesla	Randall Fay & Griffin Jay
Lord Ruthven	John William Polidori
Marguerite Blakeney	Emmuska Orczy
Alice Clarke Raffles	Philip José Farmer
Lupin	based on Maurice Leblanc
Kramm	based on Gustave Le Rouge
Gerolstein	based on Eugène Sue

Also Starring:

Napoléon Bonaparte

And:

The *Ruthvenian*	Donald F. Glut

Win Scott ECKERT Win Scott Eckert holds a B.A. in Anthropology and a Juris Doctorate. He is the editor of and contributor to *Myths for the Modern Age: Philip José Farmer's Wold Newton Universe*, a 2007 Locus Award Finalist for Best Non-Fiction book. Win's latest books are the encyclopedic two-volume *Crossovers: A Secret Chronology of the World*, and the Wold Newton novel *The Evil in Pemberley House*, about Patricia Wildman, the daughter of a certain bronze-skinned pulp hero (co-authored with Philip José Farmer). He is immensely pleased to appear in all nine volumes of *Tales of the Shadowmen*.

The Wolf at the Door of Time

Starring:	**Created by:**
Doctor Omega	Arnould Galopin
Moses Nebogipfel	H.G. Wells
Joseph Balsamo	Alexandre Dumas
Thibault (The Wolf Leader)	Alexandre Dumas
Agnelette	Alexandre Dumas
Leo Saint-Clair (The Nyctalope)	Jean de La Hire
Captain Gogol	Ian Fleming
Avakoum Zahov	Andrei Gulyashki
Oktobriana	Petr Sadecký
The Wolves:	
The Black Dog of Bungay	Historical

The Hound of the Baskervilles	Arthur Conan Doyle
The Beast of Gévaudan	Historical
The Hound of Mons	Historical
Co-Starring:	
Zoomashmarta	Philip José Farmer
Captain Strange of Arcadia	Calvert & Hughes
Also Starring:	
Jean Chastel	
Captain Yeskes	
The Companion in White	
Nurse Agatha Miller (Agatha Christie)	
And:	
The Wold Newton Meteorite	

Martin GATELY is the author of the comics novella *Sherwood Jungle* in the *Phantom: Generations* series. He is a regular contributor to the UK's journal of strange phenomena *Fortean Times*, for which he also created the *Cryptid Kid Investigates* comic strip. His writing career began back in the 1980s when he wrote for D C Thomson's legendary *Starblazer* comic-book. He lives in a decaying mansion in Nottingham that has a view of a former insane asylum. He is a regular contributor to *Tales of the Shadowmen*.

What Lurks in Romney Marsh?

Starring:	**Created by:**
Denis Borel	Arnould Galopin
Fred	Arnould Galopin
Dr. Syn (The Scarecrow)	Russell Thorndyke
Mr. Mipps	Russell Thorndyke
Josie Bauer	Spider Robinson
Co-Starring:	
Doctor Omega	Arnould Galopin
Tiziraou	Arnould Galopin
Professor Chronotis	Arnould Galopin
Rotwang	Fritz Lang & Thea Von Harbou
Doctor Nebogipfel	H.G. Wells
The Time Traveler	H.G. Wells

Travis HILTZ started making up stories at a young age. Years later, he began writing them down. In high school, he discovered that some writers actually got paid and decided to give it a try. He has since gathered a modest collection of rejection letters and had a one-act play produced. Travis lives in the wilds of

New Hampshire with his very loving and tolerant wife, two above average children and a staggering amount of comic books and *Doctor Who* novels. He is a regular contributor to *Tales of the Shadowmen*.

As Time Goes By...

Starring:	**Created by:**
Doctor Omega	Arnould Galopin
Fred	Arnould Galopin
Rick Blaine	Julius J. Epstein,
	Philip G. Epstein
	& Howard Koch
	Murray Burnett & Joan Alison
The Drexlers	Norvell W. Page
Co-Starring:	
Ferrari	Julius J. Epstein,
	Philip G. Epstein
	& Howard Koch
Major Strasser	Julius J. Epstein,
	Philip G. Epstein
	& Howard Koch
Sam	Julius J. Epstein,
	Philip G. Epstein
	& Howard Koch
The Spider	Harry Steeger
Noël Essaillon	René Bajavel
Also Starring:	
Naphuria aka Amenhotep	
V aka Akhenaten	
And:	
The Cosmic Cube	Stan Lee & Jack Kirby
The Sleepers	Stan Lee & Jack Kirby

Paul HUGLI has a degree in Zoology, and has written for everything from *Cracked* magazine to general interest pamphlets, and for most of the first, second *and* third tier adult magazines. He is the author of three published "adult fantasy" novels, and the acclaimed *Traci Lords Companion*. He has also been employed as a science/math instructor, and as a "Floor Manager" at a local "Gentleman's Club." In addition, he once owned/managed Destiny Bookstore, which dealt in SciFi, comics and adult "fantasy" magazines, for 30 years. He now has three novels in the works. He is a regular contributor to *Tales of the Shadowmen*.

Gods of the Underworld

Starring:	Created by:
The Black Coats	Paul Féval
Colonel Bozzo-Corona	Paul Féval
Aubert Lecoq and sons	based on Paul Féval
Marcel Draco	based on Ian Fleming
Doctor Lerne	based on Maurice Renard
Claude Verdier	based on Arthur Bernède
	& Louis Feuillade
Portal-Giraud	Paul Féva
Jacques Collin a.k.a. Vautrin,	Honoré de Balzac
Trompe-la-Mort	
Bibi-Lupin	Honoré de Balzac
	and Maurice Leblanc
Jacqueline Collin a.k.a Anne	based on Honoré de Balzac
de Breuil	& Alexandre Dumas
Monsieur Jackal	Alexandre Dumas
Eugène-François Vidocq	Historical
Toussac	Arthur Conan Doyle
Le Biffon	Honoré de Balzac
Fil-de-Soie	Honoré de Balzac
Auguste	Honoré de Balzac
La Pouraille	Honoré de Balzac
Co-Starring:	
Sir Percy Blakeney	Emmuska Orczy
Chauvelin	Emmuska Orczy
Henri de Lagardère	Paul Féval
Alexis Ladeau	Robert E. Howard
And:	
Black Scorpion Venom	Sax Rohmer
Mato Grosso Pestilence	Harold A. Davis
The Nemedean Chronicles	Robert E. Howard
Also Starring:	
Joseph Fouché	
Jean Henry	

Rick LAI, a regular contributor to *Tales of the Shadowmen*, is a computer programmer. During the 1980s and 1990s, he wrote articles expanding on the Weld Newton Universe concepts which have since been collected by Altus Press as *Rick Lai's Secret Histories*: *Daring Adventurers*, *Rick Lai's Secret Histories*: *Criminal Master Minds*, *Chronology of Shadows: A Timeline of The Shadow's Exploits* and *The Revised Complete Chronology of Bronze*. Rick He translated

Judex by Louis Feuillade and Arthur Bernède for Black Coat Press. His *Shadows of the Opera* is about a 19th century vigilante trained by the Phantom of the Opera. Rick resides in Bethpage, New York, with his wife and children.

Dad

Starring:	Created by:
The Boy	Richard Matheson
Glinda	L. Frank Baum

Jean-Marc & Randy LOFFICIER, the editors of *Tales of the Shadowmen*, have collaborated on five screenplays, a dozen books and numerous translations, including *Arsène Lupin*, *Doc Ardan*, *Doctor Omega*, *The Phantom of the Opera* and *Rouletabille*. Their latest novels include *Edgar Allan Poe on Mars* and *The Katrina Protocol*. They have written a number of animation teleplays, including episodes of *Duck Tales* and *The Real Ghostbusters*, and in comics, such popular heroes as *Superman* and *Doctor Strange*. They created the Mayan detective series *Tongue*Lash*. Randy is a member of the Writers Guild of America, West and Mystery Writers of America.

To Dust and Ashes, in its Heat Consuming

Starring:	Created by:
Victor Carroon	Nigel Kneale
Tug Carrington	W.E. Johns
Lord Beltham	based on Pierre Souvestre & Marcel Allain
Boothroyd	Ian Fleming
Professor Bernard Quatermass	Nigel Kneale
Harry Dickson	Anonymous
George Bulman	based on Kenneth Royce

Nigel MALCOLM lives in Kent, England. He works as a teacher of English as a Foreign Language. He is a long-term *Doctor Who*, *Star Trek* and *Prisoner* fan—long before all the new-fangled versions came along. He is currently working on a steampunk novel and an audio play. This is his first contribution to *Tales of the Shadowmen* and his first professionally published short story.

Diplomatic Freeze

Starring:	Created by:
Harry Paget Flashman II	based on George MacDonald Fraser

Sgt. Ballantine	based on Henri Vernes
Jean Saint-Clair	Jean de La Hire
Marcel Gioja	based on Paul Féval
The Lizard People	Charles Derennes
Jean-Louis de Venasque	Charles Derennes
The Black Coats	Paul Féval
Co-Starring:	
Professor Valenron	Charles Derennes
Jacques Ceintras	Charles Derennes
King Kull of Valusia	Robert E. Howard

David McDONALD is a professional geek from Melbourne, Australia who works for an international welfare organisation. When not on a computer or reading a book, he divides his time between helping run a local cricket club and working on his upcoming novel. He is a member of the Australian Horror Writers Association, The International Association of Media Tie-In Writers, and of the Melbourne based writers group, SuperNOVA. He is a regular contributor to *Tales of the Shadowmen*.

Death of a Dream

Starring:	**Created by:**
Bouzille II	based on Pierre Souvestre
	& Marcel Allain
The Phantom of the Opera	Gaston Leroux
Ellen Patrick	Lars Anderson
Mizzeia Khali	Jean de La Hire
Josephine Balsamo IV	Jean-Marc Lofficier
	based on Maurice Leblanc
The Daroga	based on Gaston Leroux
Colonel Bozzo-Corona	Paul Féval
The Marchef	Paul Féval
Pha-ho-tep	Paul Naschy
Jo Jo La Verne	Philip Wylie, Joel Sayre
	& Byron Morgan
Co-Starring:	
The Red Hand	Gustave Le Rouge
Little Nemo	Winsor McCay
Ambrose Vollmer	José Moselli
Aladdin	Antoine Galland
Leo Saint-Clair	Jean de La Hire
And:	
The Angels of Music	Kim Newman

Christofer NIGRO is a writer of both fiction and non-fiction with a strong interest in pulps, comic books and fantastic cinema, and a regular contributor to *Tales of the Shadowmen*. He may be known to some by his extensive writings in cyberspace, including his websites *The Godzilla Saga* and *The Warrenverse*, as he is an authority on the subject of *dai kaiju eiga* (the sub-genre of cinema specializing in giant monsters), and the characters featured in the fondly remembered comic magazines published by Warren. He has recently revived and expanded Chuck Loridans' classic site MONSTAAH, and has since been published in the anthologies *Aliens Among Us, Carnage: After the Fall, No Place Like Home* and *Rigorous Mortis*. He is presently at work on a novel, and works as a website administrator and freelance editor.

The Benevolent Burglar

Starring:	Created by:
Jules Maigret	Georges Simenon
Honoré	John Peel
Simon Templar	Leslie Charteris
Patricia Holm	Leslie Charteris
Roger Conway	Leslie Charteris
J.G. Reeder	Edgar Wallace
Larry O'Ryan	Edgar Wallace
Lane Leonard	Edgar Wallace
Co-Starring:	
The Black Coats	Paul Féval
Claud Eustace Teal	Leslie Charteris

John PEEL was born in Nottingham, England, and started writing stories at age 10. John moved to the U.S. in 1981 to marry his pen-pal. He, his wife ("Mrs. Peel") and their eight dogs now live on Long Island, New York. John has written just over 100 books to date, mostly for young adults. He is the first author to have written novels based on both *Doctor Who* and *Star Trek*. His most popular work is *Diadem*, a fantasy series; he has written twelve volumes to date. He is a regular contributor to *Tales of the Shadowmen*.

The Conspiracy of Silence

Starring:	Created by:
Fantômas	Pierre Souvestre & Marcel Allain
Juvel	Pierre Souvestre & Marcel Allain

Written by:
Neil **PENSWICK** was a successful theatre writer in the North of England. He submitted material for various television shows and was on the short-list to write for *Doctor Who* when it was cancelled in 1989. He adapted his script entitled *Hostage* as one of Virgin's New Adventures (1993). In recent years, Neil has written for a range of television series including thrillers, Sunday-night family viewing, a drama-documentary, and, for the first time, and contradicting his Leonard Cohen type reputation, a situation comedy. He is currently short-listed to write for a popular BBC TV children's series and has also been mentored by the brilliant and hugely talented Phil Ford and written an original three-part scary children's series. He is a regular contributor to *Tales of the Shadowmen*.

Professor Peaslee Plays Paris

Starring:	**Created by:**
Count Ferenczy	H.P. Lovecraft
Flambeau	G.K. Chesterton
Pr. Nathaniel Wingate Peaslee	H.P. Lovecraft
The Black Coats	Paul Féval
Baron Cesare Stromboli	José Moselli
Inspector Romaine	Robert Ellis & Helen Logan
Joséphine Balsamo	Maurice Leblanc
The Iron King	Les Martin based on Alexandre Dumas
Nardi	Philip MacDonald
Colonel Bozzo Corona	Paul Féval
Co-Starring:	
Sherlock Holmes	Arthur Conan Doylew
Captain Nemo	Jules Verne
Chief Valentin	G.K. Chesterton
Broquet	Victorin-Hippolyte Jasset
Guichard	Georges Simenon
Maigret	Georges Simenon
Also Starring:	
Vincenzo Peruggia	
Louis Beroud	

Pete **RAWLIK** holds a B.S. in Marine Biology and manages monitoring projects in the Florida Everglades. He has been a fan of the Lovecraftian fiction since his father sat him on his knee and read him Lovecraft's *The Rats in the Walls*. His fiction has appeared in *Talebones*, *IBID* and *Crypt of Cthulhu*. His literary criticism has appeared in *The New York Review of Science Fiction* and in *The Neil Gaiman Reader*. He is a regular contributor to *Tales of the Shadowmen*.

Nestor Burma Goes West

Starring:	Created by:
Nestor Burma	Léo Malet
Jim Anthony	Victor Rousseau Emmanuel
Irma Vep II (Pam Rive)	based on Louis Feuillade
Irma Vep III (Vera Pim, Vera Gemini)	based on Louis Feuillade and Albert Bouchard / Blue Oyster Cult
The Vampires	Louis Feuillade
Co-Starring:	
Doctor Cornelius	Gustave Le Rouge
Hélène Châtelain	Leo Malet
Doc Ardan / Doc Savage	Guy d'Armen/Lester Dent
Adelaide Lupin	Win Scott Eckert
Arsène Lupin	Maurice Leblanc
Sun Koh	Paul Alfred Müller
Jan Mayen	Paul Alfred Müller
Dolores Colquitt	Victor Rousseau Emmanuel
The Great Vampire	Louis Feuillade
Harley Warren	H.P. Lovecraft
Abner Ravenwood	Lawremce Kasdan, George Lucas, Philip Kaufman
SNIF	Vladimir Volkoff
And:	
The Mound	H.P. Lovecraft
Devil-Girl from Mars	James Eastwood, John C. Maher
Them!	Ted Sherdeman, Russell Hughes, George Worthing Yates
Tarentula	Robert M. Fresco, Martin Berkeley

Josh REYNOLDS is a freelance writer of modest ability and exceptional confidence. His sword & sorcery novel, *Knight of the Blazing Sun*, is due for publication by Black Library in 2012. Also to-be-released 2012 is *Out of Black Aeons*, the first book in *The Adventures of Charles St. Cyprian* from Pro Se Press. In other interesting facts, he was once bitten by a snake. It subsequently died. He is a regular contributor to *Tales of the Shadowmen*.

The True Cost of Doing Business

Starring:	Created by:
Buonaparte Ignace Gallia	Ian Fleming
Tee Hee Johnson	Tom Mankiewicz
Colonel Bozzo-Corona	Paul Féval
Baron Samedi	Tom Mankiewicz
Co-Starring:	
SMERSH	Ian Fleming
Marc-Ange Draco	Ian Fleming
The Matarese Family	Robert Ludlum
Pilaster Bank	Ken Follett
Albert the Alligator	Walt Kelly

Frank SCHILDINER has been a pulp fan since a friend gave him a gift of Phillip Jose Farmer's *Tarzan Alive*. Since that time he has published articles on *Hellboy*, the Frankenstein films, *Dark Shadows* and the television show's links to the H.P. Lovecraft universe. He is a Senior Probation Officer in New Jersey and a martial arts instructor at Amorosi's Mixed Martial Arts. Frank resides in New Jersey with his wife Gail and one cat. He is a regular contributor to *Tales of the Shadowmen*.

The Silence

Starring:	Created by:
Michel Ardan	Jules Verne
Jonas Drake	based on Erle Stanley Gardner
George Santee	Bradley H. Sinor
Donald Boothroyd	based on Ian Fleming
Colonel Moran	Arthur Conan Doyle
John Carter	Edgar Rice Burroughs
Co-Starring:	
Dickson	Anonymous (possibly)
Von Herder	Arthur Conan Doyle
Impey Barbicane	Jules Verne
Artemus Gordon	Michael Garrison

Bradley H. SINOR has seen his work appear in numerous science fiction, fantasy and horror anthologies such as *The Improbable Adventures of Sherlock Holmes*, *The Grantville Gazette* and *Ring of Fire* 2 and 3. Three collections of his short fiction have been released: *Dark and Stormy Night*, *In the Shadows*, and *Playing with Secrets* (along with stories by his wife Sue Sinor). His latest collections are *Echoes from the Darkness* and *Where the Shadows Began*. He can be reached via his wall on Facebook. He is a regular contributor to *Tales of the Shadowmen*.

Vampire in the Fist

Starring:	**Created by:**
The Rezeau family	Hervé Bazin
Irma Vep	Louis Feuillade

Michel STEPHAN was born and lives in Brittany with his wife and two children. He has been a fan of science fiction, fantasy and horror since age 10. He loves Universal monster movies (especially the *Frankenstein* series), sci-fi serials and collects Aurora model kits. He has submitted stories to Black Coat Press's French sister imprint, Rivière Blanche and has previously contributed to *Tales of the Shadowmen*.

WATCH OUT FOR
TALES OF THE
SHADOWMEN
VOLUME 10: ESPRIT DE CORPS
TO BE RELEASED DECEMBER 2013

IN THE SAME COLLECTION

Volume 1: The Modern Babylon (2004)

Matthew Baugh, Bill Cunningham, Terrance Dicks, Win Scott Eckert, Viviane Etrivert, G.L. Gick, Rick Lai, Alain le Bussy, Jean-Marc & Randy Lofficier, Samuel T. Payne, John Peel, Chris Roberson, Robert Sheckley, Brian Stableford.

Volume 2: Gentlemen of the Night (2005)

Matthew Baugh, Bill Cunningham, Win Scott Eckert, G.L. Gick, Rick Lai, Serge Lehman, Jean-Marc Lofficier, Xavier Mauméjean, Sylvie Miller & Philippe Ward, Jess Nevins, Kim Newman, John Peel, Chris Roberson, Brian Stableford, Jean-Louis Trudel.

Volume 3: Danse Macabre (2006)

Joseph Altairac & Jean-Luc Rivera, Matthew Baugh, Alfredo Castelli, Bill Cunningham, François Darnaudet & J.-M. Lofficier, Paul DiFilippo, Win Scott Eckert, G.L. Gick, Micah Harris, Travis Hiltz, Rick Lai, Jean-Marc Lofficier, Xavier Mauméjean, David A. McIntee, Brad Mengel, Michael Moorcock, John Peel, Chris Roberson, Robert L. Robinson, Jr., Brian Stableford.

Volume 4: Lords of Terror (2007)

Matthew Baugh, Bill Cunningham, Win Scott Eckert, Micah Harris, Travis Hiltz, Rick Lai, Roman Leary, Jean-Marc Lofficier, Randy Lofficier, Xavier Mauméjean, Jess Nevins, Kim Newman, John Peel, Steven A. Roman, John Shirley, Brian Stableford.

Volume 5: The Vampires of Paris (2008)

Matthew Baugh, Michelle Bigot, Christopher Paul Carey & Win Scott Eckert, G.L. Gick, Micah Harris, Tom Kane, Lovern Kindzierski, Rick Lai, Roman Leary, Alain le Bussy, Jean-Marc Lofficier, Randy Lofficier, Xavier Mauméjean, Jess Nevins, John Peel, Frank Schildiner, Stuart Shiffman, Brian Stableford, David L. Vineyard.

Volume 6: Grand Guignol (2009)

Matthew Baugh & Micah Harris, Christopher Paul Carey, Win Scott Eckert, Emmanuel Gorlier, Travis Hiltz, Rick Lai, Roman Leary, Jean-Marc Lofficier, Randy Lofficier, Xavier Mauméjean, William P. Maynard, John Peel, Neil Penswick, Dennis E. Power, Frank Schildiner, Bradley H. Sinor, Brian Stableford, Michel Stéphan, David L. Vineyard.

Volume 7: Femmes Fatales (2010)
Roberto Lionel Barreiro, Matthew Baugh, Thom Brannan, Matthew Dennion, Win Scott Eckert, Emmanuel Gorlier, Micah Harris, Travis Hiltz, Paul Hugli, Rick Lai, Jean-Marc Lofficier, David McDonnell, Brad Mengel, Sharan Newman, Neil Penswick, Pete Rawlik, Frank Schildiner, Stuart Shiffman, Bradley H. Sinor, Brian Stableford, Michel Stéphan, David L. Vineyard.

Doctor Omega and the Shadowmen (2011)
Matthew Baugh, Thom Brannan, G.L. Gick, Travis Hiltz, Olivier Legrand, Serge Lehman, Jean-Marc & Randy Lofficier, Samuel T. Payne, John Peel, Neil Penswick, Dennis E. Power, Chris Roberson, Stuart Shiffman.

The Nyctalope Steps In (2011)
Matthew Dennion, Emmanuel Gorlier, Julien Heylbroeck, Paul Hugli, Jean de La Hire, Roman Leary, Randy Lofficier, Stuart Shiffman, David L. Vineyard.

Volume 8: Agents Provocateurs (2011)
Matthew Baugh, Nicholas Boving, Matthew Dennion, Win Scott Eckert, Martin Gately, Micah Harris, Travis Hiltz, Paul Hugli, Rick Lai, Joseph Lamere, Olivier Legrand, Jean-Marc & Randy Lofficier, DavidMcDonald, Chris Nigro, John Peel, Dennis E. Power, Pete Rawlik, Joshua Reynolds, Frank Schildiner, Michel Stéphan, Michel Vannereux.

Night of the Nyctalope (2012)
Matthew Dennion, Martin Gately, Emmanuel Gorlier, Julien Heylbroeck, Travis Hiltz, Jean de La Hire, Roman Leary, Jean-Marc Lofficier, David McDonald, Chris Nigro, Philippe Ward.